THE GAP INTO POWER:
A DARK AND
HUNGRY GOD ARISES

THE GAP INTO POWER

A DARK AND HUNGRY GOD ARISES

STEPHEN R. DONALDSON

BANTAM BOOKS

NEW YORK·TORONTO·LONDON·SYDNEY·AUCKLAND

THE GAP INTO POWER
A DARK AND HUNGRY GOD ARISES
A Bantam Book / November 1992

Book design by Diane Stevenson, Snap-Haus Graphics

Library of Congress Cataloging-in-Publication Data
Donaldson, Stephen R.
   The gap into power: a dark and hungry God arises : a novel / by
Stephen R. Donaldson.
      p.   cm.
   ISBN 0-553-07176-9
   I. Title.
PS3554.0469G36   1992
813'.54—dc20   92-11668
                                                        CIP

Published simultaneously in the United States and Canada

Bantam Books are published by Bantam Books, a division of Bantam Doubleday Dell Publishing Group,
Inc. Its trademark, consisting of the words "Bantam Books" and the portrayal of a rooster, is Registered in
U.S. Patent and Trademark Office and in other countries. Marca Registrada. Bantam Books, 666 Fifth
Avenue, New York, New York 10103.

PRINTED IN THE UNITED STATES OF AMERICA

BVG   0 9 8 7 6 5 4 3 2 1

TO
LYNDA KEXEL
BILL PUDER
AND
RICK CARTER:

The best team.

HOLT

Shortly before Angus Thermopyle and Milos Taverner left UMCPHQ aboard *Trumpet*, Holt Fasner visited his mother.

He did this despite the fact that the old harridan had been in a foul temper for decades.

The medical advances which had kept him nearly healthy, relatively strong, almost in his prime, for a hundred fifty years had come too late to be comparably effective for her. In fact, they would have failed her thirty years ago if he hadn't insisted on plugging her into machines which first pumped blood, then digested food, and eventually breathed for her. She was technically still alive, of course; but now she was only the husk of a woman. Her skin was the blotchy color of rotting linen; she could hardly move her hands; she hadn't lifted her head from its supports for at least ten years. She no longer knew the difference when tubes brought her sustenance or carried away waste.

She retained her mind, however. Bitter as a vial of acid, Norna Fasner continued to think long after her body lost its last capacity to do anything.

That was why her son kept her alive. Many years ago she'd given up asking him to let her die. She knew from old, painful experience that he would put her off with a bland chuckle and a vacuous remark: "You know I can't do without you, Mother." And shortly afterward she would find yet another video screen installed in the room which she considered her tomb.

She studied the screens, even though she hated them. Their images were all she had to think about. If they were switched off, her brain would almost surely go null; and she didn't want that. She desired death, not unconsciousness. If even one of her screens had gone blank, she might have wept in frustration and grief. Every image, every word, every passing implication was a hint which might eventually enable her to believe that her son would be destroyed. Without hints—without the possibility that she would receive hints— all her years of paralyzed, unliving existence would come to nothing.

Her son was the United Mining Companies CEO; unquestionably the richest and beyond doubt the most powerful man alive. From his corporate "home office," his station orbiting Earth half a million kilometers beyond UMCPHQ, he ruled his vast empire: the largest, arguably the most necessary enterprise in human history. His employees were counted in millions: men and women who lived or died by his decisions and policies, in billions. Disguised by the UMC charter, and by the public democracy of the Governing Council for Earth and Space—which was nominally responsible for controlling men like him, corporations like his—he raised and toppled governments, destroyed or enriched competitors, caused potential futures to take on substance or fray away like mist. Behind his back, people who feared him sometimes referred to him as "the Dragon"—and only people who had no idea who he was didn't fear him.

He stood at the nexus of human dealings with forbidden space. All human access to that imponderable source of wealth passed through his hands. And humanity's only defense against that imponderable threat belonged to him.

The value of Holt Fasner's time couldn't be measured in pure cesium. Nevertheless he visited his mother whenever an opportunity presented itself. He treasured her advice too much to let her die.

Although he was sometimes hard-pressed to interpret it. Her wish for his ruin was so palpable that he had to be extraordinarily careful in how he sifted her insights, what valence he assigned to her pronouncements. As a result, his encounters with her were a challenge which he found profoundly stimulating.

In truth, he could almost certainly have afforded to let her die any time during the past half century. He liked talking to his mother; he profited from her advice. But he could have done without it. He kept Norna Fasner alive precisely because she wished him ill with such steady virulence; also because he took pleasure in her utter helplessness; and finally because she kept him on his toes. Otherwise he was inclined to forget that he was mortal.

Men who forgot their mortality made mistakes. Holt Fasner had paid blood—not always his own—for his successes; and now that he had them, he didn't mean to let them go glimmering in the name of a mistake.

So he visited his mother shortly before *Trumpet*'s departure. Risks were at work; small risks that might metastasize at any moment. In themselves, Angus Thermopyle, Milos Taverner, Nick Succorso, and Morn Hyland were nothing more than three men and a woman; pawns of Holt's larger policies, his grander dreams. But stirred together with Billingate and the Amnion, they might conceivably produce something more volatile, with a lasting impact, like a minor thermonuclear pile which went critical and rendered all its environs uninhabitable for centuries.

The director of the United Mining Companies Police was in charge, of course; Warden Dios himself. The risk was of his choosing, not Holt's: the negative consequences, if any, would be his to clean up. But Holt cherished the well-being of the UMCP as he cherished the health of the whole United Mining Companies. If he'd believed the risks too great, he would have forbidden them.

He hadn't.

Nor had he dismissed the situation from his mind, however. Instead of trying to second-guess Ward—who had spent the better part of three decades proving himself as the Dragon's strong right hand—Holt went to talk to Norna.

The room where he kept her immured was hidden in the obscure recesses of the home office, in a part of the station where no one ventured except men and women with extremely specialized authorizations. As usual when her several doctors weren't examining her, the only illumination in her high sterile sickchamber came from the twenty or so video screens which nearly covered the wall in front of her. That dimness was her choice: the little strength left in her fingers was enough to tap buttons that would raise or lower the lights, adjust her posture, summon assistance—or even turn off the screens. Holt allowed her that freedom because he trusted the use she would make of it.

Stark and garish in the phosphor gleam, her face looked like that of a mummy painted to appear ghastly under UV lamps. Incessantly her thin lips and toothless gums chewed food she hadn't tasted for decades. At intervals she drooled unselfconsciously; a fretwork of wrinkles spread the saliva into a sheen across her chin. She didn't glance at her son as he entered: her eyes flicked restlessly across the screens as if she could absorb and understand them all simultaneously.

From them came a steady mutter of voices and soundtracks, a muted and indistinguishable argument interleaved with at least half a dozen kinds of music—a noise like a rabble, uneasy and irate; but so blurred and distant that it might have been the tectonic grumbling of rocks, or the lost complaint of the sea. The sound alone set Holt's teeth on edge: at times it seemed to muddle his brain. It made him think there was something structurally wrong with the home office itself.

He knew from experience, however, that Norna absorbed and understood the voices as well as the images.

"Hello, Mother," he greeted her—artificially hearty, in part as a matter of policy, in part because he had to do *something* to counteract the effects of the noise. "You're looking well, better than ever. I do believe you'll be able to get out of bed soon. I can certainly use your help running the company. How are you feeling? What do the doctors say?"

She met his blather with her usual disregard. The way her eyes hunted the screens made him think of a chicken trying to peck seeds out of stony soil.

He scanned the screens himself for a moment, but their images offered him nothing. The typical collection: half a dozen news broadcasts, all trying to reinterpret life for their viewers, all reaching the same conclusions; three or four sports programs showing acts of extreme violence in varying degrees of simulation; four or five comedies and satires which gave the impression that they all repeated the same jokes over and over again; and half a dozen romantic videos—"Mother, really, at your age, aren't you ashamed?"—reveling in the kind of mindless and supernal lust which had apparently driven Morn Hyland and Nick Succorso together on Com-Mine Station. With such tripe masses of human beings were tranquilized—until those rare occasions when they woke up, saw what was really happening around them, misunderstood it, and did their best to impose the stupidest possible solution on the men who normally led them. The Humanity Riots were a case in point. The rest of the time, the world reflecting from the screens served its purpose efficiently enough. But it had nothing to give Holt himself.

For the umpteenth time, he wondered what it gave his mother. Did she see in it something that he missed? Was she simply hoping for news that some disaster had befallen him? Or was she able to snatch a secret knowledge out of the gabble—knowledge which had somehow eluded him, despite his vast resources?

The question added piquancy to his visits with her.

What *could* he have missed? Not much, obviously, since he'd demonstrated his ability to profit—and profit hugely—from those times when the human billions kicked over the traces and demanded irrationality from their leaders. He still chuckled internally when he thought of the Humanity Riots. Imagine trying to face the threat of the Amnion without genetic expertise to match their own! And yet humankind's outbreak of revulsion against genetic experimentation had effectively delivered Intertech into his hands. Owning Intertech, in turn, had given him control over first contact with the Amnion— and that had led as inexorably as a syllogism to his present position as the arbiter of fate for his whole species.

If any man in history could claim to have *not missed much,* Holt Fasner was the one. Nevertheless he kept the question—and his mother—alive to help him ensure that he didn't start missing things now.

At one hundred fifty years of age, he was almost in his prime, still close to his middle years physiologically. But his cheeks were just a shade too ruddy. He had to blink a bit too often to keep his eyes from filming over. At times he couldn't hold his hands steady: at times his prostate troubled him. His doctors had advised him against any form of strenuous exercise because they didn't know how long the tissues of his heart could last. Now more than ever it was vital to make no mistakes.

"Mother," he went on with the same bland heartiness, as if she hadn't refused to answer his polite inquiries—as if she had, in fact, given him the answer he desired most—"I need your advice. In the past few days, I've had a couple of troubling conversations with Godsen Frik.

"You remember him, don't you?" Holt knew perfectly well that his mother never forgot anything. "He's Ward's director of protocol. For some reason"—Holt showed his teeth in a salesman's grin—"he thinks he has the right to go over Ward's head when he doesn't like Ward's decisions or policies. Reprehensible conduct in a subordinate, don't you think? Ward wouldn't tolerate it if he didn't know that Godsen is a particular protégé of mine. In time—ten years or so—I think Godsen will be ready to do his duty to all humankind by accepting the presidency of the GCES. But it is a problem, isn't it? For Ward as Godsen's director. And for me, as Ward's friend, ally, and mentor. After all, I want Ward"—Holt had a malicious love for phrases like this one—"to be happy in his work. All human space depends on him."

Certainly all human space depended on the UMCP. No other force strong enough to interdict the Amnion existed. And therefore Holt's unique position also depended on the UMCP. If he hadn't owned the cops, the GCES could have dismantled his empire long ago.

Listening hard, trying to filter out the insistent mutter of the screens, he heard Norna's almost inaudible question, chewed out by her bloodless lips and toothless gums:

"What's the situation?"

Ah, Mother, you live for me, don't you? You don't want to, but you do it anyway.

Holt went on smiling.

"Ward has decided that it's time to do something about one of the worst of the bootleg shipyards that serves forbidden space by helping illegals—as well as by what they used to call 'fencing stolen goods.' It's amazing how many men want to get rich by aiding and abetting our enemies. The Amnion want our resources—our raw materials, our technologies, our genes. Pirates sell those things.

"But piracy would be"—Holt pursed his mouth—"ineffective without bootleg shipyards to build and repair ships—and without dealers to transact business with the Amnion. Ward would love a chance to blow them all to dust.

"The question is how. The particular shipyard he has in mind this time just happens to be in forbidden space. He would lose his job if he committed an act of open warfare against the Amnion. So he's planning a covert strike.

"Do you remember that situation on Com-Mine, oh, half a year ago? The one where it looked like Security was in collusion with one pirate to frame another?" Of course she did. "The one that tipped the votes to pass the Preempt Act?"

Holt had maneuvered hard to secure the passage of the Preempt Act. It gave the UMCP jurisdiction over local Security everywhere—thereby perfecting the UMCP's hegemony by emasculating the only plausible alternative to Holt's cops.

"Well, the illegal who got framed is called Angus Thermopyle—one of the slimiest characters you would ever want to meet. Ward reqqed him under the act. Now he's been welded and programmed, and he's being sent against that shipyard. Today, I think."

Right now, in fact.

"It's a complex issue. Please stop me if I'm boring you, Mother. I had the distinct impression that Ward didn't want to obey when I told him to set up that frame on Com-Mine. Our Ward is still too much of an idealist. He doesn't like to get involved in the practical side of politics. I've actually heard him make speeches against 'descending to the level of our enemies.' But he did it because he could get something he wanted out of it—which was this Angus Thermopyle. As far as I can tell, he didn't actually want more authority for its own sake." As if to himself—but watching his mother closely—Holt mused, "I wish I knew how hard I would have had to push him to make him follow orders if he hadn't wanted Angus."

If Norna said anything, he didn't hear it.

"The point, however," Holt resumed, "is that Ward did follow orders. He is following orders. The next few days should produce some interesting developments on the fringes of forbidden space."

Now Norna muttered something that sounded like, "Why does that bother Godsen?"

"Good question!" her son exclaimed jovially. "As usual, Mother, you've cut right to the heart of the matter. Why *does* that bother a dedicated public servant like Godsen Frik?

"Well, of course, we wouldn't have been able to frame this Angus Thermopyle if we hadn't had someone working for us inside Com-Mine Security. But it would be"—Holt considered his choice of adjectives—"unfortunate if any local investigation uncovered the truth. We passed the Preempt Act on the assumption that local Security couldn't be trusted—that Com-Mine had a traitor working for forbidden space. If word got out that the traitor was actually working for *us*—well, I could probably keep station votes in line, but the rest of the Council would go absolutely shit-faced.

"To protect against that eventuality, Ward reqqed our traitor at the same time as Angus—a sadistic little bureaucrat named Milos Taverner. All well and good, so far. But here comes the part that upsets Godsen. Angus is a cyborg now, programmed down to his toes. He can't clean his teeth without permission from his datacore. But he still needs a control—someone who can adjust his programming to meet unforeseen circumstances. In addition, he needs crew. And on top of that, he needs cover. He needs an explanation for why he's free, how he got out of lockup, where he got his ship."

Holt paused for effect, then said, "Ward has chosen Milos to go with Angus."

Norna chewed her silence. Traces of saliva leaked past her lips instead of words. Her eyes flicked rapidly across all her screens, but never toward her son.

"Am I making this clear enough for you, Mother?" Holt asked in a tone of cheerful solicitude. "We know Milos has the soul of a traitor because he betrayed Com-Mine Security for *us*. Ward says he won't turn against us because we've got him by the short hairs." That was another phrase Holt Fasner especially enjoyed. "If he reveals anything we don't want him to reveal—or does anything we don't want him to do—he's cooked. But Godsen has a different perspective. A more 'public' perspective. If these activities become known, what are 'the people,' 'the great unwashed masses' "—such words rolled almost gleefully off Holt's tongue—"going to think of sending out a known murderer and rapist under the control of a known traitor? What are the votes on the GCES going to think of Ward's belief that Milos won't turn against us?

"And what are the chances, really, that Milos *won't* turn against us? He can probably make a stellar fortune by selling everything he knows about us—not to mention about Angus," although Milos couldn't literally sell Angus himself, since the programming which made Angus loyal to the UMCP was unalterable.

"Our Godsen knows his duties. It's his *job* to become hysterical and froth at the mouth in situations like this. *And* it's his job to come to me.

"I haven't backed him up, however. I don't want him to forget his place—I don't want him to think he has the power to tell me what to do. And I don't want to undermine Ward." Not in a case like this, where the potential benefits were large—a dramatic victory against forbidden space and piracy, wonderful for the credibility of the UMCP—and the likely risks were small. After all, if Milos misbehaved Ward could always order Nick Succorso to kill him. "He has a talent for this kind of delicate manipulation. And he's the best UMCP director I could ask for. He may be the only man I know who might be able to threaten me—if I didn't own him down to his soul."

In fact, Holt would have feared Ward if he hadn't gained a kind of absolute complicity from Ward by winning Ward's acquiescence in the suppression of Intertech's immunity drug.

A small voice whispered out of Norna's husk. "But you're still worried."

"How right you are, Mother," Holt agreed. "I'm still worried. No matter how careful Ward is, he's still taking a risk—and you know I don't like risks. That's the reason I suppressed Intertech's antimutagen. It had at least the theoretical potential to shift the balance of power across human space. Any effective defense against the way the Amnion impose mutation could conceivably undercut Ward and the whole UMCP by making them appear less vital, less *necessary*. That might have weakened my position with the votes."

He shrugged judiciously. "Or not. Maybe none of those things would have happened. But I didn't want to take the chance. So I made sure that only Ward and Hashi know the drug actually exists—and that only Hashi can use it. To protect Data Acquisition's covert operations, don't you see?

"Now Ward's taking a risk of his own. Not without consulting me, of course. His reasons for doing it are pretty persuasive," if only because Angus Thermopyle would have a chance to eliminate the problem of Morn Hyland. She was a UMCP ensign with an unauthorized zone implant and—presumably—knowledge of the immunity drug; and if she ever left forbidden space to tell what she knew, PR and the whole of the UMCP would have a disaster of megaproportions on their hands. "It's what you might call a surgical strike." Holt licked his lips. "Extirpate a melanoma before it spreads.

"So he's taking this particular risk with my blessing. But I'm still worried about it. I think Ward is getting himself in trouble."

Norna's words were no more than a low growl against the blurred mutter of the screens, but for some reason Holt heard them as clearly as if her voice were the only sound in the room.

"I think he's getting *you* in trouble."

Holt chuckled automatically. "Come now, Mother. Don't be an alarmist. You'll get yourself all excited for nothing. This is Warden Dios we're talking about. I *made* him—he's my right hand. He can't use the san without doing it to benefit me."

He might have gone on; but his blather trailed away as he saw Norna pointing a gnarled and tremulous finger at one of the screens.

At first he couldn't tell which one. A *romance?* No, one of the news broadcasts. Somewhere in the midst of the intolerable babble a male face with an authoritative voice and no mind was saying, ". . . this special bulletin."

Special bulletin? What special bulletin? Nothing happened—nothing was *allowed* to happen—in human space unless Holt Fasner knew about it first.

"A highly placed source in the office of the UMCP director of protocol on UMCPHQ Station has confirmed that Angus Thermopyle has escaped."

Without warning, a tingle ran down Holt's nearly strong spine and tightened around his scrotum.

"Captain Thermopyle," said the male head as if he were anything more than a ventriloquist's dummy, "is an illegal captured and convicted approximately six months ago on Com-Mine Station, and later transferred to UMCPHQ by the orders of Hashi Lebwohl, Director of Data Acquisition. No explanation has ever been released for Data Acquisition's interest in Captain Thermopyle. However, as this news team reported at the time, he is no ordinary illegal. The circumstances of his arrest and conviction are widely held to be the precipitating factor in the recent passage of the so-called Preempt Act by the Governing Council for Earth and Space. Apparently Captain Thermopyle was assisted in his piracies by a traitor within Com-Mine Station Security. Doubts about the integrity of station Security across human space persuaded the members of the GCES of the necessity of the Preempt Act.

"That Captain Thermopyle was able to escape from UMCPHQ itself is sufficiently disturbing. However, our source in the office of the UMCP Director of Protocol has confirmed that the situation is worse than it appears.

"The difficulties revolve around a man who was at one time the Deputy Chief of Com-Mine Station Security, Milos Taverner."

Oh, shit, thought Holt. Anxiety spread from his groin up into his chest. His lungs hurt as if they were getting old.

Like all dummies, the male head in the news broadcast was implacable. "Because he was responsible for the interrogation of Captain Thermopyle on Com-Mine Station, Deputy Chief Taverner was brought to UMCPHQ along with Captain Thermopyle, again on orders from the Director of Data Acquisition. Ostensibly Deputy Chief Taverner was reqqed by Data Acquisition to continue his interrogation of Captain Thermopyle. He was considered to have a unique and invaluable knowledge of the prisoner.

"Now, however, our source has confirmed that Deputy Chief Taverner was brought to UMCPHQ, not because of his specialized knowledge, but because he was thought to be the traitor who had betrayed Com-Mine Station Security. He was brought to UMCPHQ so that Data Acquisition might learn the truth about him—and so that the threat he represents would be neutralized.

"For reasons which are not clear at this time, Deputy Chief Taverner was not adequately guarded. Now, it appears, he has succeeded at breaking his former partner, Captain Thermopyle, out of confinement. Together they have stolen a ship and escaped UMCPHQ.

"The implications of this apparent incompetence on the part of the UMCP are vast and frightening for a species already threatened with extinction by the Amnion—a species protected only by the same men and women who have just allowed a convicted pirate and his most dangerous accomplice to slip through their fingers."

There was more: a recap of Captain Thermopyle's arrest and conviction, and a summary of Deputy Chief Taverner's record, followed by an exhaustive analysis of events by a whole panel of self-appointed experts—genophobes, libertarians, free-market crazies, native Earthers; every political fringe group that wanted votes on the GCES and didn't have them. Holt Fasner had stopped listening, however. He was already on the intercom, securing a channel between the home office and UMCPHQ—putting the fear of the Dragon into every technician and secretary between his mother's sickchamber and Godsen Frik.

His hands shook the entire time.

WARDEN

From his personal Command Operations Room in UMCPHQ Center, Warden Dios watched *Trumpet* run out smoothly through Station control space. Except for Min Donner, his Enforcement Division director and occasional bodyguard, he was alone: he'd sent everyone else away, even the communications techs who were supposed to keep him in instant contact with every department and activity of the United Mining Companies Police. He hadn't locked the door, but he had silenced all the CO Room pickups, monitors, and logs.

Solitude was rare for the UMCP director. Silence was even rarer. Being with Min may not have been the same thing as being alone; but at least she didn't talk unless she had something important to say.

So far *Trumpet*'s departure was meticulous. The ship hadn't filed any kind of destination report, and hadn't been asked for one; but her blip on the screens showed that she was following her assigned trajectory exactly: on course at the correct speed; responding precisely to the data and demands from the navigational buoys which managed UMCPHQ's—and Earth's—heavy in-system traffic.

Had Warden Dios expected anything else? Not really. *Trumpet* had only two men aboard, and neither Angus Thermopyle nor Milos Taverner was likely to begin improvising so early. Angus was as perfectly welded as Hashi Lebwohl could make him—and Hashi was a wizard of cybernetics. The idea that Angus would ever diverge from his programming was almost inconceivable. In any case, Milos would keep him in line.

And whatever actions Milos' uncertain loyalties might inspire, they certainly wouldn't be of a kind to attract attention—or doubt—this close to Earth and UMCPHQ. He'd been too well trained, too thoroughly threatened. In addition Warden had arranged to burn Milos' bridges behind him. The news bulletin which Protocol had released through one of Godsen Frik's subordinates, announcing Angus' "escape" and Milos' "complicity," enforced Milos' cooperation. The former deputy chief of Com-Mine Station Security might eventually dare many things; but he wouldn't dare them here.

The UMCP director had no reason to stay where he was. He was a busy man. He should already have gone on to other duties. Still he valued the silence and the near solitude. Alone with Min Donner, he remained in the privacy of his CO Room, watching *Trumpet*—and a piece of his own fate—pass out of his control.

He believed the whole human species was at issue. Otherwise he would not have been able to do what he did.

He was a strong man, with a thick chest and powerful arms. The lines of his face and jaw seemed hard enough to have been cut from metal. And the patch glued over the prosthesis of his left eye, like the crookedness of his nose, only made him look stronger. But sometimes he needed more than strength to stand the strain of his oblique intentions. He needed to remind himself of the consequences if he failed.

If he failed, Holt Fasner would win.

Warden Dios had done too much to help create the Dragon's power: he couldn't turn his back on his responsibility now that he finally understood the danger of what he and Holt together had made.

For a moment the outgoing blip blurred slightly as navigational transmission shifted from one buoy to the next. In another hour, *Trumpet* would reach her assigned gap range—considerably closer to Earth than other ships were allowed, but well within the priority zone restricted for the UMCP's use. Then she would be gone. And Warden would have to live with the outcome.

Min adjusted her weight slightly; her fingers stroked the butt of the handgun she carried everywhere. Warden suspected that she wore her impact pistol to bed. Without lifting her eyes from the screens, she asked quietly, "Do you really think this is going to work?"

He glanced over at her. The strictness of her mouth never altered; her jet hair had been marked by exactly those streaks of gray ever since she'd become his most valued assistant. Her gaze was hot enough to scorch men with less iron in their souls—or less scar tissue.

In an oddly impersonal way, he loved her. More personally, he respected her moral clarity, her loyalty to her people in ED; her commitment to the law and power which preserved the fragile integrity of human space. Years ago those qualities used to swell his heart. Now they made him grieve.

Because he was grieving, he was less cautious than he should have been. "I think," he replied, "if it doesn't, the Dragon is going to force me to commit seppuku."

That brought her around to face him. Her eyes burned into his—the artificial orb behind its patch and the human one. Her whole body blazed with infrared emissions. "Then why are you doing it?"

"Min—" No question about it: he should have been more circumspect; should never have given her this opening. She was already in enough danger, simply because she was the Enforcement Division director—and honest. "What do you suppose my choices are?"

"You could send *me*," she said promptly, tightly. "Or you could let me put together a team. Instead of sending out a cyborg and a traitor, not to mention sacrificing Morn Hyland"—Min was not a woman who feared to speak her mind—"you could have let somebody you trust try to do both jobs. Put Billingate out of business *and* rescue Morn.

"It's suicide to leave her there," she pursued before he could respond. "The Amnion might get their hands on her. And she doesn't *deserve* to be abandoned like that. She doesn't *deserve* to just be put out of her misery along with that shipyard. If you think Angus and Milos are too chancy to rescue her"—Min's tone was acid; her body, the color of mineral acid—"if you think asking them to pull her out is too complex, try something else. Let me organize a team. Or go myself."

Abruptly she stopped. Dios could see the flux of tension along her jaw as she bit down on the other things she was tempted to say.

"Because," he replied falsely, hiding his sorrow, "she doesn't matter now. I don't care whether you understand or not. And I don't care how much it hurts to let go of her. Only Angus and Milos

matter. Everything depends on them. If I give them a reason to fail—
if I make their job too difficult by ordering them to rescue Morn—
they might as well not go at all."

And if they fail us, we're doomed.

Min must have known that she couldn't conceal her distress
from him. Nevertheless she turned her head away so that he couldn't
see her eyes, her expression.

He was tempted to ask, Min, do you still trust me? Are you
going to back me up? But he knew she would tell him the truth—
for reasons which had nothing to do with his ability to distinguish
lies—so he allowed her to keep her answers private. She had that
right. Instead he took his next step along the path of culpability and
sacrifice that he'd chosen for himself.

"There's something I want you to do for me," he told her. "It
can't come from me, but it's got to be done."

She waited without moving.

Stifling a sigh, Warden asked, "Have we got any supporters on
the Governing Council—I mean, supporters who are also opponents
of the UMC? I should know the answer, but I have a hard time
forcing myself to think about things like this."

He read her puzzlement as she thought. After a moment she
inquired, "Are you talking about a bloc of votes? Or individual vot-
ers?"

"Individuals. Council members."

She let out a breath like a small snort. Facing him again, she
said, "Captain Vertigus."

Warden Dios raised his eyebrows to convey the impression that
he was surprised. Captain Sixten Vertigus, commander of the SMI
probe ship *Deep Star*, was the first human being who had ever seen
an Amnioni.

"He must be all of ninety by now," Min went on, "but he's still
able to sit up straight while the rest of the Council natters. By se-
niority, at any rate, he's the senior member for the United Western
Bloc, but he doesn't wield any real power. According to the news
broadcasts, he makes periodic speeches denouncing the Dragon's 'quest
for UMC hegemony.' On the other hand, he votes on our side
whenever one of our issues comes up.

"What do you want him for?"

Warden held himself perfectly still, determined to give the ED director no hint of his urgency. In a steady, conversational tone, he answered, "I want you to talk to him for me. I want you to convince him to introduce GCES legislation that will sever us from the UMC. We need to be a separate entity, accountable only to the Council itself—we need to be the *human* police, not just the Dragon's private enforcement agency. I want him to put a bill of severance in front of the GCES, and I want him to do it *now.*"

The colors shining from Min's form told Warden that she'd been waiting a long time to hear him say something like this.

"Get everything ready yourself," he continued. "Lay it all out for him. Convince him to put all of his personal prestige, all of his experience, all of his passion behind it."

He knew Sixten Vertigus to be a man of considerable passion. Otherwise he wouldn't have violated Holt Fasner's direct orders by making personal contact with the Amnion.

"And don't let him get bogged down by details. Write the bill for him if you have to. The big thing he'll want to know—what all the members will want to know—is how we'll be financed. What kind of revenue source can take the place of the UMC coffers. The answer is, tax every company that does any kind of business in space. Most of the money will still come from the UMC. But if we're separately constituted, if we're an independent branch of the government instead of an arm of the UMC, we'll be able to function the way cops *should.*

"I want that bill in front of the GCES within forty-eight hours."

Before Holt learns what's happening on Thanatos Minor.

Min's eyes shone like her aura. Facing him straight, she said softly, "The Dragon will never let you get away with it. For one thing, he has the votes to stop you. And when he finds out what you're up to, he'll consider it a betrayal. He's still your *boss.* He has the corporate authority—as well as the personal clout—to *fire* you."

Slowly the director of the UMCP smiled. "That's why the whole business is absolutely confidential. If Godsen or even Hashi hears one word about this—if *anybody* except you, me, and Captain Vertigus so much as smells the truth—all of it," all of us, maybe all of humanity, "will be wasted.

"In fact, it's essential to keep *me* out of it entirely. Even Captain Vertigus can't know it's my idea. As far as he's concerned, it comes from you. I want him to do it because he believes in it, not because he thinks I'm trying to outmaneuver Holt."

Min nodded once, sharply. "Director—" she began, "Warden—" But she had to think for a moment or two before she said, "I'm not going to ask you what this has to do with sending Angus and Milos against Billingate. But I *am* going to ask you to watch your back. You could get killed playing a game like this."

"Min, Min"—Warden spread his hands in a gesture of humorous helplessness—"he's only a Dragon. He isn't God."

She wasn't amused. "No, and you aren't either. I bet you might even bleed if he cut your heart out. I bet—"

She might have gone on: she was charged with her own passion, and had too few outlets for it. But she was interrupted by a timid knock at the CO Room door.

The door slid open without permission. One of Center's communications techs, looking pale and more than a little apprehensive, ventured her head into the room.

"Director?"

Instinctively irritated, Warden wanted to snarl at her, Don't be such a damn sheep. When was the last time I murdered—not to mention demoted, or even reprimanded—a communications tech for simply doing her job?

He stifled the impulse, however. It was dangerous; symptomatic of a tension he couldn't afford to betray. Smiling to disguise his vexation, he waited for the tech to explain herself.

"It's the PR director," she said, fumbling slightly. "Godsen Frik. He's trying to get in touch with you. He says it's urgent. I can route it to your intercom." She nodded at the console in front of him.

Warden forced himself to continue smiling despite the sting of anxiety in his veins. "Thank you, technician." Damned if he was going to make the effort to remember the woman's name at a time like this. "Please tell Director Frik that he just missed me." When the tech hesitated, he added quietly, "Dismissed."

She pulled her face out of the doorway, and the door closed itself.

Min Donner didn't say anything. That was a relief. Maybe his love for her wasn't so impersonal after all. Or maybe he was just grateful that she still trusted him enough to let him arrange his own doom without hounding him with questions.

She should have asked her questions. She had the right. After all, she was his most valued assistant, his staunchest supporter; occasionally his bodyguard; sometimes his executioner. Unless he was *very* careful—and unless she did everything he told her to do exactly the way he told her to do it—his doom would almost certainly carry her with it, for good or ill.

That danger was one reason he grieved.

One reason among many.

MILOS

Milos' scalp itched. In fact, his whole body itched. He was dirty —too dirty. He abhorred having this much grime ground into his hands and shipsuit, this much oil on his face, this much old sweat crusting in his crotch. Even as a kid, he'd been far too fastidious to let himself get into a condition like this. He felt like he'd had excrement rubbed all over him.

That made him angrier than he'd ever been in his life.

None of this was his fault, of course. Hadn't he played straight with the United Mining Companies *shit* Police? Well, hadn't he? Yes, he had. He played straight with everybody who paid him. Even Com-Mine Security, who might conceivably view the matter in another light, had no legitimate complaint against him.

Sure, he'd risked Station supplies to help Succorso trap Thermopyle—on Hashi Lebwohl's orders, not Com-Mine's—but that gamble had paid off handsomely. And once Thermopyle was in lockup, Milos had done everything any deputy chief could have done to break him. If Security didn't like the results, let them blame Thermopyle, not Milos.

Milos Taverner played straight. He gave value for the money he received.

Unless his own neck was in the noose. Then he looked after his own safety and let the people who paid him take care of themselves. But no one could hold that against him. It was a pardonable human characteristic. An instinct for survival was as necessary—and as inescapable—as the impulse to eat and drink.

It certainly didn't justify what Hashi Lebwohl—and Warden Dios, of all people!—were doing to him now.

They were forcing his neck into the noose with a vengeance.

And they had less reason to complain about him than Com-Mine did. Caught between Lebwohl's orders to keep Thermopyle silent and Security's orders to break him, Milos had satisfied the former at the expense of the latter. The fact that Angus had obstinately declined to be broken was beside the point. Milos had met DA's requirements. Neither Lebwohl nor Dios had any reason to criticize the results he'd obtained for them.

Yet here he was: sitting at *Trumpet*'s second's station, at least nominally responsible for communications, scan, and data and damage control; about to go into tach with the same slimy illegal he'd once ambushed; about to face disaster and death in forbidden space—and not only had he been *forced* into this position by the very people he'd just satisfied, but he'd been forced into it *dirty*.

So that he would be a believable second for Captain Thermopyle, who was known on Thanatos Minor: so they said. Shit. He knew the real reason, and it had nothing to do with believability. It had to do with humiliation and control.

Milos couldn't remember a time when he hadn't understood such things.

Ever since his childhood in one of Earth's more degraded and pestilential cities, he'd been aware that the only effective way to evade the harm a guttergang might do him was to make himself valuable by passing along information about the plans and doings of some other bunch of thugs; purchase safety with other people's secrets. Then he was thought of as an important resource by the first guttergang: he was protected.

But of course that couldn't last. Eventually the second guttergang would guess what he was doing and come after him. Then the situation would be too dangerous to survive. So the only effective way to keep his skin whole was to pass information both ways: to make himself essential to both guttergangs—or to three or four, or however many there were—and to control as much as possible what the gangs knew, in order to mask his own intricate loyalties.

Yet even that wasn't enough. Guttergangs protected their sources of information—in those days, kids like Milos were called "bug-gers"—but didn't respect them. Whenever the thugs felt like it, they brutalized and tormented their buggers. Like the UMCP, they forced their buggers into dangerous and shaming tests of loyalty.

Humiliation and control.

By the time he was ten, Milos Taverner had learned how to deal with those as well.

It was amazingly easy. A word or two in the right places—not too often, not too obviously—and individual pieces of slime who degraded or scared him were destructed. Guttergangs may not have respected their buggers, but they had too much to lose by letting someone else damage their sources of information.

All Milos needed, the one absolute requirement for keeping his neck out of the noose, was to make sure that no one knew he was buggering for both sides.

So mighty Warden Dios and his precious Hashi Lebwohl—not to mention the sanctimonious Min Donner—were wrong about Milos. They didn't know what their own actions could cost them.

They thought that if they rubbed his nose in their power hard enough, if they made him feel beaten and filthy enough, they could compel him to submit to having his neck in the noose.

Milos didn't doubt for a second that the noose was real. After all, if none of Lebwohl's and Dios' plans went awry, there weren't likely to be many survivors on Thanatos Minor when their pet cy-borg carried out his programming. And Milos wasn't likely to be one of them: he didn't have Thermopyle's enhanced resources to help him escape alive.

Which of course was exactly what Lebwohl and Dios were counting on. If *Trumpet* brought anyone back to UMCPHQ, it would be the cyborg they had spent so much money on, not the relatively inexpensive human being.

They should have known better.

They shouldn't have let him have the command codes that ruled Thermopyle. If they hadn't given him the capacity to redirect Angus' prewritten exigencies, he would have had only one option left; only one place to go with his anger. Now, however, he had several.

One of his options was to make Thermopyle pay at least some of the price of his, Milos', humiliation.

But not here: not this close to UMCPHQ; not while it was still possible for the cops to monitor whatever happened aboard *Trumpet*. Milos was prepared to wait awhile. At least until this gap scout—a ship which Angus knew intimately, and which Milos understood very little—resumed tard on the other side of the dimensional gap.

So he didn't respond to the crude gibes Angus aimed at him almost incessantly. In any case, he knew perfectly well that those insults were just so much spatter and froth, an almost incidental by-product of Angus' seething malice. Angus wasn't paying any real attention to his second. All the important parts of the cyborg's mind were focused on his new ship: on feeling her energies under his hands; on studying every scrap of knowledge his databases contained about her. On imagining what he could do with her.

No, more than just imagining: *tasting*; sensing with his whole body. Milos had seen enough malevolence in Angus' eyes to sicken him for a lifetime. He felt that he and he alone—certainly not Hashi Lebwohl or Warden Dios—could gauge the sheer potency of the venom which boiled and spat inside Angus Thermopyle like a witch's brew. He knew how *alive* with hate Angus was. But he'd never discerned in Angus anything resembling the look of unholy joy which burned across the cyborg's face while he familiarized himself with *Trumpet*. As he worked his board and studied his screens, Thermopyle looked like he was having an orgasm.

Shit. And shit again.

Once *Trumpet* crossed the gap, Milos would have to begin exercising his power over his putative "captain" fast and hard. He wanted to crush that look of vile ecstasy almost as much as he wanted to live.

But not now; not yet. Instead of reacting to Angus' sneers, Milos concentrated on his own board, learning as quickly as he could how his brief but primarily theoretical training for this ship functioned in practice.

Damage control was easy: most of the systems, and all the reports, were automatic. Data wasn't much different than the kind of computer work he'd done for years as Com-Mine Station's deputy chief of Security. And, for reasons which were probably obvious, but which he never mentioned, he already knew everything he would ever need about communications. Scan was another matter, however. He'd never used doppler sensors or particle sifters or—was that a dimensional stress indicator?—and had only the thinnest under-standing of the information they provided.

None of his "duties" affected the actual operation of the ship, however. That was a problem of another kind. Command, helm, targ, engineering; even life support and general maintenance: Angus ran them all. In practice as well as in theory, Milos' survival de-pended on his capacity to run Angus.

"You about ready?" Angus asked, sounding as cheerfully de-structive as an ore-crusher. "We're coming into the fucking cops' fucking private tach range in a couple of minutes. I don't want you shitting your suit when we hit the gap. I hate that smell. I get too much of it just having you on board."

"So what?" Milos muttered, keeping his attention on his read-outs. "You hate everything." He loathed and feared the very timbre of Angus' voice; but it was essential to show Angus that he, Milos, couldn't be intimidated. "A bad smell won't change anything."

Angus snorted. "So you say. But you haven't caught a whiff of yourself yet. You don't know as much about shit as I do."

Milos didn't bother to retort. He'd been raised among gutter-gangs. And he'd spent months back on Com-Mine interrogating An-gus. He already had more experience than he would ever need with excremental human corruption.

The helm screen informed him that *Trumpet* was fifty-three sec-onds from the UMCP's reserved gap range. She was assigned to go into tach in a minute and a half.

Then human space would be out of reach.

For both of them.

Maybe forever.

When that happened, Angus Thermopyle was going to find out just how much Milos Taverner knew about shit and survival.

Eighty seconds later Angus said, almost crowed, "Hang on to your balls. As soon as we cross, everything changes. You bastards have just corn-holed me for the last time."

Milos knew that wasn't true. In an apparent effort to reassure him, Hashi Lebwohl had allowed him to watch a number of Angus' tests on UMCPDA's monitors. And he'd been given many of the test results to read. They all demonstrated incontrovertibly that An-gus had been well and thoroughly welded; that he would never be able to violate his programming. For all his enhanced capabilities, he was the most helpless being in human space.

Nevertheless, without thinking about it, without even realizing he did it, Milos cupped his hand over his crotch as *Trumpet* disappeared into the gap.

ANCILLARY DOCUMENTATION

BILLINGATE

$\sim$ Even while the power of the United Mining Companies Police was at its peak, a number of illegal or bootleg shipyards survived and occasionally flourished in and around human space.

The reason for their existence was simple. Forbidden space had a vast hunger for the same raw materials which Earth craved in such quantity, as well as for the mass-production technologies at which humankind excelled; a hunger which legal trade—both enabled and limited by the United Mining Companies—couldn't satisfy. To feed this appetite, the Amnion were willing to pay well for what they desired, without questioning how those things were obtained. This was true despite explicit treaty to the contrary. Therefore piracy became a thriving subcutaneous industry. Theft offered a higher reward for a given amount of effort than honest prospecting or mining.

That the risks were great, or that the opportunities were unpredictable, were drawbacks which had never hindered crime at any time in human history. That piracy required fast and space-worthy vessels, however, would have been a significant drawback in the absence of bootleg shipyards. Ships were far more difficult to steal than their cargoes. If they were taken while in dock, they were often stopped before their new masters could escape. And if they were attacked somewhere in space, they were usually damaged too severely to be worth much.

Illegal shipyards came into being by the blunt logic of human larceny. A passion for profit was the engine which drove Earth and her widely scattered stations. When that passion was felt by men and women with unscrupulous souls, they acted on it illegally. The law of supply and demand guided many of them, not into piracy, but into providing support for pirates.

The best-known—because the best-defended—of these bootleg shipyards was the one called Billingate on Thanatos Minor.

There were a number of such shipyards within human space, of course. However, by virtue of their locations their existence was precarious: they were vulnerable to direct attack by the UMCP. In order to exist at all they required secrecy. Therefore they hid like ferrets; they moved whenever they could; often they kept their own operations—and profits—small so that they would be less susceptible to exposure or betrayal.

Billingate had few worries along those lines. Because it had been hived into the bleak rock of Thanatos Minor, a planetoid which sailed the vacuum a few million kilometers inside the borders of forbidden space, it had little or nothing to fear from overt assault. It was protected—albeit obliquely—by treaty. It was also defended by Amnion warships: the quadrant of space it occupied lay along the most heavily patrolled boundary with human space. And it was defended as well by the ships which depended on it. In human space, any illegal might reasonably flee rather than face a UMCP destroyer or battlewagon. In forbidden space, flight was less attractive because it led deeper into the fatal realm of the Amnion. Safety from imposed mutation existed only at the fringes of Amnion territory. Illegals were inclined to feel cornered when they were threatened near Billingate; therefore they were predisposed to fight back.

This shipyard did not need secrecy to protect it.

So pirates with enough credits went to Billingate to purchase vessels—or re-creations. Illegal gap ships went to Billingate for repairs. And any brigand who could get there went to Billingate to fence his or her loot. Thanks to its location, Thanatos Minor provided an ideal clearinghouse for the raw materials, technologies, and organic tissues which the Amnion craved. The human species was betrayed more consistently, more often, and more profitably there than anywhere in human space—or human history.

For this reason, Billingate had grown populous—UMCPDA estimated between four and seven thousand inhabitants—as well as rich.

For the same reason, it had also become known.

The stories which reached the ears of private citizens and corporate officials, station security officers and UMCP ensigns, sequestered researchers and GCES undersecretaries alike, had a specificity which the tales of bootleg shipyards generally lacked. Because Billingate had been built entirely by illegals for illegals, it had good cause to be regarded as "the sewer of the universe." Internal crime was violently interdicted because it reduced profitability; but every vice known to humankind thrived there, restricted only by the available credit of its participants. Slavery was common. Chemical dependencies of every kind could be readily nourished. Sacrificial prostitution prospered for the amusement and enrichment of the men— and women?—who owned nerve junkies or null-wave transmitters too reduced to defend themselves. Bio-aesthetic, -prosthetic, and -retributive surgery enhanced or destroyed human capabilities.

It was better to be dead than poor on Thanatos Minor.

Over this morass of human desuetude and corruption, a man called simply "the Bill" presided on the strength of his evenhanded malice, his political acumen (that is to say, his ability to gauge the motivations and breaking points of his people), his talent for protecting the shipyard's profits by making sure that he got paid *first;* and on the authority he gained by being perceived as Billingate's "decisive" by the Amnion. It was he who ruled Thanatos Minor, settled disputes, punished offenders, kept the books—and made Billingate function with some approximation of efficiency, despite the manifold weaknesses and eccentricities of its populace.

Rumor suggested that he had been surgically provided with a double phallus so that he could penetrate women in both nether orifices simultaneously.

Unfortunately all this information served no purpose except to increase the outrage with which Billingate was viewed in the more conservative, genophobic, or ethical strata of human society: it did nothing to threaten Billingate itself. The UMCP was prevented by clear treaty from entering forbidden space to extirpate Thanatos Minor. Likewise, of course, the Amnion were precluded by treaty from permitting Billingate's existence; but this was an unequal, essentially toothless restriction, since the Amnion could—and did—deny all knowledge of the Bill's operations. On that basis, any UMCP incursion into Amnion space would be deemed an act of war.

In the corridors of UMCPHQ, as well as in the chambers of the Governing Council for Earth and Space, it was frequently argued that war was preferable to this kind of peace. As long as places like Billingate were able to exist, the UMCP could never prevail against piracy. However, the official position of the United Mining Companies was that the benefits of trade justified the costs of piracy— and war would put an end to trade.

Speaking for the UMCP, Director Dios took the same position for different reasons: he argued that the costs of war would be far greater than the benefits of eliminating piracy. War, he claimed, would produce an exponential increase in bloodshed and lost lives, without any guarantee of success. Despite the strength of the organization he headed, he was known to question whether humankind could ever win a war with the Amnion.

DAVIES

He had no idea why he was still alive.

Of course, there was no physical reason why he should be dead. Nick Succorso's goons hadn't damaged his body. They'd kept him locked in silence while the ship performed a long and brutal deceleration. They'd made him wait for hours as the ship coasted. Then they'd rousted him from his cell, manhandled him across the ship, and sealed him in an ejection pod. But none of that had threatened his life.

And the pod itself was designed to keep him safe. It enclosed him as tightly as a coffin, allowed him virtually no movement—and certainly no access to its controls. He could see nothing except the status screens which were supposed to help him hope; monitors which were intended to reassure him, but which instead told him his heart and lungs were working too hard. Trajectory and thrust were preset: how could anybody who needed an ejection pod be expected to navigate? Nevertheless its pads and restraints protected him from the g of launch: its systems cooled the heat of his terror, supplied him with plenty of oxygen to compensate for his ragged, urgent breathing.

Yet he should have died. Stress which had nothing to do with the treatment his body received should have killed him.

He was being sent to the Amnion—to a waiting warship called *Tranquil Hegemony*—where he would be studied down to his nucleotides to help the enemies of his species perfect their mutagens; and then he would be made one of them. Perhaps he would become simply a monstrous and immaterial part of their genetic imperialism. Or perhaps he would become a human-seeming and direct agent of their will. In either case, everything that he knew or could recognize about himself would be gone; betrayed and transformed.

Didn't men and women go mad under that kind of pressure? Didn't their hearts burst? Didn't dread clog their lungs until they could no longer breathe?

Of course they did.

But for him the situation was much worse. Born without transition into a sixteen-year-old body, he had no idea who he was. His mind was a copy of his mother's: his body replicated a man he'd never met. Unable to satisfy his instinctive and fundamental need for an image of himself, he had no basis on which to think, to feel, to make choices.

As far as he could remember, he was a woman in her early twenties, a UMCP ensign on her first mission; young and inexperienced, but passionate; a dedicated fighter in the struggle to preserve humankind's right to live or die for what it was. Yet that was nonsense. He was obviously male; so obviously male that his crotch responded when he looked at Morn Hyland—a beautiful woman, not his mother, no, not his mother at all, how could she be? His memories were incomprehensible because they belonged beyond question to someone else.

And they weren't complete. He had a black hole in his mind where he should have had transitions: at the point where his memories should have revealed how he came into being, what his birth meant, why his existence under these conditions was necessary, his recollections frayed away to nothing.

Morn had tried to offer him answers. She'd explained that he'd been brought into being by an Amnion "force-growing" technique which had taken him from her womb to physiological maturity in approximately an hour. And he'd been imprinted with her mind—education, memories, reflexes, and all—because he had none of his own. In addition she'd told him that she'd made the decisions which had afflicted him like this for the simple reason that otherwise he and she would both have died.

He believed that, not because he understood it, but because it fit the person he remembered having been.

But she'd given him nothing adequate to explain how such decisions had become necessary. And he couldn't recall it for himself.

Beyond question he should have gone nova under so much pressure, like a superheated sun.

He had no idea why that hadn't happened. He *felt* like a superheated sun. The source of his intransigent grasp on consciousness and sanity lay hidden somewhere in the black hole of his memories; swallowed by the dark.

Now the ejection pod carried him across the dark to his doom. There was nothing he could do about that; nothing at all; nothing of any kind. Yet he went on fighting for his life.

Fighting to remember.

What had Morn told him?

What you remember, she'd said, *stops right at the point where I first came down with gap-sickness.*

But she'd insisted her son didn't have the same sickness.

Nick hated him, she'd claimed, because she lied to him. By saying that Davies was his, Nick's, son.

But that wasn't enough. Davies had heard its inadequacy in her voice.

He's a tormented man, and I used that against him.

He never wanted me to have you. He wanted me for sex, that's all. So he ordered me to abort you. I told him every lie I could think of that might change his mind.

The truth was deadly. It would have killed them both. Because Davies' father was *the only man in human space that Nick hates worse than the cops.*

Nick himself had supplied Davies with the rest of the story.

Nick had talked about Angus Thermopyle.

He's a pirate and a butcher and a petty thief. Right now, he's serving a life sentence in Com-Mine Station lockup.

That may not make you think very highly of your mother. She's supposed to arrest men like Captain Thermo-pile, or kill them, not fuck them until she gets pregnant.

But it wasn't like that. Captain Thermo-pile gave her a zone implant. After she demolished Starmaster, he rescued her from the wreckage. Davies remembered none of this. He gave her a zone implant to keep her under control. He turned her on until she would have been willing to suck her insides out with a vacuum hose, and then he fucked her senseless.

That's your father, Davies. That's the kind of man you are.

But here's the interesting part. Why wasn't your father convicted? If she had a zone implant, he must have had a zone implant control. Why wasn't it found on him when he was arrested?

The answer is, she'd learned to like it. She wanted it, Davies. It wasn't found on him because he'd already given it to her. She loved using it on herself.

So what did she do with it when he was arrested? She didn't turn it over to Com-Mine Security like a good little cop. They would have removed her zone implant—and your father would have been executed. She couldn't let them take it away from her. So she hid the control and escaped with me. She used it to seduce me so that I would rescue her—not from Captain Thermo-pile, but from Com-Mine Security.

All she's done since then is perfect her addiction.

His time was running out. The pod's blips and chronometers measured his movement toward the Amnion warship like a countdown to death.

Did she tell you she refused to abort you because she wanted to keep you? That isn't strictly true. The only real reason is that she couldn't get an abortion without letting the sickbay test her. It would have recorded her zone implant.

That's your mother, Davies. That's the kind of woman you came from.

And Davies thought, No. No. If that were true—if all that were true—she could have had an abortion and then erased the sickbay log. And she wouldn't have tried to help me. She wouldn't have said, As far as I'm concerned, *you're the second-most important thing in the galaxy. You're my son. But the first, the most important thing is to not betray my humanity.*

He believed that because he recognized it.

Nevertheless he knew what Nick said *was* true. It just wasn't enough.

Nothing was enough. The status screens showed him only that he was closing on *Tranquil Hegemony.* A minute or two remained, no more. In the distance hung the black rock of Thanatos Minor; but that information, too, wasn't enough to do him any good.

He needed to be able to *maneuver.* Urgently he strove to remember everything he might have known about ejection pods. Was there some way to get at the controls, override the presets? Surely a pod designed for emergencies might encounter emergencies of its own; therefore there must be some way for the pod's occupant to take command.

Think, you idiot.

Remember.

If he'd known his father, he might have recognized Angus Thermopyle's instinctive reaction to futility and fear.

But he hadn't known his father. He couldn't remember anything that might help him as the pod cut in thrust—acceleration, not braking—and began to veer away from *Tranquil Hegemony.* He could only stare at the screens with his heart hammering in his throat and sweat streaming off his forehead, and wonder who was being betrayed now.

If *Captain's Fancy* and *Tranquil Hegemony* were talking to each other—shouting at each other?—he didn't hear it: the pod's receivers were tuned to the wrong frequencies, or the messages were tight-beamed. But he saw his course shift away from the Amnion ship; felt lateral thrust as well as acceleration until his new trajectory stabilized and thrust cut out.

Then the screens showed him that he was now running straight for the unreadable stone of Thanatos Minor.

When *Tranquil Hegemony* didn't fire on him, he knew he'd been granted a temporary reprieve.

In response his heart started beating even harder, and sweat ran into his eyes like oil.

At his present velocity, a landing on Thanatos Minor would crush him to undifferentiated pulp—if it didn't consume him in a fireball first. Precisely for that reason, Thanatos Minor would blast him out of space before he hit, to avoid being damaged by the impact.

There was nothing he could do about it.

Nevertheless he was out of *Tranquil Hegemony*'s reach, at least for the time being. Any death was preferable to the one Nick Succorso had intended for him. And according to the screens, he now had nearly six more hours to live.

Six more hours to try to wrestle some kind of understanding up out of the blind abyss which filled his head.

Six more hours to figure out who was being betrayed.

By whom.

His urgency didn't let go of him for an instant.

Davies had betrayed his father's ship.

No, it wasn't him: it was Morn. Not his father's ship: his grand-father's.

But when he insisted on the distinction, he lost the memory; so he let the strange discontinuity between himself and his mother blur.

He'd betrayed *Starmaster* himself.

Not deliberately. He'd done it because he suffered from gap-sickness, and no one knew that. There was no test to reveal it: no test except the gap itself. In his case, the stimulus which triggered the flaw in his brain was heavy g.

And *Starmaster* was under heavy g with a vengeance, slamming herself against the vacuum for both speed and agility as she chased Angus Thermopyle's *Bright Beauty* through the careening rock of the belt. Thermopyle had just fried an entire mining camp, butchered every last man, woman, and child for no known reason; their lorn cries, truncated by destruction, had reached *Starmaster* as they died. Now *Starmaster* was in pursuit, blazing with purpose and clarity.

This was the work the ship had been designed for; the work to which he'd committed himself despite his ingrained doubts about himself. He was on duty on the auxiliary bridge—emergency backup for any station which might fail—and his own purpose should have been clear; it would have been clear if he hadn't been taken over by something greater, something so lucid, precise, and compulsory that it reduced everything else to a corrupt muddle. There on the auxiliary bridge the universe spoke to him—

—and his memories stopped.

He could find no way past that clarity. It must have seared his mind; changed the chemistry of his brain somehow; burned out synapses. He knew that his—no, Morn's, he was separate from her now—*her* life must have gone on from that point. She could remember what happened next. Angus Thermopyle knew. Nick knew some of it. But for Davies Hyland the path was closed; blocked by a neural gap he couldn't cross.

For him, it was easier to figure out who was being betrayed.

Not the Amnion.

And not himself. Or his mother. Not this time.

Nick Succorso.

Davies had seen the loathing on Nick's face and trusted it: he was utterly sure that Nick would never risk cheating the Amnion to save Morn's son. And Morn had already worked miracles on Davies' behalf.

If he survived the next few hours, that knowledge might prove useful.

He had no particular reason to think he would—except that if Morn could work the miracle of diverting him from *Tranquil Hegemony,* she might also have conceived a way to keep him alive. The more he thought about her, the more powerful she appeared: a source of miracles as well as understanding. Maybe that was why the stresses of the past days hadn't destroyed him. Maybe buried away inside him somewhere was a visceral awareness of what she could accomplish, how much he could rely on her.

And maybe the son of a woman like Morn Hyland could work miracles of his own.

Eventually the pod's screens told him that he was going to be rescued.

A ship came toward him. Not a pursuit craft from *Tranquil Hegemony:* a vessel from Thanatos Minor. And she didn't fire. According to the screens, he was still an hour off the rock when she intersected his trajectory.

Her blip absorbed his on the screens.

Because of his training in the Academy—no, Morn's, dammit, *Morn's*—he knew what was happening as the pod began to decelerate. A monitor reported decreasing velocity; he felt g shove him against the pads and restraints. But the pod slowed without braking thrust. The other ship must have matched speeds with him, accepted the pod into one of her holds, then clamped it down so that she could control it.

With difficulty, he wormed his hands up to wipe the sweat off his face. He had no guarantee that this other ship wasn't Amnion.

Nevertheless he believed she was human. If the shipyard on Thanatos Minor hadn't been controlled by human beings, Succorso wouldn't
have tried to escape here from Enablement Station.

So the ship was human. And illegal. He couldn't stop thinking
like a cop, the cop Morn Hyland had been. Whoever rescued him
was his enemy, one way or another. The shipyard on Thanatos Minor served forbidden space as surely as if it were Amnion. The illegals who proxied for them here were the most malign men and women
in the galaxy; as bad as Angus Thermopyle; worse than Succorso in
some ways.

And he had no way of knowing what they wanted from him;
what his value to them was; what use they meant to make of him.

Though the prospect twisted his soul, he had to brace himself
for more helplessness, brutality, deprivation.

As soon as its sensors detected a breathable atmosphere, the
ejection pod automatically popped the locks and unsealed its hatch.

At once a hand gripped the hatch and swung it wide.

Davies found himself staring down the muzzle of an impact gun.

"Out," demanded an oddly lifeless voice.

With his mind full of Morn, Davies feared that he would start
to wail. For some reason he didn't. Instead he snarled a curse, pushed
the muzzle out of his face, and sat up.

Right the first time: he was in a hold. A cargo hold, not a
medical rescue bay designed to receive ejection pods, judging by the
look of it; by the fact that the pod was anchored with the kind of
flexsteel straps freighters used to secure crates and equipment; and by
the lack of heat.

The man with the gun sure as hell didn't look like a medtech.
His slack features and dead eyes gave him the appearance of a nerve
juice junkie who was about to follow his addiction to its logical conclusion. His shipsuit was too nondescript to mean anything. But he
must have been a guard. His impact gun wasn't a weapon he carried:
it was a part of him, a prosthesis replacing his right forearm. Instead
of a left foot, he had a metal tripod anchored to his calf. If he really
were a nerve juice addict, with most of his muscles gone flaccid and
stupid, he probably needed that support to help him stand the kick
of his gun. And the gun had to be part of his arm or else he wouldn't
be able to aim it.

Slowly he brought the muzzle back to Davies' face and repeated, "Out."

"Don't fucking rush me," Davies growled like his father.

But he didn't hesitate to climb out of the ejection pod.

The cold gripped him immediately. Hours of sweat turned to ice on his skin. He was already shivering as he looked around to see if the guard was alone; to see if he had anything to gain by kicking the guard in the stomach and ripping his gun off.

The guard wasn't alone. A man and a woman stood fifteen or twenty meters away, watching him. They were bundled in coldsuits that muffled their shapes; but their hands and boots looked normal, and their faces were human.

The man's head was so long and thin that it seemed like a caricature of itself. Because he was unusually tall, he gave the impression that inside his coldsuit his whole body was thin. A nearly lipless mouth smiled over crooked teeth. Beneath a thatch of dirty hair, his eyes glittered as if he'd artificially reinforced his concentration with enkephalins.

That glitter and his smile made him look like a madman.

The woman appeared stable by comparison. Despite its lines, her face was still handsome; gray highlights did nothing to cheapen the richness of her hair. Davies would have said she was a beautifully mature woman whose best years weren't far behind her. Only a slight stiffness in the way she carried herself suggested that she may have been older than she looked.

The man's smile widened as he studied Davies. For a moment no one said anything. Then he breathed in a gust of vapor, "Now here's a surprise." His voice was wrong for his body: it should have belonged to a kid with rosy cheeks and excessive enthusiasm. "Another surprise."

"What do you mean?" the woman asked in a vibrant contralto.

"What?" The man glanced at her with what may have been amusement. "Don't you recognize him?"

"No." The woman frowned. "Well, yes. But that's impossible. He's far too young."

"Interesting, isn't it?" The man returned his bright gaze to Davies.

Involuntarily Davies wrapped his arms around his chest, trying to contain some of the warmth which steamed from his bones. If he could climb back into the ejection pod and close the hatch, its systems would protect him from freezing. But the guard would stop him if he tried that. Unable to control his shivers—and unable to keep his mouth shut—he remarked raggedly, "I guess you know my father." Then, because he was desperate, he added, "So I guess you know he won't take it kindly if you let me freeze to death."

The guard kept his gun aimed at Davies' head and reacted to nothing. Apparently his addiction inured him to cold—or to the awareness of cold.

"Let me explain something," the man said, incongruously youthful and eager. "You're worthless to me. Other people think you're valuable, and I'm going to know why before I make up my mind about you, but to me you're just a waste of atmosphere. Threats won't help you. And your father as sure as shit won't help you." The man chuckled. "If he even knows you're alive. So don't give me a hard time. Answer my questions like a good boy and take your chances.

"How did you do that?"

Davies understood all of this and none of it. Angus Thermopyle was in Com-Mine Security lockup. He knew nothing about his son— and probably wouldn't care if he did. And Davies himself meant nothing to Thanatos Minor. His value was to the Amnion and Morn, with Succorso caught between them, fighting to make them both serve his own purposes.

His teeth chattered as he asked, "Do what?"

The man seemed to enjoy the sound of Davies' teeth. "Change course in that pod," he said liplessly.

"I didn't." Davies shivered so hard that his right knee failed. This was only a cargo hold. Nothing except the bulkheads and the infrastructure and the ship's frail skin held out the black and absolute cold of space. For an instant he caught himself with his left. Then that, too, folded, and he thudded to the deck. His mouth could hardly form words. "It's impossible."

"I told you so," the woman commented distantly.

"Then it's a game," the man assented. "Captain Nick must be playing bait-and-switch with our hosts. If he thinks he can get me tangled up in something like that, he's even more confused than I remember.

"What's your name?"

The heat leaked out of Davies, taking his life with it. He should have wailed or pleaded. He should have answered the question. But he didn't. He said, shivered, "Fuck you."

At that, anger or enthusiasm stretched the man's lips even thinner. They were pale around his words as he said, "Listen to me. I'm the Bill. You pay me before you get anything. Hypothermia is a nice death. As soon as you go to sleep, nothing ever bothers you again. You can be sure I won't let you freeze. I'm not that nice to anybody. You can answer questions now, or you can wait until I try a little BR surgery on you.

"What's your name?"

Despite the cold, Davies had no trouble reaching back among his memories *Mom's memories* to the Academy, where she'd first heard the term "BR surgery." BR meant "bio-retributive."

"Davies," he replied in a cough of steam. "Davies Hyland."

The man paused. "Now why, I wonder," he mused, "does that name sound familiar?"

"You heard the story," the woman told him. "Captain Davies Hyland, commanding officer, United Mining Companies Police destroyer *Starmaster*. It destructed somehow—or Thermopyle blew it up. He got away with the captain's daughter. Morn Hyland. She left him for Succorso when Com-Mine Security arrested him.

"You know Thermopyle. You know what he must have done to her while he had her. On top of everything else, he must have gotten her pregnant.

"This must be her son."

"That doesn't make sense," the man protested. "He's at least sixteen years too old."

The hold contracted around Davies. The cold seemed to leech vision as well as heat out of him. The ague in his muscles was so severe that he couldn't keep his head up. On his knees he huddled over himself like a penitent.

The woman sighed patiently. "Where did he just come from?"

"Captain Nick's ship."

"And where before that?"

The man let out a sigh of comprehension. After another pause he asked, "Davies, why did you go to Enablement Station? What were you doing there? What was Captain Nick doing?"

Now who was being betrayed? By whom?

Davies could feel the sleep he'd been promised coming. The chills threatened to shake his consciousness apart. Soon he wouldn't be able to connect one thought to another, and he would be able to rest at last.

What answer would Morn want him to give?

He had no way of knowing, but he did the best he could.

"She's UMCP. Morn Hyland." *I'm* UMCP, you fucking bastard, and this is one bill I'm definitely going to pay. "They sent her." He could barely force out more than one word at a time. "I don't know why. But Succorso—" The cold seared his lungs. For a moment he coughed hard enough to bring up blood. Then he finished. "He's working with her."

There. At least one small part of his debt of harm to Nick Succorso was paid.

But it didn't work. Not the way he wanted. Out of the cold and the gathering dark, the man said, "I don't believe you. Enablement is the only place she could have obtained a kid your age. That means you must have been the reason they went there. There must be something"—Davies heard relish in the word—"*special* about you. Otherwise our hosts wouldn't want you back.

"I'm quite sure you know what that something is. Eventually you're going to tell me. You're going to tell me what kind of game they're playing."

Davies couldn't see the deck in front of him.

What kind of game.

He no longer knew whether his eyes were open.

They're playing.

Maybe, he thought as he sagged dumbly onto his face, maybe it worked after all.

NICK

Nick Succorso rubbed the scars on his face as if they were tight with old pain and waited for Billingate Operations to assign him a berth.

Where he was told to dock would hint at where he stood with the Bill.

He knew perfectly well that he was pushing the Bill into a difficult position. The Amnion warships—*Tranquil Hegemony* and now *Calm Horizons,* looming out of deep space—had certainly been in communication with Thanatos Minor, transmitting their requirements. Also certainly, those requirements weren't to Nick's benefit. And the Bill had to take them seriously. He lived here on sufferance: his hosts could revoke his whole economic existence whenever they wished. In addition, two Amnion warships represented enough firepower to root him out of his rock like a rat out of a hole.

And then there was the question of selling human beings to forbidden space. The Bill had no moral, or even visceral, qualms about such things: that was sure. Nevertheless he was equally sure to have pragmatic qualms. If Thanatos Minor became known as a place where men and women were lost to the Amnion, Billingate would lose traffic. Fewer ships would come; fewer repairs would be done; fewer goods would be sold.

He wouldn't thank Nick Succorso for bringing problems like that down on his head.

On the other hand, Nick had credit for the repairs he needed;

and providing such repairs brought in much of Billingate's wealth. And the ships which came for repair were the same vessels which brought the resources and information the Amnion craved. Any ship the Bill turned away would have a double impact on his profits.

Also the circumstances surrounding the sale of Morn and her damnable brat were unique. In this situation, the Bill might believe that he could cooperate with Nick—perhaps secretly, perhaps passively—without risking too much damage.

He wouldn't thank Nick for coming to him now, like this. But he might conceivably do the work Nick needed from him.

The first indication of his leanings would come when Operations assigned a berth. A visitor's dock or a place in the shipyard? If the Bill treated *Captain's Fancy* like a visitor, Nick's troubles were just beginning.

As if Morn hadn't already done him enough harm—

He still had no idea how she'd escaped from her cabin to reprogram that ejection pod. The maintenance computer reported that the lock on her door worked fine. His crew volunteered nothing. Someone had betrayed him, but he didn't know who—or why.

"Damn them all to hell and shit," he muttered. "What the fuck's taking so long?"

Mikka Vasaczk and her watch had the bridge while *Captain's Fancy* coasted toward the rock. Sib Mackern sat at the data station because he and Alba Parmute were sharing the work of three people; but Scorz was a competent replacement for Lind on communications, Ransum could manage helm despite her jittery hands, and Karster was safe enough at targ. The scan second, Arkenhill, was no substitute for Carmel—who was?—and this close to Thanatos Minor, as well as to two Amnion warships, scan was critical; but Mikka was watching everything that came in through Arkenhill's board almost as carefully as Nick himself did.

In any case, *Captain's Fancy* was moving too slowly to survive a fight. She might inflict damage, but she would be destroyed nonetheless.

While his ship glided along her approach trajectory toward Billingate, Nick paced the bridge and studied the screens and fretted as if he had worms gnawing inside him. The electricity, the combative frisson, which usually filled his nerves like eagerness when death and ruin threatened him, was gone. The knowledge that he could beat anybody had been replaced by the fear that Morn had dug a hole too deep for him to climb out of.

There was no question about it: he should have ripped out her female organs when he first heard she was pregnant, instead of taking her to Enablement to have her brat.

He shouldn't be stewing about that now, of course. The past was the past: men who looked back got shot by what was in front of them. Until now, the only regret of his life was that he'd ever trusted anyone enough to let *that woman* scar him. Unfortunately his acid longing to take back the mistakes he'd made with Morn refused to recognize its own futility. Instead it gnawed inside him like cramps, hindering his strength, restricting his energies.

She was so beautiful— Sex with her was the closest he'd ever come to healing his scars. And every bit of it was a *lie*. Like the first time, with the woman who'd cut him. The welcoming spread of Morn's legs had been a steel trap, open to shear off his manhood, his ability to beat impossible odds; gaping to amputate the part of him that never lost.

What she'd done to him made his heart hurt as if she'd laid her knife there instead of on his cheeks.

What the *fuck's* taking them so long?

"It's not a simple question for them," Mikka answered unnecessarily. "They have to figure out whose side they're on. Probably they've never had to do that before."

For the first time since he'd known his second, her habitual scowl didn't look merely closed, defended. Instead it conveyed criticism; even hostility. It gave the impression that she no longer trusted him—*him*, Nick Succorso, who had once been as unquestionable to her as the orbits of the stars.

Morn had cost him that as well.

"This may come as a surprise to you," he snarled from the burning depths of his regret, "but I knew that already."

Mikka shrugged stolidly.

"Whatever they're talking about," Scorz reported in an abstract tone, "they're beaming it too tight for us to hear. There's some residual buzz, but I can't pick up anything else."

Struggling to put Mikka and Morn and regret out of his mind, Nick muttered as if he didn't know he was repeating himself, "Damn them all to hell and shit."

Operations continued to transmit routine traffic information, trajectory confirmation, station protocols; nothing else.

He paced the bridge and tried to think.

At some point he would have to resume his air of superiority and confidence; fake it if he couldn't actually feel it. His dread and regret were infectious: the more uncertain he felt, the more his people would doubt him. Mikka wasn't the only one—although she was the worst, because she was the most capable; because he'd trusted her the most. Sib Mackern seemed to flinch whenever Nick caught his eye. And Ransum's nervousness was spreading. Normally confined to her hands, it now affected the way she turned her head; it made her shuffle her feet as if she felt an unconscious desire to run.

Already three people on the bridge distrusted Nick enough to be unreliable.

Who else felt that way? Maybe no one except Vector Shaheed. And Vector's attitude was predictable: he had reason to think Nick was going to kill him. Hell, the phlegmatic shit deserved to be killed. He'd ignored an order. Maybe the infection hadn't spread any further yet.

But it was going to spread. It would certainly catch Pup. The kid was Mikka's brother. And he admired Vector.

And the rest of the crew would be exposed to the same illness as soon as they felt Nick's vulnerability and realized that the center of their lives might not hold much longer.

Groping for clues—for ways to pull himself out of his stew—maybe for hope—Nick stopped at the scan station and asked harshly, "Where did they take that damn pod?"

"Cargo berth," Arkenhill answered promptly without lifting his gaze from his board. He may have been trying to prove that he was as capable as Carmel. "I guess they're planning to keep the pod. The ship docked a couple of minutes ago. You want to know which berth?"

"No." Nick had only one reason for caring what happened to Davies Hyland. "I want id on the ship."

"That's easy. We've got traffic data." As a precaution against accidents, Operations transmitted information on all ships and movements in Billingate's control space. Arkenhill hit keys, consulted his readouts. "She calls herself *Soar*. Captain Sorus Chatelaine. Port of registry, Terminus."

"She's a ways from home," Mikka observed dryly. Terminus was farther from forbidden space than any other human station—at least a hundred light-years farther than Earth.

Nick turned to Sib Mackern. "What does data say about her?"

Sweat and lack of sleep made Mackern's pale mustache stand out and his eyes recede. His hands faltered as he worked his board. After a moment he reported, "Nothing, Nick. We've never heard of her before."

Involuntarily Nick's fingers curled into fists. Sib sounded like a weakling—and Nick despised weaklings. He had to stifle an impulse to hit the data second.

"Cross-reference it," he snapped. "Name, captain, registry, id codes. Give me a real answer."

Among illegal ships, there was often a considerable discrepancy between public and private id. Ships and captains could change their names as often as they liked. But they couldn't change their registrations—or the id codes embedded in their datacores. Not without swapping out the datacores themselves.

Even that was possible, of course. But then there would be other kinds of discrepancies—

"Do it by configuration, too," Mikka added for him. "Try their emission signature or anything else scan picked up on them."

Now it was his second that Nick wanted to hit. Not because she was wrong, but because she helped him when he shouldn't have needed it; because he did need it. His brain wasn't working, and he hated that more than he despised weaklings.

Morn, you goddamn bitch, what have you done to me?

Who betrayed me for you? Who let you *out*?

"Here it comes," Scorz put in abruptly. "Final approach and docking instructions."

Nick held his breath while the communications second relayed the details to command and helm.

She was being treated like a visitor. A ship without cargo. A fugitive. An illegal in search of recreation. Or a dealer in information.

Certainly not as a ship that needed—and could pay for—massive work on her gap drive.

Cursing explosively, Nick strode to Scorz' station. "Give me a channel!"

Scorz tightened the receiver in his ear, tapped keys. Almost immediately he said, "Stand by for Captain Succorso," and leaned away from his pickup to give Nick room.

"Operations!" Nick snapped. "This is Captain Succorso. Who's garbling your reception? Didn't you hear me say I need repair? Didn't you get my credit confirmation? I want a berth in the shipyard!"

"Captain Succorso." The reply which came over bridge audio was laconic; insufferably unconcerned. "Our reception isn't garbled. And we aren't deaf. We just don't like ships that come in chased by angry Amnion. You're lucky we're letting you dock at all. But the Bill wants to talk to you." A pause. "He wants to confirm your credit in person."

All at once Nick's dread became as heavy as a blow to the stomach. For a second or two he felt that he couldn't breathe; that his voice would crack like a kid's if he tried to talk.

He couldn't wait for the shock to pass, however. Half coughing, he rasped, "Make sense, Operations. This is a goddamn credit-jack," coded to be read by a computer, "not a physical transfer. He won't learn anything by *looking* at it.

"I need repairs. I can pay for them. Dock me in the shipyard!"

Operations forced him to wait for an answer. When it came, the voice from the speakers seemed to be laughing secretly.

"Apparently that credit-jack has been revoked."

"You sonofabitch!" Nick hunched over the pickup, trying to drive his anger into the face of the man he couldn't see. "It can't *be* revoked. It's *money*! You can't revoke *money*!"

The radio voice permitted itself an audible chuckle. "Try telling that to the Amnion warship behind you."

With a definitive click, Operations cut transmission.

An unnatural silence filled the bridge, as if the air-scrubbers and servos had shut down.

Karster usually kept his questions to himself. Perhaps to compensate for the fact that he looked as unformed as a boy, he tried to act like he already understood everything. He couldn't stand the silence, however.

"Confirm it in person?" he asked. "What's that supposed to mean?"

"It means," Mikka replied as if she were suddenly tired, "the

Bill wants to know what's going on before he makes up his mind about us."

Nick wheeled on the command second. If she kept this up, he was certainly going to hit her. "You said it yourself," he snarled. "It's not that simple. He's got fucking Morn's fucking brat."

The Bill wanted to know what was going on so that he could milk the situation for all it was worth. And so that he could get even with Nick for bringing him this kind of trouble.

Nick had promised Davies to the Amnion.

Trying to demonstrate that he'd never intended to break his bargains with them—as well as to conceal the true nature of his dishonesty toward them—he'd also promised them Morn.

But the Bill had Davies. If Nick's credit-jack had been revoked, he had nothing with which to buy the brat back.

Except Morn.

He'd come to a place where he had to cheat somebody—and whoever he cheated would kill him for it.

Unless—

The idea hit him like a bolt of his old lightning, the electricity which kept him and everything he valued alive.

—unless he cheated the cops instead.

Hashi Lebwohl had assigned him to undermine Billingate, do the shipyard potentially permanent harm. And the DA director had told him how to do it. A dangerous gamble: the kind Nick specialized in. That Lebwohl was willing to take such risks had impressed Nick in spite of himself.

It was a risk which could be turned against Lebwohl and the entire fucking UMCP.

Would they respond to his last message? He didn't know. Maybe not. But if they did, so much the better. They were much more of a threat to Thanatos Minor and the Amnion than to Nick himself. As far as they were concerned, Morn was the only excuse he needed for whatever he did. He could always say he was trying to rescue her.

And if they didn't respond, they couldn't interfere.

The consequences would be incalculable, of course. But that wasn't Nick's problem. Let Lebwohl clean it up. Or Dios himself. They deserved it.

In the meantime it just might work.

For a moment he simply stood still, tasting his own resources, letting the bolt's charge bring him back to himself. Then he turned away from Mikka as if her doubts no longer mattered.

"Arkenhill," he asked with a semblance of his old relaxed, deadly insouciance, "how far back are those warships?"

The scan second had this information at his fingertips. "*Tranquil Hegemony* is about half an hour. She burned for a while after we passed her—after the pod changed course. Closed most of the distance. But she's down to our speed now—normal approach velocity for Billingate." To show that the hostility of her intentions wasn't aimed at the shipyard.

"*Calm Horizons* has been coming up on us as fast as a lumbering tub like that can and still leave room to decelerate. In fact, she cut it a lot finer than we did." Which she could do because she was Amnion—and because she'd been moving much slower than *Captain's Fancy*'s imponderable .9C. "She should be in dock"—Arkenhill checked a screen—"call it eight hours from now."

Nick shook his head. "They won't come all the way in. They're going to hang off in prime range for that damn super-light proton beam, just to remind us—and the Bill—we can't hope to cross them and live.

"So," he continued as if he were thinking aloud, "I'll have a little more than half an hour to talk to the Bill before *Tranquil Hegemony* arrives. And I can stall for four or five hours after that—until *Calm Horizons* is in position to support *Tranquil Hegemony*.

"By then I'd better be ready to get us out of this mess. One way or another."

He scanned the bridge. No one disagreed with him—and no one except Mikka and Ransum met his gaze. The helm second's face conveyed nothing more profound than worry and tension. However, Mikka's expression was dour and defiant, almost openly skeptical. Minute by minute she allowed more of her distrust to show.

"Scorz," Nick said over his shoulder, approximating a poised casualness he still didn't feel, "call me when we're ten minutes out of dock. I'll be in my cabin."

Getting ready.

Then he moved to the command station and leaned close to Mikka's ear. Maybe she was the one who'd betrayed him. Ignoring the way she pulled her head back as if she didn't want him to touch her, didn't want to feel his breath on her cheek, he murmured intimately, "I'm going to do my job. You do yours. But the next time you look at me like that, you'd better be prepared to back it up."

Leaving that threat behind him, he walked off the bridge.

When *Captain's Fancy* docked, he was waiting in the access passage of her airlock as if he were eager.

He tried to believe that he'd recovered his sure genius for victory: to some extent he succeeded. Yet his new energy felt as artificial as the resources Morn's zone implant gave her.

Why were the Amnion so bloody determined to get their hands on her brat? What did he represent to them? Was he just an excuse—a way to unmask Nick's real treachery? Or did Davies have some value Nick couldn't guess?

Because he couldn't answer questions like that, he couldn't gauge his own position accurately—or the Bill's. How much did the Bill have to gain by pleasing the Amnion in this situation? How much did he stand to lose by refusing to help Nick?

The sensation that Morn had done him more damage than he could sustain continued to gnaw deep in his guts despite his efforts to believe he was ready.

"Dock in two minutes," Scorz announced over the intercom. "Secure to disengage spin."

Nick was ready for that, at least. With his hands on the zero-g grips, he waited for the transition between *Captain's Fancy*'s internal spin and Thanatos Minor's pull.

The rock's gravitic field was roughly .8g. In itself, Thanatos Minor lacked the mass to produce so much gravity. However, one of the curious side effects of the kind of fusion generator which powered Billingate was an increase in the planetoid's effective density. It had almost enough g to be comfortable.

As Nick's boots began to drift from the deck, imitating freefall, Scorz said unnecessarily, "One minute."

Nick clenched his teeth against his visceral distrust of dock. He was illegal: his survival depended on movement—*Captain's Fancy*'s as well as his own. Even when he was safe, he disliked surrendering his ship to the clamped paralysis of a berth. But now he was faced with the very real possibility that he and his ship would never move freely again.

Then the hull relayed a jolt of impact. Transmitted through the bulkheads, the sound of the grapples and limpets carried clearly across the ship. From Billingate's lock came the hiss of air-lines. As if they were magnetized, Nick's boots pulled him toward the new floor.

"Dock secure, Nick." This time the voice over the intercom was Mikka's. "We're switching to installation power now." Familiar with every hum and glow of his ship, he noticed the nearly subliminal flicker of the lights as the current changed. "Shall we keep drive on standby?"

Damn her. That was something else he should have thought of for himself. Resisting an impulse to snarl, he answered, "Good idea. Let's act like we expect to be assigned a shipyard berth almost immediately." Then he added, "Lock up behind me. Nobody goes in or out until I get back."

"Right," she acknowledged.

At the control panel, Nick checked the airlock, then hit the sequence to open the doors. His hands did everything abruptly, as if he were eager—or afraid.

As soon as he entered the lock and closed the doors, an indicator told him that Mikka had sealed the ship.

Reaching to key the outer door, he heard Sib Mackern over the intercom. "Nick?"

Nick thumbed the toggle. "What?"

"I've got alternative id on *Soar*. The ship that picked up Davies. It's tentative—you might call it hypothetical—but I thought you would want to know."

Nick dismissed the suggestion. "Tell me later. I haven't got time now." He was in a hurry. The timer was running on his last half hour before the Amnion arrived and began throwing their weight around.

He silenced the intercom; opened *Captain's Fancy*'s outer door.

It was like being back on Enablement. Billingate's airlock stood open, admitting him to the scan field passage which would search him for weapons or contaminants. And at the end of the passage, two guards waited. The only significant difference was that these guards were purportedly human—and they already had their guns trained on him.

Both of them looked like their doctors had forgotten—or never known—the distinction between bio-prosthetic and bio-retributive surgery.

Nick was accustomed to such sights, but they still filled him with contempt. Any man who couldn't shoot straight unless his gun was built into his arm, or couldn't decide when to shoot unless Operations radioed orders directly into his brain, was something less than human, no matter how much he thought he'd been enhanced. But the doctors hadn't stopped there. In addition to prosthetic fire-arms and transmitters, both guards had optical monitors where one or the other of their eyes should have been. They were machines, nothing more: pieces of equipment pretending to be human. For recreation, Nick thought mordantly, they probably stuck their fingers in power receptacles.

"Captain Succorso?" one of them asked as if his vocal cords had been replaced by a speaker.

Nick grinned maliciously. "Who were you expecting? Warden Dios?" Striding between the guards, he said, "I'm going to see the Bill. Be good boys and stay here. Make sure nobody steals my ship."

He knew the way; but the guards didn't let him find it for himself. After a momentary hesitation while they listened to orders from Operations, they came after him, bounding against the rock's g until they caught up with him. One at each shoulder, they steered him along the access passages into the reception area for the visitor's docks.

In Reception they passed more guards, as well as data terminals which would have enabled Nick to secure lodgings, establish local credit, hire women off the cruise, or prepare id verification through finger- or voice-print. He had no interest in those amenities, however. Moving at a pace that made him bounce from stride to stride, he half led, half accompanied his escort toward the nearest lift which ran down into the core of the rock; to the depths where the Bill had hived his lair.

Down there, a thousand meters of stone, concrete, and steel kept the Bill and his profits safe from any attack short of a prolonged super-light proton barrage. *Calm Horizons* and *Tranquil Hegemony* could probably dig him out, but only by blazing away at Thanatos Minor until the entire surface was slagged and the reactor in the heart of the rock reached meltdown temperatures.

The Bill may have been as larcenous and uncaring as a billy goat, but he was smart enough to be afraid. Otherwise he wouldn't live down here—and Nick's credit-jack would be good.

The ride down in the lift made Nick wish he carried a transmitter that could reach *Captain's Fancy*. But here even the kind of nerve beepers he used routinely in places like Com-Mine Station were worse than useless: they didn't function, but they did arouse suspicion.

On either side, the guards kept their guns aimed at his ribs as if they expected him to do something crazy at any moment.

"So how's business?" he asked as if he wanted to start a conversation. "Do you clowns get enough activity around here to keep you from dying of boredom?"

One of the guards smiled to show that he had no teeth: they'd been rotted away by nic or hype. The other remarked, "As long as we think we might get to shoot you, we're happy."

Nick shrugged. "Sorry to disappoint you. You can't shoot me now—the Bill wants to talk to me. And once we do that he'll realize that keeping me alive is more important than you are."

"You have to pay him first," the guard with no teeth chuckled, "and you ain't got no credit."

"Don't worry about it." Nick sneered cheerfully, trying to diffuse the tension which tightened around his chest as the car descended. "Some things are more valuable than credit—although a BR like you probably can't understand that."

"What do you think?" the second guard asked the first. "*I* think he's trying to insult us."

"Don't think," Nick advised. "You'll get confused."

Involuntarily, despite his air of confidence, he held his breath as the lift sighed to a stop.

Another access passage. More guards. Nick hardly noticed them. The mass of rock piled above him had never felt so heavy. It seemed to lean down on him, making his shoulders sag and his step falter in spite of the light g. Until his jaws began to ache, he didn't realize that he was grinding his teeth.

He needed energy *now*; needed his wits and his superiority. The problems he'd left behind aboard *Captain's Fancy* could be ignored temporarily. Another victory or two would restore his crew's confidence in him. Eventually he would discover who had betrayed him. But the problems ahead could kill him in a matter of minutes. If he didn't measure up to his reputation, he was finished *now*.

Do you think I'm done with you, Morn? he asked the echoing corridor. Do you think I've finished hurting you? You're out of your mind. I haven't started yet.

That came first, before he tried betraying the cops.

Straightening his shoulders, he walked the last meters to the strongroom which served as the Bill's personal command center, and grinned sardonically at the door guard.

Unlike Nick's escort, this individual cradled his beam gun in his hands. He didn't appear normal, however. Except for his mouth, most of his face had been covered or replaced by scanning equipment. Red and amber lights winked cryptically at his temples. The Bill didn't entrust his own security to the bugeyes—the optical monitors and listening devices—which scrutinized and reported on all the rest of Billingate.

On the wall over the door was a sign that read:

I'M THE BILL YOU OWE. IF YOU DON'T PAY ME, YOU DON'T LEAVE.

Apparently none of the guards needed to announce Nick aloud. Their transmitters did the job inaudibly. After a moment's consultation, the scan-guard keyed the door and admitted Nick to the strongroom.

His escort stayed behind. He did his best to saunter inside without them like a man who owed nothing.

The room was large enough to be a cargo hold. The Bill liked to have space about him, perhaps to counteract the claustrophobic depth of his covert. The flat surrounding walls were featureless, however. In fact, they were barely lit. Most of the illumination came from a set of ceiling spots which focused down on the Bill himself.

If recent events disturbed him, he didn't show it. Alone in his command center, he stood encircled by a neat ring of computer stations, gleaming under the spots: boards, terminals, screens, and readouts which, presumably, kept him in contact with every part of Billingate. The grotesque length of his head was mimicked by the rest of his body: he was insatiably thin. Stark in the light, he looked hungry enough to suck the marrow from Nick's bones. Shadows filled the hollows of his cheeks. Arms like sticks supported hands with fingers as sharp and narrow as styluses. Under his dirty hair and glittering eyes, his lipless smile exposed his keen, crooked teeth.

As if in welcome, he spread his arms. "Captain Nick," he said in his incongruously boyish voice. "How nice to see you. You haven't been away all that long—not as long as some—but it's always a pleasure when you visit.

"I gather you've led an interesting life recently. It isn't every day that you arrive here *escorted*"—he relished the irony of the word— "by Amnion defensives. You must tell me all about it sometime.

"But not now," he added quickly, like a solicitous host. "I know how busy you must be. For the present, tell me how I can serve you. Somewhere here, we have"—he made a gesture which seemed to encompass the galaxy—"everything you can pay for."

Nick was in no mood for blather. Nevertheless his ship—as well as his life—depended on his ability to match the Bill. Deliberately casual, he remarked, "That depends on how much money I've got. I have a credit-jack"—Nick named the sum—"but Operations tells me you won't honor it. That limits my options."

" 'Won't,' Captain Nick?" the Bill put in promptly. "Surely Operations didn't say 'won't'?"

Nick tried to grin with his old, dangerous amusement. "Maybe I've missed something. I requested a shipyard berth. They docked me with the visitors." A little of his anger leaked into his voice, but he kept it quiet. "And they told me my credit-jack has been revoked. Doesn't that mean 'won't'?"

"Not at all, not at all." Whenever the Bill moved his head, the light made his face look like it was being eaten by shadows. "It simply means the situation has become delicate. The 'issuing authority' of that credit-jack has 'instructed' us not to honor it." Apparently the Bill enjoyed euphemisms. "This is not strictly—shall we say, not strictly legal? If it were, no one would ever pay me for anything. Men in your position—not you, of course, Captain Nick, certainly not, but men with fewer scruples—would give me credit for goods or services, and then after they were gone they would simply 'revoke' my remuneration.

"I don't do business that way. I'm the Bill you owe, Captain

Nick." Behind his light, enthusiastic tone, he was fatally serious. "That means I get paid first—and I make sure the money is good before I accept it. If I accept your credit-jack, you can be certain the Amnion will honor it."

"Fine," Nick said, "good." His poise was fraying. He would have loved to hit the Bill a few times and hear those thin bones snap. "How do we get there from here? I need repairs. I have a credit-jack to pay for them. But you're suspicious. Now what?"

"Simplicity itself." The Bill smiled so that his teeth shone. "Ask the Amnion to rescind their instructions. As soon as they inform me that they no longer object to our transactions, your credit will be good, and I'll provide repairs which will satisfy you completely."

Without realizing it, Nick had tightened his shoulders, clenched his fists. By an act of will, he uncurled his fingers. But he couldn't undo the knots in his voice as he said, "I can't do that. It's up to you, not me. You have something that belongs to me. It's something I've already promised to them—payment for services rendered. As long as you have that, I can't satisfy them. And as long as I can't satisfy them, they're going to be a threat to all of us. They may decide to just take my property away from you."

Smoothly the Bill said, "I may decide to 'just' give it."

"And if you do," Nick countered, "you'll be cheating *me*." He stifled a need to brandish his fists. "I may not look very dangerous right now, but I can do your reputation a lot of damage. Ships will stay away when they hear you've started cheating.

"No," he continued harshly, "the really simple solution is for you to give me what's mine. I'll pay your costs, of course—and a salvage fee. Then I can satisfy the Amnion, and we'll all get what we want in the end."

The Bill shook his long head. "I'm afraid that's a little too simple." Boyish high spirits seemed to bubble in the background as he spoke. "Just as an example of the complexities you've neglected—salvage fees depend on the value of the goods salvaged. You're asking me to surrender those goods, but you haven't told me what they're worth."

Nick swallowed a curse. "They haven't got any value to me at all. The Amnion want them, I don't. And I can't explain the Amnion to you. I don't *know* why they think that brat is so precious." I don't even know whether it's really him they want. I don't know which one of us they were trying to kill in the gap. A bit lamely, he added, "You could ask them to set the fee."

"My dear Captain Nick," replied the Bill with cadaverous amusement, "I've already done that. They decline to place a value on your 'property.' Indeed, they decline to solve any of your problems for you. If I understand them rightly, they insist that the sole, or at least the only relevant, issue here is 'the mutual satisfaction of requirements.' They feel that they've bargained with you in good faith, and that you've cheated them. This they consider intolerable. They insist on restitution, pure and simple."

Nick clenched his teeth for a moment. Then he took a deep breath, let it out with a sigh, and said as if he were admitting defeat, "So I'm stuck. You won't return the contents of that ejection pod. And you won't accept my money. That doesn't leave me very many options." Are you ready for this, Morn? It might work. Can you stand it? "I guess I'll have to offer you something else."

The Bill beamed. "Naturally I'm interested—although I can't imagine what you have that would be worth more than money."

"Try this." Nick glanced around the dark corners of the strong-room as if to ensure that no one else could hear him. Then he moved closer to the Bill. Billingate's g made him feel light: what he was about to do made him feel light-headed. When he came up against the nearest of the Bill's computer stations, he stopped. In a quiet, conspiratorial tone, he said, "I'll trade you. You give me the kid you found in that pod. I'll give you a UMCP ensign, complete with id tag."

The Bill's face seemed to stretch as if he were feigning surprise.

"She's a cop—and she's intact," Nick articulated softly. "If that were all, she would be worth a fortune out here. The things she can tell you are priceless. But there's more.

"She's a cop, she's intact, she's gorgeous—and she has a zone implant. The control comes with her."

The shifting of the shadows on the Bill's face began to make his surprise appear more genuine.

"Think about it for a minute," Nick urged. He'd already promised Morn to the Amnion, but that didn't hinder him. They were after Davies: Morn was just "restitution" for their inconvenience. Nick would be able to find some other way to satisfy that requirement. "Her id tag alone is precious. It'll give you all the codes the cops use to access their own computers. And you won't even have to break her to get the rest. All you have to do is turn her on and let her spill everything she knows.

"But here's the best part." Are you listening, Morn? "When you're done with what she knows, she's still priceless.

"I tell you, she's *gorgeous*. And that zone implant makes her the most *effective* piece of female flesh you'll ever see. I know from experience. She'll make every other woman here look like a dry hag. In the end, you might get more for selling her on the cruise than her information and codes are worth." The idea of selling Morn into sexual slavery almost restored his sense of being sure and unbeatable. "The truth is, she's a hell of a lot more valuable than that fucking brat. Except to the Amnion, because they don't fuck women—and they don't know she's a cop. But she's about the only thing I've got left to bargain with. For the sake of surviving what you call my 'escort,' I'll trade her for that kid."

"Interesting." The Bill twisted his lipless mouth. "A tasty offer—apparently. Of course, I accept your glowing picture of her worth unreservedly. But simply out of curiosity—do the cops know you've got one of their ensigns to sell?"

Curiosity, shit. "Sure they do. Her name is Morn Hyland—she came to me off Angus fucking Thermo-pile's ship after Com-Mine Security arrested him. They probably think she's still working for them—they don't know about the zone implant—but that doesn't mean they haven't already taken precautions. *Some* of what she knows is out of date by now. *Pieces* of her information have been changed. She's still priceless."

"Then why," inquired the Bill, "haven't you simply sold her to the Amnion and solved all your problems that way?"

"Because"—Nick glared straight into the Bill's bright gaze—"I don't want to solve that many of *their* problems. I'm like you. I do business with them for what I can get out of it, not because I'm trying to help them."

Remember that. I'm warning you. I'm like you. If you mess with me, I'll burn your heart out.

The twisting of the Bill's mouth became a grimace. He looked down at his readouts, tapped a key or two absentmindedly. Etched by light, he ran his fingertips along the edges of his boards.

When he lifted his head again, he was smiling like a corpse with an orgasm.

"Captain Nick, I don't trust you. You're playing some kind of game with me—perhaps the same game you're playing with the Amnion. Why else did you divert your ejection pod here, instead of letting *Tranquil Hegemony* have it?"

Before he could stop himself, Nick protested, "*Morn* did that."

When he realized his mistake, he swore at himself viciously. How had she done him so much damage? How had she reached so far inside him with the knife of her treachery?

"And you expect me to believe," the Bill retorted as if he were pouncing, "she did it without your connivance? No, Captain Nick. You planned that with her. Or else the picture you paint of her is decidedly—shall we say, decidedly optimistic? In either case, I can be sure of only one thing. If I trade for her, what I get will not be what you say it is.

"Haven't you heard the rumors about you, Captain Nick? Don't you know people think you're a pirate who supplements his income by doing odd jobs for UMCPDA? Perhaps this entire exercise is an elaborate charade designed to plant your pet ensign on my installation.

"I'm afraid my answer is no." He sounded as happy as a kid who'd won a game of marbles. "If you can't *pay* me, Captain Nick, we really have nothing further to discuss."

Nick sagged as if he were beaten.

But not because the Bill had refused him.

Oh, the loss he felt was real. So intensely that it made his groin ache, he *wanted* to force Morn into prostitution on Thanatos Minor. As revenge that would have pleased him more than giving her to the Amnion. It would have fit the way she'd hurt him.

Nevertheless his show of dismay was a ploy. He allowed himself to appear defeated in an effort to conceal the true nature of his desperation.

"All right," he said like a groan, "all right. I'm helpless here, you know that. If I weren't, I would see you *crawl* before I did any more business with you. But I'm stuck. You won't honor my credit. Without repairs, I can't run. And you won't give me that brat you rescued. If I don't turn him over to the Amnion, they'll do worse than kill me." He recited all this in a deliberate display of prostration. The Bill liked to see people prostrated; liked it so much that he might believe it. "You haven't left me any choice.

"I've got one last thing to trade."

"Ah." The Bill gave a sigh of expectant gratification. His eyes watched Nick keenly.

"I've got—"

Abruptly a light flashed on one of the Bill's boards, distracting him. He touched a key, glanced at a readout; his long, delicate fingers tapped in instructions.

Listen to me! Nick wanted to shout. You're right—I sometimes do jobs for Data Acquisition. That's why I've got an immunity drug for Amnion mutagens. Hashi Lebwohl gave it to me. To test for him. That's why I went to Enablement. To test it. And it works. Otherwise I wouldn't be here now.

I'll give you some of it if you give me Davies.

But the words died inside him as the door swept open, and a woman with a slight stiffness in her stride came into the strongroom.

"Captain Nick," said the Bill with his usual incongruous eagerness, "do you know Sorus Chatelaine? She tells me you haven't met, but you may recognize her by reputation. It was her ship"—his grin was obscene—"that salvaged your 'property.' "

The light seemed to contract around Nick. The woman was all he could see as she approached. Baffled by surprise and old terror, he stared and stared at her while she greeted the Bill, then shifted her stance to study him with an air of detached amusement. The stiffness in her limbs suggested that she disliked even the rock's lesser g.

"As it turns out," she said in a low, vibrant tone, "I was wrong. Captain Succorso and I *have* met after all. He was using another name at the time, as I recall. That's why I didn't make the connection."

Sorus Chatelaine, the captain of *Soar*. He hadn't made the connection, either, of course he hadn't, like her ship she'd had another name then. And she was much older now. Lines and tired skin marred the structural handsomeness of her face; the light made the gray in her hair look white. Yet he recognized her instantly, absolutely, as if she'd stepped out of a recurring nightmare.

She was the woman who'd put the scars on his cheeks, the wounds on his soul.

"I see the surprise is mutual," she added archly, as if he were still only a helpless boy in front of her.

Fear and rage knotted his muscles, twisted his face. An instinct for survival stretched as thin as thread was all that kept him from hurling himself at her throat.

With a confident smile, she dismissed him and returned her attention to the Bill. "You've been busy." Her voice still had the contralto richness which had once wrung Nick's heart when she made love to him; when she laughed at him. "You may not have had time to pick up the latest bulletins. I wanted to discuss them with you—and Captain Succorso may have something to contribute." She was laughing at Nick again, secretly but unmistakably.

He couldn't stop staring at her. His muscles were so tight with strain that he could hardly breathe.

"Your timing is unfortunate," the Bill chided cheerfully. "Captain Nick was about to make what I'm sure is a most unusual offer. However, that can wait for a moment." He looked at his readouts. "Which bulletin did you wish to discuss?"

"Operations," Captain Chatelaine replied promptly, "has just had contact from what appears to be a UMCP ship. A Needle-class gap scout, presumably unarmed—if her id is honest. She calls herself *Trumpet*. She's about eighteen hours out, and requesting permission to approach.

"According to her first transmission, she has two men aboard." Sorus paused for effect, then said, "Angus Thermopyle and Milos Taverner.

"They claim they stole her."

Nick seemed to feel the air being sucked out of the room. Nailed where he stood by contracting light and too much stress, he feared for a moment that he was going to pass out.

NICK

Torn between spotlights and murder, anoxia and fear, he reeled internally. He seemed to experience the crash of lightning, the blaze of thunder, but they were all inside his head; secret; unreal. She'd left him with tears of humiliation and ruin streaming through the blood on his cheeks, and now his scars burned like streaks of acid under his eyes. If he could have drawn breath, he might have moaned.

Caught and fixed by the light, Nick Succorso went a little crazy.

Before he broke, however—before he killed himself by trying to kill Sorus—a name came to him like a spar to the hand of a drowning man. *Milos.* He clutched at it, clung to it, recited it. *Milos Taverner.* It was rescue and hope and a kind of madness inextricably tangled together, but it was all he had.

Milos Taverner was coming to Billingate.

Slowly the pressure in his chest eased, and he began to breathe again. The light loosened around him like a cut noose; he could see the walls again, dim through the enshrouding shadows. The feral grimace let go of his features. By degrees he recovered his grin.

Somewhere he'd come undone. He was no longer the Nick Succorso who never lost. But he could still grin and face his tormentors and wreak havoc.

Milos was coming.

He'd been silent, struggling with himself, too long. When he looked at the Bill and Sorus Chatelaine again, he saw that they were both watching him expectantly. The Bill held his fingers poised over one of his boards as if he were braced to call for help—or to shoot Nick himself. But Sorus appeared to fear nothing. Her gaze was amused and clinical, as if she enjoyed her effect on him and wanted to know how far it would push him.

"God, I'm tired," he murmured in a probably futile effort to explain away his reaction. "If you think it's pleasant being harried all the way here from Enablement, you haven't tried it recently." Then, because craziness was just another form of inspiration, he added, "Do you know what those bastards did to me?" He no longer needed outrage. He was calm now, almost clinical himself. His grin showed how calm he was. "They sold me sabotaged gap drive components. I damn near blew up in the gap. If my engineer hadn't panicked and tried to abort tach, I wouldn't be alive now."

And you wouldn't know how treacherous your hosts can be.

"I wonder what you did to provoke *that*," Sorus mused.

Nick ignored her. From now on he was going to ignore her. Until he was ready to finish her.

For the present he concentrated on the Bill.

In the Bill's eyes, he could see the lean man's efforts to guess what had produced this change in him.

After a speculative pause the Bill asked, "Were you expecting Captain Angus? You seem pleased to hear of his arrival."

"Not particularly," Nick answered with some of his old, casual readiness. Even a crazy man could understand how dangerous this moment was. The Bill had to be deflected from the truth. "I was thinking about something else. She"—he rolled his eyes at Sorus—"probably didn't tell you I've got an old score to settle with her. A very old score. There was no reason for her to mention it, of course. She didn't know it would be relevant. But it's sure as hell relevant now. When she first walked in here, the only thing I could think about was butchering her on the spot. Then it occurred to me"—his grin felt malign and gratifying against his scars—"that I've got better options. This could turn out to be a lot of fun."

Let her believe him as much or as little as she chose. He didn't care. The Bill's reaction was all that mattered.

"The truth is," Nick went on, "I don't give a shit whether Captain Thermo-pile is here or not. He's got nothing to do with me.

But if you want my advice, this is it. Don't let him come in. Something stinks about all this, and it isn't me."

The Bill pursed his mouth reflectively, then flexed his fingers like a dismissal. "There is cause for concern, certainly. Fortunately we have plenty of time to consider the situation. The thought of time reminds me, however, Captain Nick, that you were interrupted. As I recall, you were about to make me a new offer."

Nick shrugged. "Never mind." No matter how undone he was, he could be as dismissive as the Bill. "We'll talk about that later. I've got other things to think about. For now, a visitor's berth sounds like a good idea. Unless"—he tightened his grin—"you're planning to revoke *all* my money, not just that one credit-jack."

"Captain Nick," the Bill said in a tone of good-humored reproach. Shadows played in and out of his mouth as he spoke. "Money is money. Please spend as much of it here as you wish. I'll be delighted to honor your credit-jack as well—as soon as your other difficulties are resolved."

"Good," Nick drawled. "In the meantime, take good care of my property. I don't want to have to worry about what you're doing to that little sonofabitch."

Without a glance at Sorus Chatelaine, he turned and strolled toward the door.

"Some things never change, Captain Succorso," she murmured, taunting him. "Keep that in mind."

The door slid open in front of him. Ignoring her, he left the Bill's strongroom.

Milos Taverner was coming to Billingate.

By the time his escort returned him to *Captain's Fancy*, his time had already run out. As soon as he entered the lock, shut the door, and keyed the intercom, Mikka told him, *"Tranquil Hegemony* is in, Nick. She's been demanding to see you ever since she docked. Now I guess they're going to send another of their emissaries to talk to you."

Fatally calm, Nick asked, "Where is she?" while he waited for Mikka to unseal the ship.

"A dedicated berth in the Amnion sector. I'm surprised they

don't insist you go there. Make you deal with them on their own terms, in their own air. But I guess they don't want to give you a chance for more delays."

"All right." Nick snapped off the airlock intercom as the inner door opened. More delays? He had no choice. If he couldn't delay, he was finished. He had no levers to use against the Bill—none except the immunity drug, which he was saving to trap Sorus. So he had to rely on Milos.

Milos was here with Angus? Why? What kind of power brought those two natural enemies together? Was it a power Nick could make use of somehow?

He needed answers; needed Milos. But Milos and *Trumpet* were still eighteen hours away.

He would have to stall the Amnion.

He entered the relative safety of his ship and headed toward the bridge like a man for whom danger and survival had become simple.

Unquestionably he was losing his mind. Pieces of it seemed to fall away by the minute, uncluttering what remained.

She was his ship, *his*, and he took strength from her. She would serve him somehow, save him yet—she and Milos. As he moved through her he had the sensation that Thanatos Minor's gravitic hold was growing less, that his legs had more lift and his arms more thrust.

All his dreams of revenge on Sorus Chatelaine had a chance to come true at last.

He wished he'd known her real name before this. It would have helped make his plans against her more vivid.

Brandishing a grin, he crossed the aperture to the bridge.

Mikka and her watch were still at their stations. Some of them did nothing but sit, obviously waiting for Nick's return. Others— Arkenhill, Sib Mackern, Mikka herself—studied operational data from the installation; they may have been looking for hints of the ship's fate.

Now, however, they weren't alone. Liete Corregio stood beside Mikka. Like Mikka, she gave the impression that she was scrutinizing everything on the command readouts as well as the display screens. And Vector Shaheed was seated at the engineer's station. For a man who'd been sentenced to death, he looked remarkably phlegmatic—

which reminded Nick that he'd always liked the engineer. Vector was at least courageous enough to face facts without feeling sorry for himself. Maybe, Nick thought indulgently, Vector didn't have to die after all. Competent engineers were hard to find.

"Nick," Mikka said as if she were announcing him. Stolidly she stood up from her g-seat, offering him command.

He waved her back to her post. He felt too buoyant to sit down. In any case, there was nothing he needed to do at the command board. He scanned the bridge; for a moment he fixed a smile that was almost charitable on Vector. Then he asked nonchalantly, "So where's this fucking 'emissary'?"

"Depends on how fast he walks," Mikka muttered. "We were told he's on his way. Should be here in the next five minutes."

Nick nodded cheerfully. The likelihood that the emissary would threaten him within an inch of his life didn't trouble him. He already knew what the threats were. What he didn't know was how ready the Amnion were to carry them out.

"Nick," Sib said from the data station, "about that other ship, *Soar*—" He sounded tired and worried; scared of Nick's displeasure.

Feeling magnanimous, Nick cut him off. "I already know. She used to call herself *Gutbuster*. She was illegal a long time ago, before places like this hit their stride. In those days she sold directly to the Amnion." That was a guess—the woman who became Sorus Chatelaine had never told him who her buyers were—but he believed it. "Maybe she still works for them."

Then, on a whim, he put his head between Mikka's and Liete's. Leaning close, he whispered so that only they could hear him, "She's the bitch who cut me."

Like Mikka, Liete wasn't especially pretty. Her features were too blunt: her competence was too obvious. But Nick thought that the surprise, the instinctive anger, on her small, dark face made her lovely.

Quietly she breathed, "Are we going after her?"

Is that what this is all about?

"We sure are," Nick promised.

Facing him straight as if to offer him everything she had, Liete murmured, "Good."

"Terrific," Mikka snarled. Nick's news deepened her scowl to a grimace. "That's just what we need."

Her hostility threatened to curdle his mood. Turning his mouth to her ear, he said distinctly, "I warned you. If you want to take that attitude with me, you'd better back it up."

Her reaction startled him. As unexpected as a flash fire, she flung herself away from him in revulsion. Springing out of her g-seat, she confronted him across the command board.

"I'll fucking *back it up*, you bastard!" she yelled. "I'm your god-damn *command second*! I've backed *you* up too often—I've saved your fucking *ass* too often—to be treated like this.

"Things aren't bad enough for you already? You think you're the only one here who cares what happens—the only one whose life is on the line? We're all hanging by our fingernails because *you* took us to Enablement, *you* cheated the Amnion, *you* traded Davies away. And after swearing to give him back, *you* lost him. Now the Bill has him. Our credit isn't worth crap. You haven't got anything left to trade. If we try to leave, those warships will fry us—and if we stay here, we'll starve. That's assuming we aren't murdered where we sit because *you* haven't kept your bargains.

"And now"—she pounded the station with both fists—"*now* you're going to turn this whole disaster into a fucking *grudge match* with some woman who works for the Bill and probably the Amnion as well!

"This is *shit*, Nick!" Abruptly her anger seemed to run out of energy. Sounding as weary as Sib—but not scared, not even a lit-tle—she finished, "And *I* would be shit if I didn't try to stop you."

The bridge was as silent as a tomb. No one aboard had ever seen Nick challenged like this. Even Orn Vorbuld, who had tried to rape Nick's woman—and had left a virus in the computers to protect himself—hadn't done anything like this.

All at once Nick started laughing. He had to laugh to prevent himself from screaming. Mikka's protest brought back the firestorm of fear and fury which had nearly engulfed him in the Bill's strong-room. In another minute he was going to kill the command second with his bare fists.

"That's all right, Mikka," he chuckled. "I can see you're upset. But you're working from a false assumption. You're assuming you know what the issues here really are." You're assuming I'm already beaten. "That's why you're wrong. And *that's* why—"

"Nick," Scorz put in anxiously, "that emissary is here."

Nick opened his throat to roar, Why you'd better shut up if you want to live! But the look on Liete's face stopped him. Her eyes were shining with excitement—no, with *trust;* with the precise utter confidence in him, the willingness to surrender herself absolutely, that he craved from the bottom of his heart.

Mikka didn't feel that way about him now. Being Mikka, she may never have felt that way about anything.

But Liete Corregio was on his side to the end.

So he didn't need to scream. Or kill Mikka. Or defend himself. Suddenly calm again, as casual as ever, he asked Scorz, "Who is it this time?"

A sigh of relief or trepidation seemed to spread away from him around the bridge. "He didn't say," Scorz reported as if he were fighting a knot in his throat, "but I think it's the same bastard they sent last time."

Involuntarily Nick recoiled as if he'd been hit. *"Him?"* he snapped. His calm was gone in an instant; forgotten. *"Here?"*

"I *think* so," Scorz offered hesitantly. "He sounds the same."

A laser of inspiration shot along the synapses of Nick's brain; his nerves were ablaze with coherent light. The same bastard they sent last time. Not some regulation Amnioni off *Tranquil Hegemony.*

Marc Vestabule.

Which meant that somebody on Enablement, some Amnion "decisive," had anticipated this situation. Anticipated *Captain's Fancy's* survival in the gap. Anticipated Nick's escape to Thanatos Minor. Otherwise why was Vestabule aboard *Tranquil Hegemony?*

"By damn," Nick murmured in wonder, "they weren't trying to kill us with those gap drive components." He was impressed in spite of himself. "They were *testing* their equipment. Using us to see if those components worked."

None of Mikka's watch understood him: he was too far ahead of them. Mikka herself scowled like a shout of frustration. Arkenhill and Karster stared at Nick with their mouths open. Ransum squirmed in her seat as if she had skinworms. Liete seemed caught between Nick's excitement and her own incomprehension.

Only Vector was quick enough to follow Nick's reasoning.

"But what are they *for?*" he protested quietly. "They would have killed us if we hadn't aborted tach." He may have been trying to remind Nick that he'd once saved *Captain's Fancy.*

"Not for the gap," Nick answered as if he were sure. "For acceleration." Almost in awe, he added, "Imagine what a tub like *Calm Horizons* could do at .9C."

"Oh my God," Sib groaned.

Around the bridge voices swore. Nick ignored them and went on thinking.

Nothing on Earth—nothing in human space—could be defended against a super-light proton beam fired from a warship traveling at .9C. If the Amnion ever decided to abandon their strategy of nonviolent imperialism, they wanted to be sure they would win.

So Davies Hyland was just a smoke screen. What the Amnion really wanted was to kill Nick; kill *Captain's Fancy.* Before he or his ship warned human space.

But they had to do it in a way that concealed the truth. A way that kept their secret hidden—and preserved their reputation for honest trade on Billingate.

No, it was too big: the conclusions were too large to be drawn from such small evidence. Nevertheless Nick felt the presence of possibilities so vast that he could only guess at their dimensions.

Milos Taverner was coming to Billingate. With Angus Thermopyle. Superficially that made no sense whatsoever. Beneath the surface, however, it stank of Hashi Lebwohl. Nick had no trouble making that kind of intuitive leap.

He could only speculate about the nature of Lebwohl's intentions; but he didn't really care what they were. The important point was that when Milos and Angus arrived, he would have a direct conduit to the UMCP.

Together that conduit and his new information might be enough to make the entire United Mining Companies fucking Police back him up.

All he needed was time.

"Scorz," he said as if he were calm again; as if his excitement were a kind of peace, "tell Vestabule an escort is on the way. We'll open the door for him in a couple of minutes."

As the communications second hurried to obey, Nick turned to Liete. "You're on. Get a gun—take Simper with you." Just to remind at least this one Amnioni that Nick Succorso was prepared to defend himself. "Bring that fucker here."

Her eyes flashing like a salute, Liete Corregio left the bridge.

As he watched her go Nick felt a stirring in his groin. For the first time since he'd learned of Morn's treachery, he wanted a woman.

Scorz was right: the emissary was Marc Vestabule. Anyone who saw him once would recognize him again.

He was a failed—or an incompletely successful—experiment: a human being who'd been given a mutagen which the Amnion had hoped would make him one of them—genetically, psychologically—while leaving his physical form intact. Only pieces of his former self remained, however; the stubborn residue of his humanity. He retained some areas of his brain, some human habits or resources of thought. Much of his body was still human: one arm, most of his chest, both shins, half his face. And he was able to breathe human air without much difficulty. But his knees were knots of Amnion skin so thick that his shipsuit had to be cut away to let him move freely. His other arm looked like a metallic tree limb gone to rust. And half his face was distorted by an unblinking Amnion eye as well as by sharp teeth with no lips to cover them.

He entered the bridge between Liete and Simper as if he had no fear—as if he'd been made oblivious to his own mortality by the essentially Amnion knowledge that he had no individual significance; that his uniqueness among his people was only a tool, not a matter of identity.

That was his strength. It may also have been his weakness.

"Don't tell me," Nick drawled as soon as the emissary stood before him. "You want to sit."

Marc Vestabule blinked his human eye at this reference to their previous encounter. In a voice like flakes of rust scraped off an iron bar, he replied, "No, Captain Succorso. I want you to honor your bargains with the Amnion."

Nick shrugged. "Well, *I'm* going to sit. Looking at a shit like you makes me weak in the knees." A small flick of his hand sent Mikka away from the command station. Sprawling casually into the g-seat, he turned it to face Vestabule.

As he grinned into the emissary's gaze he said, "Scorz, set up a recording of this. Put it on automatic relay. If anything happens to us—for instance, if we're attacked while we aren't looking, or if Vestabule here is on a kaze mission—I want Operations to hear everything we say. But only," he cautioned, "if we're attacked or damaged. As long as this clown plays straight with us, we'll keep the conversation to ourselves."

"Right." Scorz went to work promptly.

"Now," Nick said to Vestabule, "why don't you start by telling me exactly what bargains you want me to honor—and why. Just so we all know specifically what we're talking about."

Including Operations.

The blinking of Vestabule's eye was the only hint that he may have experienced human agitation or anger. Like his expression and his posture, his tone revealed nothing as he replied, "Captain Succorso, this is foolish. You protect yourself from dangers which do not exist, and at the same time you aggravate your true peril. You have entered into agreements with the Amnion"—he appeared to grope for the right word—"voluntary agreements. 'The mutual satisfaction of requirements.' We satisfied your requirements. You did not satisfy ours."

"That's not my fault," Nick put in amiably. "I told you—the mother of that brat went crazy. You might call it a mutiny of one. I got her back under control—but she was crazier than I thought. She escaped again."

As if Nick hadn't spoken, Vestabule continued, "On more than one occasion you have promised to fulfill your part of the agreements. But you have not done so. You have accepted our demand for recompense for the difficulties you have caused us. But you have not provided that recompense. This is not honorable trade."

Nick sharpened his grin. "You aren't listening. I said she escaped again. I had her locked up, but she got out. That's the only reason you didn't get what I promised you. She reprogrammed the ejection pod."

"That," the emissary pronounced flatly, "is not our concern."

"The hell it isn't." Nick feigned a little anger. It came easily, but it was pure charade. He was having too much fun to be angry. "*She* did that—*I* didn't. *I* wasn't trying to cheat.

"And now it's out of my hands. The Bill has the pod. He's got the 'human offspring' you're so eager for. And there's nothing I can do about that. You've goddamn *revoked* my credit-jack, so I can't buy the brat back. You've left me helpless, and now you want to hold me accountable for it. You say you want me to honor my bargains. *I* say trying to do business with you is like eating shit."

"Captain Succorso—" Vestabule made a gesture that appeared to have no meaning. It may have been intended to placate Nick, or threaten him. Or it may have been merely a neural atavism.

"Keep listening!" Nick interrupted, bringing up more anger to disguise what he was about to do. "I'm not fucking done!

"I traded with you *honorably.* I gave you my blood. Then you wanted to change the deal. You wanted that brat. You offered me gap drive components in exchange. So I gave you the brat. And *you* gave me faulty components. Damn near killed me in the gap." The louder and more angrily he spoke, the more his body relaxed. "I can only think of three explanations.

"Remember," he warned, "this is being recorded. If you mess with me, Operations is going to hear it.

"One"—he held up his index finger—"you were planning to cheat me right from the beginning. You think I'm immune to your fucking mutagens, and you want me dead so I can't pass my immunity along.

"Two"—he waggled his middle finger at the emissary—"you decided to cheat me after Morn took over my ship. Punish me for letting one of my own people trick me. And make sure she didn't get away with it."

Ransum and Sib watched as if they were about to be sick. Vector's round face revealed nothing. But Liete's eyes were shining again, and Karster looked like he could almost understand what Nick was doing.

"Three—are you still listening, Vestabule?" Nick's hand closed into a fist. "This is the explanation I really like. You were *using* me to test those components for you. You've figured out a way to use tach to generate acceleration, and you wanted me to see if it worked.

"Now it's your turn," he rasped like the blade of a knife. "Give me a reason why I shouldn't relay this recording to Operations whether you threaten me or not."

Vestabule showed no disconcertion. He may have been incapable of it. On one side of his face, his human eye blinked like an appeal. On the other, his Amnion teeth were bare and brutal.

"Relay it," he replied simply. "Your first explanation will cause your death. Your own kind will kill you to discover the nature of your immunity. Your second will appear only logical and reasonable to such men and women as inhabit Billingate. And your third will not be believed. If we possessed the technology you describe, we would have more reliable means of testing it."

"More reliable," Mikka put in unexpectedly, "but not cheaper. Your manufacturing methods are too expensive. You might not be able to afford the dozens or even hundreds of probes or ships you could lose trying to calibrate the parameters."

Her support surprised Nick without pleasing him. He'd already given up on her: he didn't want her help now.

In any case, Vestabule ignored her. He kept his dislocated gaze fixed on Nick. "Captain Succorso, I repeat—relay your recording if you wish. Your threats have no meaning to us. I"—again he appeared to grope for a word—"recognize them. They are bluffs. Empty of substance. I waste time listening to them.

"Now you will listen to me." His Amnion arm made another indecipherable gesture. "If you do not honor your agreements with us, you and your ship are forfeit. We will take you and your people and your ship, and leave you nothing.

"The Bill will not defend you. He will be given a plain, *honorable* account of our actions. And we have the means to prevent you from defending yourself. If we choose, we can paralyze you completely."

"How?" Nick demanded.

"You must deliver to us the human offspring called Davies Hyland," Vestabule continued as if he hadn't heard. "You must deliver to us the woman who cheated us, his mother. If you do not, we will take all you have in restitution."

Nick wanted to repeat his demand. *How* can you prevent me from defending myself? If I wave a finger at Liete, she'll shoot you where you stand. But an instinctive fear warned him away from challenging the emissary on this. He knew in his guts that Vestabule wasn't bluffing.

"Come on, Vestabule," he urged. "Think it through. You're overreacting. If you go that far, you'll take damage. Once the Bill hears my recording, he'll know any *honorable* account of your actions is phony. You're probably right—he won't contest the point. But he'll stop trusting you." As much as the Bill could be said to trust anybody. "Every ship here will stop trusting you. That will hurt you in subtle ways—ways you can't fix.

"It's better for you to deal with me.

"But you're making that impossible. Consider the position you're putting me in. You want me to get Davies from the Bill and give him to you. Do you really believe how I do that isn't your concern? How do you imagine I'm going to pay for him?

"You've only left me two things I can sell. One is the idea that you've learned how to use tach for acceleration. But if I try to do that, I'll have to supply proof. To be honest, I can't." This was a calculated risk, an effort to distract Vestabule. "Those components were slagged.

"So I've only got one other option." Abruptly Nick leaned forward, bracing himself on his board to thrust his threat straight into Vestabule's face. "I'll have to sell the Bill the secret to my immunity."

And you don't want me to do that, do you, you oxidized lump of Amnion shit?

"Nick," Mikka whispered; a moan of protest.

No one else spoke.

"Unless," Nick added almost as an afterthought, "you give me time to come up with some other solution."

Blinking furiously, as if *Captain's Fancy*'s atmosphere hurt his human eye, the emissary regarded Nick. Nothing betrayed his reaction: no twitch of the muscles in his cheek, no flexing of his fingers. Nick's people sat frozen as Vestabule contemplated the situation, thinking his hidden, Amnion thoughts.

When he was done, he said in his rust-rough tone, "Very well."

Ransum let out an audible breath.

Fortunately every one else kept quiet.

But Vestabule had attention for no one but Nick. "Captain Succorso," he continued, "if you will immediately provide the recompense you have promised, as a demonstration of your intention to deal with us honorably, we will grant you one of your standard days in which to come to an accommodation with the Bill.

"I warn you plainly, however, that this accommodation must make no mention of your presumed 'immunity.'" The very expressionlessness of his voice gave his words power. "Such information cannot be kept secret—not in this place, among illegals like yourself. We will learn of it. Then the time for talk will be past. We will exercise our power to paralyze your defenses and take your ship. We will take you and all who remain with you in restitution.

"And if that does not suffice, we will go further. We will destroy Billingate itself before we will permit the knowledge you claim to possess to be disseminated."

Nick dismissed that threat: it was too big to worry about. Again he wanted to ask, Paralyze our defenses? How? And again he stifled the impulse. He'd gained the only thing he wanted—time—and he didn't mean to risk losing it.

He summoned a sarcastic laugh. "So you say. If you want to go that crazy, be my guest. But short of that—"

He glanced around the bridge: at Sib's pale, stricken features; at Mikka's intractable glower; at Vector's clear blue gaze and contemplative frown; at the concentrated readiness which seemed to fill Liete's whole body. Milos was coming to Billingate. Sorus Chatelaine was finally within reach.

"Short of that," he repeated as he returned the line of his grin and the heat of his scars to Vestabule, "we have a deal. I don't know what's going to happen, but I'll try"—he bared his teeth—"anything and everything to make it work."

Marc Vestabule stared back at him, blinking/unblinking, and said nothing.

Abruptly Nick stood. "Liete, escort this fucker off the ship."

Without hesitation, Liete pointed Vestabule toward the aperture. She kept one hand on the butt of her gun.

Obedient and unconcerned, as if he'd been given everything he could have wanted, the emissary turned and left the bridge between Liete and Simper.

As soon as they were out of earshot, Nick swung around to face Mikka. "Now." He was poised like a predator. "We've succeeded at stalling them for one day. That changes the whole situation. Now we've got something to hope for.

"Go get Morn. Wake her up—flush the cat out of her. I want her on her feet and ready to leave in ten minutes."

Mikka didn't move. For a moment she didn't meet Nick's gaze. When she raised her eyes, they were hot and moist. Far back in her throat, as if she feared her voice might choke her, she asked, "Do you call that stalling?"

"I do," he snapped because her question and her emotion affected him like a betrayal. "She isn't the one they want."

"But she's still a human being," Mikka replied, as guttural as a growl. "You're giving them a human being." Like a woman who had no words strong enough for what she felt, she said, "I don't like giving human beings to the Amnion."

Unexpectedly—so unexpectedly that it stopped Nick's retort in his chest—Sib Mackern said, "I don't either, Nick."

"Make that three of us," Vector added quietly. Scanning the bridge, he asked, "Anyone else? How about you, Ransum? Would you want to be turned into something like Vestabule? Would you do that to your worst enemy? Arkenhill? Scorz? Karster?"

They all should have said, We'll do whatever Nick tells us. We trust him. He's saved our lives more times than we can count. And he knows more than we do. This is his ship, and he's the best. We're on his side to the end.

None of them did, however. Karster drummed his fingers on the targ board, studying his readouts as if he wanted to shoot someone. Ransum was breathing too hard, like a woman on the verge of a heart attack. Arkenhill had turned as pale as Sib: he may have been about to puke.

At last Scorz murmured in a small voice, as if he were belittling them all, "We've done worse."

It wasn't enough; not for Nick Succorso; not now and not ever. The only women he'd ever given himself to had betrayed him. The Amnion were on top of him, threatening to *paralyze his defenses* take his ship and his life. The Bill had Davies—and refused to repair *Captain's Fancy*. Sorus was still laughing at him. He'd already lost more pieces of himself than he could count.

He might have predicted a reaction like this from Vector. The engineer had never really belonged aboard *Captain's Fancy*. And Sib was weak enough to be bent in any direction. But for Mikka Vasaczk, his command second, to oppose him like this—

Scorz' support didn't come close to being enough.

Nick wanted to scream at Mikka, rage and rant at them all; he wanted to beat her face to pulp. Was this the best they had to give

him? Then he would see them in hell. He would sacrifice every fucking one of them to the Amnion, and he would *laugh* when they
begged him to rescue them—

But he didn't have the strength for it. Energy and hope seemed
to drain out of him like water, as if Mikka had knocked a hole in
the bottom of his heart. While everyone on the bridge waited for
him to go up like a supernova, he took one slow breath and another,
and let his shoulders sag.

Then he said softly, "What makes you think I have a choice?"

They couldn't argue with that. Even Mikka couldn't. If Nick
Succorso was beaten, what choice did any of them have?

Wheeling away from him, she strode off the bridge as if she
were taking the last vestige of his invincibility with her.

NICK

He waited in his cabin for Mikka to tell him that Morn was ready; but he wasn't idle. Sealed by his priority codes, one of his lockers served him as a personal safe. He opened it to stow Morn's id tag and zone implant control securely: the Amnion had no discernible interest in the latter; and his negotiations with Marc Vestabule had gone well enough to spare him the necessity of offering the former.

Of course, there was always the possibility that the Amnion would make her into something like Vestabule. If they did, she would retain some—most?—of her human mind; and they would learn that she was more valuable than they'd realized. But Nick couldn't help that. It was out of his hands.

From his locker he took a vial of capsules—his precious store of the immunity drug—and poured two into his palm. A small tic pulled at his cheek, but he ignored it. One capsule he swallowed immediately, just as a precaution; the other he shoved deep into one of the pockets of his shipsuit. Then he put the vial away and relocked the safe.

Rubbing his hands over his scars, he glanced at his chronometer. How long would it take to flush enough of the cat out of Morn's veins so that she could walk? Not long. In another minute or two he would be on his way to the Amnion sector of Billingate: the place reserved for them, where they could breathe their own acrid air—and set up their own defenses.

To go there was dangerous; but it was necessary. And it would give him at least a measure of revenge for Morn's lies.

While he thought about such things, another part of his mind was busy imagining how he might kill Mikka Vasaczk.

Women; always women. No sooner had he found a way to get rid of Morn Hyland than Mikka turned against him. And the question of how he would revenge himself on Sorus Chatelaine was still unresolved. He would simply shoot her, if that was the best he could do; but he wanted more, *needed* more. He was being undone by women: he owed it to himself to exact as much female pain as he could in recompense.

Marc Vestabule talked about "recompense," but he didn't use the word with Nick's intimate intensity.

Sorus would have to wait, however. First Morn. And when that score was settled, he would turn his attention to saving *Captain's Fancy*. He felt sure that somewhere during that process he would be able to rid himself of Mikka.

Without realizing it, he'd begun to pace back and forth in his cabin as if he were shuttling feverishly between real and imaginary possibilities for revenge.

The sound of the intercom stopped him. "Nick," Mikka said flatly. "I've got her up. She's groggy, but she can walk."

To vent some of his tension, he snap-punched the intercom toggle. "Meet me at the airlock. I'll take her from there."

Mikka clicked off without acknowledging him.

Promising murder, Nick keyed open the door and strode out of his cabin.

For the second time in little more than an hour, he had to leave his ship. And the second occasion was deadlier than the first: the Amnion were more likely than the Bill to do him active harm. Nevertheless he didn't delay. Tension wasn't the same thing as energy or confidence, but it could serve the same purpose.

He caught up with Mikka and Morn in the access passage of the airlock. They moved slowly: Morn's steps were nothing more than a stupefied shuffle; without Mikka's support, she would have folded to the deck. From the back they looked like sisters with their arms around each other for encouragement.

Sneering his disgust, he noticed that Mikka had taken the time to put Morn into a clean shipsuit. Presumably Mikka had also cleaned

Morn herself, washing off twelve or so hours' worth of accumulated filth. Wasted dignity. A woman who was about to lose her humanity entirely didn't need it. And he didn't want her to have any left when he handed her over to her ruin.

"Far enough," he growled at Mikka. "You can go back now.

"I'm leaving you in command. I don't expect you to like what I'm doing. I don't expect you to forget about it when it's over. But I do expect you to take care of the ship while I'm gone. You aren't any safer without me." Nick had guaranteed that by telling Scorz to record his discussion with Vestabule. "And I still know more about what's at stake here than you do. As matters stand, I'm the only hope you've got."

Mikka glared at him. "I'm not stupid, Nick. Don't make that mistake."

"I'll be lucky if I get the chance," he retorted, driven by bitterness. "You're too busy making it for me.

"Go to the bridge," he ordered so that he wouldn't have to listen to her anymore. "Pull a raiding team together—the best people we have for weapons, demolition, stealth work. Take them off duty, get them rested, ready, equipped. I'm not sure what I'm going to do yet"—he admitted this because he knew it would make Mikka more likely to comply—"but when the time comes we'll need to give it our best shot."

Maliciously he encouraged her to think that he might try to recapture Morn from the Amnion.

She replied with a shrug of acceptance; but she didn't hurry away. Carefully she disentangled herself from Morn, checking to be sure that Morn wouldn't fall when she stepped back.

Morn wavered as if the muscles of her legs had gone to jelly. She stayed on her feet, however.

Giving Nick one last black look, Mikka walked away.

He keyed the inner door of the lock. The tic in his cheek tightened as he paused to evaluate Morn's condition.

Even when she'd been with Thermo-pile, helpless against his brutality, she'd never looked so pitiable. She was still half-drugged, that was obvious. Her face wore its ineffable beauty like a bruise, as if she herself were the source of all her suffering. Her hair stood out from her head like the tag ends of her life. As the cat relinquished its hold, she would begin to suffer zone implant withdrawal. And yet, despite long days of hunger and strain, days which had cut lines around her eyes and carved flesh from her bones, her breasts were still full, still seemed to yearn against the fabric of her shipsuit, and the line of her hips beckoned him to her legs.

Tension wasn't enough. If he couldn't be the Nick Succorso who never lost, sure of himself and his power over her, then he needed anger; pure incandescent rage to sustain him.

Grabbing her arm as if he were about to beat her up, he drew her into the airlock.

She made no effort to pull away; but she murmured, "That hurts," as the ship's inner door closed and locked.

At least she was recovering consciousness. Soon she would be awake enough to know what was happening; enough to be appalled. That was something, anyway.

He engaged the sequence that opened the outer door. Still grinding his fingers into her arm, he took her off the ship to face the Bill's guards.

To his surprise, there were no guards. Apparently the Bill had decided to keep his personnel out of the cross fire if the Amnion decided to stage an assault on Nick's ship. Guards still watched over Reception—the Bill hadn't abandoned his own security—but none of them took any notice of Nick and Morn. They may have been instructed to ignore anything that took place between *Captain's Fancy* and the Amnion sector.

"Fuck you," he muttered to everyone and no one as he hauled Morn through Reception into the corridors which led toward the Amnion. Did the Bill like to get paid? So did Nick. Grimly he put this detachment of security, this diplomatic dissociation from *Captain's Fancy*'s needs, on the Bill's tab.

That tab was getting longer by the hour.

"Please, Nick," Morn breathed between clenched teeth. "I'm not going to fight you. You don't need to break my arm."

He tightened his grip for a moment until he heard her gasp. Then he eased the pressure—not because she asked, but because his hand was tired.

"So you're awake," he sneered at her softly. "Good. Do you know where we are? Do you know where we're going?"

She didn't reply. Her only answer was the increasing stability of her strides and the way she carried herself to minimize the strain on her arm.

"Good," he said again, nodding as if he were sure she understood. "There are several reasons why we're doing this." I want to. You earned it. It's necessary. "One is that I've had another talk with that mutated bastard Marc Vestabule. He issued any number of threats, but one in particular got my attention. He told me they 'have the means to prevent' me from defending myself." The same intuition which had restrained him from challenging Vestabule on the subject inspired him to broach it now. "He said they can 'paralyze' my ship. Completely.

"What do you know about that?"

She was silent for a few steps. Then she sighed, "God, Nick." She sounded utterly exhausted, frayed to the ends of her soul; but she didn't sound scared enough, not nearly scared enough to satisfy him. "What makes you think I can answer a question like that?"

He didn't have to grope for explanations. "First, you're a cop. Before you joined me, you had sources of information I didn't. You could easily know more about their technological resources than I do. And second"—reflexively angry, he squeezed his fingers into her arm again—"you talked to them when you took over my ship," *my ship,* you bitch.

She bit down on another gasp. She hadn't looked at him since he'd taken her from Mikka; she didn't look at him now. But she was listening. "All right," she said through her teeth as if she, too, were threatening him; as if even now, on her way to the Amnion, she thought she could still oppose him. "I'll trade you. You tell me why you were talking to the UMCP before we ever went to Enablement. Tell me what your deal with them was. What they hired you for. Tell me why they let you have me in the first place. And I'll tell you why the Amnion think they can paralyze your ship."

She astonished him; surpassed him. Why wasn't she terrified? —stricken to the core? She should have been sobbing in revulsion and supplication, not trying to bargain with him.

The corridor was empty in both directions. The Amnion kept themselves apart from the rest of the installation—and nobody with any sense went looking for them. The Bill's bugeyes were watching, of course; but they probably couldn't pick out voices at this range.

Nick let go of Morn's arm, clutched her by the shoulders, and swung her around to face him.

"Look at me, damn you." Why aren't you out of your head with fear? "*Look* at me."

Her gaze came up to his slowly. When he saw her eyes, the mad, dark passion in them almost made him flinch. The extremity of her suffering, the depth of her abuse, was matched by a focused, absolute, and predatory conviction. She looked like a woman who could come back from her grave—or from Amnion mutagens—to destroy him.

Roughly he shoved her away. Helpless to defend herself, she stumbled against the wall; he caught her on the rebound and compelled her into motion again. He needed movement to control the dread rising in his guts.

"I already told you," he said as soon as he trusted his voice. "I was dickering for you. I wanted the damn cops to pay me for not selling what you know to the Bill."

"Bullshit," she retorted. "I knew that wasn't true when you first said it. Now I'm sure.

"You knew how to contact them. You knew where the listening posts are. That means you were dealing with them long before you headed for Thanatos Minor. And I finally figured out that you must have had their permission to take me off Com-Mine."

"How do you get to that conclusion?" he demanded.

His question was unnecessary: she was already answering it. "You needed a source in Com-Mine Security to frame Angus. But you needed more than that. You and your source needed a contact at UMCPHQ—somebody who could give you the codes to make that bogus supply ship look genuine. So the UMCP knew what you were doing. You had their cooperation. Maybe you were just following their orders. Maybe that's what your whole precious reputation is based on. You do what the cops tell you, and they make sure you look good in the process.

"So you weren't trying to *dicker* for me. As far as I was concerned, your deal with them was already set. Why *were* you talking to them? What did they hire you for?"

Nick tried to laugh, and couldn't. His mouth was too dry; his throat was too tight. A spasm in his cheek tugged at his scars as if they were fresh.

Nearly panting against his tension, he said, "Hashi Lebwohl wanted me to do a job for him here."

"What job?" she insisted.

He was going to tell her; he was suddenly eager to tell her. He wanted to hurt her with it, wanted to do anything in his power that might erode the lunatic conviction which protected her from her fear. And he was going to hold her to her bargain.

"The point," he said, although he could hardly breathe, "was to do Billingate some damage. Maybe enough damage to put the Bill out of business. I already had Lebwohl's immunity drug. He wanted me to sell it to the Bill."

This was the truth. Nick hoped that it would crack her heart.

Morn didn't gasp or protest; but he had the satisfaction of feeling her go rigid in his grasp, as if she were in shock.

Gradually the knots in his chest loosened, letting him inhale more easily.

"I was supposed to give the Bill the real thing to test on a live subject, and then supply him with an inert substitute to duplicate in his labs. He could sell his substitute to the illegals or the Amnion, it didn't matter which. As soon as the truth got out—he was selling an immunity drug that didn't work—he would be in deep shit."

Live with *that*, you bitch—while you can. That's the kind of people you work for, the kind you believe in.

"I may still do it," he continued, "if I can't get the Amnion off my back any other way. But if I do, I won't bother with substitutes." Like the truth, this lie was intended to do Morn as much harm as possible. "When I told Lebwohl I was in trouble, he cut me off. Now I don't mind selling him out."

Thinking that he'd finally broken her, he put his arm around her and pulled her ear close to his mouth. "Now it's your turn," he whispered almost companionably. "Tell me how the Amnion think they can paralyze my defenses."

"Oh, that," she muttered as if she hadn't felt a word he said; as if she were too numb or blind to be reached by his malice. "You should have figured that out for yourself."

Here it comes, he thought. Now she would try to get back at him.

"Back on Enablement, I needed to show them *Captain's Fancy's* self-destruct was real. If I let them believe I was bluffing, they wouldn't have given Davies back. So I dumped a copy of everything in the auxiliary command board into my transmission. Including," she finished like an act of violence, "your priority codes. They can override every instruction you key in."

Nick thought his heart was going to stop.

Of course, he also had those codes. He could override their override. And they could override again—

Paralysis. Eventually the computers would shut down to protect themselves from burnout.

For a moment the shock left him white and blank. She wasn't trying to hurt him. Her revelation didn't damage him: it helped him. What the Amnion knew about his ship was only dangerous as long as he didn't know they knew it. Once he got back to *Captain's Fancy*, he could simply write in a new set of priority codes. The whole job would take less than an hour.

Morn had given him an unexpected and imponderable reprieve.

"Why?" Surprise seemed to leave him naked beside her. "I might not have figured it out. Why tell me?"

Why help me?

Her exhaustion had returned. "Because," she answered as if she were too tired to fight anymore, "I don't want them to get you. I don't want them to get anybody. If you were in that pod, I would have done exactly what I did. Otherwise my own humanity wouldn't be worth having."

Defensive and bitter, he snarled a curse. "And I suppose it never entered your head that if you gave me the answer, I might feel *grateful* enough to change my mind?"

Even in his own ears he sounded petulant, petty.

"No," Morn said flatly. "I know you better than that."

Nick couldn't reply. Grinding his teeth to steady himself, he pushed her on down the corridor.

Another hundred meters along an empty passage brought them to the Amnion sector.

The entrance was nothing more than a faceless door in a blank wall. He'd never been inside; but he assumed that the door was the outer opening of an airlock which protected the sector's atmosphere. With a shudder, he remembered the acrid taste of the air on Enablement, the pain and coughing— His lungs still felt tender. He had no intention of going through that ordeal again.

Tightening his hold on Morn in case she panicked at the last minute and tried to get away, he reached up a hand to the intercom beside the door.

"Nick, please."

For one wild instant he thought she was going to beg him to release her; spare her.

But she didn't. Instead she murmured, "Just tell me why they let you take me." She'd returned to her original question, to her escape from Com-Mine Station. "It can't hurt you—and I need to know. Why didn't they try to rescue me themselves?"

"Shit," he sneered because he was disappointed. Even here, standing on the threshold of hell, she refused to break. "What makes you think you were worth the effort? You'd already spent too much time with Captain Thermo-pile. The cops knew there wasn't enough of you left to rescue."

But then he saw that the truth would be harder for her to bear; so he continued, "They let me take you because you're what I wanted for pay. I don't mind doing their dirty work sometimes, especially when the target is a fucker like Thermo-pile, but I like to get paid. I didn't know I was about to lose my gap drive, so I didn't ask for credit. I took you instead." He forced out a harsh chuckle. "They probably considered it a steal. They got to nail Thermo-pile, and all they had to give up was a piece of his wreckage."

She hadn't looked at him since he'd forced her to; she didn't look at him now. Nevertheless her damaged voice seemed to drive straight through him.

"If you believe it's that simple, you've been trusting them too long."

She was more than he could stand. Hitting the intercom with his fist, he snarled, "I'm Captain Nick Succorso. I've brought the fucking 'recompense' you fucking wanted. Her name is Morn Hyland—she's the mother of that 'human offspring' bastard you're lusting after. Open the door. I'm going to put her inside and leave her. I've got other things to do."

The response from the intercom was immediate. "Captain Nick Succorso, the delivery of the female is acceptable. Your departure is not. You will enter with her. Suitable breathing masks will be provided. She will be taken from you. You will remain."

"The hell I will," Nick growled in instant fear. Automatically he backed to the far wall, pulling Morn with him. "That wasn't the deal. Your fucking *emissary* didn't say anything about keeping me."

"You will not be kept." The Amnioni voice sounded mechanically flat, imperturbable. "You will not be harmed. That is unconditional."

Abruptly the door slid open.

Marc Vestabule stood in the airlock.

He had two other Amnion with him; but there was nothing humanlike about them except for the masks over their faces and the weapons in their hands.

They aimed their weapons squarely at Nick and Morn.

"Please, Captain Succorso," Vestabule said as if his vocal cords were incapable of inflection. "We wish only to talk to you. If the thought of entering our sector frightens you, we will talk here, although the place is less convenient."

"Don't you mean less secure?" Nick pointed at the nearest bug-eye. "Out here the Bill can see and hear everything."

"No." Vestabule appeared certain. "Our agreement with the Bill empowers us to neutralize these surveillance devices at our discretion. The question is solely one of convenience. If you choose to enter, we will provide you with the comfort of a seat. And guards will not be necessary."

That surprised Nick. He ached for a gun. Maybe if he shot someone the tension building in his chest again would be released. The tic under his eye felt like the stress of a valve with too much pressure behind it.

"What the hell have we got to talk about?" he demanded. "We've already made a deal." He brandished Morn's arm. "I'm keeping my part of it right now."

Vestabule didn't nod; only his human eye blinked. "As we have said, her delivery is acceptable. However, we wish to relieve the confusion which makes our negotiations with you dangerous. It has occurred to me that there may be questions which you would consent to answer if none of your own people—also none of Billingate's personnel—were present to hear you. If our confusion can be relieved, perhaps the ways in which we make it 'impossible' for you to satisfy our requirements may be diminished."

For the first time, Nick thought that Marc Vestabule was more human than he looked. The emissary had retained some portion of his ability to think like a human. Pure Amnion lacked the tools to understand intraspecies duplicity or manipulation.

"In other words," Nick countered, "if I'll consider answering your questions, you'll consider unrevoking my credit-jack."

"I promise nothing." The emissary's alien knees, rust-coated arm, and distorted face promised nothing except the destruction of humankind. "The possibility exists."

Nick didn't hesitate. Shoving Morn toward the Amnion, he growled, "Get her out of here. Then I'll listen to your questions. 'The possibility exists' that I'll answer them."

An Amnioni caught her with one of its arms. She didn't struggle, made no attempt to break away; didn't look back. Without protest, as if she'd accepted her ruin long ago, she let the Amnioni steer her into the airlock.

Her escort touched the interior controls, and the door swept shut, as silent and fatal as an ax.

At the sight, Nick felt unexpectedly savage. Before he could stop himself, he began to yell at Vestabule.

"And tell that piece of shit to point his fucking gun somewhere else! I'm not going to answer your goddamn questions while you're threatening to burn holes in me if you don't like the goddamn answers!"

Vestabule made guttural sounds that meant nothing to Nick. At once the other Amnioni lowered its weapon. After a further word from Vestabule, the Amnioni clipped the weapon to a harness at its waist and moved its hands away.

Shaking with useless anger, Nick bit his lips so that he wouldn't go on shouting. His scars seemed to be pulling at his cheeks as if the skin were about to tear. Between one heartbeat and the next, his loathing for Marc Vestabule and all things Amnion became so intense that he could barely swallow. "I swear to God," he rasped harshly, "this is the sewer of the universe."

Vestabule may have retained significant vestiges of his human mind, but he was impervious to insult. "You have made similar references in the past," he observed, "but their applicability is imprecise. Correctly speaking, only humankind has 'sewers.' Our techniques for processing waste are different."

"Forget it," Nick snapped. "Forget I ever mentioned it. Now we're alone—just you, me, the intercom, a few bugeyes, and your pet bozo with the gun. Ask your questions, so I can figure out what my chances of being able to use that credit-jack are."

Fiercely he rubbed at his cheek, trying to quiet the spasm. But the muscle went on clenching and releasing convulsively, twisting his expression into a grimace.

"Captain Succorso"—Vestabule moved his arms as if he were attempting a gesture of appeal which his body had forgotten how to perform—"we have only one question, although it is complex.

"Why did you come to Enablement Station?"

Nick knotted his fists to contain his anger and waited for the emissary to explain.

"Your stated reason," Vestabule said flatly, "was that you required 'help for a medical difficulty,' in addition to credit that would enable you to repair your ship. Plainly, however, the credit itself was not the primary reason. Our data indicates that you were within reach of this installation before you left human space. This implies that you were on your way here to obtain repairs—which in turn implies that you had the means to pay for them—until you altered course and risked crossing the gap.

"Superficially we are left with the matter of your 'medical difficulty.'

"We can understand that in only one of two ways. Perhaps your desire or need for the human offspring Davies Hyland was genuine. That is difficult for us to understand. However, we do not need to understand it, for you have proven it false. Your willingness to sell the offspring demonstrates that he was not your motive. Therefore we must speculate that your true interest was not in the offspring himself, but rather in the ability to produce him."

Urgent with fury, Nick wanted to shout, Get to the point *get to the point!* But he held himself rigid, betraying nothing, while fire throbbed in his scars and burned in his eyes.

"More specifically," Vestabule continued, "we speculate that you wished to test the usefulness of what you call a 'zone implant' in protecting a human mother from the normal consequences of force-growing her fetus." *A total and irreparable loss of reason and function,* the birthing doctor had said. "Yet that proposition has also been shown to be false. You have made it clear that you did not know of the existence of the female's zone implant when you brought her to us.

"We must conclude that all reference to a 'medical difficulty' was spurious.

"Yet what remains?" Vestabule asked before Nick could protest. "Only your offer to permit us to test your blood. We are forced to conclude that this offer represents your true reason for coming to Enablement Station.

"That is not satisfactory, however. During your previous approach to us, you voluntarily submitted to the administration of a mutagen which should have transformed you much as I was transformed. Obviously it did not. Returning to us, you made us aware of that fact. Further, by permitting us to test your blood you showed us that your 'immunity' to our mutagens is not inherent. Your blood differs in no meaningful particular from other human blood. Thus you have made us aware that you possess the technical or medical means to block our mutagens, to render them ineffective.

"Captain Succorso, why did you do this? You are not a friend to the Amnion. And we judge that you are not self-destructive, despite the hazardous nature of your conduct. What explanation remains? What conclusion should we draw in order to resolve our difficulties successfully?"

Vestabule faced Nick without expression. At his side, his companion or guard was completely immobile, like a creature that had been turned to salt.

Nick glared at the two of them, watching his hope that his credit would be restored fray away like smoke.

"I get it." He was so full of violence that he could hardly contain it, but he forced a harsh laugh. "For a minute there I didn't know what we were talking about, but now I get it.

"You think I'm playing some kind of deep covert game for the cops. You think this is all a ploy—I was ordered to make you aware that we can neutralize your mutagens. As a way of convincing you to scale back your ambitions against human space. Let you know we're ready for you, it's too dangerous to challenge us. And what you're afraid of"—involuntarily his hands clenched and unclenched at his sides, aching for Vestabule's throat—"is that it's a trick. That the immunity doesn't really exist—or doesn't work well enough to be much good.

"Then the cops would have a reason to make you aware of it.

They're using me to bluff you. Encourage you to worry about a threat that isn't real.

"Is that about right?"

Even Vestabule's human eye didn't blink as he stared back at Nick.

If Vestabule had set fire to Nick's hands and feet—if the Amnioni with the gun had flamed open his belly, spilling his guts to the deck—Nick would not have told them the truth. *I loved her, goddamn you! I thought letting her have her brat was the only way I could keep her!* Vestabule probably wouldn't have believed him anyway. Some hurts were too human for any Amnioni to understand.

"You're half-right," he rasped, wishing that every word were keen enough to draw blood. "I do jobs for the cops once in a while. That's why I went to Enablement the first time. Test their new immunity for them. But I hate them. Do you hear me, you asshole?" *Are you human enough to remember hate?* "I *hate* them. When I do jobs for them, I like to make sure the results aren't quite what they were expecting. I like to do work for them that looks good and turns out bad." *Otherwise the bastards on my ship would have cut my heart out long ago.* "That's why I went back this time. To make sure the job I did for them last time turned out bad."

The emissary considered Nick for a long moment before he said passionlessly, "Captain Succorso, this is unsatisfactory."

Do you think I don't know that, you disgusting lump of shit? Do you think I don't know you're going to assume I'm betraying you, too? The truth is worse.

Turning on his heel, daring the Amnioni to shoot him in the back, Nick strode away in the direction of *Captain's Fancy.*

Taverner, you dishonest shit-licker, where are you?

By the time he reached his ship, his anger had failed. Like hope, it eroded and was washed out of him. Instead he felt an acute longing to be with someone who adored him.

Once the doors were safely locked behind him, he went, not to the bridge, but to his private quarters. Ignoring Mikka's hostility—and his own doom—in the same way that he'd ignored the Amnioni with the gun, he used the cabin intercom to ask Liete Corregio to join him.

MILOS

M ilos had to wait.

It was time for him to crush out the spark of dangerous enthusiasm in Angus' eyes, *time* for him to erase the look of malign hope on Angus' face. The longer he allowed Angus to experience anything other than hopeless domination, the more precarious Milos felt.

Nevertheless he was forced to wait while Angus obtained permission to approach Billingate. He had to trust Angus' core programming that long. By some standards, the next few hours were the most vulnerable part of Angus' mission. Thanatos Minor had the firepower to laugh at any gap scout, no matter how many secret weapons she carried. Human ships all around the installation would protect it. And—Milos had already gleaned this information from scan, as well as from Billingate's routine navigational transmissions—there were two Amnion warships in the vicinity of the rock.

If Operations refused to let *Trumpet* dock, Angus was in trouble.

Milos could solve that problem himself, if Angus failed. But he didn't want to. It would force his hand; coerce him to commit himself when he wanted to keep all his options open.

While Angus dealt with Operations, Milos lit a nic and fretted.

Angus had sent out the data that Operations needed: ship id and registration, the names of her captain and crew. He'd requested a visitor's berth. Now he ran arcane sequences on his board, comparing them to the databases hidden inside him, and murmuring softly under his breath as if he were humming.

But Operations hadn't answered.

What was the delay?

Time lag was negligible. And Angus had been here any number of times before: presumably he knew how to approach the shipyard. So where was the reply? What was Operations doing?

No, Milos couldn't wait. He should, but he couldn't. In the privacy of his bowels, he feared Angus too intensely, despite Hashi Lebwohl's reassurances.

Smoke dissipated into the air-scrubbers as he exhaled. First he checked to be sure that *Trumpet* wasn't sending anything, that all her broadcast channels were silent. Then he unbelted himself from his g-seat and floated free.

The ship was too small to use internal spin for g. He'd received some zero-g training at UMCPHQ, however. He steadied himself on the back of his seat, then thrust gently in the direction of the command station.

"Sit down," Angus muttered over his shoulder. "I'm concentrating."

Milos coasted the two meters to Angus' side. Carefully he pulled himself close to Angus until their heads almost touched.

"Joshua." His voice was soft, but distinct. "I'm going to give you a standing order. Jerico priority." That was the highest authority Milos could assign to his instructions. According to Lebwohl, only the most fundamental commandments in Angus' datacore would override a Jerico priority order. "When I tell you to open your mouth, you will always obey. You won't wait to hear the word 'Joshua.' " To be on the safe side, he added, "After that you'll chew and swallow normally. And you'll follow this order without letting it interfere with anything else you have to do."

The idea that these words were being recorded in Angus' datacore—that Dios or Lebwohl might find out about them—didn't bother Milos. He was more interested in the extent to which Angus' programming allowed him to protect himself from damage. Jerico priority was supposed to override any instinct less compelling than self-preservation.

Angus tapped a couple of keys on his board and checked one of his readouts as if he weren't listening.

An uncharacteristic grin stretched Milos' face as he breathed, "Open your mouth."

Angus opened his mouth.

Carefully Milos dropped his burning nic onto Angus' tongue.

A flash of recognition lit Angus' eyes—a black glare of hate. His toadlike face twisted in a spasm of pain. Autonomic revulsion made his hands twitch.

Nevertheless he chewed the nic briefly; swallowed it. After flexing for a moment, his hands went back to his board.

"Enjoy it," he whispered thickly, as if the pain stiffened his tongue. "It won't last."

"Yes, it will. You know it will." For some reason, Milos still felt endangered. His power over Angus should have calmed him, but it didn't. Deep in his guts, where common sense and rationality never reached, he feared that Angus' essential malignance was indomitable. Unfortunately he couldn't undertake a more elaborate reassurance right now. "Bluffing me is a waste of time," he asserted in an effort to disguise his apprehension. "I've never been as stupid as you think I am."

"Is that right?" Angus slurred. "Then I guess you knew all along that I could have proved you were in collusion with Succorso whenever I wanted. I guess you knew I was doing you a favor by keeping my mouth shut. That's why you were so fucking grateful. All that stun and beating and abuse was just your sweet way of saying thanks."

"Oh, stop it." In disgust, Milos drifted back to the second's station. "I tell you, you can't bluff me. DA trained me for this. I know what you can do and what you can't. Probably better than you do." He wanted to put as much distance as possible between himself and Angus: if he'd been willing to miss Operations' answer, he would have left the bridge. Pulling his weight down by the straps, he secured himself in his g-seat. "If you could have proved anything like that—if you even suspected it—you would have sung your head off about it."

As he tapped one of his readouts, Angus Thermopyle laughed— a sound like the pulping of flesh and the breaking of bones. "Operations' approach protocols give us id and status on every ship here— illegals don't like to come in when they can't tell who's in the vicinity. It looks like *Captain's Fancy* has already docked. Maybe we'll get to discuss what I knew and didn't know with Captain Succorso him-fucking-self."

"You're a liar," Milos retorted because he was viscerally sure that Angus was telling the truth. "If you could have rescued yourself that easily, why didn't you? What are you using for a reason today?"

Angus started to laugh again, then stopped abruptly to read a screen. "Here it comes."

"*Trumpet*, this is Billingate Operations." In spite of distance and distortion, the voice on the bridge speakers sounded laconic, humorously cynical. "Are you sure you don't want to reconsider? You might be safer if you got the hell out of here."

With a snap, Angus toggled his pickup. "Operations, I hear you." He spoke slowly to overcome the pain in his tongue. "If you said something that made sense, I might even understand. What's the problem? Do you want me to start over? I'm Captain Angus Thermopyle. My second is Milos Taverner. There are only two of us aboard. Ship id follows—"

"We have your ship id," Operations cut in. "Come on, Captain. You're supposed to be smart—if you really are Angus Thermopyle. You know what the problem is."

"Give me a hint," Angus retorted. "I've been out of circulation for a while. I don't know what's changed since the last time I was here."

"It's your ship id." Operations and Angus might have been playing a game which they both secretly enjoyed. "That's what the problem is. *Trumpet*. A Needle-class gap scout. Unarmed. A *UMCP* ship, it says here. Are you getting the picture, Captain? Do you understand now?"

"What I understand," Angus replied in a tone of belligerence which may have been feigned, "is that you aren't doing your job. I'll talk real slow so you can get a good recording. I'm Angus Thermopyle. I've been here before, so I know you can do a voiceprint comparison to verify that. My second is Milos Taverner. Until recently"—Angus grinned fiercely at Milos—"he was deputy chief of Com-Mine Station Security. You can talk to him if you want, but it won't do you any good. *He* hasn't been here before.

"Call me back when you're sure who I am. Then maybe you'll ask some questions smart enough for me to answer.

"*Trumpet* out."

Milos lit another nic and inhaled hard so that he wouldn't do or say anything to show Angus how scared he was. He waited until he was sure he could keep his voice steady before he asked, "Now what?"

"Now nothing. They'll call again when they're ready to talk." Angus didn't sound worried. "They've already done their voiceprints. They're just shitting us to see how we react."

Milos sucked on his nic and did his best not to worry. *Of course* Billingate was suspicious. So *of course* Angus' programming had been written to deal with Billingate's suspicions. There was nothing to worry about.

Milos worried anyway. His neck was already in the noose. The tighter the rope pulled, the more risks he would have to take to extricate himself.

A slight intensification of Angus' posture warned him an instant before the speakers relayed, "*Trumpet*, this is Billingate Operations. It's time for answers. And you'd better make them good. We're in no mood for crap."

Angus snapped a toggle. "Operations, this is Captain Thermopyle. Of course you're in no mood for crap. You've already got yourself to put up with. But it would help if you gave me a hint what you want me to say."

"You bloated bastard"—Operations didn't sound particularly offended—"you know perfectly well what we want you to say. We want you to account for yourself. The last we heard, you were in Com-Mine lockup. Now suddenly here you are, in a UMCP ship, with Com-Mine Security's deputy chief for crew. Call me a gap-eyed dreamer, but that sure as hell sounds like a setup to me. We want you to give us a reason why we shouldn't fry you down to your pubic hair as soon as you're in range.

"Is that enough of a hint, or do you need more?"

"Oh, it's enough," Angus snorted without hesitation. "I can fill in the blanks. You think I've done a deal with the cops. They let me out of lockup, and all I have to do in return is take one of their ships into forbidden space, with one of their pets for crew, and do some kind of job for them. Like blowing you up, maybe? Is that about right?

"How fucking *stupid* do you think I am? How stupid do you think *they* are? Has the Bill gone null-wave in his old age?"

"Captain Thermopyle," Operations retorted tartly, "we're going to believe what we damn well please until you offer us something better. You've got three choices. Get the hell out of here. Come on in and let us fry you. Or start talking. We don't care which one you choose—but I personally guarantee that you're going to choose one of them."

"Bullshit!" Angus grinned like a sneer. "Who says you don't care what I do? Even if the Bill is brain dead, he's bound to realize he needs to know what's going on here. If you fry me, he won't learn anything. And if I decide to go somewhere else, he won't learn anything. Either way, you'll be a prime candidate for some BR 'improvements.' If you haven't already had them.

"So pay attention. I don't want to go through this more than once. And put a stress monitor on my transmission so you can at least guess I'm telling the truth.

"I was in lockup on Com-Mine. A life sentence for stealing Station supplies. You heard that part right. But Security was pissed because they couldn't convict me of anything worse. They assigned Deputy Chief Milos Taverner to break me. Tear me apart and dig out"—Angus snarled the words—"my innermost secrets.

"That didn't work, so after a while the cops—the United Mining Companies fucking Police themselves—decided to take over." Angus probably didn't need the help of his zone implants to lie as calmly as he told the truth. "They reqqed me, took me to UMCPHQ. Along with Milos here, since he presumably knew more about me than anybody else. I guess this new Preempt Act gave them the authority. And maybe they were glad Milos didn't break me. Maybe they wanted to keep what I know for themselves."

Milos dropped his nic on the deck and lit another, hiding the tremors of his hands with smoke.

"This is where it gets interesting," Angus continued. "I've done a lot of things in my life, but the one they convicted me for I didn't do. I was framed. If you don't believe me, ask Captain Succorso. He's in dock there, right? Ask him. He set me up. And eventually the cops figured out that if Succorso set me up, he must have had help. From Com-Mine Security.

"Now Milos knew he was in trouble. He provided the supplies Succorso used to frame me. They must have been working together for years. It was only a matter of time until the cops nailed him. So his little scam was finished. The cops were going to catch him—and

as soon as they broke him they were probably going to execute him
for his crimes.

"He didn't like that much. But how could he get out of it? He
was stuck in UMCPHQ. He never expected to be reqqed, so he
hadn't planned an escape. He can't run a ship himself. What else
was he going to do? Before the cops revoked his clearances, he got
me out. We went to the docks, jumped *Trumpet*'s crew, and used
their id tags to get ourselves aboard. Then we used his codes to clear
her for a training run. Before UMCPHQ knew what was going on,
we hit the gap and came here. End of story.

"How do you like it?" Angus asked sardonically.

On an impulse that resembled panic, Milos keyed his own pickup
and said to Angus so that Operations would overhear him, "They
don't have to like it. Don't be so hostile. We can't go back. All they
have to do is let us stay."

He thought Angus was going to cut him off. But Angus left
both pickups active as he growled, "Oh, shut up, Milos. You're just
making it worse."

Milos flushed involuntarily. This was simply another calculated
gambit in Angus' game with Operations. In all likelihood, both he
and Operations already knew what the outcome would be. Only Milos
himself was left to sweat in ignorance and dread.

Operations was silent for a moment. Then the speakers asked,
"So what are you selling, Captain Thermopyle?"

Faking abrupt outrage, Angus shouted back, "I'm not selling
anything! I'm running away! Get it through your head! I'm fucking
running away from the fucking cops! I only came here because I
couldn't think of anyplace better!"

"Then how," Operations inquired in a tone of suave malice,
"do you propose to pay for the use of our docks and facilities?"

At once Angus pointed a finger like a command at Milos.

Sighing, Milos leaned over his pickup. "Operations, this is Milos
Taverner. I made a fair amount of money working with Captain
Succorso. But I couldn't leave it lying around on Com-Mine.
It's in a safe account on Terminus." This falsehood, which Hashi
Lebwohl had prepared for him, was so close to the truth that Milos
was able to deliver it with a minimum of distress. "Verification
follows."

As steadily as he could, he tapped his keys, dumping the information Operations needed along *Trumpet*'s transmission.

"Data received," Operations reported in a more impersonal manner. "Steady as you go until you hear from us again, *Trumpet*. Operations out."

Obediently the speakers went dead.

Milos should have kept his mouth shut: he knew that. But he couldn't. He had too much tension in him; he was too dependent on people he didn't understand and couldn't control. Fighting to keep his voice flat, he asked for the second time, "Now what?"

Angus' grin was as sharp as a taunt. "Now they're going to talk to your buddy, Captain Sheepfucker himself."

Milos tried to think of everything he knew about Nick Succorso; tried to imagine what orders DA had given *Captain's Fancy*. Doubtfully he asked, "Will he back you up?"

Angus swore. "Of course not." Nevertheless his voice carried a note of grim satisfaction as he added, "Which is exactly why they're going to let us come in."

Milos couldn't restrain himself. "That doesn't make sense."

"Sure it does. You're just too stupid to see it." Angus' yellow eyes were full of threats. "Look at this from the Bill's point of view. He's got two Amnion warships on his hands. *Captain's Fancy* is in—and she came from deeper in Amnion space, from Enablement Station. So Captain Sheepfucker has been screwing with them somehow. That's why those warships are here. They may even be after Donner's precious Morn Hyland." Angus said her name like a curse. "The Bill is already up to hips in shit he didn't ask for and doesn't want.

"Now suddenly we arrive." More and more, Angus' explanation itself sounded like a threat. "About the best thing you can say for us from his point of view is—we're dangerous. Especially at a time like this. But now we're linked to Captain Sheepfucker. We claim he'll back up our story. Sure as hell looks like we're here because of him, doesn't it?

"As soon as Succorso refuses to confirm us, the Bill won't have any choice. He'll have to bring us in. Once we're docked, he'll have us under control. That way he can try to protect himself from all the different things that might be going on."

At last Milos found the determination to stifle his questions. They betrayed too much: ever since he'd been cursed with the job of trying to break Angus, his questions had betrayed too much. No matter how much he reminded himself that he still had secrets and options which Angus—and therefore Hashi Lebwohl—couldn't guess, every passing hour seemed to bring him more under Angus' power. He needed reassurance, *needed* it—

Sucking smoke into his lungs while his crotch and armpits oozed and his heart labored, he forced himself to continue waiting.

Scarcely ten minutes passed before Billingate spoke again.

"*Trumpet,* this is Operations," said the laconic voice. "You have permission to come in. Approach vectors and berth assignment follow."

Numbers began to scroll across the helm readouts.

"Don't keep me in suspense, Operations," Angus put in quickly. "What did Captain Succorso say about me?"

"Pay attention," Operations snapped. "I'm not done. You have permission to come in, but it's conditional. You won't be allowed to leave until you satisfy us."

"You mean"—Angus concealed his grin with a sour growl— "Captain Succorso refused to back me up?"

"He refused to talk to us at all," replied Operations. "We aren't going to let you out of here until you convince him to convince us we can trust you.

"If you're going to turn tail, you'd better do it right now. You're already in range for fire from Amnion defensive *Calm Horizons.* Operations out."

The sudden silence seemed to throb in Milos' ears like the pressure of his pulse. A shudder that should have been relief came over him. For a moment he couldn't force himself to breathe.

Then Angus hammered his board with one fist and snarled, "*Got you, you bastards!*"

Milos exhaled as if he'd been released.

Now.

Finally he was done waiting.

He hadn't put his own neck into this noose. And he hated it. Now he could do something about that.

As Angus processed Billingate's instructions, Milos dropped his nic and unbelted himself for the second time. Drifting toward the command station, he said with his own kind of satisfaction, "That can wait. I want to talk to you."

Angus didn't respond. The screens showed that he was programming helm to follow Operations' instructions automatically.

When he'd anchored himself on the back of Angus' seat, Milos ordered, "Joshua, stop what you're doing. Listen to me."

As obedient as a piece of equipment, Angus dropped his hands. He started to turn his head; but some instinct or prewritten commandment stopped him.

"Joshua," Milos said softly behind Angus' head, "you know everything they want you to know about why we're here." He didn't need to explain who "they" were. "They've given you access to some of their databases, some of the information you need. You'll get more as you go along.

"But they haven't told you why *I'm* here."

A muscle spasmed in Angus' shoulder. He may have been fighting his zone implants.

"They think they have," Milos went on. "They think they've explained me well enough to let you function." And they think they know the truth, whether they told it to you or not. "But they're wrong. I've got my own reasons.

"It's time for us to start on them.

"Angus Thermopyle," he said from the bottom of his heart, "I loathe you. Your violence sickens me. Your person nauseates me. I despise your morals. Everything you do and everything you are is offensive to me. But more offensive than anything else is the fact that I have to act like your subordinate. Taking your orders is bad enough. Looking and *smelling* like you is much worse.

"We're going to change that right now."

As Milos unsealed his shipsuit he urged quietly, "Go on, Joshua. Ask me what that means."

Angus' voice came out as if the muscles of his throat were in knots. "What does that mean?"

From the core of his bones to the ends of his nerves, Milos Taverner understood humiliation and control. For the first time in months—perhaps for the first time in years—he felt a moment of happiness. Dropping his shipsuit, he moved his grip from the back to the arm of Angus' g-seat. "It means," he said with a complex smile, "you're going to use that foul tongue of yours to keep me clean."

Careful to invoke the appropriate codes so that nothing could go wrong, Milos described exactly what he wanted Joshua to do.

Later, when the dirtiness of his body and the fear in his soul had been relieved, he gave Angus a Jerico priority order which ensured that from now on Angus would allow him unrestricted access to *Trumpet*'s communications.

ANCILLARY DOCUMENTATION

UNITED MINING COMPANIES

A BRIEF HISTORY

Publicly the history of the United Mining Companies was a study in the exercise of economic muscle.

How did the UMC become so big? How did it come about that humankind's activities in space were not only directed but policed by the UMC? How were the governments of Earth finessed out of their familiar—if essentially arbitrary—sovereignty over their own citizens? By what right did the UMC become the sole legal bargaining agent, and therefore the sole viable defense, between humankind and the Amnion? How did a mere "private" commercial enterprise become responsible for the fate of the human race?

The answer to all these questions was the same: economic muscle.

If a corollary was required, it could be found in the development of the gap drive. Without the ability to cross—that is to say, explore and expand across—interstellar distances, questions of this scale would never have arisen.

At the time when Dr. Juanita Estevez was in danger of destructing herself and SpaceLab Station with the first gap drive prototype, Earth was in a period of political and economic stagnation; a period of atrophy so profound that more than a few analysts concluded the planet had exhausted not only its resources but its ability to solve problems. One hundred fifty or so sovereign nations had become so interdependent that warfare was no longer viable as a means of economic and political revitalization. By the same token, mutual interconnection compelled each nation to share the deterioration of its neighbors. In other words, the inhabitants of the planet were being killed by precisely the same thing that kept them alive.

Without enough fossil fuels to make energy cheap (except in space, fusion generators were prohibitively expensive to build and maintain); without enough trees to recycle the atmosphere; without new raw materials to replace the old; without any adequate way to make productive use of garbage, or to dispose of it in a nonpolluting fashion; without frontiers or wars to provide the sense of excitement or urgency which inspired creative problem solving: Earth had become a seemingly endless list of things her people had to do without. The planet appeared to have outrun its own future.

In a last-ditch effort to save themselves, a number of commercial enterprises and quasi-commercial conglomerates put up space stations. These were research facilities, primarily, exercises in hope: huge orbiting labs, hydroponics tanks, launch platforms for probes toward the other planets, and high-tech development centers. The stated purpose for such vast expenditure was to make the discoveries that would restore the future of humankind. However, the actual result was to drain the planet's waning resources so severely that stagnant economies around the globe sank into active decline.

Paradoxically, the more these commercial and quasi-commercial adventures cost, the more necessary they seemed and the more powerful they became. Earth didn't simply need them: it needed them to succeed.

By the time SpaceLab Station did what it was supposed to do—that is to say, by the time Dr. Estevez discovered the gap drive which made exploration and development beyond the solar system first feasible and then practical—the Station's parent conglomerate (then called simply SpaceLab Inc.) had become so necessary to the several nations from which it sprang that none of the relevant governments was able to take control of the Station's products.

That, in brief, explained why what followed was an exercise of commerce rather than of sovereignty. The only concession SpaceLab Inc. made to its governments—not to mention its competitors—was an agreement to license the gap drive patents for a bearable royalty.

For a time, SpaceLab Inc. (now Sagittarius Exploration) naturally became the most potent commercial concern in existence. And its dominance was confirmed when one of its first missions brought home news of a rich asteroid belt. This was not the belt on which the UMC founded its wealth. It was a far smaller and thinner find, played out early; but it supplied enough raw ore to enable most subsequent exploration.

However, despite its access to huge capital in the form of royalties, Sagittarius Exploration found itself without the corporate resources to take advantage of its find. Here the UMC (then Space Mines Inc.) entered the picture.

At that time SMI was a relatively small and apparently harmless ore-smelting enterprise: it existed to make what it could out of the asteroids which were within reach from Earth at space-normal speeds. It was big enough to do the work Sagittarius Exploration (now popularly known as SagEx) needed, but not big enough to be a convincing competitor. Naturally, SagEx tried to absorb the smaller company. SMI managed to avoid that fate; and as a reward for its creative tactics it eventually gained a partnership with SagEx in the development of the belt.

There Space Mines Inc. began the rise which eventually transformed it into the United Mining Companies.

The SagEx belt—and Sagittarius Unlimited Station, in which SMI was also a partner—produced wealth on a previously unimagined scale.

Because of its earlier smallness and pedestrian activities, SMI had no support from any of Earth's governments, therefore no governmental restrictions. And the company's new wealth gave it muscle. Using that muscle with both vision and cunning, SMI soon became one of the primary players in the exploration and development of space.

If the story had ended there, however, Space Mines Inc. would never have become the source of so many interesting questions.

Earth and its conglomerates still faced a limited future. Despite the gap drive, human space was effectively finite, limited by its own population base. Therefore wealth—and the opportunities for wealth—could only grow in proportion to the expansion of the species. That expansion took place steadily, in the stations around Earth and elsewhere, but the process was slow. As always, the economy could only support so much growth; after that, growth had to stop.

Contact with the Amnion changed this equation.

In a display of profound foresight, SMI used its new wealth, and every other dollar the company could scrape together, to acquire Intertech, like SpaceLab Inc. a research and development company which had expanded into exploration. At the time, Intertech was uniquely vulnerable to acquisition. In the aftermath of the Humanity Riots—which had been triggered by Intertech's efforts to understand humankind's first encounter with an Amnioni mutagen—the company itself was devastated. And no one else wanted it: no one else realized the potential implied by its role in the riots. The takeover of Intertech put SMI in the position of being the only human enterprise capable of both reaching the Amnion and responding to what they offered.

To capitalize on this position, SMI used all of its recently achieved vigor and muscle to pursue trade with the Amnion.

Suddenly a door of vast opportunity opened, and SMI held the knob in one hand, the key in the other. Intertech owned everything humanity knew about the Amnion: SMI owned the ships and facilities needed to take advantage of that knowledge. And Earth had a nearly bottomless hunger for new resources—as well as new markets. Rather than risk failing to gain the benefits offered by the Amnion, Earth's governments rechartered Space Mines Inc. as the United Mining Companies and gave it the mission of developing Amnion trade for the sake of all humankind.

Ultimately trade with the Amnion provided the UMC with both its reason and its means for being.

That was the public history.

WARDEN

Eventually, of course, Godsen Frik caught up with Warden Dios. The director of the United Mining Companies Police couldn't avoid his own director of Protocol indefinitely.

Before Godsen found him, however—and before the first peremptory, predictable demand for a video conference came in from the Governing Council for Earth and Space—Warden managed to sequester himself with Hashi Lebwohl for more than an hour.

Their conversation took place in one of the several secure offices which Warden maintained throughout UMCPHQ. Naturally no room, however private, could be secure from what Milos Taverner might have called "buggery." But the director of Data Acquisition was no "bugger": where secrets were concerned, he was as safe as a tombstone. The distinction of being the only person in UMCPHQ who might reveal what was said in one of those offices belonged to Frik himself. And the offices themselves, with their baffled walls and electronic shielding, were proof against any kind of eavesdropping.

As an additional precaution, the techs and guards who tended those offices had strict orders never to acknowledge that Warden Dios ever used them. While he was inside, he ceased to exist in every official sense. Even Min Donner would have been turned away with a blunt, "We haven't seen him, sir," if she'd tried to locate the UMCP director while he was sequestered.

As a result, Godsen had no idea where Warden had hidden

himself, and therefore no idea in which direction events were moving, when he finally succeeded in confronting Dios.

Warden wasn't usually a petty man; but he took a certain small satisfaction in Godsen's ignorance. Ignorance led to discomfiture—and Warden liked seeing the PR director discomfited. Relations between the two men left him few other grounds for satisfaction.

By this time he was in his formal office—a huge, expensive, and generally useless space which he reserved for those occasions on which a display of status was more important than the status itself. At the moment when his public secretary informed him that Godsen wanted to see him immediately, he'd just settled himself behind a wide mahogany desk—polished wood hydroponically grown at immense cost—in an armchair, also of polished mahogany, which rolled on old-fashioned casters. Both desk and chair, like all the furnishings and appurtenances of the room, had been given to him several years ago by Holt Fasner: a congratulatory gift on the completion of the UMCP's orbiting headquarters. Perhaps that was the real reason he never used this office if he could avoid it. Now, however, he had no alternative.

He quickly reviewed the arrangements he'd made for the next hour. Then he keyed the intercom and told his secretary—a woman whom he privately considered to be as polished and useless as the furniture—to let Godsen Frik in.

The PR director entered at once, looking harried.

The look didn't suit him. His fleshy self-confidence and rather flagrant dignity were effective masks for his schemes as well as his pleasures; but they did nothing to conceal a sense of harassment or an air of grievance. His pontifical head with its panoply of white hair, which usually gave him the appearance of the quintessential elder statesman, now made him resemble an aging boy who'd been caught in a particularly shameful act of sodomy.

Observing this was another of Warden's small satisfactions.

It changed nothing, however. Godsen Frik was always transparent to him, thanks to his prosthetic eye. In this Godsen was unlike his fellow directors. Hashi Lebwohl could have betrayed the universe without giving so much as a hint to Warden's infrared sight, not because he was a natural traitor, but because he made no essential distinction between the many levels of his natural duplicity. And

Min Donner's intense concentration and devotion were inherently honest. But Godsen exposed himself by physiological clues too obvious for Warden to miss—every scheme, every mixed motive, every falsehood showed in the rate of his heart, the temperature of his sweat, the aura of his skin.

Whenever Warden Dios dealt with his PR director, he knew he had to be prepared for the consequences, which ranged from Frik's own simple obstructionism to active intervention by Holt Fasner.

That was a curse. Nevertheless Warden counted on it, planned for it; used it.

"Come in," he said unnecessarily. "Sit down." Because he disliked Frik, he always treated him with mildness and courtesy.

Godsen seemed unconscious of his director's dislike. As soon as the door closed behind him, and the indicators showed that the room's monitors were inactive, he came toward the desk, hitched one of his hams onto the gleaming surface in an effort to appear self-confident, and said, "I did what you told me. Now I'm getting my ass roasted."

The effort failed. His voice was too tense to project its usual assured rumble.

Warden spread his hands in a gesture of helplessness. "I don't suppose it occurred to you that you don't have to deal with him? You could always leave him to me."

"He" in this context could only be Holt Fasner.

Unfortunately Godsen had no difficulty choosing among his disparate loyalties. Harried but unrepentant, he replied, "You know I can't do that. For one thing, you didn't hire me for this job. He did. He says he has plans for me. You can't expect me to ignore that. And for another, there isn't a man or woman here—hell, there isn't a skeleton in the damn closet—that can refuse to accept a call from him."

This last assertion wasn't notably accurate. Neither Min Donner nor Hashi acknowledged any authority outside UMCPHQ. Nevertheless Godsen believed what he'd just said; that was obvious.

Warden resisted the impulse to respond, I've got plans for you, too. Instead he inquired, "So what did he say?"

"He said"—Godsen was good at mimicry—" 'What the fuck do you think you're doing, telling the whole world Thermopyle and Taverner got away? Don't you know what's going to happen now?' "

STEPHEN R. DONALDSON

"And what did you reply?"

"I told him I was acting on your direct orders." Godsen's aura was crimson with tension and vulnerability, undermining his efforts to sound staunch. "I told him we did it to back up Joshua's alibi, so he can get into Billingate. And I told him"—the fluctuation of his readings signaled a lie—"I think you made the right decision. It's worth the risk. Everything we've done with Joshua won't be worth spit if Billingate decides not to trust him."

Warden dismissed all this. "And you didn't mention Morn Hyland?" His tone was particularly mild because his question was especially threatening. "You didn't point out that by risking public exposure of our operation I'm increasing the pressure on myself to rescue her? You've been eloquent in your desire to see her saved." Or eliminated. "You've often pointed out that we'll have a serious disaster on our hands if anyone ever learns we've deliberately left one of our ensigns in her position. Did you perhaps suggest to him that he should urge me to reconsider Joshua's programming where she is concerned?"

He didn't expect a true answer. But he'd posed his question to glean as much information as possible from Godsen's readings.

IR sight was wasted on Godsen: he exposed himself by body language alone. In blustery indignation, he retorted, "No!" Pulling himself off the desk, he retreated a few steps, nearly turned his back as if he wanted to hide his face. "That's ancient history. I lost that argument long ago."

So. Godsen hadn't been given any special instructions. He'd played the Morn card—again—and Holt Fasner had left it lying on the table. The Dragon had decided that the situation didn't call for intervention. Yet.

Warden permitted himself an entirely private sigh of relief.

"That's good," he said kindly. "You ought to know he doesn't care about her. I'm not entirely sure he cares about you. You're both just means to an end." He wouldn't have said such things to anyone but Godsen Frik. Only Godsen might be alarmed by them—and only he might report them. In a subtle way, Warden was trying to tell both Godsen and Holt the truth about himself. "If I knew what that end was, I would be easier in my mind."

Palpably striving to recover his balance, Godsen lowered himself into a chair. For a moment he braced his hands on its arms; then he pulled them together on his thighs. Studying them as if they had notes written on the palms, he asked, "What *is* going to happen now?"

Warden dismissed that as well. "It's not your problem. PR isn't an easy job, but it does have one advantage. Nobody expects honesty.

"Still, I'm glad you're here. You've saved my secretary the effort of tracking you down." Warden smiled at his own irony. "I want all of us to be absolutely clear about what our position is from now on."

Unobtrusively he pressed a button which relayed a private signal to his secretary. On cue she chimed his intercom to announce, "Director, Min Donner and Hashi Lebwohl are here."

"Send them in."

At once the door opened, and the remaining UMCP directors entered the office.

"Come in," Warden said by way of greeting. Because he hadn't stood to greet Godsen, he remained sitting. In any case neither Hashi nor Min needed courtesy from him. They both knew more than Godsen did about why they were here. "I hope I haven't kept you waiting."

Min's shrug said, It doesn't matter.

"Not at all," the DA director wheezed equably. "When I am in the presence of a woman as lovely as your secretary, I am never 'waiting.' "

"Good." Warden pointed out chairs and said, "Sit," in a tone he didn't use with Godsen Frik.

The ED director seated herself as if she were coiling into the chair, poised to spring.

Perhaps to acknowledge the importance of the occasion, Lebwohl had put on his dirtiest lab coat over stained pants and an appalling shirt. That and his scrawny frame made him look like a scarecrow. The laces trailed from his ancient shoes, threatening to trip him at every step. Slumping from his thin nose, his glasses were so badly scratched and smeared that they seemed to blur everything he saw—or everything other people saw when they looked at him. His movements and even his posture appeared somnolent: the boundless energy hidden inside him showed only in his charged eyebrows and the conceptual purity of his blue eyes.

As he sagged into a seat, he had the look of a man who was

ready only to be measured for a winding sheet. But Warden Dios knew better. In his own fashion—a style utterly unlike Min Donner's—Hashi Lebwohl was coiled and poised; ready for everything except death.

Still Warden didn't explain what was "going to happen now." Min and Hashi already knew—although only Hashi had been briefed—and Godsen could be allowed to sweat a little longer. He glanced at his desk chronometer: twelve minutes left. There was never enough time; but twelve minutes would probably suffice. If they didn't, he could always fake a brief transmission delay.

"Now." He faced each of his subordinates in turn, scanning their emanations like a craftsman checking the condition of his tools. On the most fundamental level, he didn't believe in using human beings: not as tools; not as genetic raw materials. That more than any other aspect of his personality explained why he'd become a cop. The fact that his personal dilemma required him to do so many things he abhorred gave him another moment of nausea. It didn't show, however. He'd perfected the art of keeping the worst cost of whatever he needed and did to himself.

Bland and careful, as if all his defenses were impenetrable, he announced, "*Trumpet* is gone. For better or worse, Angus and Milos are on their own.

"You all know this is the most hazardous position we've ever put ourselves in. Never before have we risked so much on people in situations so far outside our control. And never before has so much depended on our ability to keep what we're doing to ourselves. So it's time for us to be clear." Warden said this despite the fact that he had no intention whatsoever of being clear himself. "If you still object to this operation—if you believe it's misguided or doomed—if you think I haven't adequately considered the difficulties—I want you to say so now."

Godsen went back to studying his hands. Hashi smiled around the room as if he didn't know what doubts or objections were.

Min didn't hesitate, however. "Why bother?" she asked bluntly. "As you say, *Trumpet* is out of reach. Assuming we could give Milos new orders, we have no way of knowing when, how, or even if he would put them into effect."

"You aren't listening." Warden spoke more harshly than he intended. Min sometimes had that effect on him—or rather his own falseness toward her did. "I didn't offer to change Angus' programming. Whether sending him out this way is a stroke of genius or an act of suicide, he's out of our hands. I'm concerned about us here, not him.

"If *we* fail to back him up effectively, we might as well not have sent him at all. No, it's worse than that. If we aren't going to back him up, we should have left him rotting on Com-Mine. If we lose him, we'll expose all the knowledge and expertise that went into him, as well as all the information he carries about us.

"I want to deal with your objections and problems now, so they won't interfere later."

"Then there is no need for me to speak." The DA director coughed like a man who'd spent a lifetime breathing Earth's clotted atmosphere instead of processed station air. "Much of this operation I designed. The rest I approved. And I do not doubt that it will succeed.

"However, I suspect that my colleagues"—he grinned through his glasses—"differ with me on this."

Warden glanced at Min, at Godsen. "How so?"

Min glared grimly at Frik.

Seeing that she wasn't going to speak first, Godsen raised his head. Covering his uncertainty with fulsomeness, he announced, "Well, I've said before that I think Taverner is a terrible choice. That man has the morals of a stoat. Even Hashi will admit we didn't have any trouble suborning him—which means no one else is likely to have any trouble either. But I think the situation is worse than that.

"I've read his records"—Godsen appeared to consider this an act of great diligence—"and I can tell you, it isn't a simple question whether we approached him or he approached us. He was too slick about it to be obvious, but I'm convinced selling out Com-Mine Security was at least as much his idea as ours."

Under her breath, Min muttered, "What does that prove?"

Portentously Godsen continued, "So Taverner is a terrible choice for two reasons. He'll sell us out as soon as someone—anyone—offers him enough money." He seemed to draw confidence from the sound of his own voice. "And if the great unwashed public we're all sworn to serve and protect ever *ever* gets a hint that we released a cyborg as powerful as Joshua with only a proven bugger to control him, this whole operation will turn to shit faster than you can say 'righteous indignation.' Even the Dragon might not be able to keep the votes from pulling the plug on Data Acquisition."

"Meaning what?" asked Warden calmly.

"Meaning"—Godsen was in full spate—"the mighty and for-ever-to-be-respected GCES might decharter Hashi's little game room. The votes might decide Data Acquisition is too sensitive for mere cops to play with. They might even consider a bill of severance."

Warden noticed Min's increasing tension, but betrayed none himself. "Do you consider this realistic?"

For a moment Godsen was torn between his love of rhetoric and his deeper loyalties. Then he sighed. "No. The Dragon won't let it happen.

"But he's the real issue here, isn't he? If this gamble goes against us, he's the one who will have to clean up the mess. And he won't be amused. *That* I guarantee."

"Neither will I," Dios promised. Because he was speaking for Godsen's benefit, he faced the other directors and kept his tone quiet. "And I won't put up with being second-guessed. If I ever get *any* hint—from *anybody*—that one word of our conversation has left this room, I'll extract blood for it. Finding fault after the fact is easy. The four of us are going to leave the easy jobs to other people."

That was another message aimed at Holt Fasner. When Godsen repeated it to the Dragon, it would take on a different meaning.

Leave Min and Hashi out of this. If you decide you want to punish someone for what happens to Angus' mission, concentrate on me. I'm at least big enough to pay for my own mistakes.

The fact that Hashi and perhaps Min as well were probably as doomed as Warden Dios himself didn't deflect him.

"Other objections? Other problems?" he asked bluntly.

Like a woman who knew that her moment had come, Min said, "Morn Hyland."

The passion of her aura, the intensity of her emissions, was vivid. All her doubts and fears were focused in that one name.

Involuntarily Warden stiffened. Precisely because he valued his ED director and ached to spare her, he often found that he couldn't be as gentle with her as he was with Godsen. Close to anger, he demanded, "What about her?"

The curse as well as the blessing of his position was that Min

Donner trusted him too much to fear his anger. The fact that she challenged him so rarely was a mark of respect, not an indication of timidity.

"Like Godsen," she said, as clear as a blade, "I don't trust Taverner. I don't care about the PR implications. I worry about betrayal. But now that I see how this operation is running, I understand why you wanted him. Thermopyle probably wouldn't get into Billingate alone. And anybody else we sent with him wouldn't be much of an improvement. Taverner may be a shitty choice, but he's probably the best we could hope for.

"Morn Hyland is another matter. I don't understand what you're doing to her." Min glanced at Frik as if giving him a chance to support her, then continued on her own. "For some reason, you refused to let Thermopyle be programmed to at least try to rescue her. I don't understand that—and I may never understand it until you tell me why you let Succorso have her in the first place.

"I don't care if she's the price we were supposed to pay for Succorso's help. That isn't good enough. He's accepted money before. For a chance to hurt a 'competitor' like Thermopyle, he would have accepted money again. In any case, he couldn't have stopped us. If we'd ordered Com-Mine Security to take her after he got her away from Thermopyle, there's nothing he could have done about it.

"She's one of ours, one of *mine*. She'd been raped and abused for weeks. She had an unauthorized zone implant—and by the time Thermopyle was done with her, she was almost certainly an addict. We're the *police*, for God's sake. If there was ever a human being who needed our help, she was it. But we didn't help her. We abandoned her to Succorso.

"I want to know why."

Even though Warden was braced for this, it still hurt him. Of the people in his office, only she had the power to cause him so much pain. He had to stifle his impulse to say, Min, forgive me. I'm so sorry.

He glanced at his chronometer. Two minutes left. Apparently he would be on time.

"Other problems?" he asked Godsen. "Worries?" he asked Hashi. "Objections?" he asked Min.

The three of them regarded him without speaking. Godsen's apprehension, Hashi's hidden excitement, Min's outrage: each had its own distinct infrared flavor; but none struck him as a reason for delay.

Because he was a man who acted on his commitments, he took the next step along the path he'd chosen.

"All right. Unless I've completely misjudged the situation, you're about to get the answers you want.

"You won't be surprised to hear that Godsen's news release is already stirring up trouble. Specifically the GCES is in an uproar. I don't know what the council members are saying, but I would guess that terms like 'incompetence,' 'dereliction of duty,' and even 'mal-feasance' are being shouted in all directions. An emergency session has already been declared to probe the situation.

"The Council has demanded a video conference with Hashi and me so that we can account for ourselves. In fact, we're supposed to downlink with them"—Warden checked the time—"right about now. As you know, our charter doesn't require us to obtain GCES approval for our operations, but it does require us to honor requests for disclosure. So Hashi and I are going to talk to them."

He looked at Godsen and Min. "I want you to listen. What you're going to hear is our official position—the position you'll swear to from now on. Is that clear? If the explanation we give the Council doesn't resolve your objections, I'll go into more detail afterward."

Godsen nodded to demonstrate his dutiful loyalty. Min tightened her grip on herself and said nothing.

"Hashi," Warden continued as he tapped buttons which activated the broadcast equipment in his office, "we'll sit on the edge of the desk. A little informality"—he hoped that his bitterness didn't show in his voice—"might make us look like the kind of men who tell the truth."

While cameras and pickups came to life, and partitions unfolded to reveal a wide screen in one wall, Lebwohl pushed himself out of his chair and shambled to the desk. At the same time lights dimmed around the office so that only the desk remained bright. Warden chimed his secretary and told her to complete the downlink with the GCES on Earth. Then he joined his DA director on the front of the desk.

Min Donner and Godsen Frik watched from the gloom outside the reach of the cameras as Warden Dios and Hashi Lebwohl settled themselves to talk to the Council.

After a brief burst of static, the screen resolved into an image of the formal meeting hall of the Governing Council for Earth and Space.

Much of the room was filled by a large, half-oval table. The twenty-one council members sat around the outside of the table, with small data terminals as well as hardcopy notes in front of them, and their personal advisers behind them. Usually individuals being questioned by the Council sat at a testimony table within the half oval, equally accessible to all the members. Now, however, the screen which showed Warden to the Council had taken the place of the table and chair. His own perspective on the hall came from cameras above and behind the testimony seat; but what Holt Fasner called "the votes" faced him as if he were seated in front of them.

A quick scan told him that all the members were present. That didn't surprise him: this wasn't an occasion that any of the elected representatives of Earth and her far-flung stations would choose to miss. Somewhere in the back of his brain, he knew all twenty-one by name, as well as a fair number of their advisers; circumstances would refresh his memory at need. And at any given moment Hashi could probably recite verbatim the UMCP file on every person in the hall.

For the present Warden made a deliberate effort not to take notice of old Sixten Vertigus, rigid as steel in his chair despite his years, or of any of the other members who might conceivably support a bill of severance. He didn't want to give even the slightest indication that he was going to damage—perhaps ruin—their careers.

The screen in his office had a distressing flicker. Sunspot activity, no doubt. Numbers running across the bottom of the image told him that his communications techs were attempting to filter out the distortion. Unfortunately the unsteadiness of the picture touched a sore place in his optic nerves, gave him the impression that he was coming down with a migraine.

Members shuffled papers, verified or canceled their data readouts. In a moment every eye was fixed on Warden's image. Because of his own angle of view, the members appeared to focus their attention on his crotch. He missed being able to make eye contact with them, just as he missed the IR dimension which video denied him; but he was accustomed to the discrepancy.

"Director Dios. Thank you for responding so promptly."

The man who spoke sat in the middle of the half oval. Only the position of his chair indicated his rank: he was Abrim Len, president of the Governing Council for Earth and Space. In the private rooms of UMCPHQ, ensigns and techs sometimes joked that Godsen Frik was a Len clone. Both men were capable of the same public posturing, the same orotund cadences. Len was no Fasner stooge, however. He was simply a man who preferred any sort of consensus, no matter how fatuous, over any form of confrontation.

Prominent teeth and a receding chin made him look like a rabbit.

"As you can imagine," he was saying, "the news released by your director of Protocol a few hours ago has given us all grave cause for concern. It's our hope that you can explain what's happened in a way that will relieve our fears."

The president paused expectantly.

"Mr. President," Warden replied in greeting, "members of the Council. As you know, I'm Warden Dios, director of the United Mining Companies Police." He announced this as if he were stating his loyalties. "With me is Hashi Lebwohl, who serves as my director of Data Acquisition. I don't need imagination to understand your concerns. We're more than a little concerned ourselves. Hashi and I will do our best to answer your questions.

"I must tell you immediately, however, that my investigation is incomplete. Events are too recent—I haven't yet had time to study them fully. Please keep that in mind if some of our answers don't seem entirely adequate."

"Certainly, certainly." Len's impulse to soothe ruffled feelings was instinctive and automatic. "In any case, we're all acutely aware of the rather specialized nature of the relationship between the GCES and the UMCP. It's gratifying to see that you take the commitment to disclose so seriously."

"Mr. President," Warden put in sternly because he didn't like wasting time, "I take all my commitments seriously."

"I'm sure you do," Len responded at once. "Your record is admirable in every particular. I speak for everyone here"—he gestured around the hall—"when I say that we hold you in the highest esteem.

"Director Lebwohl, we appreciate your presence as well." One of Len's techniques for avoiding conflict was to keep talking. "This level of cooperation benefits all of us who are charged with the duty of guiding and protecting our people."

"Make no mention of it, please, Mr. President," Hashi replied with a grin. "I am always eager to do whatever I can to redeem my own errors."

Despite his confidence in Hashi, Warden feared for a moment that the conference was about to go badly awry.

" 'Errors'?" a woman snapped aggressively. "Do you admit errors?"

With an effort, Warden identified the junior member for the United Western Bloc. Her name was Carsin.

At the same time he flicked a look at Godsen and Min. They emitted nothing except tension.

"All in good time, my dear, all in good time," Len interposed quickly. "We must consider every aspect of this unfortunate situation in its proper order. It is premature to discuss errors"—another man would have said, *to assign blame*. "Director Dios, Director Lebwohl, can we first agree on the facts?"

Warden folded his arms across his chest. "Of course."

"Are the news broadcasts accurate?" Len pursued. "Is it true, Director Lebwohl, that a convicted illegal held for questioning by your department has escaped?"

When Hashi nodded, his glasses slipped farther down his nose. He pushed them back up with a hand like a spider. "In substance, yes."

"This illegal was a man named Angus Thermopyle?"

"Unquestionably."

"Has he escaped from you altogether?"

"Do you mean, has he escaped from UMCPHQ, as well as from Data Acquisition? Yes."

"Do you know where Angus Thermopyle has gone?"

Hashi shrugged delicately. "How could I? If we possessed such knowledge, we would already be in pursuit. However, we have no data except the tach parameters of the ship Captain Thermopyle has stolen. Certainly we can do the calculations to predict the direction and distance of his first crossing. But why should we trouble ourselves? Nothing in all space can prevent him from changing course when he resumes tard and then reengaging his gap drive with altered parameters. Under these conditions, we lack the means to trace him."

"Would you consider it *trouble* to do those calculations any-way?" the UWB junior member demanded sarcastically. "Just on the off chance that we might learn something useful?"

"Not at all." Hashi made a show of writing a note and handing it to an offscreen aide. For the sake of appearances, Min came for-ward to accept the piece of paper, then sat down again.

"Please, Junior Member Carsin," Len protested. "I'm sure that Director Dios and Director Lebwohl are willing to answer any and all questions. But everything will be easier if you'll wait your turn."

Frowning as if she'd received an official reprimand, Carsin turned her attention to her data terminal.

Len consulted his notes. "Let us continue with the facts. Is it true, Director Lebwohl, that this Angus Thermopyle was assisted in his escape by a former deputy chief of Com-Mine Station Security, a man named Milos Taverner?"

"That also appears unquestionable. Considering the conditions of his imprisonment, I sincerely doubt that Captain Thermopyle could have effected his own escape. Indeed, in this context I would say that the term 'escape' is fundamentally imprecise. Captain Thermo-pyle did not escape. He could not have escaped. He was *released* by Deputy Chief Taverner."

Perhaps to preserve an air of impartiality, Abrim Len chose not to ask the next obvious question himself. Instead he nodded to the senior member for the Pacific Rim Conglomerate.

"Director Lebwohl," this man said immediately in a firm voice, "we're in the dark here. We hardly know where to begin analyzing this mess. Instead of waiting for individual questions, why don't you simply tell us what we all want to know? How did this happen?"

Static split the screen momentarily. The sensation of migraine tightened in Warden's temples. He resisted an impulse to rub his eyes.

With his usual deftness, Hashi managed to convey both exag-gerated patience and geniality as he replied, "It is no mystery, ladies and gentlemen. As a deputy chief of Com-Mine Security, Milos Tav-erner had certain clearances and authorizations at UMCPHQ. He used them to secure Captain Thermopyle's release, as well as to obtain access to a ship. Because of the nature of those clearances and authorizations, only the most routine requests for confirmation were forwarded to me. By the time I received them, Captain Thermopyle and Deputy Chief Taverner were already beyond reach."

"That's not the question, and you know it," Junior Member Carsin sneered. "We aren't interested in the mechanics. If your incompetence were that obvious, Dios would already have your head on the block."

"Then perhaps," Hashi wheezed as if his lungs pained him, "you would be good enough to phrase your question more precisely."

"We want to know," Carsin retorted, "how this whole situation became *possible*. According to the news broadcasts"—she pointed at her readout—"you reqqed Taverner from Com-Mine because you thought he might be a traitor. So why in *hell* did you let him have all those 'clearances and authorizations'?"

Min's emanations were as sharp as a snarl. The PR director radiated a stew of anxiety and concentration.

Hashi did a convincing imitation of a man who was gratified by Carsin's explanation. "Thank you, Junior Member." He placed no discernible stress on the diminutive. "Now I understand.

"*You* must understand, ladies and gentlemen, that our position in relation to Deputy Chief Taverner was not as simple as the news broadcasts may have made it appear. None of you have forgotten, I think, the original case concerning Captain Thermopyle. He was convicted on Com-Mine Station of the burglary of Station supplies. He was a notorious illegal, however, believed to be the perpetrator of many, far more serious crimes—and yet insufficient evidence was found to convict him of anything worse than mere burglary. Later it became clear that even this crime could not have been committed without the assistance of someone favorably placed within Com-Mine Security itself."

Around the hall, members keyed their readouts or turned to whisper questions to their advisers. However, the member for Com-Mine Station didn't need to refresh her memory. It was significant, Warden thought, that she kept her mouth grimly shut.

"Because of the palpable absence of damning evidence," Hashi continued, "Com-Mine Security quite naturally declined to let the matter rest. Deputy Chief Taverner was the officer assigned to Captain Thermopyle's ongoing interrogation. Unfortunately no results were forthcoming.

"It was at this point that we acted on our interest in the case. We were interested from the first, I must confess—Enforcement Division no less than Data Acquisition." Carefully Hashi prepared the way for the issues on which Warden Dios hoped the Council would focus. "As you may recall from the original case concerning Captain Thermopyle, we had reason to suspect that he was involved in the destruction of the UMCP destroyer *Starmaster*. This suspicion revolved around his arrival at Com-Mine Station with *Starmaster*'s sole survivor, an ensign named Morn Hyland. What happened to *Starmaster*? How did Ensign Hyland survive? Why was she in Captain Thermopyle's company? More to the point, why did she remain with him? We were interested—I might well say *passionately* interested—in the answers to these questions.

"Unfortunately we had no jurisdiction. We were required to abide by the results of Com-Mine Security's investigation."

By this time most of the members appeared to have obtained the records or reminders they needed from their data terminals or advisers.

Hashi adjusted his glasses again, then steepled his fingers like a lecturing professor.

"The Preempt Act altered the question of jurisdiction, however. And it raised an additional consideration. Its recent passage gave us a clear responsibility for the integrity of Com-Mine Station Security. Why were no results forthcoming from Captain Thermopyle's interrogation? Why had he been convicted of only so minor an offense? Had the records been expunged? If so, had they been expunged by Deputy Chief Taverner? Was his failure to obtain further information explained, perhaps, by complicity in Captain Thermopyle's crimes?

"Ladies and gentlemen, I found these questions too fascinating to ignore. On my authority as the Director of Data Acquisition, I reqqed both Captain Thermopyle and Deputy Chief Taverner, so that I could learn the truth for myself."

Warden had no criticism of Hashi's performance so far. Hashi kept his instinct for innuendo and misdirection in check: he sounded as plausible as Warden could wish. Still the communications techs couldn't keep the screen from flickering as if it were distorted by Hashi's—and Warden's—duplicity.

"But how to go about learning the truth?" the DA director asked rhetorically. "That was the complex question. If I made my suspicions obvious to Deputy Chief Taverner—for example, by revoking his clearances and authorizations—he would certainly do his utmost to protect himself. Then I might never gain the information I desired. Therefore my best hope was to preserve the illusion that I had reqqed him because of his special knowledge of Captain Thermopyle. There was, after all, no reason why this should not be the truth.

"Indeed, where Captain Thermopyle was concerned, I was daily given reason to believe in Deputy Chief Taverner's honesty. My own interrogations were as unsuccessful as it is possible to imagine. Despite my most advanced techniques—within the limits of the law," Hashi added piously, "I gained nothing which Deputy Chief Taverner had not gained before me.

"Therefore what grounds did I have to treat Deputy Chief Taverner as a suspected illegal? Among the UMCP, we hold the principle sacred that a man is innocent until proven guilty." Hashi was starting to play his part too thickly, but Warden didn't interfere. "The more I interrogated Captain Thermopyle, the more my distrust of Deputy Chief Taverner evaporated.

"Ladies and gentlemen, I did not revoke his clearances and authorizations because I had no evidence against him. Until he released Captain Thermopyle and fled, I had no foundation for my suspicions."

Now Warden cut in. Impelled by the pain in his optic nerves, he asked roughly, "Does that help? You should be able to ask accurate questions now."

"Thank you, Director Lebwohl," said Len. "An admirably lucid account. Do I understand you to mean, then, that the 'error' you made reference to earlier was an error in judgment concerning Milos Taverner?"

"Just so, Mr. President," Hashi agreed placidly, as if he were at peace with the universe.

"In that case," Len returned in the same vein, "please accept my condolences. Everyone makes mistakes—but not everyone can afford them. Men who hold as much responsibility as we do, Director

...Warden looked away from the
...odsen Frik.

...She was too sure. In a sense, she'd
...nt to her ideals. As her director,
...things she didn't like; but he had no
...the nature of her beliefs. Despite his
...is personal respect, he couldn't get what

...the other hand—
...sing—of Warden's prosthetic eye was that it
...never blind to the aura and sweat, the respi-
...he people around him; could never turn off his
...n's hypocrisy. For him, Godsen was the UMCP
...ather, he was what the UMCP had become; what
...been turned into by Dios himself, under pressure
...er. Warden couldn't lose sight of that fact.
...emanations consoled him by reminding him that every
...was justified; that everything he did to make restitution
...he risk.
...aced the cameras and the migraine flicker of the screen
...Len began saying, "Thank you, Director Lebwohl. You've
...ost forthcoming. I believe you've satisfied those of us who are
...le of being satisfied in this difficult situation. And I'm sure the
...—he didn't so much as glance at Carsin—"understand the need
...contain their dissatisfaction until the Council can resume its
...mergency session in private.

"Director Dios, do you wish to add anything before we go on?"

Warden shook his head. Steadying himself on his core of anger,
he said, "Hashi Lebwohl has my complete confidence. He's already
answered your questions more fully than I could myself."

Len bowed slightly. "Very well, Director Dios. We will proceed."

The whole Council seemed to pause as if the broadcast image
had frozen. Members held papers motionless in their hands; advisers
leaning forward to speak remained still.

The throbbing in Warden's temples sharpened noticeably.

He wondered how much trepidation his IR vision would have
picked up from the president in person as Len said, "You mentioned

Lebwohl, m
'errors' aff

"M

as th

ma'

I

As if he wanted reassurance,
cameras toward Min Donner and C
Min had no comfort in her.
been purified by her commitm
Warden could require her to d
power to make her question
impersonal love, as well as
he wanted from her.
The PR director, o
One curse—or ble
never closed. He was
ration and pulse, of
awareness of Gods
in miniature. Or
the UMCP had
from Holt Fasn
Godsen'
price he pai
was worth
He
again a
been
capab
rest
to

proc

At

ceiving a r.

"Junior Memb

appears that Capta

den space. If he does

planetoid called Thanatos

tion of a bootleg shipyard cat

pirates." With a shrug, he added,

such as Captain Thermopyle, if I ma,

Amnion preclude all possibility of pursuit.

Then he resumed his answers as if he w

He was calm the entire time; unruffled; almo
wheeze of his voice betrayed any strain. He was well
challenge. And he was temperamentally equal to it: he
tale indignation at being pushed to defend lies with more
cause he made no necessary distinction between truth and falseh
he was in his natural element.

Warden should have paid attention, but his mind wandered. The Council's questions, like Hashi's answers, were chaff; a way of filling the time until Abrim Len felt ready to broach "other matters." As a good politician, the president wanted his fellow GCES members to satisfy their appetite for trivialities before he raised more sensitive issues. The real questions—the real threats—hadn't begun yet.

Angus Thermopyle's arrest and conviction on Com-Mine Station. As you know, those events have played a large part in the debates of the Council on other occasions." For instance, in the debate over the Preempt Act. "You may not be aware, however, that certain of our members have asked questions concerning those events for which we have never obtained satisfactory answers. Angus Thermopyle's escape gives those questions a new urgency.

"Member Martingale, will you continue?"

Martingale was the member for Com-Mine Station.

"Director Dios," she said without raising her eyes from her data terminal, "my constituency was more intimately involved in the Thermopyle case than any other. I'm better placed to ask questions than my fellow members—and my responsibility to Com-Mine Station requires me to ask those questions. At the same time, Com-Mine is anxious"—she stressed the word carefully—"to avoid any taint of personal interest. Our Security has been extensively challenged. We wish to defend ourselves—and yet any self-defense smacks of special pleading.

"Therefore, at my urging, the Governing Council for Earth and Space has appointed a Special Counsel to investigate these matters independently. For the record, I remind my fellow members that the Special Counsel was chosen without consultation with my office or Com-Mine Station. Director Dios, both my office and Com-Mine Station have been questioned as rigorously as I hope you will be questioned now."

Warden blinked at the pain of the flickering screen. Here it comes, he thought as Martingale finished, "Let me introduce Special Counsel Maxim Igensard. Special Counsel Igensard, will you take the floor?"

"Thank you, Member Martingale." The man who spoke left his seat behind the Eastern Union senior member and moved to stand at the table.

After a restive moment the Council grew still again.

Muttering silent imprecations against the IR blindness of the downlink, Warden studied Maxim Igensard intensely.

He'd known of Igensard's appointment for some time, of course. However, the fact that the GCES wanted Igensard to question him and Hashi now should have come as a complete surprise.

Warden wasn't surprised. He was relieved—so profoundly re-lieved that for a moment he nearly made the mistake of letting it show.

"Director Dios," Igensard began. "Director Lebwohl. This is a rare opportunity for me. I hope we'll be able to shed light on some troubling issues."

The Special Counsel had a diffident voice which matched his colorless appearance. Although he was the only man in the hall standing, he appeared short. His formal gray suit had been cut—unsuccessfully—to conceal an incongruous potbelly; incongruous be-cause his limbs were slight and his face carried no fat. He looked like a man who could be blown in any direction by the winds of circumstance.

Yet he alone seemed to understand that in order to create the illusion of eye contact with the UMCP director he had to face the cameras rather than the screen. As a result, he was the only member who didn't appear to be scrutinizing Warden's crotch.

Despite the flicker of the screen, Igensard's straight gaze showed no diffidence at all.

Warden's throat tightened in hope or dread. "Ask whatever you want," he said gruffly. "We'll answer as well as we can."

Igensard didn't hesitate. "As it happens, I don't know to whom I should address my questions." He had no notes; apparently he needed none. "I'll tell you what I want to know, and you can answer as you see fit.

"Morn Hyland," he announced as if the subject had no partic-ular significance, "was an ensign aboard the UMCP destroyer *Star-master*. When her ship was lost, she came into the hands of Captain Thermopyle. His testimony is on record—he claims to have rescued her after her ship was destroyed, purportedly by Com-Mine Station sabotage."

To control his own tension, Warden interposed, "Are you going to ask us if Milos Taverner had anything to do with *Starmaster*'s destruction? We don't know."

Igensard continued as if Warden hadn't spoken. "She remained with him after he returned to Com-Mine Station. He claims she did so because she didn't trust Com-Mine Security. But when Security arrested him for stealing Station supplies, she immediately left both him and Com-Mine with a Captain Nick Succorso aboard the frigate

Captain's Fancy. Captain Succorso himself has frequently been suspected of illegal activities, but has never been convicted. Is this substantially correct?"

Warden shrugged. "You've got the records. You know it is."

"In that case, Director Dios, Director Lebwohl, all my questions can be summed up in one. Why did you allow this to happen?" The diffidence of Igensard's voice was a sham; a way of disarming people. "A known illegal is caught and convicted by Com-Mine Station. He is later reqqed by Data Acquisition. At the same time, a UMCP officer, the sole survivor of a UMCP ship, Captain Thermopyle's only companion—the only witness to what he may have done—is allowed to depart Com-Mine, untouched and unquestioned, again in the company of a known illegal. She is set free, presumably so that she can rejoin Captain Thermopyle—who by some monumental coincidence has just contrived his escape from Data Acquisition.

"Director Dios, Director Lebwohl, this stinks of complicity." Igensard's straight stare made Warden forget his potbelly and his shortness. "It stinks of malfeasance. It suggests that Captain Thermopyle is one of your operatives—that his crimes were whitewashed to preserve his life—that he was reqqed from Com-Mine Security so that his interrogation would not succeed—that he was allowed to escape in reward for his services, and in order to serve you further. It suggests that the UMCP is in league with known illegals to subvert Station security, protect illegals, and preserve piracy, all of which work to the aid of the Amnion in their aims against humankind."

Warden feared that Min was going to come out of her chair and start yelling. Only an iron discipline held her still.

"Before you answer," Igensard concluded, "let me inform you that I've seen Com-Mine Station's records of the entire affair. They are explicit. Com-Mine Security allowed Ensign Hyland to depart with Captain Succorso on your orders. She was UMCP—outside their jurisdiction. So they contacted UMCPHQ for instructions. Your instructions were to take no action concerning her.

"I ask you again. Why did you allow this to happen?"

Now, Warden thought. This is it. The whole thing stands or falls here.

The sensation of migraine from the screen made him feel that he was going blind in both eyes.

"With respect, Special Counsel Igensard," he drawled sardonically, "aren't you being just a bit global about all this? You're drawing large conclusions from some very small evidence."

"Just answer the question, Director Dios," Igensard retorted. "The Governing Council for Earth and Space will draw its own conclusions."

With a mental lift of his shoulders, Warden Dios trusted his fate to people he couldn't control; to Hashi Lebwohl, who made no distinction between one fate and another. "This is your department, Hashi," he said softly. "You'd better answer."

Hashi had been thoroughly prepared: he squirmed as if he were sweating for his life. For the first time since he'd seated himself on the front of Warden's desk and faced the cameras, he started to tell the truth.

"Special Counsel Igensard, your concern is misplaced." Now his voice held a tremor so convincing that Warden almost believed in it. "Again the situation is more complex than you realize.

"Captain Thermopyle is not numbered among Data Acquisition's few operatives. If you have studied the psy-profiles prepared on him by Com-Mine Security, you will believe me. Such a man—how shall I say this?—is utterly beyond trust. I could not use him as an operative because he would not submit to being used.

"On the other hand, Captain Succorso *does* serve me upon occasion.

"For the most part, his crimes are putative rather than real. They serve as a smoke screen. Therefore we had no reason to permit Com-Mine Security to interfere in the matter of Ensign Hyland. We had cause to doubt their integrity—and a useful alternative was available to us."

"Then where is she?" Igensard demanded promptly. "What kind of rescue do you call this? My God, Director Lebwohl, she was in Thermopyle's hands for *weeks*. You mentioned his psy-profile. He's a certifiable psychopath—and she's a *cop*. Haven't you thought about what he must have done to her? Com-Mine Station has hospitals, therapists, neural medicine. What help can Captain Succorso give her? Where did he take her?

"What kind of *use* are you trying to make out of her?"

"Special Counsel Igensard, you must understand." The tremor in Hashi's voice became more pronounced. It made him sound frail; cornered. "Human space is at peace with the Amnion. With considerable difficulty, the United Mining Companies Police strives to maintain this peace. But Data Acquisition is another matter. Data Acquisition is at war. It is a war for facts, for comprehension—for the means by which the Amnion and humankind may be spared overt conflict—but it is a war nonetheless. And in warfare men and women become tools. They must be used for what they can accomplish, without regard to the personal cost.

"Data Acquisition cannot afford to neglect opportunities when they are presented. Ensign Hyland presented me with an opportunity which it would have been malfeasance to ignore."

Min Donner was on the edge of her seat, listening hard. Godsen Frik chewed his knuckles as if he might bite off his fingers.

"You must recall," Hashi continued, "that Captain Succorso is universally thought illegal. Therefore he has access to places and powers which no UMCP officer may approach directly. And Ensign Hyland was irretrievably compromised. You ask if we have considered what Captain Thermopyle must have done to her. I tell you that we *have* considered the harm she has undergone—that we believe Captain Thermopyle's vileness toward her beggars description—and that in our opinion no hospital or therapy can restore her.

"Therefore"—Hashi took a shuddering breath—"we elected to make use of her in another way."

"Don't stop now," the Special Counsel put in. His tone was incisive enough to draw blood. "You're painting a fascinating picture of what passes for ethics in UMCPHQ."

At once Warden snapped, "That's uncalled for. *You* aren't charged with the duty of protecting humankind from the Amnion. *We* are."

"Certainly, of course," Abrim Len interposed, as smooth as oil. "Director Dios, Director Lebwohl, we appreciate the honesty of your answers. Special Counsel Igensard, please refrain from passing judgment on what you hear. That is the responsibility of the Council as a whole, not of any one man or member."

Igensard bowed his head momentarily, but didn't respond.

Council members rearranged their papers or peered at their readouts as if they were embarrassed by the reproach. Some of them watched Igensard and the downlink screen avidly: others appeared to want to move their chairs farther away from the Special Counsel's position.

"As I say," Hashi resumed, sounding a bit steadier, "we elected to make use of Ensign Hyland in another way. Again I insist that these matters are complex. Before the case of Captain Thermopyle and Ensign Hyland came to our attention, we were at work preparing an operation for Captain Succorso. I made reference earlier to Thanatos Minor and a bootleg shipyard in forbidden space. That shipyard is beyond our reach, by virtue of its location. Yet it is accessible to Captain Succorso. Seeking to damage its effectiveness, we—no, I must say I—conceived a way to strike against it through Captain Succorso.

"My plan was to send him to Thanatos Minor armed with a drug which he would claim supplied an immunity to Amnion mutagens."

Min drew a sharp breath which must have been audible over the broadcast pickups.

"We would provide Captain Succorso with fabricated proofs of the efficacy of this drug. He would sell it to the illegals of Thanatos Minor—who would in turn no doubt sell it to the Amnion. Even the rumor of such a drug would cause them considerable alarm. When the actual uselessness of the drug was discovered, Thanatos Minor would naturally blame Captain Succorso. But many illegals—and perhaps the Amnion themselves—would blame Thanatos Minor. In my opinion, the bootleg shipyard would suffer a loss of credibility from which it might never recover.

"That is my *job*, Special Counsel Igensard—to do such damage as I can to the forces which weaken us against the Amnion."

Igensard's mouth twisted into a sneer. "And what use were you going to get out of Morn Hyland in all this? Were you going to use her as a guinea pig to prove the drug worked?"

"No!" Hashi protested as if the idea horrified him, although the truth was worse. "We gave her to Captain Succorso for his own protection. I have already said that she was irretrievably compromised. And we had already taken steps to protect ourselves from the revelations Captain Thermopyle presumably extorted from her. Yet she was a *cop*, in your terms. And Captain Succorso, by his very nature, is a man of malleable loyalties.

"We gave Ensign Hyland to him so that he would have something to sell if he were trapped or caught—if he found himself in circumstances which tempted him to expose the falseness of our drug."

Min Donner sprang to her feet. Radiating outrage, she moved

right to the edge of the cameras' view. Her fists were clenched to strike out. If Warden hadn't stopped her with a quick glare, she might have jumped at Hashi.

But the DA director appeared oblivious to her fury—or to Godsen's consternation. As if he wanted to make himself look as bad as possible, he added, "I had another reason also. She is a beautiful woman, Special Counsel Igensard. Because of Captain Thermopyle's treatment, we suspect that she is aptly suited to satisfy the appetites of such men as Captain Succorso. We gave her to him to lessen the likelihood that he would turn against us if his mission on Thanatos Minor proved"—pushing up his glasses, Hashi finished—"difficult."

Through the shocked silence which gripped the Council, Igensard said softly, "Director Lebwohl, you used the word 'vileness' to describe Captain Thermopyle's behavior. Don't you think the description fits your own as well?"

Like Min, Warden leaped to his feet. "That's *enough!*" he roared. "Call off your dogs, Mr. President!"

He wasn't worried about Igensard or the Council: his overriding concern was to restrain the ED director before she disrupted what he was trying to accomplish through Hashi.

"I didn't agree to this conference so that my people could be abused," he stated loudly. "I did it because my charter carries the duty of disclosure. But I remind you that there's no duty of consultation. We aren't required to let you second-guess us! We did what we did with Ensign Hyland for the same reason we do everything else—because *at the time* that seemed like the best way to fulfill our Articles of Mission. It was a gamble, nothing more, nothing less. It either works or it doesn't. Either way, we don't deserve insults from small men with big titles."

If that didn't achieve what he wanted, nothing would.

Right on cue, Abrim Len burst into a flurry of placatory phrases and gestures. But Maxim Igensard was already shouting, "Director Dios, what do you make of the fact that Angus Thermopyle is heading for the same place you sent Succorso and Hyland?"

More quietly Warden repeated, "I said, that's enough. We've answered your questions—we've done our part. As far as I'm concerned, this conference is over. Mr. President, if you want to pursue any of these subjects further, we can arrange another occasion. But before we do, I want you to teach your Special Counsel better manners. My people and I have done nothing to deserve this kind of hostile interrogation."

Turning his back on the cameras, he keyed his intercom and told his secretary to sever the downlink.

Almost immediately the screen went blank.

He didn't bring up the dimmed lights around his desk. He wanted to switch them off completely and spend some time alone in the dark, rubbing his temples, letting his sore eyes rest; cradling his lacerated ideals. But he couldn't do that; not yet. The PR director came toward him, broaching the concentrated illumination like an indignant lion.

"Director," Godsen blared, "that was an outrage! Do you know what you've done? You've made us look like garbage, like weasels! You've curled their moral hair to the roots! There's going to be hell to pay for this. If I know Carsin and Igensard, they're already howling for our blood—and after that stunning performance, the rest of the members will be ready to listen. I tell you, Holt Fasner is going to be—"

Warden's headache was spreading. Godsen's voice hurt his ears. But he didn't look at Frik. His attention was caught by Hashi's aura.

Warmth and moisture left a glowing curve down Hashi's spine. Despite his calm, organic duplicity, the DA director had sweated through his lab coat. In contrast, his face was pale, leeched of blood, as if he'd been drained by the effort of so much selective truth.

Conserving his energy, moving as little as possible, Warden stopped Godsen by simply pointing one finger at him. Warden's stance was firm, his manner unruffled. Yet his very stillness seemed to frighten Godsen, as if his finger were fatal.

"I didn't ask for your evaluation of our 'performance,'" he said quietly. "I asked you to tell me if I've answered your questions. You wanted to know what insurance we have that Milos won't betray us. The answer is, none. But we've put him in a position where there's only one direction he can go if he turns against us. And Angus' programming watches for that automatically. We can't prevent him from trying to sell what he knows about Joshua, or us—but if he does that we'll have a recording of it. And he can only sell what he knows. We've been very careful about what we've allowed him to learn."

"As soon as he starts trying to play some kind of bugger game against both sides, we'll be able to use him in ways he doesn't suspect.

"*That's* what makes him worth the risk."

Warden knew that Godsen considered this issue trivial compared with the consequences of the GCES conference; but he didn't care. Dismissing the PR director, he forced himself to face Min Donner's more profound outrage at last.

"How about you?" With an effort, he kept his tone mild. "Have I answered your questions?"

As fierce as a hawk, she confronted him across the focused light. One hand closed and unclosed involuntarily; the other plucked at her gun as if she required a constant exertion of will to leave the weapon in its holster.

"Was all that true?" Her voice was as soft as his, but immeasurably more feral. "All that about Morn?"

Sighing with weariness, Warden Dios replied, "Yes." At the moment he had no more stomach for lies.

She winced: that one word seemed to hurt her more than any other. "But how—?" she pursued as if her pain came to her in pieces. "I don't understand. That doesn't explain—" With a sudden shiver like a spasm of revulsion, she took hold of herself. "It doesn't fit. How did you know Com-Mine wouldn't give Angus the death penalty. How could you?"

She wasn't thinking straight yet; but Warden saw where her reasoning would go. He accepted the accusation as stoically as he could.

"I didn't. We all knew Angus was going to be arrested—but I had no idea how significant he was until they only got him for burglary. Hashi told the truth. We were planning to send Nick against Billingate before we ever had the opportunity to frame Angus and pass the Preempt Act."

"Then Hashi told the truth?" Min couldn't have stopped now to save her soul. "That's why you let Succorso have her? So he could sell her to get himself out of trouble? And so he could use her along the way?"

Warden nodded once. He couldn't say *yes* to her again.

"But it still doesn't make sense!" she protested. "Getting Angus changed everything. You knew you could never really trust Succorso.

Welding Angus and sending him against Billingate is a lot better. It's much more likely to work."

Warden nodded again.

"Which means," Min continued, "you don't need Succorso now. You don't need to let him keep her. That's all been superseded. Why wasn't Angus programmed to rescue her? Why did you refuse to let him be programmed to rescue her?"

Godsen appeared to think Min was breaking down Warden's defenses. As if he were supporting her, the PR director put in, "*I* wanted her rescued. I argued for that as hard as I could. It's a terrible mistake to leave her with Succorso. But you wouldn't listen."

Warden ignored Godsen. He would have ignored Hashi, if Hashi had had enough energy to join the accusation. Only Min Donner mattered to him here.

Wielding anger like a scourge, he drove himself to tell one more lie.

"Because both Nick and Morn have been what Hashi calls 'irretrievably compromised.' They've been to Enablement. I don't know why—that was never part of our plans." Not since Nick Succorso first traveled there to test the immunity drug. "But they went. And they got away again. I'm afraid to guess what it means."

Unexpectedly Hashi spoke. As if he were coming to Warden's aid, he wheezed, "It may mean that the Amnion have perfected mutagens which enable them to transform human beings without altering their bodies or destroying their minds. In that case, both Captain Succorso and Ensign Hyland have become appallingly dangerous. We must hope"—he might have said *pray*—"that our Joshua succeeds in destroying them."

Min faced this for a moment as if she still believed she could face anything.

Then she turned away, wrenched the door open, and strode out of the office.

Warden looked at Godsen. "You, too. I want to be alone."

The force of Warden's single eye was enough to make Godsen leave. He may have wanted to put as much distance as possible between himself and the UMCP director.

Only Hashi remained. "I, too," he said when Warden glanced at him. "I need rest as well." He started toward the door.

Halfway there, however, he paused. Peering through his smeared glasses, he said, "Warden Dios, you suffer too much. I am at a loss to explain why I esteem you so highly.

"Yet I must say this. The conference which we have just endured—that was well played. I can only guess at your intentions, but I do not doubt that you have accomplished them."

Without waiting for an answer, he left Warden alone.

By some standards, the DA director's compliment was a worse insult than anything Maxim Igensard had said. Nevertheless Warden smiled wanly and said, "Thanks," at Hashi's departing back.

Like Morn Hyland—not to mention Angus Thermopyle—Warden Dios was now irretrievably compromised.

ANCILLARY DOCUMENTATION

UNITED MINING COMPANIES

A BRIEF HISTORY *(continued)*

Privately the history of the United Mining Companies was a study in the unscrupulous brilliance and overweening ambition of two men: Holt Fasner and Warden Dios.

Experimenting with rejuvenation techniques developed by Intertech, Holt Fasner lived for more than a hundred fifty years. In his late thirties, he became chairman and CEO of Space Mines Inc. During the next one hundred ten years or so, he built the original company from a small orbital ore smelter into one of ten or twelve major players in the exploration and development of space, and then into the biggest player, the UMC. He did this by a display of foresight, cunning, manipulation, and willingness to take risks which none of his competitors could match.

He did it by simple acquisition—e.g., Intertech—as well as by subterfuge. For example, corporate espionage paid rich dividends when he was able to drive Sagittarius Exploration into bankruptcy by exposing the attempts of SagEx's directors to suborn the political process which chartered space companies. In addition, he had a gift for being in the right place at the right time: contact and trade with the Amnion was established by SMI on the basis of information gained through the acquisition of Intertech. His policy of bold exploration served him well: his ships discovered the tremendous asteroid belt—dangerously near forbidden space—which eventually came to be served by Com-Mine Station. And he did not shrink from betrayal: on one occasion, he reneged on a deal to help pay for a new orbital smelter—much needed to process the growing influx of ore—with the result that the company which had been relying on him lost several credit ratings and became vulnerable to SMI greenmail. Nor did he balk at bribery: perhaps his greatest coup came when, for a few billion dollars, he succeeded at buying the votes which chartered the UMC with a monopoly on dealings with the Amnion. In fact, Holt Fasner lived long enough to see the UMC become so powerful that it controlled the safety or ruin of the human species.

His ambitions didn't end there, however. Having achieved an apparently impregnable dominance for the UMC, he focused his attention on the United Mining Companies Police.

In one sense, this was easily explained. The Amnion were a vast source of wealth: they also represented the most lethal external threat humankind had ever encountered. Vigilance and muscle were essential. A force effective enough to oppose Amnion imperialism was required. Presumably if human space were capable of defending itself efficaciously that capability in itself would suffice to stave off overt aggression. So ran the rationale for developing the resources of the UMCP dramatically, as well as for granting it jurisdiction over every other form of human security. In a relatively few years, the UMCP became the most extensive and vital of all the UMC's enormous concerns. The UMCP may have grown out of the UMC originally; but eventually the Police grew to be the engine which drove all the United Mining Companies' enterprises.

Unfortunately this explanation ascribed to Holt Fasner an altruism which no one had ever observed in his character. As a matter of protocol, he always claimed for himself the best possible motives; but people who either suffered or profited from their dealings with him dismissed those claims.

On the other hand, if his stated reasons for assigning so much of the UMC's energy and resources to the UMCP could be dismissed, what alternative explanation remained? What were Holt Fasner's true ambitions? Did he simply covet the power for its own sake? For the illusion it created that he and he alone stood between humankind and ruin? For the reassurance that his legacy to his species would never be forgotten?

Or was the whole question being asked backward? Was the real issue not, What did Holt Fasner want? but, What did Warden Dios want? Had Holt Fasner himself, the most dominant man in human space, fallen under the dominance of the director of the United Mining Companies Police?

This perspective did not make the question easier to answer.

Who *was* Warden Dios? What were his ambitions? How did he come to his present position—and what did he want to make of it?

Without an adequate understanding of one—or both—men, the true role of the UMC, as well as the UMCP, in human affairs was difficult to estimate.

Warden Dios had no wife and no children; no brothers or sisters; no known lovers, dependents, playthings, or weaknesses. To all appearances, he had no mother or father. What did such a man value, if he had none of the normal bonds which web men and women to their contexts? What did he desire, if he had no use for those bonds?

In the opinion of some observers, he had sprung full-grown from the mind of Holt Fasner: he was a pure tool of the Dragon's, working his master's will with all his considerable diligence and cunning.

However, other analysts insisted that this was not the case. In their view, he was one of those rare men who had become an idealist through experience with its opposite. Orphaned young in one of Earth's more toxic cities, he grew up among guttergangs and violence, and from those things learned to believe in the utter necessity of what police have tried to do throughout human history—i.e., to impose order on destruction; to protect the weak or vulnerable from abuse within society; to protect society itself from threat, whether internal or external. His idealism—so the argument went—was the idealism of a man who believed in what the police stood for; a man who lived to serve those beliefs.

If this perception was accurate, he and Holt Fasner formed a strange and volatile partnership. Holt Fasner was many things, but no one ever accused him of being an idealist.

Certain facts were known. Warden Dios was a much younger man than his boss and mentor; but he looked older, in part because of his prosthesis, in part because he lacked Fasner's enthusiasm for rejuvenation experiments. He was only in his early thirties when Fasner picked him to head SMI Internal Security, which became the United Mining Companies Police as soon as the UMC was chartered shortly thereafter; he was the only director the UMCP ever had. So he had little or nothing to do with the process by which Fasner built Space Mines Inc. into the UMC: the worst accusation from that period which could be brought against him was that he may have participated in the operation against Sagittarius Exploration. From that point of view, his record was unblemished by his association with Holt Fasner's more questionable dealings.

Yet he was responsible for the growth of the UMCP from nothing more than SMI Internal Security to its present status as the single most powerful division of the UMC. The more virulent the problem of piracy became, and the more dangerous relations with the Amnion came to seem, the more necessary his Police grew to be. From his headquarters orbiting Earth, he ruled human space by defending it. He imposed order, which enabled the UMC to function; ultimately he enabled the UMC to exist. In his hands, he held the only power which stood between humankind and the ambiguous threat of the Amnion.

In some circles, Warden Dios was revered. That was natural enough: powerful people frequently were. Holt Fasner himself received reverence from men who were astonished by his achievements.

Elsewhere, however, Dios was considered the most dangerous individual who had ever lived: more dangerous than Holt Fasner because more crucial to humankind's survival. In that view, the most fatal tyranny was that which disguised itself as the protector of its victims. After the passage of the Preempt Act, few could argue that the UMCP had not become a form of tyranny.

Any useful study of the United Mining Companies had to take into account both the public and the private histories; had to confront the almost paradoxical intersection between economic muscle—which deals only in aggregates—and personal power—which by its very nature resides only in individuals, not in charters, chains of command, or official positions.

MORN

The guards had locked her in a room. The genetic technicians had come and gone.

Shivering like an invalid, Morn Hyland sat with Amnion mutagens in her veins and waited for the organic convulsion which would bring her doomed humanity to its end.

Lit by the sulfuric glow her imprisoners preferred, the small, sterile cell around her seemed lambent with insidious yellow threats. It was a bare chamber, not a lab; empty of everything except cleanliness and light, a small san and the couchlike chair where she sat. Any monitors were so unfamiliar or so well disguised that she couldn't identify them: she was apparently alone in a naked room. Perhaps the Amnion wanted to observe her transformation without inhibiting her reactions—and without risking damage to valuable equipment. Or perhaps their facility on Billingate wasn't supplied for research; perhaps she'd been put in this cell because it was the only space available to hold her. Whatever the reason, she was free to pace the floor or sit still, as she chose.

She sat as still as her shivers and the fear storming through her permitted. Transfixed, she studied the spot on her forearm where the mutagen had been injected as if it were venomous; as if the wound was made by a fang.

A breathing mask protected her lungs against the mordant air: that was her only defense. The Amnion hadn't given her anything to soften her terror, or muffle the violence of the change. Of course not. They had no reason to: here, in the section of Billingate which they had built for themselves, the concept of compassion was as alien as the Amnion themselves. They lacked the psychological, the societal, perhaps even the genetic tools to think in such terms. From their point of view, what they imposed on her was no doubt profoundly good. It satisfied the ribonucleic imperative which shaped their purposes. So of course they did nothing to make her plight easier. They wanted to study her distress as well as her transformation as accurately as possible, in order to refine their methods accordingly.

Where had they gone wrong with Marc Vestabule? Why was it that they could alter human beings entirely, but not by increments? What element of the human mind—or genetic code—made necessary this all-or-nothing sense of identity? Why were the Amnion unable to master the brain without changing the body?

When they learned the answer to this question, they would be able to create Amnion that could pass as human beings.

Perhaps they could discover the secret by studying Morn as she changed.

Staring at the sore red injury on her forearm, Morn waited to discover the secret for herself.

How bad would it be, when her genetic abhorrence met its ruin—when her cellular being was blasted apart and made new? Would she be afraid enough to go mad at the crucial moment? Was her fear itself her last defense? Was terror her sole protection against becoming the most effective traitor possible, the most useful imaginable weapon against her own species?

And was that the only mystery which gave her human life—or any form of life—its uniqueness in the wide universe? If an Amnioni were set in this chair and subjected to a mutagen which would alter its essential being, would the creature feel the same way she did? Or did the chemistry of alien nuclear identity bring with it other defenses, other mysteries?

Such questions obsessed her because she had no answer for the one that really mattered.

Was Nick's immunity drug going to work?

If it failed, she had nothing left to hope for except that fear would destroy her mind before she knew what she had become.

A DARK AND HUNGRY GOD ARISES

On the other hand, if the drug worked she would be no better off. Not really. She would gain only a little time. The Amnion would inevitably notice that the change didn't take place on schedule. Then, because they were careful—and wanted to learn—they would draw some of her blood and test it in order to determine why the mutagen had failed. They might or might not allow her an opportunity to swallow another of the capsules hidden deep in the pocket of her shipsuit. In the end, that was irrelevant. If this facility lacked the resources for refining new mutagens, her humanity might be prolonged for a while; but that possibility was ultimately irrelevant as well. The significant, the damning fact was that the enemies of her kind would learn from her the secret of the immunity drug. By stealing these capsules from Nick's cabin, she had made certain that the Amnion would gain the knowledge they needed to counteract the drug.

To keep herself whole for a few more hours—a day or two at best, if neither this facility nor the warships were equipped to design new mutagens—she'd betrayed her entire species.

She didn't care, did she? Not now: not here. How could she? At any moment the red patch on her forearm might swell and suppurate, carrying a change as dramatic as a volcanic eruption to every cell in her body. The UMCP had betrayed humankind long before she did. Whether the Amnion learned about it or not, the drug had already been withheld from the men and women who needed it most. Her own treachery only completed the job begun by people who had sworn to protect the human race.

And in the meantime it might gain her a few more hours.

She looked no further ahead than that. Nick Succorso had deprived her of any larger future; he'd cost her everything except the immediate crisis. Deflecting Davies' ejection pod from *Tranquil Hegemony* to Billingate hadn't solved anything: she knew that. It had simply been the best she could do.

Gain a few more hours.

By the same token, stealing a few of Nick's capsules had also been simply the best she could do. When she'd stuffed a little wadding into the bottom of his vial so that the absence of six or eight capsules wouldn't be too obvious, her sole intent had been to prevent him from noticing the theft in time to stop her. And when she'd questioned him about his dealings with UMCPHQ, she'd wanted nothing more than to understand the scale of the corruption which engulfed her. She had no other goals.

Her only alternative was to give up—and she wasn't going to do that.

Not while Nick was still alive.

Not while he and people like him—the UMCP—remained free to barter her son and her species for their own purposes.

Her family had taught her convictions which she couldn't set aside without an abrogation of identity as profound in its own way as anything the Amnion might do to her.

Her family had also taught her how to hold a grudge.

So she stared at the small red pain on her forearm and waited while fear stormed through her. Her nerves were strung so tight that she shivered as if she were feverish—as if her body were fighting frenetically to fend off an organic invasion.

Sweat dribbled like saliva from the edges of the breathing mask. The mask itself felt stifling over her mouth; claustrophobic. If she could have looked at her own face, she might not have recognized herself. Bruises and emotional starvation distorted her beauty; her eyes were as deep and fatal as wounds; her hair straggled wildly, as damaged and unkempt as a nerve juice addict's.

Yet within her an essential passion burned as if it were unquenchable. Nothing short of an absolute transformation could snuff it out.

For perhaps the first time since Nick had taken the control to her zone implant, she didn't miss it. With its artificial strength, she could have escaped the Amnion by committing neural suicide. Or she could have spared herself this ordeal of dread and horror by muffling her emotions; re-creating the state of psychic numbness which had enabled her to endure her son's birth.

She didn't want to die, however. And she believed that anything which softened her terror would help the Amnion get what they desired out of her.

She had come to a place inside herself where neither death nor imposed capabilities and addiction were as important as the struggle to keep her humanity intact. Was fear the defining mystery of life? Then let her be afraid. That was preferable to any kind of surrender.

Feverish shivers built into a shudder; tremors shook her muscles as if the convulsion had begun. She might have been suffocating on her own CO_2. For a moment she was so frightened that she seemed to see the red patch on her skin swelling like an infection. It would suppurate and burst; mutagenic pus would seep from the wound, gnawing at her flesh and her DNA until she screamed and went wild in stark simple revulsion; until her horror became as vast as the void between the stars, and all things died—

But then the shudder passed. Her vision cleared, and she saw the truth. The redness around the place where the mutagen had been injected was fading. Her skin was as pallid as the underlying bones—and as whole.

In the Academy, she'd been told what to expect from Amnion mutagens. They were supposed to be faster than this; swift as well as violent.

Maybe the immunity drug was working.

What had Nick told her?

It's not an organic immunity. It's more like a poison—or a binder. It ties up mutagens until they're inert. Then they get flushed out—along with the drug.

The immunity is effective for about four hours.

Maybe she was going to live.

For a while longer.

And it was possible that the Amnion sector of Billingate lacked the resources to design new mutagens which could overcome the drug. It was possible that she would be able to take another capsule before her enemies tried her again. If she kept track of the time. If she did what Nick had once done: if she held a capsule in her mouth and didn't bite down on it until after her blood was drawn. And if the Amnion failed to guess how her immunity had been accomplished.

When she allowed herself to think that, flashes of dopamine ran through her blood like little epiphanies; bits of hope. Her breathing shuddered inside the mask as if she were about to faint.

A few more hours.

That was all she asked.

Please.

ANGUS

His tongue hurt as acutely as his zone implants allowed: it should have hurt much worse. He had shit and sweat ground into his blisters. Every inhalation stank; his whole mouth tasted like ash and excrement.

As he took *Trumpet* into Billingate, Angus Thermopyle fought the fragmentation imposed on him by his welding; did what he could to stay sane.

Hashi Lebwohl had made him schizophrenic, as dissociated as a multi-tasking computer. What was left of his volition handled the details of approach to Thanatos Minor. Databases fed him information indiscriminately, whether he asked for it or not: facts about *Trumpet*; UMCP speculations concerning the Bill and Billingate; classification on the Amnion warships; charges against the other illegals in the vicinity; descriptions of fusion generator disasters. At the same time preprogrammed exigencies monitored and sifted everything Milos said and did; recorded every byte of Milos' complex transmissions and labored to decode it.

Such things were abstract. He did them without choosing them; occasionally without understanding them.

Other pieces were more personal.

With every inch of his skin from the crown of his skull to the soles of his feet, he felt *Trumpet* alive around him: capable of anything; built full of possibilities and surprises. Schizophrenic with a vengeance, he approached the cold rock of Thanatos Minor almost gleefully, reveling in the power of his ship, and in his ability to command her. His tactile pleasure was so acute that his palms itched as if they could remember the time before his hands had been cut open to install his lasers. An emotion like joy flushed across his face as he tapped keys, tested systems, listened to servos.

Then it fell into the cracks between the pieces of himself, the fragmentation gaps, and was lost.

From out of the cracks came crying instances of confusion like kids abandoned in their cribs.

Why did he have to look at all this stuff about fusion generators? According to his databases, some of these generators used magnetic containment vessels for the forces they unleashed; and some of those bled gravitically, increasing the effective mass of bodies around them. He knew that already. Why did he have to review it now?

And what in hell was Warden Dios up to?

We've committed a crime against your soul.

What the fuck did that mean? Why had Dios switched his datacore? Who was the UMCP director trying to betray now?

It's got to stop.

More fragments—

Randomly among them, like electrons bereft of their nuclei, ran small bursts of fury; hints of violence as precise and pure as the noradrenaline in his synapses—and as meaningless as the unguessable physics of tach. An organic human brain was the wrong tool for the work he did. Only expert programming and pervasive zone implants enabled him to go on multi-tasking when he should have been flung apart like a ship in an explosive decompression.

It made no difference to his datacore whether he stayed sane or not. Machine requirements controlled him by electronic compulsion: madness or sanity meant nothing. Nevertheless he fought to hold the pieces of himself together.

He wanted the joy of running *Trumpet*.

He wanted to see Morn Hyland again.

He wanted revenge on Milos.

And Warden Dios had given him something to hope for.

We've committed a crime against your soul.

It's got to stop.

Angus knew nothing about men who said such things. As far as he could tell, they didn't exist. He had to assume that Dios was driven by malice, just like everybody else.

Nevertheless he considered it possible, just barely conceivable, that he wasn't the target of Dios' malice. Not this time. Dios' plotting might be aimed at someone else. In which case everything might change when the differences between his datacore and Lebwohl's began to make themselves felt.

Screams Angus couldn't utter rang in his head: screams of rage and frustration, loss and hope; the screams of a small boy being tortured in his crib.

They kept him from losing his mind. On a level his zone implants couldn't reach, those voiceless cries focused his hard-earned cunning and his malign intelligence, his hate and his strange expertise, in a struggle to bridge the gaps between the pieces of himself.

Because he lacked the power to vary *Trumpet*'s preordained course, or to stifle the databases he didn't want, he concentrated on his second.

Prewritten commands required him to record everything Milos said and did. Apparently Lebwohl and Dios didn't trust the former deputy chief of Com-Mine Station Security. Fine. Neither did Angus. But his distrust—no, his visceral and compulsory loathing—was both more global and more specific. Lebwohl and Dios presumably suspected that Milos might betray Angus' mission. Angus knew in his bones that Milos would go farther; much farther. Weeks of stun and starvation and abuse—not to mention the taste of nic and shit— had made Angus a more searching judge of Milos' character than any cop.

He wanted to know everything about Milos because he intended to castrate and then disembowel his second with his bare hands, and any fact he could glean, any hint of intention or weakness, was a tool which might help him reach his goal.

In this way, he fought to make himself whole.

Trumpet was still six hours out of dock when Milos finished his communications. The nic dangling from his mouth disguised his smugness; the characteristic mottling on his scalp and the uncharacteristic stains on his shipsuit hid it. Nevertheless Angus felt it pour off his second like an electromagnetic aura. He knew Milos intimately, understood every shade of his second's stolid fastidiousness.

Milos was *smug*. The things he did to humiliate Angus fed an old hunger. And his transmissions—tight-beamed and coded for secrecy—had given him a sense of power which he probably thought didn't show.

One part of Angus glowered at this; he ached to strip it from Milos' bones. Another worked with mechanical efficiency to decipher those messages. Yet another calibrated the distance to Milos' g-seat and the distance to Billingate, measuring possibilities. And another waited—

Trailing smoke, Milos lifted himself from his seat; he bobbed in the absence of g. "I need rest," he said as if he weren't talking to Angus. "Let me know if anything changes, Joshua."

Like a badly inflated balloon, he floated toward the companionway which gave access to the rest of the ship.

Angus felt an almost tangible relief as Milos left the bridge. Now maybe he could concentrate on cracking those codes.

The idea that he could improve on—or even affect—the efforts of his computer was an illusion, however. His microprocessor ran at its own speeds, for its own reasons. And it made other decisions for him as well. Despite his fragmented fury and need, he found himself growing unexpectedly sleepy. Apparently his programming had decided that he, too, needed rest.

Helpless to do anything else, he leaned his head back against the g-seat and drifted into the dark interface between his mind and the machinery which ruled it.

As he lost consciousness, he swore viciously at Hashi Lebwohl; but that changed nothing.

If he dreamed, his datacore took no notice of it.

He came back to wakefulness four hours later, as alert as if he'd never been away. As soon as he opened his eyes, he realized with an odd sense of dislocation that he knew everything that had happened while he slept. Traffic information from Billingate; *Trumpet*'s relative position; the movements of other ships: all were recorded—and accessible. When he reviewed the data, he half expected to learn that he'd spoken to Operations while he slept; that his programming controlled him so perfectly that it didn't need him to be conscious at all. However, his recordings showed that *Trumpet* had been entirely passive, apart from her automatic responses to Billingate's approach protocols.

Ignoring the sensation that he existed simultaneously in several different places across the gap, Angus began preparing himself for the state of affairs which awaited him on Thanatos Minor.

Operations didn't broadcast political bulletins, of course; but Angus felt sure that the shipyard was awash in plots and counter-plots. This was apparent from the presence of *Captain's Fancy* in one of the visitor's berths and *Tranquil Hegemony* over in the alien sector, as well as from the fact that another Amnion "defensive," *Calm Horizons*, had parked herself in prime firing range over the installation. Captain Nick Sheepfucker had come here from the direction of Enablement, trailing two of the biggest hostiles Angus had ever seen. That implied covert agendas and conflicts—

—which in turn might make Angus' mission a hell of a lot easier.

His datacore told him nothing about *Captain's Fancy*. He only knew Morn Hyland was aboard because Dios had said so.

But he'd overheard Lebwohl tell Donner and Frik that his programming made no provision for Morn's survival. That alone would have been enough to make him want her alive.

If he'd been in charge of his own actions, his position would have been more complex. Morn was potentially lethal to him: she had information which could wipe out his last hope. For that reason—among others which he didn't want to think about because they were profoundly disturbing—he'd made a deal with her and kept it.

Left to himself, unwelded, what would he have wanted to do about her now? Kill her where she stood? *Yes.* Ask her to rejoin him? *Yes!* Beg her to believe that he'd kept faith with her as long as he could? *Yes!* and *yes!* again.

The thought that he might have to stand by and watch her die brought old anguish up through the cracks in his dissociation.

Where Nick was concerned, the questions were less personal, but no more ponderable. What the hell was he doing at Enablement? Were those warships here to chase him down, or protect him? Whom had he betrayed this time?

Angus didn't really care. For himself he wanted revenge, pure and simple: the exact nature of Nick's plots and alliances changed nothing. And for Angus' mission the only significant danger Nick represented came through his association with Milos.

The messages which Milos had sent earlier had been beamed, not toward Operations or any other part of the installation, but to *Captain's Fancy*—and *Tranquil Hegemony*. And both ships had answered.

That made Succorso at least as fatal to Joshua as Morn was to Angus.

With an emotional violence which had no effect whatever on the steady precision of his hands, Angus Thermopyle chimed Milos' cabin and growled like a demonic cherub, "Wake up, baby boy. Come back from dreamland. We've got reality dead ahead, and it's closing fast."

Then he silenced the intercom so that he wouldn't have to answer Milos' demands for an explanation.

Trumpet's final approach went smoothly. Milos did his job with inexpert but unobjectionable care. And Operations had no reason to treat the gap scout worse than any other ship. After all, the installation was more than adequately protected by its own guns, as well as by *Calm Horizons'*. Whether or not *Trumpet* would ever be allowed to leave was less clear.

Finally Billingate's grapples thunked into their sockets in her hull; power, air, and communication limpets were attached to her receptacles. Because his datacore left him no choice, Angus began shutting down the ship.

Putting himself, Milos, and *Trumpet* in debt to the Bill.

At the same time he growled to Milos, "If you've got any special instructions"—his tongue still tasted like hell—"you'd better give them now. This isn't a good place for surprises. Unless you improvise better than you use that board."

Milos dropped his nic into the growing pile beside his seat and lit another. Without looking at Angus, he muttered, "Is that what you call 'reality'? A place that isn't good for surprises?"

Angus rasped a bitter laugh. "You haven't got a clue what I call 'reality.' " He gibed at Milos because he needed some outlet for his random bursts of anger. "When you find out, I fucking guarantee you won't like it.

"For your first lesson," he added as he unbelted from his g-seat, "we're going to go out and act like we really came here because we wanted to. Even if you spent your whole life in guttergangs until you left Earth"—a guess, but Angus trusted it—"you haven't seen anything like this before."

Milos' eyes flicked uneasily. "Is that a fact?" he drawled; but his attempt to sound unconcerned wasn't a success.

"Trust me," Angus leered. Flexing his knees, he tested the pull of Thanatos Minor's g. Then he moved, deceptively light on his feet, toward the companionway.

Gripping its rails, he paused. "By the way," he advised, "don't make the mistake of thinking you can carry weapons here. You'll be scanned down to your balls before you reach Reception. The Bill makes damn sure nobody but him has any firepower."

Nobody but him and the Amnion.

Alarm forced Milos to look at Angus. "Will you get caught?"

Angus grinned. "That depends on whether fucking Hashi Lebwohl knows what he's fucking doing."

As he started up the treads he saw Milos furtively pull a stun-prod as small as a dagger out of his pocket and slip it into the padding of the second's g-seat. Milos looked like he could no longer remember what smugness felt like.

He definitely wasn't going to enjoy Billingate.

Angus took that as a form of reassurance.

He was a coward: he wanted all the reassurance he could get.

Together he and Milos rode the midship lift down to the airlock. There Angus stopped. Pointing at the control panel, he announced harshly, "Seconds are supposed to do jobs like this. Are you going to open it, or do I have to hold your hand?"

Milos' eyes were nearly opaque with anger and anxiety. In a tense rasp, he retorted, "You're going first, Joshua. I'm not coming out until you make it through the scanners."

Angus had no response to a Joshua command. He couldn't even shrug. He simply moved to the control panel and keyed the airlock doors.

One window in his head showed him the time: 22:07:15.53 standard; late in Billingate's artificial evening. Another reminded him of the security codes which would lock everyone else out of *Trumpet* until he or Milos returned. With his prosthetic vision, he watched the evanescent electromagnetic emissions of the servos and locks as the interior hatch lifted. Rage fumed and spattered through him, and accomplished nothing.

After Milos joined him in the airlock, he closed and sealed the interior door, then opened his ship to the complex atmosphere of Billingate.

The access passage ahead was awash with EM fields. Gossamer, multihued, and insinuating, they looked like webs or veils which his crude body would tear when he passed through them. But he knew that he was safe before he touched the first veil. His enhanced sight confirmed what his datacore told him: his computer and its zone implants, his lasers and powerpacks, caused no ripple in the shimmering aura of Billingate's detection scan. Hashi Lebwohl had unquestionably known what he was doing when he designed Angus' equipment.

Impersonally Angus noted the absence of guards. That was good—from Lebwohl's point of view. It meant the Bill had decided not to challenge Angus' story directly. Instead he would rely on time and observation to reveal the truth.

Angus wasn't surprised. As a matter of policy, the Bill treated his sources of revenue politely. He spied on everybody; but he didn't willingly offend paying customers.

Over his shoulder, Angus muttered to Milos, "Come on. It doesn't get much safer than this."

Without waiting for his second, he headed toward Reception.

There were guards in the reception area, of course; but he ignored them. By the time Milos caught up with him, he'd already used one of the data terminals to verify his credit and link it to voiceprint id. Brusquely he motioned for Milos and said, "Your turn. Tell the nice computer your name so we'll be able to spend your money."

Grinding his teeth, Milos gave the terminal a voiceprint to use for id. His glare suggested that he was thinking of new ways to humiliate Angus.

With a grin to conceal the twist of fear in his stomach, Angus asked the terminal for two rooms in a bar-and-sleep on the cruise.

Of course, he and Milos could have stayed aboard *Trumpet* in relative privacy. And the Bill was sure to monitor any rooms they hired on Billingate. But for that very reason they were safer in a bar-and-sleep. The Bill would worry less about men who didn't try to hide from him.

Because he wanted to nauseate his second, he booked rooms in a place called Ease-n-Sleaze, which was located near the center of the cruise. Then he took Milos by the arm and said in an acid whisper, "Look on the bright side. This way all those bastards you've been talking to can find you just by"—he logged off the terminal—"checking. Won't that be nice? And you can see anybody you want without"—he tapped his head—"asking Lebwohl's permission."

"Thanks so much," Milos replied, making an effort to match Angus' malice. "I didn't know it was going to be this easy."

"It isn't." Angus bared his teeth. "I'm just trying to lull you into a false sense of security."

"Please don't threaten me anymore," Milos muttered darkly. "I'm already so scared"—he glared straight at Angus—"I could just shit."

Angus tightened his grip for a moment. "I know. But you ought to be careful what you do about that. Someday you're going to get your balls bitten off.

"Shall we go?" Dropping Milos' arm, he gestured toward the lifts.

Milos complied like a man who was so busy devising complicated forms of murder that he couldn't think about anything else.

The cruise wasn't Billingate's sole lodging sector, but it was much larger than the alternatives. Occasionally the Bill had guests for whom he catered privately. And sometimes ships were willing to pay the extra charge for rooms which were better furnished and less exposed; perhaps because the captain feared he would never get his people back if he let them loose; perhaps because the crew had vices they didn't want to share. But every other human who came to Thanatos Minor stayed either aboard ship or on the cruise.

It filled several of the middle levels of the installation. Toward the surface were the various worksheds and storehouses which supported the docks and the shipyard, as well as the hermetic Amnion sector; toward the core were the Bill's personal strongroom, his surgical facilities, and Billingate's power station. Between the surface and the core lived, drank, slept, worked, caroused, cheated, fucked, raped, pandered, pleased, and fought the people who supplied—and the people who enjoyed—Billingate's more personal resources.

Perhaps because of the constriction of the halls which the denizens called "streets," or perhaps because there were millions of tons of rock impending overhead, the cruise seemed to throng with people. Billingate's population was reputed to number roughly five thousand; but the cruise gave the impression that twice that many men and women were here at any given moment. Of course, some of them came from the ships docked around the installation. The rest must have been missed by uninformed estimates.

After the first assault of smell and light, after the first look at the crowded streets and windows, bars and dens, the most remarkable aspect of the cruise was the proportion of women. Women were rare in what human space called "entertainment/lodging sectors." Those who lived on stations generally had their work or their families, and little reason to mingle with transients. And women who were themselves transient—who traveled or crewed on ships—visited entertainment/lodging sectors for what those places supplied, not because they wished to be used as supplies.

On the cruise, however—

The Bill must have scoured human space to attract so many. From sinkholes on Earth and the depraved recesses of stations, from illegal shipyards and desperate ships, he must have begged, purchased, and betrayed them by the hundreds to get them here. According to how they were viewed, they were either the glory or the slime of the cruise: women who enjoyed what they did, what they got, and became rich; women on nerve juice or other drugs who barely kept themselves alive; women with surgical adjustments, bioretributive and otherwise, who had no choice. No spacefaring illegal who came to Billingate could honestly say that he'd ever had so much beauty and ruin to choose from.

On special occasions, Angus himself had taken advantage of a woman or two here. But that was before he'd known Morn; before he'd debased her as far as his hate and his considerable imagination could go; before she'd begun to break his heart.

Now he tasted the air, watched the lights, and leered at the women as if he were in his natural element at last. But neither he nor his datacore had any interest in female recreation.

For his part, Milos pursed his mouth and frowned like a man who found most women—and perhaps sex itself—vaguely disgusting.

Angus had no time to enjoy his second's disgust, however. He had other priorities.

The air which greeted him as he left the lift was exactly as he remembered it: too hot; inadequately processed; clotted with smoke, perfume, sweat, rot, estrogen, vomit, booze, and every other human stench he could think of. The lighting may have been deliberately garish, full of colors that screamed and shades that whimpered; or it may have simply been made garish by the accreted grime of the atmosphere.

Nevertheless neither the air nor the light blinded him to the EM aura of the bugeyes which ranged along the ceiling in all directions, or the telltale emissions of the guards and wires with communications prostheses. As impartial as death, the Bill tried to keep track of everything that happened on Thanatos Minor.

Some of the guards were easy to spot. They were obvious because they patrolled the cruise as if they had nowhere particular to go; and because they carried weapons—or had weapons installed in their arms. Angus counted six within fifty meters. But others—the "wires," he called them—were disguised. Their communication equipment was hidden in their clothes or their bodies, or camouflaged as something else—an artificial hand here, a prosthetic jaw there. Still Angus recognized them all. Their EM emissions were as plain as placards. Anything he said in their hearing would be instantly recorded in the Bill's data banks.

The computers and personnel charged with sifting and collating such information must have been inundated by it.

One of the wires had a more complex emission signature. That attracted Angus' attention. When he located its source amid the jostling surge, he found himself looking at a man whose head had been cut off and attached to a mechanical neck which could swivel in any direction. That, Angus decided, was the duty officer in command of this section of the cruise.

With a slight nudge, he turned Milos to glance at the man. "Watch out for that goon," he whispered. "If we do anything the Bill might not like, he can react faster than Operations."

Milos nodded. Scowling at a woman with a pneumatic bosom, he breathed, "What are we going to do that the Bill might not like?"

Angus grinned humorlessly. "Don't ask me. You probably know more about that than I do."

Satisfied that he'd located all the guards in his vicinity, he launched himself into the throng, heading down the congested street toward Ease-n-Sleaze.

Milos probably did know more than he did about what he might do. His datacore didn't answer that kind of question. It kept track of the guards for him, collating auras and vectors so that he seemed to know where they all were without effort; but so far it hadn't unlocked any new information—or issued any new directives. Apparently his only immediate assignment was to install himself on the cruise and behave as normally as possible.

That meant a room in Ease-n-Sleaze; it meant a seat in the bar and a few cheap drinks. Which suited him fine: for a while longer, he could cherish the totally false impression that he was doing exactly what he would have done anyway.

Some distance down the street, Milos caught up with him. Anchoring himself at Angus' elbow, he muttered, "I hope you're having fun. You probably think this place is heaven."

"Don't you like it?"

Milos didn't appear to notice Angus' contempt. In a low, raw voice, as if he needed to swallow and couldn't, he said, "It's like a city that's been taken over by a guttergang. Just one. Completely. No factions, no levers—no way to change anything. No escape."

"Nobody to betray in exchange for a little protection," Angus put in. Then he added, "Except me. And if you do that, you'll have to live in places like this the rest of your life. The cops'll fry you as soon as they get their hands on you."

Milos' expression gave Angus another piece of reassurance. The nausea lurking at the back of his gaze was unmistakable.

The crowd rolled around Angus. Men and women bumped into him and stumbled or strode past; on their way, some of them flicked light fingers along his shipsuit, looking for valuables he didn't carry. Just for exercise, he would have liked to catch one of those hands— he could have done that easily—and break it. Nevertheless he let them go. He didn't want the guards and wires to focus their attention on him.

A woman stopped in front of him and offered to sell him a vial of nerve juice. A man lurched into his way and asked if he had any nerve juice to sell. A creature, apparently hermaphroditic, paused to clutch his/her crotch and stroke his/her breasts invitingly. Angus dismissed all such interruptions with a snarl and steered Milos on toward their destination.

The sign was like a shout blazoned up one wall, aggressive yellow and green:

EASE-N-SLEAZE
BAR & SLEEP
FUN & FROLIC
YOU NAME IT:
IT'S HERE

As if he were coming home, Angus pulled Milos into the crowded doorway.

Left to the bar: right to what passed for the front desk. Angus went right. At a small counter with nothing on it except a data terminal stood a man with a doomed and bitter air; he gave the impression that to punish a no-doubt minor infraction his employer—the Bill or some subsidiary profiteer—had implanted an unstable explosive in his stomach. He didn't look up as Angus slapped a palm on the counter and said, "Rooms." Instead he asked distantly, "Id?"

"Voiceprint," Angus replied.

The man snorted as if this were an inferior answer. He touched a key on his terminal, then waited for Angus to go on.

Distinctly Angus articulated his name.

After a glance at his readout, the man sighed as if he were contemplating the gulf of his fate. "Four twelve."

At a nod from Angus, Milos announced his name.

"Four thirteen," the man responded in the same tone.

"Messages?" Angus inquired.

Still without raising his eyes, the man pointed at his readout. "There's a message here for me. It says to make sure you pay for everything up front."

Milos frowned a question.

Angus shrugged. "The Bill just wants us to remember he doesn't trust us."

Turning his back on the counter, he moved to the lift.

On the fourth level they found their rooms directly opposite the lift. Milos hung back as Angus approached four twelve, scanning hard for electromagnetic data.

Bugeyes along the corridor *there* and *there*. An intercom, id tag jack, and palm plate outside the door: normal wiring; no booby traps. If the room itself held any surprises, their emissions didn't leak through the door.

"Anything to worry about?" Milos asked tensely.

Angus ignored the question. He wasn't worried himself: he was simply cautious. Balancing his weight so that he could jump in any direction, he told the intercom his name.

The door slid open.

The room was bigger than his cabin aboard *Trumpet*, but not much. The air was no better than the atmosphere outside Ease-n-Sleaze: apparently the room had recently been occupied by someone who liked to smoke nic laced with dorphamphetamines. The nacreous walls were rank with stains; some of the splotches looked like old grease or blood. Two ersatz stainless steel chairs slumped against them. A ratty fabric like exhausted Velcro covered the floor. Light the color of defeated neon spread from reflectors in the corners of the ceiling. A data terminal set into one wall gave him the means to contact people—or spend money—without leaving his quarters. The bed probably knew almost as much about desperation and hate as he did.

Before his heart beat again, he was sure that the room was safe. It had its own bugeye, sure—privacy was an ambiguous concept anywhere in the Bill's domain. But the room itself wasn't dangerous—he could do whatever he wanted here. As long as he didn't mind being watched.

For completeness he checked the bathroom. Then he returned to Milos.

"Home sweet home," he announced. "Let's see if yours is any better."

Compelled by his zone implants to take care of his second, he confirmed that there was no material difference between his room and Milos'. Only the shade of the stains varied.

Milos hardly glanced at the room. He studied Angus' face, looking for dangers; hints of alarm.

Concerned that Milos might feel driven to demand reassurance by issuing a Joshua order in the Bill's hearing, Angus growled sourly, "It's like living beside a bugger. Everything's recorded. You're safe— as long as you never do anything." By now he was sure that Milos knew enough about buggers to understand him.

Milos shrugged stiffly, as if he could feel the bugeyes pressing against his shoulder blades. Nevertheless he made an effort to play his part. "If we never do anything," he asked plaintively, "how are we going to have any fun?"

Angus snorted. Torn between what he wanted and what his programming required, he said, "You should have thought of that before you got yourself on DA's shit list." Then, as if he were re- lenting, he added, "We can at least get drunk. We probably won't get in trouble doing that. The Bill doesn't trust us, but he'll let us spend your money."

Just for a second, Milos looked so cornered and exposed, so full of self-pity, that Angus thought he might burst into tears like a whipped brat. An instant later, however, his features tightened, and darkness gathered behind his eyes. He'd remembered his anger.

"I'm ready," he said flatly. "Let's go."

Good, Angus sneered to himself because his programming wouldn't let him say the words; wouldn't let him gibe at his second in a public place. I love it when you're pissed. That's when you make your worst mistakes.

Chewing useless fantasies in which Milos begged for death while Angus played cat's cradle with his guts, Captain Thermopyle led his second down to the bar.

Nick Succorso was waiting for them at a table in one of the dim, dirty corners.

ANGUS

The bar itself was a long stretch of simulated wood, old with stains and gouges. Both men working back and forth in front of the ranks of vats, dispensers, and vials had the vacant look of null-wave transmitters: men who couldn't cheat anyone because they'd given up or lost the ability to make that kind of decision. Light reflected in smears from the grimy fixtures and fittings, the glasses and metal.

The bar had been set against one wall, so that it seemed to lead toward the stage at the far end of the room. No one was performing at the moment: the acts playing there were between sets. That was too bad. The din and glare of a performance would have hampered the Bill's bugeyes. Inevitably the pickups and cameras would have been less discerning. A show might cover the audience enough to make private conversation safe—

—might cover Angus enough to let him ease forward and stab a laser into the base of Nick Succorso's brain without being effectively recorded.

But he didn't care whether he was recorded. He didn't give a shit who knew what he did. As soon as he saw Nick, his brain went black with hate, and he started forward with bloodshed in his mouth and murder in his fists. Fuck the Bill. Fuck Milos and Lebwohl and zone implants. Nick Succorso was the man who'd caused *Bright Beauty*'s destruction. He'd trapped Angus, deprived him of space and choice. The fact that Angus was here now, welded and cursed, was a direct result of Nick's treachery.

Worse than that, Succorso had taken Morn. Angus refused to admit his pain, even to himself; nevertheless the thought of Morn with Nick hurt him as acutely as the dismantling of his ship. Morn had wanted Nick from the first moment she saw him, Angus never doubted that, and after Angus was framed she'd given Succorso the one thing Angus had failed to extort or coerce from her: her willingness; her self.

Because he denied the laceration of his heart, he didn't realize that losing her to his betrayer had only reinforced the abject fidelity with which he'd struggled to keep his end of their bargain.

In his mind he was already moving. A few steps to reach the tables. Between them toward the corner where Succorso sat. A look of slaughter on his face so that Captain Sheepfucker would know what was about to happen. A quick grab, at microprocessor speeds; too fast to be stopped: a fist to the side of Succorso's neck, aiming a laser while he fought and failed to break loose. Then one quick mental command, one fierce squeeze of will, and Nick would slump in his hands, all that brave buccaneering superiority and manliness turned to dead meat in an instant of coherent light.

Angus did it, *he did it.* No inhuman lump of circuits and restrictions could stop him; no zone implant could defuse this hate. No matter how much it cost him, no matter what neural excruciation it exacted, he *did* it. Succorso hung lifeless in his fists, and he was free again, *free,* alive at last to kill or connive for his own survival—

But of course he didn't do it. The whole idea was a mirage. He could see it in his mind as if it were real: his datacore and his zone implants paid no attention. While he faced Nick's mocking grin and his scars across the bar, Angus couldn't move or speak; could hardly breathe. He would have been unable even to sweat in his agony if his programming had decreed otherwise.

"Maybe," Milos breathed as if he'd recovered his smugness, "this is going to be fun after all."

A sound like a wail squalled in Angus' head; but his datacore stifled every hint or whimper of his distress.

His mouth against Angus' ear, Milos whispered, "Come on, Joshua. Do your job."

Involuntarily, as bloated with mortality as a toad, Angus lumbered into motion.

Entirely against his will, he located the bugeyes, then began scanning the room for wires. He spotted only two. One, a man perched at the bar itself, sat hunched over a pair of mechanical hands as if the fact that they also served as transmitters nauseated him; he was out of range to eavesdrop on Nick. The other, a woman with virtually no clothes and an unmistakable EM signature, sat at a table near Nick's corner. She wasn't alone: two men huddled beside her, alternately buying her drinks, whispering in her ears, and fondling her breasts. But they were nothing; she was the only danger.

Angus' datacore advised him to get rid of her. But it didn't say how—and didn't exert any pressure.

Nick remained sitting as Angus and Milos approached. His back was in the corner so that he could watch the room. Angus would have preferred that position himself; however, his programming decreed otherwise. He'd already identified the emission traces from the wall which showed where the wiring for the nearest bugeyes ran. He would be closer to those traces if he took the seat on Nick's left.

"Milos." Nick went on grinning. "Captain Thermo-pile. It would be nice if I could pretend I'm surprised. Unfortunately every fucker on this rock who isn't brain dead already knows you're here. It might have been better," he added to Milos, "if we could have talked on my ship."

Nudged in that direction, Milos sat down on Nick's right. Angus took the chair on Nick's left and reversed it so that he could straddle it with his back against the wall.

"Better for you, maybe," Milos answered warily. "Not for me. I'm already compromised enough."

Nick's scars looked the way Angus' tongue felt, ashen and hurt. "I offered to come to you. You turned me down."

Milos frowned unhappily. "This is safer. The Bill doesn't trust us. It helps if we're all behaving normally." Only his tone hinted at the truth: according to Angus' datacore, Milos had been ordered to avoid situations in which he might be tempted to expose his power over Angus. And Angus' awareness of the order made it compulsory. Keeping his head down and his voice low, Milos informed the table-top, "Angus has a talent for spotting guards. He says. He says he can keep us out of trouble. Since he's got his neck in the same noose we do, I believe him."

"Are you sure?" Nick didn't glance at Angus. "A lot has happened since the last time we talked. I've been busy—and you sure as hell look like you have. How do you know he's got his neck in the same noose?"

"Drinks, Milos," Angus put in roughly because he wasn't allowed to scream. "What the fuck are we sitting here for, if we aren't going to get drunk?"

Milos was Angus' second; he was supposed to take orders. Nevertheless he let a little of his anger show in his eyes before he stood up and moved toward the bar.

"Captain Thermo-pile," Nick drawled, "you're getting rude in your old age. I get the impression you don't want Milos to answer my question. Now why is that, I ask myself? Have you got a game of your own going on the side?"

Angus was busy assessing the dangers of this conversation. The bugeye in the ceiling above him could see well enough, but might not be able to hear accurately. On the other hand, the nearly naked woman and her companions were only a couple of tables away; definitely in range for her pickups. That wasn't a problem yet: he had things to say which he and his datacore didn't mind letting the Bill overhear. But the hazards would increase rapidly—especially when Nick and Milos broached the subjects they were presumably here to discuss.

"You've got it wrong, Captain Sheepfucker," Angus rasped. "Milos is my second now. I don't know what you clowns said to each other, and I don't care. The question isn't what game I've got going. It's what are you two playing at."

"Fascinating." Nick sneered. "I hope you'll forgive me for not believing you. If you're telling the truth, something pretty serious has changed since the last time I saw him. He's had the shit kicked out of him. Maybe it would help if you spent a while trying to convince me you're *capable* of making a deputy chief of Com-Mine Station Security take on the job of being your second."

He sounded as cocky and casually dangerous as ever; but Angus wasn't fooled. He had a coward's intuitive hearing: he registered the stress hidden in Nick's tone. It was like the pallor of Nick's scars and the almost febrile way he watched the bar; a symptom of fear. Something essential was unraveling inside him.

Angus couldn't express his fury in any other way; but his programming let him show it in his voice. Like concentrated mineral acid, he retorted, "I'm on the level here, Captain Sheepfucker. I made Milos my second the same way I made him get me out of lockup. I had *proof*"—he snapped the word like a blow to the head— "you spaceshits framed me, you and him together. You're fucking right he's had the shit kicked him out him. I got him by the balls. After I twisted them for a while, he agreed to do what I wanted."

No matter how much he unraveled, Nick wasn't easily intimidated. "You're talking, Captain Thermo-pile," he snorted, "but I don't hear anything. If you want to sit around passing gas, why don't you go to another table and do it by yourself? You didn't have any *proof*. If you did, you would have used it to keep yourself out of lockup in the first place."

"Wrong." Angus wanted to crush the superiority off Nick's face; wanted that so acutely it made his hands hurt. "It took months. I had proof, but I couldn't get anybody to listen. Milos blocked me. I didn't get an ear until I was reqqed to UMCPHQ."

Milos had obtained three drinks from one of the bartenders; he was turning away. The wire at the bar had apparently fallen asleep with his face in his mechanical hands.

Without transition Angus hammered his fist on the table, snarled a curse, and jumped to his feet. Surging between the tables, he moved to confront the wired woman and her groping companions.

"Sister," he grated at her bare skin and her drink-stupid expression, "I don't like the way you're looking at me."

She didn't need to be alert to serve the Bill; she hardly needed to be alive. In all likelihood she was a hooker who'd been offered a better deal, one which spared her the necessity of actual sex. In exchange for being wired, all she had to do was float around in public places like this and let men think she was available long enough to buy her drinks.

Startled by Angus' attack, she tried to focus her eyes on him, but couldn't; so she muttered thickly, "Fuck off, asshole."

Angus was in his element—and his hate had nowhere else to go. He lashed a fist at each of the woman's companions, knotted his fingers in the fronts of their docksuits. With reinforced ease, he hauled both of them up out of their chairs.

"I said," he blared like a klaxon, *"I don't like the way she looks at me!"*

That got their attention. They were small, lost individuals, probably minor machinists or tool handlers who worked for the shipyard; too drunk to want anything except a chance to screw their companion—and probably too drunk to do anything about it if they got the chance. Angus' strength seemed to frighten them witless. One of them looked like he was going to faint. The other blurted out, "What do you want us to do about it?"

From the vicinity of the bar, Milos gaped as if Angus had initiated self-destruct. Both bartenders stood like statues: Angus could see their fingers poised over the keys which would summon guards. The wire at the bar remained in his slump; everyone else stared at Angus.

He put the men down. When they recovered their balance, he released them. Then he pointed toward a vacant table farther away; out of range. In a calmer tone he articulated precisely, "I want you to take this collection of female body parts and"—abruptly he began yelling again—"go sit over *there!*"

"I wasn't looking at you," the woman protested. "I've never seen you before."

She didn't appear to notice the difference as her companions pulled her to her feet and tugged her away, stumbling drunkenly among the tables. Obviously neither of them had the vaguest idea what she was doing here.

Milos came toward Angus anxiously. Ignoring him, Angus turned his back and moved to rejoin Nick.

"What the hell was *that* all about?" Nick asked sardonically. "Do you have a death wish, or do you just *like* making everybody want to shoot at you?"

Angus ignored that as well. When he'd straddled his chair again, he resumed, "I wasn't sitting on my hands while we were on Com-Mine." His rage was harder now, more focused, as if venting some of it had made it stronger. His pulse racketed in his veins; but his respiration was steady and slow despite his exertion. "I may not have been smart enough to keep you from framing me, but that doesn't mean I was stupid. While you and Milos were dicking with each other, I went EVA."

With one finger, he traced the word "wire" on the tabletop.

Nick's eyes widened slightly, perhaps because of what Angus said, perhaps because of what he wrote.

"I went to your ship," Angus continued, "and I put a current sensor on your cables until I found the one that carried your computer link to Com-Mine. Then I wrapped a magnetic field around it and ran a line back to *Bright Beauty*. That way I was able to read the fluctuations in your data stream. I recorded an echo of everything you and Milos said to each other."

Milos arrived at the table and stopped as if he'd been hit with a paresis dart. He hadn't heard this explanation before; but he couldn't betray his surprise without also betraying Angus—and Hashi Lebwohl as well.

The intensity of Nick's attention gave Angus a grim satisfaction. Nick looked like he'd just discovered that his ship's computers no longer answered his priority codes.

"I couldn't break your cipher, but I didn't need that for proof." Angus' voice sounded like breaking bones. No words were enough to articulate his outrage; but he did the best he could. "The routing was embedded in the messages. It always is. And my recording was copied in *Bright Beauty*'s datacore. The proof was *there*. All I had to do was convince somebody to look for it. Then Milos was finished.

"So don't make the mistake of thinking you can plot with him behind my back. That's over. You fucking nailed me once. I'm telling you now, you are fucking *never* going to nail me again. If you want Milos for something, you include me—or you forget him."

Record *that*, motherfucker, he told the Bill. Make something out of it if you can.

Nick stared at Angus for a moment. Then he threw back his head and started laughing. He wanted Angus to believe that he couldn't be touched; that his superiority was a gap Angus couldn't cross. But Angus knew better. In Nick's laugh he heard fraying nerves and shaken confidence—the muffled hysteria of a man who was being eaten alive by doubts.

You're *mine*, Captain Sheepfucker, Angus promised. Remember that. Somehow, somewhere, I'm going to get you. You can count on it.

With a shudder, Milos thunked his drinks down on the table. His fingers trembled as he dug a packet of nic out of his pocket, took one, and stuck it between his lips. Trying to sound calm, he said, "I should have known better than to leave you two thugs alone. The next time I turn my back, you'll probably kill each other."

"Oh, shut up, Milos," Angus said. "The next time you turn your back, we'll probably kill *you*."

Milos' gaze threatened a variety of complex retributions as he sat down and lit his nic.

Nick picked up a glass and drained it as if he didn't care what it contained. "Don't listen to him, Milos," he advised. "He's so busy hating everybody, he can't think. He hasn't figured out yet that this situation is too complicated for hate. There's more going on here than he realizes—and it's more dangerous than he imagines."

Angus was in no mood for drink; but he sampled one of the glasses and decided that a little liquor wouldn't hurt him. For a fact, the situation *was* complicated. Like Milos, Succorso was a UMCPDA stooge. He'd been shaken by Angus' attack, that was all; not really upset. Angus read his mood as if it were legible on EM wavelengths. The pressures gnawing at him came from some other source.

Because he knew of Milos' relationship with Lebwohl, he probably guessed that Angus' claim of power over Milos was a fabrication; guessed that Angus and Milos must be here on DA's orders. Angus saw that clearly.

Nevertheless he didn't care: he trusted his own judgments. Under the Bill's bugeyes none of them could risk revealing what they knew, or thought, or needed.

"I don't need his help," Nick was saying to Milos. "I need yours."

A burst of light from the stage signaled that some kind of performance was about to start. Good. Angus was ready to take advantage of anything that confused the cameras and pickups.

"I just got here," Milos protested through a cloud of smoke. "And I'm on the run. I'm not exactly in a position to help anybody." For Angus, he added, "Neither of us is."

Nick grinned like a manic-depressive. "Don't bullshit me, Milos. I know something about your *resources*." The way he stressed the word made it a reference to Data Acquisition. "If you were destitute, the Bill wouldn't let you in here. You've at least got enough money to make him tolerate his distrust. And you've probably got a few secrets you can sell, just for insurance. We've worked together a long time, off and on. I've earned some credit with you." He didn't appear to be as concerned about the bugeyes as Angus was, but he still chose his words carefully. "Don't tell me you can't help me until you hear what I want."

"All right," Milos sighed. He was smoking hard enough to clog the air. "Don't keep me in suspense. I'm in a hurry to get to the part where I say no. What do you want?"

A crash which was meant to sound like cymbals came over the stage speakers. The abrupt brilliance as the lights focused into a tight spot on the stage created a temporary zone of darkness around it. Men and women at the tables and the bar looked in that direction expectantly.

As if he were dissociating himself from Nick and Milos, Angus leaned back against the wall, letting his arms dangle on either side of his chair.

"I'm in some trouble here," Nick explained unnecessarily. "You may have figured that out. There's a fucking Amnion 'defensive' in dock because of me, and another hanging out there where it can strip us all down to our subatomic particles." He glanced at the stage as if he were waiting for the show to start before he came to the point. "I'm in deep shit, and there aren't any easy ways out of it. I think you could say"—his scars were pale under his eyes, the color of fear—"I've made a couple of serious miscalculations recently. If I don't get some help soon, I'll have to start selling everything I own just to stay alive."

Selling what? Angus wondered. What did Nick have to sell? DA's secrets? His stomach knotted. Morn herself?

The thought that Captain Sheepfucker might sell her to save his ass made Angus want to snap Nick's neck.

We've committed a crime—

Wasn't that what Angus himself had done? Sell her to save his ass?

No. *No.* He'd made a bargain with her. And he'd *kept* it.

Until Lebwohl put electrodes into his head and forced the truth out.

It's got to stop.

"How much money do you have?" Nick asked Milos.

Milos snorted. "What makes you think I'm going to tell *you*?"

Another crash from the speakers. As if she were being disgorged by the surrounding gloom, a woman appeared in the spotlight. Like a shout, emissions hit Angus' sight. Around her heart and deep in her belly, electromagnetic nodes revealed themselves like stars to his artificial vision. But the woman wasn't a wire: her aura was wrong for communications. The equipment implanted in her served some other purpose.

She wore a quilted jacket and pants that looked like they might have been designed to deflect stun-prods. An immaculate wreath of hair caught the light around her head and shone. Her face, too, was lovely; delicate and vulnerable. But a grimace twisted her mouth as if she were on the verge of sobs, and a stare of old pain filled her eyes.

Nick rolled his glass between his palms. "The Bill has something that belongs to me," he explained. "I promised it to the Amnion, but he won't give it back. That's why I'm in trouble. I haven't got the money to meet his price—and if the Amnion don't get what they want they're going to have me for fucking lunch. I want you to help me pay off the Bill."

Angus stifled an impulse to interrupt. He had no real desire to interfere with what Nick and Milos said: he simply wanted to prevent Nick from incriminating himself while the Bill could still record it.

The woman stood motionless in the center of the spotlight, staring into a gap of dismay. When the speakers crashed again, a stagehand pushed a box of props out of the gloom.

As soon as the box arrived beside her, the woman stooped and picked out a gleaming knife with a twenty-centimeter blade.

Some of Ease-n-Sleaze's patrons gasped as if they were shocked; as if they hadn't known what kind of act to expect.

Like the rest of the audience, Angus watched the stage. Without shifting a muscle, he rested the knuckles of his right fist against the wall. While the woman raised her knife into the light, and the audience gasped, he fired his laser.

From between his knuckles, a needle-thin stab of ruby pierced the wall and severed the leads to all the bugeyes in this end of the bar.

A fierce grin bared his teeth as the emissions of the bugeyes winked out.

No one in the bar noticed the difference. Nick and Milos were blind to what Angus had just done. They leaned toward each other across the table, unselfconsciously conspiratorial as Nick explained what he wanted; but now they were safe. Temporarily, anyway: as long as they were discreet. One of the requirements programmed into Angus' datacore had been satisfied.

"You're crazy," Milos muttered around his nic. "That money is all I've got. I've lost everything else. "Why"—he seemed to need an expletive which eluded him—"should I let you have it?

"What are you offering me in return, Nick?"

Nick's smile was distorted and sickly. "I'll give you what you came for. I can do that."

Milos pulled his nic from his mouth as if he were about to vomit. After a moment he threw it vehemently to the floor and snatched out a fresh smoke. "What"—again he gaped as if language failed him—"is that woman doing?"

One at a time she lifted pieces of fabric and sheets of plastic into the spotlight. Each one she held in front of her face while she stabbed the knife through it. The apparent purpose of this ritual was to demonstrate the blade's keenness. But Angus—and the aficionados in the bar—recognized another, more tantalizing motivation. By showing off the knife's sharpness, she dulled it.

So that it would hurt more.

Abruptly Angus shifted his weight forward. Folding his heavy arms across his chair back, he rasped, "Cut the crap, Captain Sheepfucker. No more empty euphemisms. Let's take it one detail at a time and call a spade a fucking shovel."

Milos' eyes showed a flare of alarm, which Angus ignored. He didn't mind letting Milos think the bugeyes were still dangerous.

"Exactly what," Angus continued, "has the Bill got that belongs to you?"

Nick stiffened; a hint of darkness touched his scars. "I was right. You've got a goddamn death wish."

Undisturbed, Angus held Nick's stare and waited.

Suddenly Nick relaxed. Smiling with unexplained malice, he said, "All right. Have it your way.

"You remember Morn Hyland. She still probably gives you wet dreams. Well, she had a kid. That's what we were doing on Enablement—force-growing her kid. She calls him Davies Hyland, after her pure, dead father."

On the stage, the woman had finished cutting up cloth and plastic. Now she put the knife down by her feet and started unsealing her jacket. Under it she was naked. Her breasts looked unnaturally large and erect in the intense light. A slight suggestion of puckering in the skin around them implied that she'd performed this act at least once before. Her fear was born of experience.

"Now the Amnion want him back," Nick went on. "It has something to do with the fact that she didn't lose her mind when he was born. They say force-growing is supposed to make plant life out of the mother, but it didn't happen to her. They think that's because of the zone implant you used on her. So they aren't particularly interested in her. But they want her brat. They want to study the consequences of having a mother who didn't lose her mind.

"The Bill has him. If I can buy him back, I can give him to the Amnion—and then *poof*"—he spread his fingers—"all my problems disappear."

For a moment the woman hesitated as if she were unsure what to do next. Finally she decided to postpone her dread by removing her pants. As she shrugged them down from her tight hips, someone in the audience whistled appreciatively.

Her belly showed the same slight puckering which marked the skin around her breasts.

"How nice for you." Angus put as much challenge as he could into his voice: he wanted to uncover what lay behind Nick's malice. "Everything's fine—as long as we help you." The information that Morn had a son meant nothing to him, aside from a minor disgust that she'd done something that stupid. "What the fuck makes you think we've got that much credit? What does the Bill want for this brat?"

When she was completely naked, the woman retrieved her knife. But then she hesitated again. The impacted fear in her eyes seemed to paralyze her.

With another nauseated, treacherous smile, Nick named a sum nearly as large as the one Milos had available.

Transfixed by the woman—or by what he heard—Milos wiped sweat off his forehead. The nic trembled in his mouth. "You're crazy. I said that already. It's true—you're out of your entire mind. I can't come within an order of magnitude of what you want."

From the far end of the bar, two or three people started stamping their feet. Almost at once they took rhythm from each other, beating a demand against the floor. The demand spread and grew as more and more of the audience put their heels into it.

As far as Angus could tell, his datacore contained no provision
for giving Nick Milos' money. Simply as an experiment, he changed
his tack: he wanted to see how Nick would react.

"But money isn't the only way to get things done," he said less
aggressively. "Even here. The real question isn't what the Bill wants.
It's what you're going to give us. You said you can supply what we
came here for. Maybe I'm being stupid again, but I don't know what
the fuck you're talking about."

The stamping spread until it seemed to hammer at the woman.
Her face quivered at every blow.

Nick leaned forward urgently. Without transition he seemed to
pass from treachery to desperation. "Listen to me, asshole," he whispered. "I'm in too much trouble here, and I haven't got time for
games. You can play *let's pretend* when you're by yourself. You can
fuck yourself senseless for all I care. Right now I won't put up with
it.

"I'm here because Hashi Lebwohl sent me. So are you. You
didn't blackmail Milos into helping you. Lebwohl gave him to you
for cover so you could come here and try to earn a reprieve."

Angus couldn't resist: he batted his eyes. The pressure mounting
on the stage didn't touch him. "I'm astonished. How do you know
all this? How am I supposed to earn this reprieve?"

"You came," Nick articulated as if he were suddenly hungry for
murder, "to rescue Morn Hyland. If you solve my problem with the
Bill, I'll hand her over. Otherwise"—his voice cracked as he crushed
a shout—"I'll sell her to the fucking *Amnion* to save my ass, and
then they'll have a fucking *cop* they can work on."

With an abject shudder, the woman tightened her grip on the
knife. Milos took the nic out of his mouth and clamped his teeth
onto one of his knuckles as she put the knife against her skin and
began cutting off her right breast.

Blood sprang from the incision, swarmed down her belly; more
blood burst from her lip as she bit through it to keep herself from
screaming. When her right breast flopped to the stage, she started
on the left.

Shaking, Milos turned his chair, put his back to the stage. With
both hands he lifted his glass to his mouth and emptied it. Then he
replaced his nic, sucked smoke deep into his lungs.

"Go away, Nick," he breathed as if he'd just suffered a wound—

or had an orgasm. "Go away and leave us alone. You're completely crazy. We don't have anything to talk about anymore."

Angus didn't want to think about Morn: he couldn't bear it. Nick was perfectly capable of selling her to the Amnion. Then she would be lost forever. And there was nothing he could do about it, *nothing he could do about it,* even Min Donner hadn't been able to get his datacore rewritten to let him help Morn. Paresthetic fire flushed along his arms until his zone implants quenched it: rage stung his heart until they denatured it. Morn, he thought, oh, *Morn!* But he could do nothing; show nothing. His programming held him, as cruel as the dimensional gap.

Nearly paralyzed by rage and protest, he watched the woman on the stage out of the corner of his eye while he continued to study Nick. He'd seen self-mutilation acts before. After she finished her left breast, she opened her belly and let her guts spill down her legs. At first she bled like a pig; but now he understood what her implanted equipment was for. The nodes he saw were pressure clamps. When the initial dramatic rush of blood was over, the clamps closed on her major arteries so that she wouldn't lose too much fluid; wouldn't die before someone took her back to the surgeons. Once they healed her, she would be ready to perform again.

As the spotlights went out, a few people applauded. Somewhere in the bar, someone retched.

—*a crime against your soul.*

Without warning, a window in Angus' head opened—the dark interface between his mind and his datacore. He seemed to fall into the gap between what he understood and what he could do as if he were going into tach; a black rush of possibilities and compulsions seemed to translate him to a whole new state of being.

It's got to stop.

Entirely without volition, he put his palm down like a promise on the table in front of Nick and said, "It's a deal. We'll get Davies Hyland for you. You give us Morn."

As if he were lost in the dimness which the spotlights left behind, Milos cried out, "Angus, you bastard!"

Nick rolled his eyes and cackled with laughter.

ANGUS

If he could have laughed or cried out himself, he might not have been able to hold back. Everything seemed to come at him at once. Behind the false stoicism of his zone implants, he was shaken to the core by inferences, dismay, and hope.

Morn!

He wanted to rescue Morn. Even to protect his heart from Nick and Milos, he couldn't pretend that wasn't true. Yet the decision wasn't his: his promise to Nick had come out of his mouth without one iota of free will behind it.

But Hashi Lebwohl had made it unmistakably clear that Angus wasn't programmed to risk his mission for Morn—

This was why Warden Dios *you bastard! you fucking sonofabitch!* had switched his datacore. So that Angus could try to rescue Morn, when everyone in UMCPHQ had written her off. Dios had some reason for pretending that he didn't care what happened to her. He'd prepared his instructions in secret, plugged them into Angus secretly, in order to conceal his true intentions from the people around him.

He wanted her back.

It's got to stop.

Unfortunately he hadn't foreseen that she could be saved by mere money. The simple expedient of buying her from Nick with Milos' credit wasn't available.

Even Lebwohl had been kept in the dark. And Milos certainly

hadn't been let into the secret. His face was gray and lost, as if he were in the grip of an infarction, and his eyes rolled with panic, trying to look in all directions at once, measure the extent to which he'd been betrayed. No one knew the truth.

I'll give you what you came for.

Except Nick Succorso?

How had Nick known Warden Dios' secret?

No, stop it, Angus told himself harshly, don't panic. All Nick knew was that Morn was UMCP—and *Trumpet* had come from UMCPHQ. The rest was just a lucky guess. When he laughed like that, the stark pallor of his scars under his wild eyes made him look crazy enough to have guessed anything.

Why did Warden Dios want to keep what he was doing hidden from his own people?

Who was the real target of Joshua's mission?

Angus wanted to laugh at Milos' consternation, and at Lebwohl's. Those motherfuckers deserved to be corn-holed like this.

And he wanted to cry out like a stricken child because none of the decisions were his.

We'll get Davies Hyland for you.

You give us Morn.

Those words meant the exact opposite of what Milos so obviously believed about the purpose of their mission.

But he had no choice in any of this. The link to his computer gushed like a conduit: commandments and data flooded him.

A man in the sterile suit of a medtech wrapped the performer in pressure bandages, then carried her off the unlit stage. Apparently Ease-n-Sleaze considered her good enough for a return engagement. A scrub robot followed the medtech to clean up the blood.

"Shut up!" Angus grated at Nick and Milos. "Both of you. We haven't got much time. If we give the Bill a chance to send more wires in here, we may never get to talk again.

"We have two problems. We don't know where the kid is. And the Bill is going to raise total hell when he finds out what we're doing. We need to make decisions fast. Then we need to *do it.*"

Nick stopped laughing as if he'd thumbed a toggle inside himself. "Captain Thermo-pile, you amaze me," he drawled in a tone of casual danger. "I thought I was going to surprise you, but you don't sound surprised. You sound like you already have the whole thing figured out."

A biting retort came to Angus' lips: his datacore quashed it. Instead he said, "The way to handle the Bill is, force him to suspect the wrong person. That's *you*, Succorso." His programming gripped him so tightly now that he couldn't insult Nick. "First you're going to get us the information we need. You'll do it in a way he can't help noticing. Then we'll arrange an alibi for you." Angus grinned like a grimace. "Hell, we'll use the Bill himself for an alibi."

Nick started to ask a question, but Milos pushed himself forward. His face was a knot of fear and fury; sweat made the splotches on his scalp gleam like the marks of a disease. "Angus," he hissed, "this is wrong. I thought you understood. It isn't why we're here. I don't care what he says. *It isn't why we're here.* I don't want this kind of trouble.

"I'm warning you, Angus. Don't force my hand."

His threat was as plain as a Jerico priority command. Stop this, or I'll override your programming. I'll show everybody here which one of us holds the real power.

Just for an instant Angus faltered. Dread crawled through his belly. Milos could stop him; could doom Morn. Dios would be helpless to save her if Milos said the right words—

But then Nick would hear them. He would see their effect: he would guess what they meant.

And then nothing Milos said or did or wanted could prevent Nick from simply killing him and taking control of Angus for himself. Even if Milos ordered Angus to defend him, Nick would probably succeed: the restrictions which protected UMCP personnel from Angus probably applied to Nick as much as to Milos. And Milos on his own was no physical match for Nick Succorso.

Angus saw all this in the furtive, involuntary glance Milos flicked at Nick. So quickly that his datacore had no time to compel him, he decided to call Milos' bluff.

"I told you to shut up," he returned. "You're my *second*—you take *my* orders. As far as I'm concerned, you've already done the only thing I needed you for. If you don't like the job, I can replace you without leaving the bar."

Milos opened his mouth; a rush of blood darkened his face as his anger gained the upper hand. But a second or two later he dropped his gaze, and his passion drained away.

"You're going to regret this," he muttered. "I swear to God you'll regret it."

Nevertheless he lacked the courage to carry out his threat in front of Nick.

"You two spaceshits ought to go on the stage," Nick sneered. "You're at least as much fun as the rest of the 'entertainment' here."

Angus' attention snapped back to Succorso. "You'll have more fun in a minute," he growled sourly. "That woman's still here." He nodded toward the table where the Bill's wire sat. "She looks like your kind of meat."

Softly, distinctly, he outlined what he wanted Nick to do.

While Angus spoke Milos' expression changed from defeat to disgust, and then to a look of settled nausea. He'd been pushed too far: he was beginning to reach decisions. Angus saw that look and knew what it meant. The next time Milos made a threat, he wouldn't back down.

The knowledge gave Angus a nausea of his own, which his zone implants concealed for him.

Before Angus finished, Nick objected, "This is some deal. I can see why everybody likes to work with you so much. Why should I trust you? What're you going to do while I take all the risks? So far you haven't given me any reason to think you won't just go back to your ship and laugh your fucking head off."

"You should trust me," Angus returned, "because you haven't got anything to lose." His tone was cold and bitter. "You're already in as much trouble as there is. It can't get any worse." Then he lowered his voice. "Besides, you're covered. You'll have an alibi—one of the best."

He consulted his chronometer, named a time. "That's about three hours from now. You'll go see the Bill, tell him you want to talk to him. Don't be late—you won't have much of a window. Tell him you're ready to buy back the kid. All you have to do is agree on the price.

"Every log and bugeye he's got will tell him you were with him when Davies disappeared. If that doesn't cover you, nothing will.

And Milos and I'll be in the clear. That's important to you. If the Bill knows *we* snatched the kid, he'll storm our ship and grab him back. The whole thing'll be wasted. But even if we can't pull it off, you're covered."

Quietly Angus repeated, "You really haven't got anything to lose."

Nick consulted his hands as if he wondered how much strength—or sanity—they still held. In a voice full of mixed intentions, he asked, "Why are we in a hurry? Why does the timing have to be so tight?"

"Because," Angus answered heavily, "if we don't catch the Bill off guard, we won't catch him at all. It won't do any good to just break Davies out. We have to take him someplace the Bill won't look for him."

Milos puffed smoke at the ceiling as if he fed on nic.

Nick let out a fragmentary laugh like a croak. "Then of course *you'll* have him. What the fuck makes me think you'll hand him over when I need him? Never mind—it doesn't matter. If I'm crazy, so are you. I've got my own insurance." Complex purposes seemed to pull his scars tight against the bones of his skull. "I can always tell the Bill where he is."

Abruptly he got to his feet. "I'll do it."

Angus nodded. Instead of sneering, Sucker! he said, "Four twelve. We'll be waiting."

Succorso ignored him. Facing Milos, Nick asked, "Aren't you going to reassure me before I go? We've worked together for years. You should at least promise you'll back me up, even if you don't mean it. Send me off to my execution with a good taste in my mouth."

Milos didn't glance at Nick. His eyes were focused on the smoke streaming from his mouth. Quietly he said, "I would tell you to go to hell, but you're already there. We all are. You two are supposed to be desperate illegals, full of hate and cunning—and too smart to be caught. But I think neither one of you has the vaguest idea what's going on here."

"Maybe not," Nick snorted. "But you don't either. *That* I guarantee."

Snarling at Angus and Milos, he moved away between the tables.

Here it comes, Angus warned himself. The new hardness gathering beneath Milos' pudgy features conveyed a guarantee of its own. The decisions he'd made were going to be expensive.

"Tell me something, Angus," he murmured past his nic. "How do you know the Bill isn't already studying a copy of this conversation?"

Angus would have kept his mouth shut; but his datacore saw no reason to avoid this question. "That woman is the only wire in this end of the bar," he replied. "She's out of range now. And I cut the power to the bugeyes. The Bill has a blind spot right where we're sitting."

At once Milos shifted his weight forward. Dull heat sprang to fire in his eyes. "In that case, Joshua," he said without shifting his nic, "I have instructions for you. Jerico priority. Forget all this. Forget Nick—forget Morn Hyland. They aren't why we're here. You're pushing me into a corner for nothing."

When Milos said the word "Joshua," buried commandments took hold of Angus. He sat still, unwillingly passive, while the link in his head prepared itself to receive and enforce Milos' orders. As Milos invoked *Jerico priority*, Angus' brain seemed to shut down: zone implants and programming controlled every neural flicker and muscular contraction while his datacore registered Milos' orders and compared them with its prewritten exigencies. His heart beat once or twice, and his lungs drew a shallow breath, but he remained blank and helpless, like a computer with no operating system. During that brief interval, Milos could have killed him, if Milos had known what was happening inside him—if Milos had wanted him dead.

At the table occupied by the wire and her companions, Nick had taken a position which kept her back turned to Angus and Milos. His eyes shone at her; a smile like a barracuda's bared his teeth. As he talked he leaned slowly closer and closer to her, covering her with his sexual magnetism.

But Milos missed his opportunity. The moment passed; without warning Angus began to talk.

"Message for Milos Taverner from Warden Dios." The words seemed to reach his mouth directly from his datacore. " 'Milos, this was recorded before you left UMCPHQ. You've just been given a rather nasty shock. I regret that, but it was necessary. On this one subject, you were misled. Everything else you were told concerning Joshua, your mission, and yourself remains true. Joshua has not diverged from his programming. Your command codes still function. You have not been betrayed.

"'When you return to UMCPHQ, I will personally explain why it was necessary to mislead you.'

"Message ends."

At the same instant Angus' mind came back on-line.

Grinning with relief, he jeered, "Too bad. Better luck next time. I guess it just doesn't pay to trust those bastards." As if nothing unexpected had happened, he twitched one hand in Nick's direction. "He won't take long. She hasn't got a prayer against a seductive fucker like him. You'd better be ready to move in a couple of minutes."

He was thinking, Clever, Dios. Nice ploy. Too bad it won't work. You're too late—you've already lost him.

What kind of game are you playing?

The whole point of admitting a lie—the only reason Dios could have for admitting that he'd lied—was to conceal other, more crucial falsehoods.

"Oh, shit," Milos breathed as if he were in shock. "Oh, shit. He set me up."

Confident and mocking, Nick looked at one of the woman's companions and said something which made the man go pale. Uncertain of his balance, the machinist or tool handler stumbled out of his chair and retreated from the table.

Her other companion appeared to ask her for support. She ignored him, however: her attention was fixed hungrily on Nick. As he seated himself beside her and reached with the back of one hand to stroke her cheek, her remaining escort stood up so awkwardly that he knocked over his chair. Swearing with empty resentment, he also retreated.

Angus knew how the woman felt. Like her, he was nothing more than a tool, a means to an end. Nobody could betray him: he could only be lied to or abused.

But Milos, on the other hand—

Milos was just beginning to grasp how profoundly he'd been betrayed.

A shudder like a convulsion ran through him. As if he were choking, he gasped out, "Open your mouth."

Angus had no defense against that order. His datacore didn't protect him: it enforced Milos' authority. Sick with recognition and helplessness, he obeyed.

Deliberately Milos took his nic and stubbed it out on Angus' tongue.

In his mind Angus let out a roar. Heaved up the table, used it to knock Milos backward; then pitched it out of his way and jumped at his tormentor. He had the strength of a great ape, he could beat anybody. With a series of kicks, he snapped Milos' sternum, shattered his ribs, crushed his larynx; with his hands, he gouged out Milos' eyes. He didn't stop until there was nothing left except a bloody pulp—

But only in his mind.

In reality he closed his mouth on a flame of pain and a sick taste of ash. While his tongue burned and blistered, he chewed the nic until he could swallow it.

His stomach would have puked its contents onto the tabletop if his zone implants had allowed that.

"That doesn't make sense," Milos whispered. "The codes still work—I can still control you. But they lied about why we're here." He fought to contain his fear. "Why let me control you—why pretend I can control you—if I don't know what you've been programmed to do?"

"I can think of a reason," Angus croaked past his pain.

"So can I," Milos countered. "This whole thing is aimed at me. I swear to God!" he raged without raising his voice, "they are going to *regret* treating me like this."

By now Nick was so close to the woman that she practically sat in his lap. One of his hands had moved from her cheek downward to stroke her neck, her shoulder, the exposed curve of her breast. The other was buried in her hair at the back of her head. Exactly as instructed.

"It's time," Angus announced. His tongue and stomach felt like he'd just eaten quicklime; but his programming ignored those discomforts—and Milos' anger. He pushed himself to his feet.

Glaring bitterly around him, Milos delayed long enough to light another nic. Then he stood up and followed Angus toward Nick and the woman.

Angus chose an approach that kept him behind the woman, out of her sight. He understood her equipment as clearly as if he'd designed it himself. Her eyes and ears were wired: she was like a video camera with an audio pickup. In consequence she only transmitted what she herself saw and heard.

The noises of the bar covered him as he moved toward her.

Leads from her receptors to her powerpack ran down her neck just beneath her skin. Nick's hand on the back of her head served two purposes: it distracted her sense of touch; and it would demonstrate his innocence. Angus flicked a glance at him to confirm that he was ready; but he was too practiced at seduction to look away from his victim. As Angus neared her, Nick lowered his head to lick a kiss into the hollow of her throat.

Scarcely touching the base of her neck with his knuckles, Angus pricked her with a tiny burst of laser fire which went only millimeters deep; so shallow and keen that she might not feel it; just deep enough to cut the leads to her wire. Then he moved on toward the door, leaving behind only a small red droplet of blood to mark the harm he'd done her.

He felt her stiffen as he passed; heard her say, "Ow," in a tone of fuddled protest. But he didn't look back to see whether she turned her head in his direction. That was Nick's problem: it was his responsibility to make sure she didn't know—therefore couldn't tell the Bill—who might have hurt her.

With Milos trailing after him, Angus took the lift back up to his room.

When the woman's wire stopped transmitting, the Bill would assume at first that she'd cut him off intentionally so that she could have a little more privacy with Nick. And he wouldn't take that kindly. However, one look at her neck and the leads would convince him she hadn't done the damage herself. If she couldn't report that Angus or Milos had been anywhere near her, he would believe Nick was to blame.

That was the real point of the gambit. As a secondary consideration, it might give Nick a lever to use on the woman. If he needed one; if his famous virility and charm weren't enough. Nevertheless the primary purpose was to focus the Bill's distrust away from Angus and Milos.

Which was fine, as far as it went. Unfortunately it did nothing to solve Angus' more immediate problems.

Caustics filled his mouth, and his stomach kept trying unsuccessfully to make him vomit. His head was a wilderland, as bleak
and fatal as the gap. Milos had come to the end of his sufferance:
Angus' sufferings had just begun.

Dios had said, *It's got to stop.* Whatever that meant, it obviously
didn't refer to Angus' distress. The UMCP director had no intention
of easing Angus' helplessness, letting him out of the crib—

He was a coward: he knew what was about to happen to him.

Grimly he said his name to the intercom outside his door. When
the door slid aside, he entered the room as if he expected to be
executed.

Milos joined him before the door closed. For a moment the two
men stood watching each other like mortal enemies. Then, simply
because he didn't want to look as scared as he felt, Angus sat in one
of the chairs and tilted it back until it was propped against the wall.

"Make yourself comfortable," he mumbled past his sore tongue.
"We haven't got all night, but you can probably count on at least
an hour." Nick would take at least an hour, if for no other reason
than to demonstrate his virility.

"You've got that long."

Milos dropped his eyes as if he were ashamed—or as if he had
something to hide. Poking another nic into his mouth, he wandered
over to the data terminal and tapped a few keys, apparently just to
be sure the thing worked. After that he took the other chair, set it
beside Angus', and lowered himself into it.

"You know something about this, Angus. Something you haven't
told me. Maybe something you heard from Dios."

If he was worried about the bugeye, he didn't show it. On the
other hand, he made no effort to invoke Angus' command codes.

"I know a lot of things I haven't told you," you cheap, deranged
piece of shit, Angus replied with as much sarcasm as he could mus-
ter. "I know a lot of things I haven't told myself. I wouldn't share
them with you if I could."

"Well, let me guess," Milos murmured as if he were deaf to
Angus' tone. "Saying we're here to destroy the Bill is just a trick.
The real reason is because of me. And Morn Hyland. That doesn't
sound very plausible—until you think about what she and I have in
common."

"She's been to Enablement. To the Amnion."

Prompted by visceral caution, Angus returned thickly, "Don't guess. It just shows you don't know what you're doing."

"Oh, I know what I'm doing, all right," Milos promised. "Open your mouth."

Although his nic was only half-finished, he dropped it on Angus' tongue. While Angus chewed and swallowed miserably, Milos lit a fresh smoke.

"It's my neck in the noose, and I'm not going to let you or anybody else hang me.

"I suppose," he continued with his own bitterness, "you really can't tell me what you know. It probably isn't much anyway. You're just an incidental victim. From that point of view, you're worse off than I am.

"We all need somebody who's worse off than we are." He regarded Angus thoughtfully. "Or who can be made worse off."

Angus didn't say anything. At this moment he believed he would have been willing to sell his life for the simple freedom to throw up.

As if he'd made his point, Milos also fell silent. He appeared relaxed in his chair. Only the passionate intensity with which he smoked revealed his underlying agitation.

For over an hour while they waited together, he made Angus eat each of his discarded nics in turn. Keeping the room tidy by using Angus as a human ashtray seemed to give him an obscure satisfaction, as if it helped put the moral grime of his circumstances into perspective.

NICK

It was too bad, really. She was a lovely creature in her frail, drunken way. She could have done so much more—she might even have been worth his effort—if she hadn't already spent most of her life pickling her brain. All the alcohol she consumed hadn't done her body any harm; not yet. Her scant clothing made that obvious. Her breasts were full and taut; the line of her hips was seamless. Nevertheless the blur in her eyes and the slackness of her mouth showed that she'd abandoned herself, not to him, but to numbness.

That took some of the fun out of what Nick was doing.

He considered this as he pretended to comfort her distress at the small pain Angus had left on the back of her neck. Women: why was it always a question of women? Wherever he went, whatever he did, they were always the means to his ends—and the reason those ends proved hollow when he gained them.

Apparently this one was too drunk to care what had happened. The disfocused accessibility on her face was like a glimpse into the future, a precognition that what he got from her would be as hollow as everything else.

But he didn't stop; maybe he couldn't. The forces which drove him were fundamental, almost autonomic. With the fingers of one hand, he massaged her tiny hurt; the knuckles of the other stroked the sweet curve between her breasts; his mouth made consoling noises against her ear. Even if his brain had decided to pull away from her before he became helplessly enmeshed in Angus' plots, Angus' be-

trayals, his body might have remained where it was, delicately stok-
ing her bleary responses until she could no longer control them.

As always, he would deal with the danger later.

The danger was real: he knew that. None of his dealings with
Milos had given him any reason to trust the former deputy chief of
Com-Mine Security. And Angus was treachery personified; so malign
that his falseness was virtually metaphysical.

On the other hand, they were both vulnerable here. The fact
that they'd come to Thanatos Minor together in a stolen UMCP ship
showed how precarious their position was. In addition—Nick admitted this with professional detachment—Angus' plan made sense.

Angus had left a number of interesting details unexplained, such
as how exactly he proposed to snatch Davies. Nevertheless his reasoning was irreproachable. Nick didn't like taking orders from Angus
Thermopyle; but he liked the way Angus thought. He wished he
hadn't lost the capacity to think that way himself.

Well, maybe he hadn't lost it entirely. He still had ideas; still
saw opportunities. But even as incomplete as he sometimes felt, he
hadn't lost his power over women like this. She may have been able
to refuse offers or entreaties from the slime on the cruise; but after a
few minutes in his company, a few minutes of his touch, her stunned
gaze begged him to possess her.

Simply to build up tension, he postponed the next step. While
he murmured vacant descriptions of her beauty and how he felt about
it, his fingertips eased under her garments to caress what little they
concealed; his grin grew sharper, as if to cut away defenses she no
longer had. But he didn't move to leave the table until she finally
breathed in a voice made husky by drink, "Take me somewhere."

Humorously avid—and secretly contemptuous—he answered, "I
was hoping you would say that."

Then he guided her to her feet.

Unsure of her balance, she leaned against him in a way that
urged him to wrap his arm around her as he moved her out of the
bar toward the front desk.

Rooms in Ease-n-Sleaze weren't expensive by the standards of
the cruise. Nevertheless the right to use six twenty-one for a while
made a noticeable dent in his small account. He didn't care, however. If he'd measured his life by his accumulated credit, he would
have had to call himself a failure. But he *wasn't* a failure, no, nobody

except Sorus Chatelaine had ever called him that; and he was going to teach her to think otherwise. His plans against her continued to take shape as he rode the lift to the sixth level. The drunk in his arms nuzzled his neck as if she knew what he wanted, but his mind was far away. After too many distractions—Angus, Milos, Morn herself—he returned to the only subject that really mattered to him.

Sorus Chatelaine.

Revenge.

Thinking about that gave him more real pleasure than the woman he was with.

When the lift opened, he pulled away from her kisses long enough to locate his room. Supporting her, he walked the unclad floor to six twenty-one and opened it by pressing his hand on the palm plate, then took her inside.

She wasn't too drunk to wrinkle her nose in distaste at the splotched walls and sagging bed. For carrying his wire around inside her like a stillborn, the Bill probably paid her well enough to live more comfortably than this. She didn't object, however. She made a small noise of protest when Nick disentangled himself to verify that the data terminal worked; but that had nothing to do with the depression of the room.

In fact, the terminal worked fine. Now Nick could have simply extracted the information he wanted, coded a message for Milos by way of *Captain's Fancy*, and left. That would have had several advantages. It would have spared him the effort of sex—would have freed him to spend more time thinking about Sorus. And it would have made his behavior look even more suspicious to the Bill. He could almost hear the woman telling her boss in a stupefied whine, I swear to God, all he did was take me up to that room and make me talk. Then he walked out. That's *all.* I told him what he wanted because I knew you were listening.

Nick grinned at the idea hard enough to stretch his scars.

But he couldn't do it: his body refused. Maybe he would be able to pretend that this woman was Morn—that her drunkenness was the abandonment he craved—

Before leaving the terminal, he spent a little more of his money to pipe in a program of modulated white noise, the kind of sound null-wave transmitters and nerve juice junkies liked when they slept; the kind that would muffle the bugeye's reception.

A DARK AND HUNGRY GOD ARISES

Holding the woman still with a kiss, he stripped away the small scraps of her clothes, then carried her to the bed and tried to bury his own needs deep enough in her flesh so that they would be quenched, at least for a short time.

Unfortunately he couldn't do that either. She came alive in his hands, of course; desire overcame her numbness. She writhed under him and gyrated over him and moaned at his kisses as if he gave her exactly what she wanted; as if she'd never felt this way before, or for so long. But she couldn't supply what *he* wanted. He had no interest in her: he'd never wanted a woman for herself. What he wanted was her passion and surrender; he wanted her to desire him so much that she ceased to exist for herself. And only Morn had ever given him that: Morn Hyland, with her zone implant and her dishonesty, her absolute commitment to her own choices.

Liete knew less about sex, but she was still better than this woman.

So he kept going until the inadequate sweat at the woman's temples and the hollow flush in her cheeks told him that she was worn-out; then he quit. Now was probably his best chance: fatigue and numbness would make her suggestible. If he caught her before she fell asleep, she might tell him almost anything.

Incomplete and unfulfilled, he wrapped her in a grasp which would keep her under control if she reacted badly. Stroking her ear with his tongue, he whispered, "There's one more thing you can do for me."

She laughed unsteadily. "I don't believe it. I thought we already did everything. If there's anything *more* any woman could do for a man like you, I want to know what it is."

He ignored the implicit challenge. Keeping his voice low, he breathed, "It's just something you can tell me. The Bill has something that belongs to me." As if he hadn't felt her stiffen, he went on, "I want to get it back. You can help by telling me where it is."

Weakly she twisted against his arms. When she'd turned enough to look directly into his face, she asked, "What makes you think I know anything about *him*? I don't. I just work here. I sell sex." Suddenly flustered, she said, "I mean, not to you. I'm not asking you for money. I already got"—she smiled awkwardly—"something a lot better.

"But I don't work for him. That's what I mean. I'm not that

important. I just fuck men who buy me drinks and pay me after-ward."

Nick gave her a lazy, warning grin. "Bullshit," he whispered pleasantly. "You're a wire. I know because"—he told the first lie that came into his head—"I've got a nerve beeper that tingles when it gets near any kind of transmitter. When I sat down beside you, it went wild."

The flush faded from her cheeks. Drink, satiation, or natural stupidity left her unable to doubt him. She swore pitifully for a moment. Then she protested, "But if you know that, you know you can't ask me questions about him. It isn't safe. He can hear you. He's recording you right now."

Natural stupidity, Nick decided. Even a drunk should have recognized the potential consequences of warning him like that.

"Oh, it's safe, all right," he told her with some of his old insouciance; but softly, in case the white noise didn't cover him. "I killed your transmitter. That was the pain you felt in your neck. I poked you with a needle and cut the leads."

For an instant her eyes rolled: she was close to fainting. But then panic brought her back.

"Unfortunately," he continued, articulating her fear for her, "that puts you in a difficult position. The Bill is going to think you switched yourself off. He's going to think you're protecting some kind of plot against him. Or maybe you're plotting yourself. When he gets his hands on you"—Nick shook his head sadly—"I'm afraid he'll tear you apart. You can tell him the truth, but he'll assume you're lying."

"You shit," she moaned, not in anger, but in desperation, "you bastard. Why—?"

He shrugged without releasing his grip. "Well, I couldn't count on persuading you to trust me, could I? I needed a lever." He kissed her strained mouth as if he didn't know the difference between fear and arousal. "This way, you need me. I can protect you. I can take you with me, so he won't hurt you.

"But I am not going to do that," he promised slowly, "unless you tell me where he keeps his prisoners. *Soar* intercepted an ejection pod from my ship. What was in that pod is mine. Tell me where it is, and you'll never need to be afraid of him again."

She stared at him as if she were too stricken to see him; as if her fear of the Bill filled her sodden horizons.

Putting his mouth to her ear, Nick murmured, "Do you really think you'll be worse off on my ship—with me—than you are here?"

Suddenly urgent, she panted, "Take me there now." She may have remembered the bugeye in the room. "I don't know anything about your pod. But I know where he keeps prisoners. I can tell you how to find it. I'll tell you as soon as I'm safe."

Nick didn't shift his hold or his mouth. "You know better than that. If I were willing to let you change your mind"—if I were that stupid—"I wouldn't have killed your wire in the first place."

She still wasn't angry. She was a frightened drunk: her life on the cruise hadn't left room for anger. For a moment longer she remained indecisive, paralyzed. Then she surrendered.

Barely audible, she sighed, "All right."

Looking as pale as if Nick had drained the blood from her heart, she told him how to locate the section of Billingate which the Bill used for his lockup.

"Is that enough?" she finished weakly. "Will you protect me now? Will you take me with you? If you don't, he—" She stopped: the thought of what the Bill would do to her was too appalling to be put into words.

Nick laughed shortly. "No." Women this stupid—no, *anybody* this stupid, man or woman—deserved what happened to them. "I can always get better sex than this, and you haven't got anything else to offer." The Bill would know at a glance that she hadn't switched off her wire herself. "I'm afraid you'll just have to take the consequences of betraying him yourself."

Dropping her from his arms, he rolled off the bed and moved to the data terminal.

"Oh, please," she begged his back, "please don't do this to me, please, I'll do anything you want, you can have all of me, I'll never let another man touch me, I'll stop drinking, I can do better if I'm not drinking, *please*—"

Nick hardly heard her. The fact that she didn't get angry only increased his contempt. At the terminal, he coded a complex message; sent it. Then he climbed back into his shipsuit and boots.

For a minute he faced the woman's pleading. When she finally ran down and began to sob, he growled, "Face facts, bitch. You're shit out of luck. All this whining isn't going to help you. I never did like whiners."

Grinning as if this victory weren't as hollow as all the others, he left the room.

As soon as the door closed, he felt so exposed that he wanted to run.

He wasn't worried that the Bill would intercept—much less decipher—his message. On Angus' instructions, he'd sent it in two parts, each differently coded, to *Captain's Fancy*. One was for Liete Corregio, ordering her to relay the other to *Trumpet* ship to ship, bypassing Billingate communications. From his room, Milos could talk to *Trumpet*'s automatic systems; could receive Nick's message without exposing its source.

No, Nick's only immediate concern was that the Bill might react to the loss of the woman's transmission by sending guards to track her down. If he dispatched them promptly enough; if they caught up with Nick before he had a chance to blur his traces among the crowds of the cruise—

Even then Angus' plan might not fail. But Nick would be in trouble. At best he would lose his freedom of movement; his ability to put his own plans into effect.

And the longer he was kept away from *Captain's Fancy*, the more time Mikka's disloyalty, and Vector's, would have to fester.

No wonder his success with the woman felt hollow. By itself each one was trivial: all he gained from it was the opportunity to go on to the next problem.

Sorus was going to pay for this. If it was the last thing he did, he would exact blood for what she'd done to him.

He fought down the urge to run; but he allowed himself a brisk stride on his way to the lift.

As he rode the car downward, a tic of tension began again in his cheek, pulling like small claws at his scars. When he tried to rub it away, the skin Sorus had cut felt tight and dead; but the tic persisted.

After he left Ease-n-Sleaze, he began to see guards, but none of them took any notice of him. Apparently the Bill had decided to give him leeway; leave him free to condemn himself. That was another mistake which he meant to make the Bill regret.

Grimacing involuntarily, Nick returned to his ship.

·　　·　　·

He should have felt better when he'd cycled the locks and sealed himself back aboard *Captain's Fancy*. She was his ship, *his*. There was no safety anywhere if not here. Nevertheless his sense of exposure and incompleteness remained. The tic refused to relax its grip on his cheek. He sampled the air as if he could smell something evanescent and subtly threatening from the scrubbers; but after a moment he realized that the atmosphere felt wrong, not because of a scent, but because of a sound.

More precisely, the absence of a sound. The almost subliminal hum and throb of *Captain's Fancy*'s thrust drive was missing.

When he'd first left her to talk to the Bill, he'd ordered Mikka to keep the drive on standby. And he'd renewed his instructions before leaving to meet with Milos: he wanted the drive active, not as a means of escape—that was impossible—but as a way of reminding the Bill that *Captain's Fancy* could do the installation a lot of damage if Nick was pushed too far.

But Mikka had shut down the engines.

Swearing brutally, he started to run.

By the time he reached the nearest lift, however, he'd regained control of his urgency. He'd left Mikka and her discontents alone too often, too long: he had no way of knowing what she'd been saying about him, or to whom. His people were volatile at the best of times. Now, under pressure from the Amnion and Morn, as well as from Nick himself, they were unstable enough to go critical. Without much effort Mikka could set them at each other's throats.

Or at his.

That should have been inconceivable. He was Nick by God Succorso, *Nick Succorso*, and *nothing* should have been able to threaten him on his own ship, among his own crew. But he knew in his scars and his twitching cheek that his hold over *Captain's Fancy* was fraying. Like his invincibility, he'd lost it somewhere in the midst of Morn's treachery.

He couldn't afford to act panicked. If he did, Mikka and her supporters—Vector? Sib Mackern? Pup?—might think they could beat him.

So he lowered his respiration, calmed his pulse, stopped cursing. Again he tried to massage the tic away from his cheek. By the time the lift opened on the passage which led to the bridge, he'd convinced himself that no one would be able to see how close he was to the end of his resources.

When he crossed the aperture onto the bridge, he found it as crowded as the cruise.

He'd left Liete and her watch in charge of the ship: Mikka was supposed to be readying a team for a raid. But now at least two thirds of the crew were packed into the small space.

To some extent, the crowding was caused by the lack of internal spin. His people could only stand on that section of the floor which was oriented toward Thanatos Minor's mass. When *Captain's Fancy* first docked, the bridge stations had adjusted automatically to the rock's g by sliding along their tracks until they rested almost shoulder to shoulder in the bottom of the curve. Because of that, the crew didn't have much space.

The entire group watched him enter the bridge as if he were an emissary of the Amnion.

A quick scan told him that Liete and her watch were still in their g-seats. But Arkenhill had replaced Allum on scan; Karster had taken Simper's position. That made sense: Mikka had almost certainly included Simper and Allum on her team. Yet both men were here, as were Mikka herself, Sib—who should have been resting while Alba Parmute had data—Scorz, Pup, Lind, Carmel, and several others. Vector sat at the engineer's station as if he were on duty.

Scowling in an effort to conceal the way the tic pulled at his cheek, Nick drawled, "All right, boys and girls. The party's over. If you aren't working, get off the bridge."

No one moved. A mild smile curved Vector's mouth; his eyes were blue and cloudless, as steady as a clear sky. Carmel watched Nick with her customary bluntness. Pastille's nose wrinkled as if his own reek disgusted even him. Except for the cut of his features and the spread of his hips, Pup bore no particular resemblance to his sister, Mikka: his face expressed naïveté and chagrin instead of her glowering competence, her clenched old ire. Allum and Simper, dissimilar in every other way, both grinned with exactly the same unsatisfied hunger for violence. Sib was sweating as if he were feverish: moisture made his pale mustache look like dirt on his upper lip.

While he was gone, Nick had apparently lost them all.

He didn't hesitate. That part of him remained undamaged, at any rate. The worse the danger, the more quickly he moved.

"Liete"—he let his voice uncurl like a lash—"is this the way you run things when I'm not here?"

The command third faced him miserably. Strain darkened her small features until they were nearly black. But she didn't try to apologize. "We're all under a lot of pressure, Nick," she said almost firmly. "I figured it was better to let them get together and talk. Get what's eating at them out in the open. At least that way we know what we're up against."

Her tone made it clear that "we" meant Nick and Liete herself.

"Don't blame her," Mikka put in before Nick could respond. "It was my idea. I still outrank her—I told her it was all right."

Nick stifled an impulse to retort, You don't outrank her *now*. You've got five minutes to get off this ship. But he knew intuitively that a premature show of authority would make the crisis worse. Before he did anything else, he needed to take the temperature of this gathering, learn how hotly the infection against him burned.

"I'll talk to you in a minute," he told Mikka. "I'm not done with Liete."

Precisely because he still trusted Liete, he let his anger show in her direction. "I sent you a message. Did you get it?"

"I got it." Liete was tough: she didn't flinch or falter. Despite appearances, she was the same woman who'd flung herself at him to prevent him from killing Morn when Morn's finger was on the ship's self-destruct. And she was still on his side.

"Did you do what I told you?"

"Of course." She sounded slightly insulted.

Nick permitted himself an internal sigh of relief. That was one less worry. Feeling marginally stronger, he demanded, "So what the hell happened to the drive? I left it on standby."

Liete had more than one reason to look unhappy. Her eyes seemed to beg him to let her apologize as she reported, "Operations sent us an ultimatum. I guess they got tired of ordering us to shut down. They told me if I didn't comply they were going to undock us. Seal their locks, drop the lines, unclamp. You would have been cut off— you couldn't get back." As if she were holding her breath, she finished, "So I did what they said."

Nick needed time to absorb this; time he didn't have. Instead of sending guards when his wire stopped transmitting, the Bill had taken action in other ways. But Nick couldn't afford to consider the implications now. He had a more immediate crisis on his hands.

With an effort of will, he gave Liete a nod. "All right." Then he turned his attention back to Mikka.

Facing his second as if he dared her to challenge him, he said, "I told you to put together a team for a raid. Did that get done?"

Mikka's capacity to confront him was more pronounced than Liete's. "We're ready," she answered harshly. "I've got Allum for demolition. Sib knows as much about electronic jamming as any of the rest of us. Simper can supply firepower." She shrugged. "I'll handle the rest myself. We can go as soon as you give us a target—and tell us what you want brought back."

" 'Brought back'?" A laugh burst out of him before he could stifle it. Mikka was thinking about Morn: he was certain of that. But he had no intention of trying to recover Morn. She was simply bait; a way to get what he wanted from Milos and Angus—and maybe from Mikka herself. In any case, Morn was an Amnioni by now, as lost and damned as if she'd fallen into the gap. Mikka should have realized that the only thing Nick could possibly want "brought back" was Davies.

Now that wasn't necessary.

But he wasn't going to say so; not yet. "All right," he drawled again. Although he faced Mikka, he directed his voice to the rest of the bridge. "You're still following orders, so I'll assume this isn't an active mutiny. You've been talking about it, but you haven't actually decided to *do it* yet.

"Why don't you tell me why you're even willing to consider that kind of self-destruct?"

"You've got it wrong, Nick," Mikka began. "We haven't gone that far. We—"

"We want to know," Carmel put in, "what's going on."

At once Lind, Scorz, and several others nodded. Sib and Pup looked like they'd forgotten how to breathe.

"We've all been to Billingate," the scan first explained, "but you've never locked us in before. There's an Amnion warship in dock and another out there ready to blast us. Without a gap drive, we might as well abandon ship—but Operations won't let us at the shipyard. You gave Morn to the Amnion"—Carmel never hesitated to say what she was thinking—"which makes some of us wonder if we're next. You keep leaving the ship and coming back, but we don't know what you do when you go out. Liete says you're trying to find a way to save us. Some of us think you're making arrangements to sell us so you can save yourself.

"You know me, Nick," she concluded. "I like an explanation. I always feel better when I know what's going on."

Nick glared at her so that he wouldn't grin. The tic in his cheek wanted him to grin; it tugged at his scars to make him bare his teeth. If he gave in to it now, he might never recover.

Glowering darkly, he retorted, "Is that all? Why didn't you say so in the first place?" A yell rose up in him; he fought it down, forced himself to speak quietly. "What do you idiots use for brains? If I could save myself by selling you, I would be *tempted*. But most of you aren't worth betraying.

"*I'm the one who's in trouble here.* Haven't you figured that out yet? It's all on my head. The Amnion wouldn't accept any or all of you as a substitute for me—and the Bill sure as hell won't. If you want to come out of this whole, all you have to do is keep your fucking heads down and don't get in my way."

His people watched him as if he were about to go nova in front of them.

"You want to know what's going on?" he growled. "I'll tell you. *Morn Hyland is a fucking cop!* At first that wasn't a problem. We had her with Hashi Lebwohl's permission. But after we went to Enablement, DA and the whole goddamn UMCP stopped trusting us. Now they want her back. But since they don't trust us—since they assume we've already sold her *and* ourselves—they aren't just going to ask us nicely if we would please hand her over. They're coming after us for blood.

"That's why *Trumpet* is here. Lebwohl has always had a hand in Taverner's pocket. Most of the time when we worked with Milos he was working with DA at the same time. And Captain Thermo-pile may be the worst motherfucker in the galaxy, but he knows it when he's been strung up by the balls. He gave Morn a zone implant—and by now the cops know that. So DA has given him a chance for a reprieve by letting him come here with Milos to get her back.

"I found *that* out," he went on before the crew could react, "by leaving you here to talk about mutiny behind my back. And I gave

Morn to the Amnion so *we* wouldn't be Captain Thermo-pile's target—so he'd go after the Amnion instead of us.

"Hell," he snorted, "they're only two men. All they've got is a
gap scout. Do you think we don't need to be afraid of them? *I* don't
think that. They've got the whole UMCP behind them. They probably have an entire flotilla right at the edge of forbidden space, just
waiting for an excuse to come in and slag us. They could do that if
we still had Morn. They could tell the Amnion, they could *guarantee,* they wouldn't touch anything but us. This 'incursion' isn't an
act of war, just a rescue mission."

Now he had them. He could see it in Simper's open face and
Liete's dedication, in Scorz' astonishment and Pastille's unwilling respect and Sib's dismay. They may have wanted to reject his explanation, but they were seduced by it in spite of themselves. Only
Vector Shaheed managed to look unconvinced.

"I've already saved us from that," Nick pronounced. "I've saved
myself, as well as all of you. And now I've got a chance to solve the
rest of our problems. Milos and Captain Thermo-pile are going after
Morn. They can't exactly negotiate her release, so they're going to
try to cut her out of the Amnion sector. And when that happens—
when the fighting starts—we'll be ready.

"Unless"—he sneered—"we can't move because we're in the
middle of something suicidal, like a mutiny.

"While the UMCP and the Amnion are exchanging raids and
threats and maybe even fire, we'll do what we came here for in the
first place. We'll sell the Bill DA's immunity drug—or what looks
like DA's immunity drug. He'll buy—he won't have any choice. He'll
believe that's what the UMCP and the Amnion are really risking a
war over. And he won't have time to test it. This whole fucking
installation will be in chaos. So he'll do the only thing he can to
protect himself. He'll slap a new gap drive in here so fast it'll make
you dizzy because he'll want us gone before the Amnion or the cops
realize what we've done.

"I'm going to save us—unless you idiots manage to get us all
killed first." At last he allowed himself to shout, *"Have I made myself
clear?"*

It was a tissue of lies, of course; almost entirely fabricated. Nick
believed that Taverner and Thermopyle had come to rescue Morn:
he'd invented the rest as he went along. Nevertheless it worked.

Before any of the crew responded, he knew that he'd gained the time he needed for his other plans.

His people were accustomed to believing him. Some of them were no longer looking at him: they were too shaken by their own thoughts to notice his wild grin and the flaring spasm in his cheek as he lost control of himself for a moment. Others clung to him with their eyes full of nausea or hope.

"Jesus, Nick," Lind breathed as if he were in shock. Carmel nodded to herself like a woman whose uncertainties had been relieved. The tremor of Mackern's lower lip made him look like a kid being yelled at by his parents. Pup's gaze flashed back and forth between Mikka and Vector, hunting for reassurance.

Liete didn't smile or sigh; yet her eyes shone as if she'd been given a gift—as if Nick had proved once again that he was worth everything she ached to offer him.

Vector kept his opinion to himself. Of all the people on the bridge, only Mikka struggled against Nick's explanation, trying to find the lie.

"If what you say is true," she asked slowly, sounding uncharacteristically hesitant, "why do you want a raiding team?"

"I don't," Nick snapped, "not anymore." He couldn't help himself: he raised a hand to cover his tic. "It was just a precaution anyway, in case I was wrong about why *Trumpet* is here."

Mikka frowned doubtfully. She may not have believed him, but apparently she couldn't think of a way to challenge him further. "In that case," she said grimly to the scan third, "you'd better go stow your gear, Allum. I don't want to leave all those explosives and detonators lying around."

Nick had won: that was obvious. It showed in the way Allum looked at him and waited for his nod before moving to obey the command second.

Rubbing his cheek, Nick tried to feel that this victory wasn't hollow.

Liete would have reassured him, if he'd given her the chance. He could have tested his success by probing the people around him. But he didn't have time: the chronometer was running on Angus' deadline. And if his victory was hollow he needed to act on it now, before its illusions dissipated.

Mikka had started to turn away. He put his hand on her arm to stop her. Swallowing a sudden lump in his throat—the distress of his awareness that she was the best of his people, and if he didn't dispose of her soon she would eventually turn others against him—he said, "I've got a job for you." His tone was casual and false. "While we're waiting for Captain Thermo-pile to win his reprieve, we need to set up our own plans.

"I want you to take somebody"—he made a show of scanning the bridge for candidates—"take Sib and go to the cruise. Find out where *Soar*'s crew is. Their captain has some kind of special relationship with the Bill." Unnecessarily he pointed out, "Otherwise he wouldn't have used her ship to pick up our pod." Then he resumed, "Make sure you've put yourself where some of her people can hear you—and where the Bill's bugeyes can pick you up. It's important that what you say gets back to both of them.

"I want you to start a rumor about the immunity drug. Talk to Sib about it. Say you've heard *Soar*'s captain has a drug that protects her from the Amnion. That's why she's so close to the Bill—why Billingate gives her special status. Talk about it until you're sure her crew hears you. Then move on.

"That should prime the Bill. When I'm ready to deal with him, he'll be salivating for a chance to do business.

"Don't come back here right away. I don't want them to think I sent you out just to start a rumor. Stay on the cruise for a while. In fact, stay there until I come get you. I'll wait until Captain Thermo-pile makes his move. That way I can be sure the timing is right."

If this worked, Nick could launch his plans against Sorus Chatelaine and rid himself of Mikka and Sib with one stroke.

Mikka's eyes were dark with doubt. He knew her well: he could see her uncertainty in the lines of her frown and the angle of her hips. But while his illusions held the bridge she couldn't oppose him. If she gave him a reason to demote her now, she was finished.

"Do you think you can handle it?" he asked maliciously. "Or should I send somebody else?"

"Oh, I can handle it." Mikka's gaze couldn't hold his; it drifted almost involuntarily toward her brother. Pup was her only weakness—the only vulnerability she couldn't ignore. As long as Nick sent her out and kept him, she would have to do exactly what she was told. In a beaten tone, she added, "Just don't forget us. I don't want to be stranded here." As she turned toward the aperture, she sighed over her shoulder, "Come on, Sib. We might as well get started."

Mackern's face twisted as if he were trying to screw up the courage for an objection. But his bravery was like his mustache, indistinguishable most of the time. The sweat on his face might have been tears as he followed Mikka off the bridge.

And good riddance, Nick thought. He studied his crew again as if he needed more candidates: he didn't want to make the fact that he'd already decided whom to get rid of too obvious.

Like a man who'd just had a good idea, he turned toward Vector.

The engineer looked at him squarely. Vector should have been grateful that he was still alive; should have been eager to make restitution for his mistakes. But he didn't appear grateful—or alarmed. His smile was calm and impersonal, as if he'd used up his ability to worry about what happened to him.

"That was clever, Nick." He sounded as mild and unthreatening as he looked. "Now I'm the only one left."

Because his tic was hidden by his hand, Nick let himself grin. "You and Pup," he amended. "I've got a job for you, too."

Vector laughed softly. "Imagine my surprise."

Nick didn't care how much of the truth Vector guessed. As long as Mikka thought he had Pup, she was helpless. And without Mikka—without her support, her determination, her expertise—Vector was nothing.

"This is crucial," Nick said past his hand. "You're the engineers, so it's up to you. I want you to take all the repair specs for our gap drive and go find the shipyard foreman. Make sure he has the parts to get us fixed.

"He won't want to talk to you without orders from the Bill. It's up to you to convince him. Tell him it's official—I'm talking to the Bill right now, all we have to do is work out the details. Tell him he'll get his orders"—for an entirely different reason, Nick consulted a chronometer—"in about four hours, and when he does they're going to have emergency priority. If he doesn't fix us and fix us *fast*, the Bill is going to string his guts from one end of the cruise to the other.

"If he hasn't got the parts, make him scavenge them. Help him if you have to."

Holding Vector's eyes—daring him to refuse—Nick waited for a response.

Vector went on smiling like a man who'd already made the only decision that mattered and had nothing more to say.

"Why do I have to go?" Pup put in with a hint of Mikka's truculence. "I'm just a kid—I'm not going to *convince* anybody."

Simply to release tension, Lind laughed like a crackle of static.

"Shut up, Ciro," Vector instructed. *Ciro* was Pup's real name. Vector said it in the same tone he would have used to offer Pup coffee. "This isn't what it looks like. If I'm leaving the ship, I want you with me."

Pastille made a sour gibe, which the rest of the bridge ignored.

Spasms pulled at Nick's cheek like an erratic heartbeat; but he went on grinning because he couldn't stop.

By the time he left *Captain's Fancy* himself to meet his deadline with the Bill, the people he distrusted most were no longer aboard. Mikka and Vector—and maybe even Sib—might have caused Liete trouble; but she could certainly handle everybody else.

And he was sure she would follow all the orders he'd given her.

He was no more than a minute or two late when he reached the strongroom and demanded to see the Bill.

DAVIES

Davies Hyland paced his cell as if he were measuring a grave. Six steps on one side, five on the other. Room for a head and a cot; a few push-ups: nothing more. Walls and loneliness were his only companions.

At times he wanted to scream. At other times he wanted to sob. Occasionally he wondered why he was sane. Human beings weren't designed by nature or trained by society to withstand the stress of circumstances like his.

His mind and his body were fundamentally wrong for each other. He was male, yet he couldn't remember being anything except female.

And he was a prisoner: a pawn in a conflict over which he had no control—a conflict which he could scarcely comprehend because of the black hole in his head where crucial memories should have been. As far as he knew, no one wanted him alive except his mother, whose plight was probably even worse than his; and the Amnion, who intended to make him one of them.

Beyond question he should have collapsed into raving or withdrawn into autism.

But he didn't.

Despite all the force and harm arrayed against him, he was charged with survival; primed to fight for his life. Behind his isolation, underneath his fear, every pulse and shimmer of energy was ready for battle.

Because of the black hole, he couldn't guess that a strange and fertile interaction had taken place between his father's biochemistry and his mother's use of her zone implant. He couldn't imagine that he'd been conditioned in Morn's womb to meet his impenetrable dilemma.

Angus Thermopyle had given his son a genetic inheritance of toughness, stubbornness; a grim and bloody-minded refusal to be broken. And Morn Hyland had spent months driving herself to sexual, psychological, and physical extremes which she could never have endured without the artificial pressure and control of her zone implant. In a sense, her son had been inured to stress as a fetus. Every cell of his tiny body had grown accustomed to levels of stimulation which could have triggered cardiac arrest in anyone else. In effect, he was an adrenaline addict—and his addiction kept him whole when he should have snapped.

So he roamed the confines of his cell more like a caged predator than a sixteen-year-old boy. Ignoring the obvious monitors and the impersonal concrete, he paced from wall to wall, toning his strange muscles, training his mind to accept them. He already had his father's thick strength, if not his father's bulk: he tested it with push-ups, sit-ups, handstands, leaps. Exercises and skills his mother had learned in the Academy he repeated until his alien shipsuit was rough with sweat and his hands began to understand how the blocks and punches could be used. Then he continued pacing.

At the same time he chewed on his memories and his predicament with a doggedness which came from both his parents: trying to force himself to remember; trying to reason his way across the gaps in what he knew and understood.

He'd told the Bill that Morn and Nick Succorso were working together for the UMCP. Now the Bill was holding him here, rather than turning him over to Nick—or to the Amnion. Was there a connection? Did the Bill think the plot was aimed at him? Or was he afraid to take sides in Morn's—and Nick's—presumed connivance against the Amnion? If his only loyalty was to himself, in which direction would he move to protect himself from danger? To profit from the Amnion was one thing: to risk exposure to their mutagens was something else entirely.

Davies assumed that the Bill had no intention of letting himself be made Amnion. He wouldn't hesitate to sell his prisoner, but he would never sell himself. Therefore he had to keep his options open until he knew what was at stake. *Other people think you're valuable, and I'm going to know why before I make up my mind about you.* That was probably why Davies was still a prisoner—still safe.

So it was only a matter of time before the Bill came to question him again. Sooner or later, the Bill would ask him for more information about Nick and Morn.

He wanted it to be sooner. Right now. While his tolerance for stress still protected him.

His cell contained a head, but no san. He would have liked to get clean. Even a fresh—a human—shipsuit would have been nice. Apparently the Amnion didn't sweat; the shipsuit he'd been given on Enablement didn't absorb much moisture. By now it was damp enough to chafe when he exercised.

Grimly he continued working under the eye of the monitors as if he never needed rest.

Come on, you bastard. Question me again. Ask me to tell you what's going on.

Give me another chance.

Before it's too late.

Nevertheless he did need rest. Despite his conditioning, he was only human.

No doubt because the Bill wanted it that way and was willing to wait for the opportunity, Davies was asleep when his captor came to talk to him.

Lost in dreams of sweat and Amnion, he heard the Bill's mocking voice. "Ah, the innocent slumber of the young." At first he thought it came from an Amnioni. But it smelled like the souring musk of his own body. "What a joy to be able to sleep and dream so cleanly."

Adrenaline brought him back to consciousness like an electric charge. Nevertheless he was cautious. With deliberate slowness, he opened his eyes.

Tall and incongruously enthusiastic, as thin as a cadaver, the Bill stood by the door. This time his only guard was the woman Davies had seen with him before—the beautiful middle-aged woman with the rich voice and the stiff carriage. She had a stun-prod tucked into the front of her shipsuit as if she felt sure she wouldn't need it.

Davies knew nothing about her, not even her name. But she was the Bill's ally. On Thanatos Minor, in Amnion space, anyone who needed an ally was vulnerable.

Totally alert, and determined to conceal it, Davies fumbled for the edge of the cot to pull himself into a sitting position. Scrubbing at his face as if he were trying to wake himself up, he muttered, "What do you want?"

Sounding deceptively happy, the Bill said, "I want to ask you some questions. Be a good boy and answer them."

Davies made an effort to look bleary-eyed. "Are you going to let me out if I cooperate?"

The Bill chuckled shortly. "Of course not."

Groaning, Davies stretched back out on the cot. "Then why should I bother?"

"Because it's less painful," the Bill replied with a grin. "If I were feeling charitable—which I'm not—I could give you drugs to make you talk. Or I could install a zone implant in your ugly skull and take the matter out of your hands. Or"—he shrugged—"I could do BR surgery on you until you begged me to let you cooperate."

"Sure, sure." Davies dismissed the threat. "You could do all that. But I'm only merchandise here. You made that clear. If you want to make a profit on me, you won't damage the merchandise."

The Bill studied Davies for a moment. Then he remarked to his companion, "Snotty little bugger, isn't he. Maybe *you* should tell him why he wants to cooperate."

The woman didn't hesitate. "Davies, you're smart enough to understand the position you're in. Nobody ever accused your father of being stupid, and if your mother were, she wouldn't have made it through the Academy. Sure, you're nothing but merchandise. But you care who you're sold to. Believe me, you care."

"What has that got to do with answering questions?" Davies interrupted. "You're just trying to figure out how much you can get for me. You aren't going to let me choose who buys me."

"It's not that simple," the Bill snapped; but his tone wasn't angry. "Events are moving in too many different directions at once. There's too much at stake. I'm not worried about how much profit

I'll make on you. I'm worried about selling you to the wrong party. Until I know what's going on, I can't decide whether to deal with Captain Nick or the Amnion."

"If you're sold to Succorso," the woman put in, "you'll go back to your own people. The cops. That is, if you're telling the truth about Succorso and Morn Hyland working together. But if you go to the Amnion, you'll end up like Marc Vestabule."

Davies remembered Vestabule. Noradrenaline crackled through his synapses like static. The pressure in his veins was too intense to let him remain horizontal. Surging off the cot, he gained his feet and retreated to the wall opposite the door. With his back to the concrete, he faced the Bill.

Succorso intended to give him to the Amnion. Davies had told the Bill the lie that Nick and Morn were working together in a blind effort to weaken Nick's hand, strengthen Morn's. From that point of view, he had no reason to care who got him.

But if events were *moving in too many different directions at once*, the Bill might soon be forced to a choice, regardless of whether or not Davies cooperated with him. Then Davies' relative safety in his cell would end.

And he did care. The route which led to the Amnion through Succorso was less direct; maybe less inevitable. If he went by that route, he might live a little longer. He might even get the chance to do Succorso some harm along the way.

Swallowing at the tension in his throat, he asked, "What do you want to know?"

The Bill smiled. "That's better," he said approvingly. "I like cooperation.

"Why don't you start by telling me why Captain Nick went to Enablement?"

Davies' heart pounded in his chest. Alive with fear and energy, he said, "As far as I know, it was so Morn could have me. She was pregnant, but she knew she couldn't raise me from a baby. They went to Enablement so I could be force-grown."

"Why?" the Bill demanded shortly. "What's so special about you?"

"I don't know." Davies didn't have to feign the distress in his eyes. "They didn't tell me. Maybe it didn't have anything to do with me. I mean, anything personal. Maybe she just wanted to keep me, but she couldn't afford what it would cost to have a—a normal son. All that time and care." Maybe she needed an ally so desperately that she wanted her mind imprinted on me rather than letting me learn my own. Maybe she couldn't wait sixteen years for me to be old enough to help her. "Maybe what she and Nick are doing is so important that she couldn't afford to be hampered by a baby."

The Bill twisted his mouth to one side. "That is a provocative notion, young Davies. You're saying *she's* so special that she can demand and *get* that kind of risk from Captain Nick—so special that the cops would rather chance losing her to the Amnion than say no to her. Or else being pregnant is part of what made her special— perhaps because it gave her an excuse to go to Enablement. The cops had a reason of their own for sending her and Captain Nick there."

"I guess," Davies murmured thinly.

The Bill's eyes glittered. "You can do better than that."

"No, I can't," Davies protested. He didn't like sounding so frightened. It came to him too easily. "You must know something about how the Amnion force-grow babies. You know I got my mind from her. That's why you think I can answer your questions. But I have some kind of memory block. Maybe it's amnesia. Or maybe those memories were never transferred. I can remember her whole life until *Starmaster* was destroyed. After that it all stops. I only know what she told me.

"She didn't have time to tell me much. The Amnion came after us—we were running for our lives all the way here."

"So what you're saying"—the Bill ran his tongue around his thin lips—"is that our Captain Nick had the colossal and imponderable gall to cheat the Amnion on one of their own stations. Is that right?"

"It's more than that," the woman interposed. "He's saying Succorso had something so valuable to offer them that they were willing to trade force-growing for it. And then he cheated by not giving it to them."

"Is that right, Davies?" the Bill repeated. His eyes caught and reflected the light like polished steel.

Here Davies was on surer ground. The Bill couldn't possibly guess how the Amnion had been cheated, or by whom. Turning his fright to truculence, Davies answered, "I don't know. I wasn't born yet when they made their deal. All I know is, they came after us.

They tried to blast us a few days ago, but Succorso evaded them somehow."

"That could be true," the woman said to the Bill. "Maybe force-growing did leave holes in his memories. We don't know enough about it to be sure. But didn't you say Captain Succorso was about to make you some kind of offer when I walked in and"—she smiled sardonically—"distracted him?"

"I did," the Bill confirmed. "He was. He had a deal in mind. He may have been about to offer me the same thing he offered the Amnion.

"But you weren't the only distraction, you know," he added. "Without belittling your effect on Captain Nick, I must point out that there *were* other factors."

The woman shrugged. "I'm not so sure. You saw the look on his face—he nearly had an infarction. I think you'll be making a mistake if you believe *anything* is more important to him than getting even with me."

The Bill considered this as if Davies weren't present. "Then you don't credit the notion that he's working with Morn Hyland for the cops?"

"Of course I credit it," she returned calmly. "It's quite possible. He should have died after what I did to him. How did he survive? He must have gotten lucky—must have been rescued. That would have brought him to the attention of the cops. They could easily have recruited him them. Trained him, supplied him with a ship and cover, given him everything he needed. All I'm saying is that I think now his priorities have shifted.

"Which," she concluded, "only makes him more dangerous."

"On that we agree, at any rate," the Bill said in his boyish voice. "Captain Nick is dangerous. If he weren't, I wouldn't have to take his demand for young Davies seriously."

His long head swung back toward Davies. "But there is just one small flaw in your intriguing theory that Captain Nick and Morn Hyland are working together—that they went to Enablement in order to cheat the Amnion and draw them here, so that they could spring some kind of unexplained UMCP trap. For the moment we'll ignore the question of who the trap's intended victim is. Could it be aimed at me? Is it designed for the Amnion themselves? Or is it merely a means to recapture Captain Angus? Never mind.

"Young Davies, the flaw in your theory is this. A few hours after Captain Nick visited me and nearly made his mysterious offer so that he could buy you back, he personally delivered Morn Hyland to the Amnion sector. She hasn't been seen since their airlocks closed behind her.

"How do you account for this?"

Like Nick, but for very different reasons, Davies nearly had an infarction—

delivered

—and couldn't afford to show it. He ducked his head to shroud his eyes, but that wasn't enough; he had to conceal the way his muscles bunched and knotted to fling him at the Bill's long throat—

Morn Hyland

—had to conceal the passion and panic firing through him as if his nerves were high-tension cables; absolutely couldn't afford to rage or cry out—

to the Amnion.

If he unlocked his heart for an instant, he would go berserk. Sobbing Morn *Morn MORN* he would attack the Bill and the woman until they killed him.

As if his larynx were full of sand, he gritted out, "I'm not sure. I keep telling you she and I didn't have much time to talk. And I can't remember anything that happened to her between when *Starmaster* went down and I was born."

Nick had given his mother to the Amnion. To punish her for rescuing her son from Enablement. For using her zone implant to mislead him. And to compensate them for his failure to deliver Davies now. But *Davies* was the one the Amnion wanted, not Morn; he should have gone to them in her place. He had nothing to lose except the few days since he'd climbed out of the crèche: she would lose an entire life.

Yet it was already too late to save her. By now her genetic ruin was certainly begun and probably complete. Even if he threw himself on his knees and begged *begged* the Bill to trade him for her, even if he told the Bill everything he knew or could guess about her so that the Bill would understand how valuable she was, it was too late. Nothing could reach her now.

Nothing of her remained human except the part Davies himself carried—the part he used for a mind.

He couldn't hide the focused yellow glare in his eyes as he raised his head.

"But it fits, doesn't it?" he said in the same abraded tone. "It's consistent with the rest of what they're doing. It looks worse, but it's really no different than going to Enablement. They're putting her neck in the noose because they've got something to gain by it."

The woman watched him steadily, as if she were starting to respect him. Softly she pronounced, "That's absurd."

A wail Davies couldn't quash rose up in his chest. Clenching his fists until his arms shook, he shouted, *"Did she look like she was trying to resist? Did she fight him?"*

His loss seemed to recoil from the concrete and fall to the floor. Abruptly he regained control of himself. Almost quietly, he continued, "Or did they just talk to each other along the way?"

The Bill, too, watched Davies. Shadows muffled the brightness of his eyes. "They talked," he admitted. "I have it recorded. But their voices aren't clear. I don't know what they said."

"In that case"—because he was desperate, Davies let nothing wild or impossible stand in his way—"I think you should consider the possibility that she's protected somehow. Maybe Succorso didn't cheat the Amnion. Maybe he made a deal with them. The pursuit might be a ruse. Maybe the Amnion have already agreed not to touch her—and she has some good reason to trust them.

"Or maybe she's immune."

"Immune?" The Bill kept his tone low, but his voice cracked like a lash.

Inspired by urgency, Davies replied, "The Amnion design mutagens. Why can't"—he searched Morn's memories for names—"Intertech or some other UMC research facility design antimutagens?" Hurrying so that he wouldn't have time to falter, he finished, "Maybe that's what Nick was going to offer you. Before he was distracted."

The Bill stared at Davies with his mouth open. Past his teeth and tongue, his throat gaped like a hole—a gap into darkness. When he closed his jaws, he had to swallow twice before he could murmur, "This is chaff, starshine. He's inventing it."

Color flushed the woman's cheeks; her eyes were wide with surprise. "But it makes a certain kind of sense."

The Bill swung around to face her. "What *sense?*"

"Suppose it's true," she replied without taking her gaze off Davies. "Suppose Succorso and Hyland are working together. For the UMCP. Against us." Her voice was vibrant with implications. "And they have some type of antimutagen. That's the bait, the trade—that's what they offered the Amnion. They went to Enablement to make a deal. Using her pregnancy as an excuse. Then they came here. With a retinue of defensives.

"The whole point is to destroy us—destroy Billingate. The Amnion want the antimutagen. Succorso and Hyland offered to trade it for our destruction. But the Amnion can't just come here and blast us. That would ruin their credibility with every illegal in human space—it would set them back decades, maybe centuries. They need an excuse."

Davies stared back at her as if he were stunned by what he'd started; but he didn't interrupt.

"So the deal," she went on, "is that Succorso would offer you the antimutagen. Then, after he had time to get away, the Amnion would fry Thanatos Minor. And Succorso would spread the story that you were dealing antimutagens—that the Amnion destroyed Billingate to stifle the secret. A lie like that might pacify the rest of the illegals enough to keep them in business.

"What went wrong is that Succorso changed his mind when he saw me. Suddenly revenge was more important than the cops. So he didn't offer you the antimutagen. He's got other ideas now. But the Amnion aren't going to take that lying down. They sent Marc Vestabule to *Captain's Fancy* to demand Hyland as a hostage—a way to guarantee Succorso keeps his part of the deal. She's safe as long as he doesn't renege."

In silence Davies pleaded with the Bill to believe her. He wanted to believe her himself.

"It still doesn't—" the Bill protested.

"Listen!" the woman insisted. "It *does* make sense. Politicians think the same way you do. The fastest way to get rich is to work the middle between enemies. But that's less effective if the enemies are actually fighting. To really get rich you need the conflict—and you need peace. You need the kind of peace that preserves the conflict. What Succorso and Hyland are doing gives both sides something they want. The cops get rid of us—the Amnion get the antimutagen. Which makes a war less likely in the short term, and makes both sides stronger over the long haul. If you were in Holt Fasner's position, you might do the same thing."

The Bill couldn't contain himself. Like an angry child, he shouted, "But we don't have any reason to think it's true! Just because a scared brat with an imprinted mind *says* it doesn't make it a fact! For all *we* know, he's inventing the whole thing. He's probably just trying to frighten us because he figures the more frightened we are, the longer we'll hold him, and while we hold him he's *safe!*"

"Then tell me something." Now the woman faced the Bill. Neither of them paid any attention to Davies. Holding her companion's gaze hard, she asked, "What's Succorso doing with Thermopyle and Taverner? Plotting something, obviously—but what? Why? Com-Mine only caught Thermopyle because Succorso set him up. What have they got to talk about?"

"No." The Bill shook his long head unsteadily. "You tell me."

Her gaze sharpened. "Didn't you hear them? What happened to all your bugeyes—your wires? What good are they, if they can't pick it up when something important happens?"

The Bill shrugged as if he were slightly embarrassed. "They were in a public bar. Not by coincidence, I'm sure. There was a lot of background noise. And Captain Angus took offense at the nearest wire. He chased her away. Also not by chance, I'm sure—although I have no idea how he identified her—because Captain Nick later singled her out for one of his notorious seductions, and by that time he knew enough about her to disable her transmitter.

"Then the bugeyes in the bar developed a fault. So far *that* looks like a coincidence."

If the woman was surprised, she didn't show it. "What did he want her for?"

The twisting of the Bill's mouth suggested distaste. "Sex, of course. And he wanted to scare her, apparently so she would tell him where his merchandise is being held. As far as I can discover, that was his only reason for disabling her transmitter—to scare her. Otherwise he wouldn't have left her alive to tell me what happened."

"All right." The woman nodded sharply. "Then it *does* fit.

"Seducing and disabling your wire is just a distraction. He did

it to confuse you. I think what he really wants Thermopyle and Taverner for is to help him against me.

"Right now, his position is too weak. The antimutagen is his
only lever. He's hanging on to it—risking his deal with the Amnion—because it's all he has. But if he can persuade or possibly trick
Thermopyle into helping him, he'll have an ally. Then he can go
ahead with his original plans and still have a chance at revenge."

The Bill met her gaze for a moment longer.

Slowly they turned together to face Davies again.

"Well?" the Bill asked, nearly whispering. "You started this.
What do you make of the fact that Captain Nick has been seen
drinking on the cruise with your father?"

Davies could hardly speak. Nick Succorso had turned his mother
over to the Amnion for reasons which had nothing to do with antimutagens. The loss of her made him feel orphaned, maimed. And
the reaction to his lie was dramatic—so dramatic that it stunned
him. The first couple of times the Bill and his companion mentioned
Angus Thermopyle's name, it made no impression on him. As far as
he was concerned, his father was unreal: an abstract concept; a man
who may never have existed.

But as they repeated Angus' name and turned toward him, he
began to hear what they'd said. Captain Angus Thermopyle was here.
With a man called Taverner.

Apparently out of nowhere, Davies' father arrived just when his
mother was lost.

His heart jumped as if the two events were connected.

Angus was fatal, of course. Morn had implied as much. And
Nick had called him *a pirate and a butcher and a petty thief.* He was
the kind of man Morn—and Davies with her—had dedicated her life
against.

But he was still Davies' father.

His arrival now meant something.

Davies couldn't afford to ignore the Bill's demand—or betray
what he thought and felt. With an effort, he crushed down his distress. Almost meeting the Bill's gaze, he breathed, "I didn't know
my father was here. I thought he was in lockup on Com-Mine. I
wasn't sure he was still alive."

"That," the Bill rasped, "doesn't answer my question."

"Yes, it does." Davies let himself sound truculent. "I've never met my father. I can't remember him. How should I know what he and Captain Succorso are doing together?" But he didn't stop there. The Bill's companion had given him the hint he needed. More bitterly by the moment, he continued, "Maybe it's what she said. Maybe Succorso is using him to plant the story that you've got an antimutagen for sale."

Like a kid experimenting with profanity, the Bill retorted loudly, "Damnation! Damn both of you! You're making me dizzy. How many conspiracies and plots do you think you can find in situations you know nothing about? You"—he jerked his long head at his companion—"are pinning everything on what you hear from a scared, force-grown child who probably isn't even sane. And *you*"—he poked a finger at Davies—"admit you've got holes in your head where you should have facts. You want me to believe you can't remember anything Morn Hyland knew or saw between *Starmaster*'s destruction and your own birth a few days ago, and at the same time you want me to take you seriously while you *speculate* about things you can't remember.

"This isn't an interrogation. It's a *farce*."

Davies blinked as if he were on the verge of tears. The woman didn't reply.

In a whirl of joints and limbs, the Bill turned back to her. "I'm leaving this with you," he said through his teeth. "We agree Captain Nick is dangerous. And we agree he wants to get even with you. So you're at risk here at least as much as I am. It's your job to learn the truth.

"Torture him"—the Bill indicated Davies—"if you want to. The Amnion will accept damaged merchandise, even if Captain Nick won't. As long as he's human, they won't worry about the details. Or capture a few people from *Captain's Fancy* and torture *them*. I don't care how you do it. Just find out the truth.

"Come talk to me when you've got something we can count on."

Without waiting for an answer, the Bill left the cell.

The woman fixed her attention on Davies again. Her hand rested lightly on the handle of her stun-prod.

He glowered back at her, as belligerent as his father.

As she regarded him gravely she said in a contralto murmur,

"You may be wondering why Captain Succorso wants to 'get even' with me. It's simple, really. I gave him those scars. But when I see you glaring like that, I can't help thinking that if he'd ever looked at me the same way I wouldn't have cut him. I would have killed him where he stood.

"I'll be back as soon as I figure out how to get the truth out of you."

She left Davies alone.

The door closed behind her. He heard it lock.

The monitors watched him as if his interrogation were still going on.

Sick at heart, and determined to reveal nothing, he stretched out on the cot, covered his eyes, and pretended to rest.

ANCILLARY
DOCUMENTATION

GOVERNING COUNCIL
FOR EARTH AND SPACE

In some ways, the Governing Council for Earth and Space was a haphazard organization. No one designed it: it simply grew over time. And as it grew it suffered mutations and grafts, like a burdock which a group of biogeneticists had arbitrarily selected for an experiment in whether weeds could be made to bear apples.

Like most haphazard organizations, the GCES was protective of its position. In reaction to the fact that there was nothing organic or inevitable about its form—or indeed about its actual existence— the Council took itself extremely seriously. Its members debated policy, passed legislation, imposed charters, and reviewed jurisprudence as if they had the authority of their entire species behind them; as if the survival and integrity of humankind were in their care.

As a bureaucratic entity, the GCES was blind to the realities of both history and politics.

The reality of history was that the Council came into being as a reaction to rather than as a control for events. It was a fact long since forgotten by most GCES Members that their political body began as a minor subdivision of another governmental entity.

During the period of Earth's history in which commercial enterprises and quasi-commercial conglomerates began to put research facilities and industrial platforms into space, most of the planet's sovereign nations slowly came to recognize the need for an agency to coordinate launches, trajectories, and orbits—to ensure, for example, that corporations such as SMI and SpaceLab Inc. didn't build stations which would interfere with each other's activities, or which might—at worst—collide someday. The original Agency was constituted as nothing more than a clearinghouse for launch-and-orbit-related information; as a means for avoiding disasters.

In a short time, however, it naturally took on a corollary function: it became a mechanism for processing disputes. Its advisory papers and proposed protocols accreted until they had the force of law. This development was considered beneficial because it permitted conflicts to be resolved without the unwieldy expedient of involving Earth's vast array of sovereign governments. From that small seed, the eventual weed sprouted.

As the competition for Earth's last great resource—space—grew more and more desperate, the Agency came to be seen as increasingly vital: sometimes as a means to gain advantage; more commonly as a means to prevent the opposition from gaining advantage. There began what might be called the hybridizing process. Sovereign nations and commercial enterprises alike began to insist on "representation": they wished to have their own people assigned to the Agency so that their interests would be protected.

This was predictable, even though it was not foreseen when the original entity was created. Because space was a political as well as physical vacuum, chaos threatened to render the Agency useless as nations and corporations clamored to seat their representatives.

The danger was averted, however, when the Agency itself was conceded the right to choose whom it would represent, which interests and organizations were empowered to supply it with Members. An eminently sensible solution in many ways, this development nevertheless had the effect of making the Agency much more powerful—as well as considerably larger—than the bureaucracy of which it was technically a subdivision. Soon, therefore, the Agency—now called the Governing Council for Space—succeeded at rechartering itself as a separate, independent organism.

Still the pattern of responding to events rather than anticipating them held sway. Space was Earth's only effective future. Even before the development of the gap drive, with its concomitant influx of resources and opportunities, and certainly before contact with the Amnion, with its strange admixture of wealth and peril, Earth had

no hope which did not derive from space. And the GCS was responsible for space. Therefore the GCS was almost responsible for Earth.

Predictably—and yet almost accidentally—the Council found itself
unable to meet its responsibilities unless it expanded its function to
include overseeing the conduct of its constituent nations and corporations on Earth as well as in space.

By this time, Earth was in no position to protest the shift of
authority from individual sovereign nations to the Council. Ration-
alizing their dependency on space, Earth's governments elected to
view the shift of authority as a change in semantics, not in substance. Where did the Council's Members come from? From Earth,
of course; perhaps by way of one station or another, but always from
Earth. Therefore Earth's nations had suffered no fundamental loss of
primacy. Their leaders were simply called Members rather than pres-
idents or dictators; the only real difference was that they exercised
their powers in a wider arena.

As a practical matter, however, relatively few of Earth's nations
and corporations were literally represented on the Council. Their
numbers would have been too large to be effective. For that reason,
the Council spawned its own subdivisions, on Earth as well as in
space. Earth's nations were somewhat artificially combined to form
six distinct bodies: the United Western Bloc, the Eastern Union,
the Pacific Rim Conglomerate, the Combined Asian Islands and
Peninsulas, Continental Africa, and one quaintly named Old Europe. In contrast, each space station outside Earth's solar system represented itself: Valdor Industrial, Sagittarius Unlimited, Com-Mine,
Terminus, Betelgeuse Primary, SpaceLab Annexe, New Outreach,
Aleph Green, and Orion's Reach. However, in recognition of Earth's
vastly greater population, each of the planet's six units was autho-
rized to supply the Council with two members; the stations seated
only one apiece.

By accretion rather than by public choice or policy, the Council
became the Governing Council for Earth and Space.

The reality of politics was that the Council had been invested
with authority solely and squarely on the assumption that this authority would never be effective. The corporate leaders who precipi-
tated the inception and encouraged the growth of the Council did
so to secure their own enterprises, not to impose restrictions on
themselves.

Consider the position of a man like Holt Fasner, in the days when SMI was young, and Earth was dying of its complex self-strangulation. Unless he were gifted with prescience, he could hardly have forecast the development of the gap drive—or the discovery of the Amnion. On the other hand, he could easily have grasped that Earth represented the single biggest obstacle to his own future, the single biggest threat to his company's growth.

Driven by planetary hungers, Earth would suck dry any development or discovery which occurred on a scale smaller than interstellar travel or alien species. And the prejudices and constraints of Earth-bound thinking—genophobia, for instance—would work to block any researcher, or any corporation, from developments or discoveries large enough to outsize Earth's hungers.

From the first, men like Holt Fasner understood the need to separate space from Earth's control.

This goal they achieved by mutating and grafting the original Agency until it became the GCES. At every stage in the process, they supplied the ideas—as well as the votes—which enabled the Council to take charge of Earth, rather than allowing Earth to retain authority over space.

On the other hand, men like Holt Fasner had no intention of simply replacing one set of governmental obstacles with another. The power which had been gradually accreted to the GCES would become a threat rather than a benefit if it were allowed to exercise itself unchecked. Precisely because the Council solved so many problems for men like Holt Fasner, it was dangerous to them.

Therefore the number of members had to be kept small, manageable. And it was necessary to own a significant proportion of the "votes": it was necessary to guarantee that enough members would speak for the men they truly represented, rather than for the people who elected them. In some cases, this necessity was easily satisfied. For example, since Com-Mine Station belonged to the United Mining Companies, the member for Com-Mine Station naturally defended the UMC's interests. In other cases, pressure was required. And in still other cases, the "votes" had to be frankly purchased.

Regardless of how the "votes" were obtained, however, the purpose of obtaining them remained the same: to ensure that the real power on Earth and in space belonged not to the GCES, but to men like Holt Fasner.

The seriousness with which the Council performed its functions was in direct proportion to its refusal to recognize the realities of its own position.

Therein lay Holt Fasner's greatest strength—and perhaps his only weakness.

MIN

No more than two hours after Warden Dios' video conference with the Governing Council for Earth and Space, Min Donner, sometimes called his "executioner," rode a UMCP shuttle down from UMCPHQ to Earth; to Suka Bator, an island in the Combined Asian Islands and Peninsulas archipelago, where the GCES had built the sprawling complex from which it presumed to defend and govern the human species.

The shuttle's logs and manifests made no mention that the UMCP Enforcement Division director was aboard. She was recorded as one of a platoon of data clerks and legal advisers sent by Dios to supply substantiation—or obfuscation—for the things he'd revealed during the conference. No one announced her arrival; no one met her. Apparently UMCP officers stationed on the island as support for GCES Security failed to recognize her: certainly they failed to react when they saw her. Instead she was waved through the checkpoints and past the guards as casually as the rest of the platoon.

There was no particular cause for caution. The shuttle had been tracked continuously from the moment it left UMCPHQ to the instant of its touchdown on Suka Bator. The GCES worried about many things, but treachery that arrived by shuttle from UMCPHQ was not among them. Attacks on the Council's authority, like threats to the Council's safety, came not from the police, but from disenfranchised political groups on Earth—libertarians who opposed both UMC and UMCP hegemony; genophobes who opposed all dealing with the Amnion; pacificists who opposed the "militarization" of human space; "native Earthers" who opposed the planet's dependence on space. Any number of those groups were capable of terrorism in the name of their beliefs. On the other hand, the UMCP worked hard to help GCES Security keep violence away from the island.

Apart from her air of command and the coiled readiness of her movements, none of the guards or functionaries had any reason to look twice at Min Donner.

She was known here, of course—any one of the Members, and most of their staffs, would have identified her on sight. But she didn't give them the chance. From the entrance to the Members' Offices wing of the complex, she disappeared into a stairwell which led to a fire exit and was therefore virtually never used. Her codes let her through doors which should have set off alarms when they were opened.

If possible, she wanted to get on and off the island in complete secrecy.

No matter how profoundly she'd been shaken by Warden Dios' recent revelations, she was loyal to him. The same dedication which kept ED almost fanatically clean, free of the taints and ambiguities which clung to Data Acquisition like a miasma, also ensured that she would carry out her director's personal instructions as purely as she could. The old commandment which had once guided the police in human society—"to serve and protect"—wasn't written anywhere on her certificates of commission. It didn't need to be: it was written in her blood.

She wasn't impervious to doubt, not by any means—especially not now, when the very nature of the organization to which she'd committed herself was being called into question. But she understood with the clarity of pure conviction that doubt and action were fundamentally irrelevant to each other.

She wasn't responsible for Dios' integrity, or for the UMCP's. She was responsible for ED's and her own. And that was a function of action: she had integrity to the extent that she gave herself wholly and simply to the goals and duties of her position. Doubt was something she set aside in the name of her service to Warden Dios, to Enforcement Division, to the United Mining Companies Police, and to humankind.

This was essential to her. Without it she would have been paralyzed. Doubt by its very nature was omnivorous: it consumed every-thing. Recent events provided a good example. In his conference with the GCES, Warden Dios had given her reason to doubt his honesty. But other things he said and did—for example, the instruc-tions which brought her to Earth now—cast doubt on the image of himself he'd presented to the Council. Whom should she believe, the private man who had sent her here, or the public figure who had effectively accused himself of selling human beings for tactical gain; of selling Morn Hyland, whose plight made Min Donner's loyal and uncompromising heart ache like a personal wound?

If she let doubt choose her actions for her, she would be useless. She needed another standard by which to make decisions.

For her that standard was *service*.

Now she served by making her way with as much stealth as a terrorist up through the Members' Offices wing to the floor occupied by the United Western Bloc. If she had any say in the matter, no one except the man she'd come to see would ever know that she'd been here.

That man was Captain Sixten Vertigus, Senior Member for the UWB. She'd arranged this meeting with him several hours ago; well before Dios' video conference. If what he'd heard then hadn't made him change his mind, he would be waiting for her.

Alone, if he could manage it.

A small sensor she cupped in her palm informed her that the corridor on the other side of the door was empty. That wasn't un-usual, since the corridor only existed to reach the fire exit. The real test of her planning—and of Captain Vertigus' cooperation—would occur when she opened the door, walked down the corridor, and turned the corner. Her route so far avoided UWB reception, which was an open hive of secretaries, flunkies, and newsdogs. But no hall in the GCES complex was ever entirely empty. After Min turned that corner, she would have to pass the Senior Member's squadron of personal and legal aides in order to reach his office.

Captain Vertigus had agreed to clear the area so that Min Don-ner could visit him unseen.

Well, did he do it, or didn't he? She couldn't hear voices; but her sensor's indications weren't encouraging. There was at least one person in range—

Secrecy was crucial here. What Warden hoped to accomplish

would become impossible if any rumor linking her with Captain Vertigus reached the wrong ears. Personal aides were sometimes trustworthy: legal aides, never. And a stray newsdog would be a disaster.

As silent as oil, she moved along the wall and peered past the corner.

Hashi had promised that she could rely on this small sensor. For once she wasn't irritated by the discovery that he was right. One person, ten meters down the hall—

All the desks and cubicles were deserted. Alone, Sixten Vertigus sat on the edge of a desk, obviously waiting for her.

As soon as he spotted her, he motioned for her to join him and retreated into his office.

During the heartbeat or two while he crossed to his door, she noticed the frailty of his movements. He was a very old man; and unlike other personages Min could have named, he hadn't availed himself of rejuvenation techniques which would have muffled the entropy gnawing at his genetic code. That, in fact, was one reason why he was regularly, if otherwise ineffectively, reelected: the UWB's population included a higher percentage of native Earthers than any Council constituent except Old Europe; and native Earthers considered it a virtue that Captain Vertigus refused to prolong his life artificially.

As the first human being ever to lay eyes on an Amnioni, he was a legendary figure. On that occasion, he had demonstrated his willingness to die for his beliefs. In addition his unfailing support of the UMCP, combined with his unswerving opposition to the UMC, gave him an aura of moral authority. He was the "esteemed elder statesman" of the GCES. As Hashi Lebwohl had once said, with his usual double-edged humor, "If Captain Vertigus didn't exist, it would have been necessary to invent him."

Still, for a man his age, he was quick enough to gain the relative seclusion of his office. By the time Min caught up with him and closed the door, he was seated at his desk as if he'd been there all along.

While she took a few compact security devices out of her pocket and attached them to the doors, the intercom, his data terminal, and the video pickup, he watched her with his hands folded on the crystallized Formica desktop. The skin of his hands was so translucent that she seemed to see the bones and veins through it; his eyes were so pale that he looked blind.

When she'd finished her precautions, he asked in a high, thin quaver, "Can we talk now?"

Min nodded. "I think so. As far as the rest of the complex is concerned, this room has ceased to exist." She grinned bleakly. "If we killed each other, nobody would know about it until someone opened the door to check on you."

Captain Vertigus leaned back in his chair; with one unsteady hand, he rubbed a wisp of hair off his forehead. "In that case, Director Donner"—if she listened only to his voice, not to what he said, he sounded like an invalid—"I hope you're not disappointed to find that I'm practically dead already. Hardly worth killing."

Apparently he'd misunderstood her. "I'm not—" she began.

He dismissed her interjection. "In fact," he continued, "I'm hardly worth all this secrecy. As you saw, I was able to send my people away"—he fumbled a shrug—"on various pretexts. That shouldn't have been possible. Not for an important man like the Senior Member for the United Western Bloc, who might reasonably be expected to start raving or froth at the mouth in the absence of his retinue. But I'm sad to say that it was easy.

"I'm a relic here. My time has passed. If you let yourself be seen coming or going, Director Donner, you would give me more status than I've had for many a year."

Min studied his features for a moment. If he already felt this defeated, this useless, he would be difficult to persuade. Suddenly she wondered whether she was the right person for this job. Presumably she'd been chosen because Warden Dios trusted her. Also because she had a reputation for single-minded devotion to her duties: the perception that she was immune to purely political agendas and manipulations enhanced her credibility. But precisely because she *was* single-minded in her devotion, she couldn't be sure of her position here. Whose game was she playing? Whose game was Warden playing?

With her ingrained lithe readiness, she took a seat across the desk from the Senior Member. To mask her uncertainty, as well as to learn what she was up against, she asked, "How did that happen, Captain Vertigus? How did you become a relic?"

"I made a political mistake," he replied frankly. He may have wanted to be sure she had no illusions about him. "One morning I sat here—at this very desk—and realized that I was old.

"For some reason, this struck me as grievous, because it meant that my work would not continue. You probably know what I considered my work to be. One quality I've observed in Warden Dios' people is that they are exceptionally well prepared. You wouldn't have come here—or wouldn't have been sent—if you didn't know what my work, my 'mission,' was on the Council."

"Nobody sent me," she put in abruptly. "This is my idea." She was always abrupt when she lied. Honesty was a compulsion which she suppressed with difficulty.

Captain Vertigus put her assertion aside with another shrug and resumed his explanation.

"In simple terms, Director Donner, I considered it my duty to oppose Holt Fasner in all his ambitions. And I considered it my work to investigate him—to study what he did and how he did it until I could learn the facts which might persuade other people to oppose him with me.

"I won't bore you with a long account of my reasons. My only personal contacts with him occurred when he briefed me before *Deep Star* first went into what is now forbidden space, and when he debriefed me afterward. However, they were enough to set me on the road I've followed for the rest of my life."

Caught by curiosity, Min tried another interruption. "What did he say to you?" She was inherently interested in anything anyone might tell her about the Dragon.

Captain Vertigus squinted at her as if he had trouble focusing his eyes. "Nothing definitive, I'm afraid. Nothing objective enough to sway other people. He's too cunning for that. All I can tell you is this. He left me with the settled impression that in his own mind nothing larger than himself exists. In his own person he considers himself bigger than the United Mining Companies, bigger than the Governing Council for Earth and Space, perhaps bigger than all humankind.

"This proves nothing, I know. Nevertheless I found it profoundly disturbing.

"But I can't expect other people to understand that, Director Donner. I can't expect other people to act on it. So I don't usually talk about it. Instead I look for objective evidence to back up my fears."

Min nodded. She felt that she understood perfectly.

"Isn't Maxim Igensard doing the same job?" she asked.

"Perhaps." The Senior Member considered the question. "He's more recent, of course. You might say he's after my time. And I"—he pursed his mouth—"distrust the quality of his ambitions. Like my own Junior Member, Sigurd Carsin, he appears to have set himself against Warden Dios and the UMCP rather than Holt Fasner and the UMC. I consider that suicidal. In my darker moments, I consider it culpable."

Then he shook his head. "But it doesn't matter what I think of him. He came along long after I made my mistake.

"On the day when I realized that I was old, I decided to entrust my investigations to my subordinates. Let younger and more energetic men and women do the work, while I used my position and what I hope I can call my credibility to act on what they learned.

"You probably know the rest. My subordinates turned out to be in Holt Fasner's pay—directly or indirectly, it doesn't matter which. My investigations disappeared, never to be heard of again. It's a sad story, in its way"—the sorrow he conveyed was complex—"but its sadness has to do with the foolishness of old men. I'm afraid you're wasting your time here."

"I doubt that." Min found herself on stronger ground than she'd expected. He may have been trying to warn her against relying on him; in effect, however, he'd identified himself as a kindred spirit. "I think I've made an unusually good choice."

He adjusted the posture of his fragile bones. Trembling slightly, he raised his hands to rub his forehead and cheeks as if to soften the strain of focusing his gaze. "In that case"—his voice was thin with age, but it seemed to carry an odd echo of hope—"maybe you should tell me why you're here."

Min Donner wasn't a woman who hesitated. "It's a sensitive matter," she began, "as I told you when we spoke. Too sensitive to be discussed without elaborate precautions." She gestured at her security devices. "Even the downlink isn't safe enough."

In fact, she'd first placed her call to the Senior Member in Godsen's name rather than her own. The PR director always had public, unquestionable reasons to talk to GCES members: she didn't. She hadn't revealed herself until Captain Vertigus had assured her that her call was private.

"The problem is simple," she explained. "I want you to do something for me. But if anyone ever realizes that I had a hand in it—that you're doing it for me—you won't succeed."

The Senior Member waited without lowering his hands or shifting his gaze.

"I want you to introduce a piece of legislation for me. And I want you to do it fast—say tomorrow morning. In case I haven't already made this clear, I want you to do it entirely in your own name. Keep me out of it. Take the fact that we talked about this to your grave with you. Otherwise it won't pass."

As an afterthought, she added, "And don't trust it to any of your aides."

"Director Donner," Captain Vertigus retorted with a hint of asperity, "I'm not stupid. I learn from my own mistakes almost routinely. And"—he shifted forward to face her more closely—"I make my own decisions. Just because I'm old and defeated and would like to end my life—shall we say, on a more positive note?—doesn't mean I'm willing to be your puppet. If you want me to do something for you, you'll have to *convince* me."

Min permitted herself an iron smile. "I know that, Captain Vertigus. I wouldn't be here otherwise."

He snorted his disbelief. Nevertheless he sounded mollified as he muttered, "Flattery will get you nowhere." Leaning back again, he demanded, "Well, what *is* it? What do you want me to put my name on?"

Frowning because she was suddenly reluctant to carry out her commission, she reached inside the data clerk's plain worksuit she wore and pulled out a sheaf of hardcopy. The longer she talked to Captain Vertigus, the more she liked him—and the less she wanted to get him into trouble. However, her loyalty to Warden Dios and the UMCP compelled her.

Grimly she tossed the hardcopy onto the desk.

"I want you to introduce a Bill of Severance which will take the police away from the United Mining Companies. Decharter the UMCP completely. Reconstitute it as an arm of the Governing Council for Earth and Space."

Then she paused to wait for the captain's reaction.

He sat still, as if he'd stopped breathing.

She faced him squarely. Because of the paleness of his eyes, she couldn't be sure that he was able to see her.

After a long moment he let out an unsteady sigh. "Director Donner, you think big."

That didn't require a response, so Min didn't offer one.

He glanced down at the hardcopy she'd dropped on his desk; touched the pages gingerly with his fingertips, as if their edges might be sharp enough to cut. "And you want this done by when? Tomorrow morning?"

"If you can."

"Oh, naturally. Of course. A bill of this magnitude, with these repercussions— Is there anything else I can do for you in my spare time? Write a novel? Assassinate the Amnion trade legation? Really, Director Donner, I think I need a breathing mask. There isn't room in this office for your ideas and air at the same time."

"If you'll take a look," Min retorted with her own asperity, "you'll see that I've already done most of the work. Of course, I've had to make a number of assumptions which you might not consider appropriate—concerning how the new GCESP should be funded, for example, or how authority should be transferred. But you can change anything you want when you put what I've written into the proper form. I'm not particular about the details. Only the central issue matters to me."

Captain Vertigus made no pretense of examining her work. "I'll take your word for it," he murmured. "I said myself that Dios' people are well prepared. Now that I think about it, I'm sure most of your assumptions are acceptable. I can probably have a bill prepared—I mean, prepare it myself—to put in front of the Council tomorrow.

"But that's not the important question, is it?" His tone sharpened. "In any case, neither of us can afford the time to haggle over details. Let's go straight for the heart, shall we? Tell me *why*.

"Why this?" He flicked the hardcopy. "Why now? And why me?"

Min restrained an impulse to stand up, pace the floor. "Because it needs to be done," she replied. "Because the timing is good. And because the Dragon doesn't own you."

The captain fixed her with a pale glare. "Don't be cryptic. I need real answers."

She shrugged. "All right. But I don't want to talk about that video conference. You were there—you saw everything, heard everything. Unfortunately Morn Hyland is one of *my* people. When I think about how she's been used, I get too angry. And I don't want to give the impression that I'm here simply because I'm angry. What you saw and heard didn't determine my position. I made my decision earlier—I called you before the conference took place. So let me make my point another way.

"You may recall hearing a rumor several years ago that Intertech was on the verge of developing an immunity drug for Amnion mutagens. Then later the research failed and was abandoned."

Captain Vertigus didn't nod; didn't react.

"Well, the rumor was true. Intertech *did* come close, very close. But the research didn't fail. It wasn't abandoned. It was quashed, suppressed."

Slowly his jaw dropped.

"I was there," she rasped, "when the UMCP directors debated the subject. Hashi Lebwohl presented a report on the state of the research. Then Godsen Frik," may he rot in hell, "argued that the research should be stopped. On the grounds that it represented a threat to the UMCP itself. First, he said, an immunity drug would force the Amnion to abandon peaceful imperialism and risk actual warfare." A sneer tightened around her nose. "Second, he said, an immunity drug would undermine the 'necessity,' the 'moral authority,' of the UMCP—which would in turn undermine funding and support—which would in turn leave the UMCP less able to face the threat of a real war."

We've been waiting a long time for this, Frik had said. *We can wait a little longer.*

"Warden Dios listened to Frik." On this subject as well she couldn't swallow her anger; but she tamped it down as hard as she was able. "He listened to all of us." He heard me insist that stopping the research would be a crime against humankind. "Then he gave Intertech authorization to continue.

"Frik was outraged. He threatened to 'go over Dios' head.' And a week later the research was quashed. On Warden Dios' orders. After Frik talked to Holt Fasner, enough pressure was put on the director to make him reverse his position."

The Senior Member gaped as if he'd swallowed his larynx. "Are you saying," he gulped, "Holt Fasner personally stopped that research? Can you prove it?"

Min scowled. "Of course not. It all happened behind my back. And Warden Dios' name was on the order.

"You didn't ask why I'm here," she rasped, "on my own, without approval or permission. Now you know. I'm a cop, Captain Vertigus. I believe in what cops are supposed to do. This isn't it. I want to stop this kind of thing, if I can."

Harshly she continued, "I think that video conference was another example. The director made himself look like a man with no ethics, no scruples. That isn't the case." Whatever her doubts, she acted on that conviction. "But as long as the UMC own the police—as long as the Dragon has the power to determine and impose policy—the real director of the UMCP is Holt Fasner, not Warden Dios.

"That's why this bill is necessary. It will free the police to defend something larger than Holt Fasner and the United Mining Companies."

Now Captain Vertigus nodded. He closed his mouth carefully.

After a moment he said, "Go on."

Min's stomach twisted. "When I called you earlier, I wasn't in a hurry. All I wanted was support, not immediate action." Some of her anger was directed at herself. She hated telling lies. "But when I heard the conference, I realized that right now may be the best chance we'll ever get for success."

That, at least, was true.

"You don't need me to tell you the Dragon will fight a Bill of Severance with everything he has. The UMC may be the biggest thing in human space, but all of it, everything Fasner does and has and wants, rests on the police. His greatest power derives from the fact that humankind depends on the UMCP for survival—and he owns the UMCP. If the police were reconstituted as an arm of the GCES, he wouldn't be the Dragon anymore. He would be just another CEO with megalomania.

"Ordinarily a bill like this wouldn't stand a chance. He owns too many votes. Too many Members think they have too much to gain by giving or selling him their support. But I think that conference opened a window. It scared a lot of people. You were there—it probably scared you.

"As far as the Council is concerned, there's only one excuse for voting against a Bill of Severance—for supporting Fasner on a subject that could determine the future of the human species. That excuse is *honesty*. As long as the cops are *honest*, severance isn't necessary. Therefore voting against the best interests and possibly the survival of humankind is just pragmatism, not malfeasance.

"After that conference, the Members have to ask whether the UMCP really is honest. Maybe Igensard is right. In which case, a vote against a Bill of Severance becomes suddenly indefensible. Even Members who've already sold themselves may think twice about supporting the Dragon when it looks like treason."

As sudden as an epiphany, she thought, And if that's what Dios had in mind all along—if that's what he was aiming for when he commissioned her to come here and then besmirched himself in front of the whole GCES—he must have been living in hell for longer than she could imagine, and may God have pity on his soul.

Abruptly Captain Vertigus lifted his hands. Small red spots of excitement or trepidation had appeared on his translucent cheeks. "Just a minute. Just a minute. This is all too plausible. I don't trust it.

"If what you're telling me is accurate, why do you want to be kept out of it? Why does this legislation have to come from me, instead of from you—or from Warden Dios? Wouldn't a Bill of Severance have even more authority if the UMCP proposed it?"

Min shook her head. "Only if you believe we're honest. Otherwise it's just another ploy—but this time it's Warden Dios' plotting, not Holt Fasner's. The same man who didn't mind selling one of my people to illegals now wants complete power for himself, without even the Dragon to restrain him.

"I don't think that's true, but I can't guarantee it." Sneering at herself now, she added, "If I could, I wouldn't have had to come here on my own. However, that's beside the point. If we proposed the bill ourselves—if the director did, or I did—the Dragon could stop us. For one thing, he could fire us. But he could also go further—a lot further. In the time it would take the Council to *read* a bill, never mind debate or act on it, he could dismantle the entire UMCP. Leave human space defenseless. The GCES would be forced to create a new police force from scratch.

"If he's provoked into a threat that extreme, we're all lost. I have no way of knowing whether he would go that far, but I'm not willing to take the chance."

Captain Vertigus look vaguely nauseated as he murmured, "I see what you mean."

A moment later he shook himself as if he were trying to clear his head. Small beads of saliva had gathered at the corners of his mouth; he wiped them away. Leaning forward to face Min closely again, he said, "This is still too plausible. It's happening too fast. You want me to take on Holt Fasner and the whole Council for you, and you want me to make up my mind right now. I'm an old man, Director Donner. I can't stay awake through any entire Council session. Sometimes I can't stay awake through an entire sentence, even when I'm the one talking.

"Why do you want *me* to do this? Why not somebody else?"

Min spread her hands. "Who else is there?" She held his pale gaze. "Who else has your 'credibility'? President Len? He's probably honest—I'm not sure—but he hates conflict. If he proposed a Bill of Severance, the first thing he would do is attach an amendment postponing the effective date for five years.

"*You* tell *me*, Captain Vertigus. Who else could I ask?"

"But tell me *now*," she added roughly. "I'm running out of time. I want to be back on the shuttle to UMCPHQ"—she flicked her eyes to a chronometer—"in eleven minutes."

For several heartbeats he continued studying her as if he wanted to peer into the back of her brain. While he hesitated, she felt that more things hung in the balance than she knew how to name; the possible futures of the human race seemed to fade in and out of existence.

Why had Warden Dios sent her here? Why had he waited until now? What game was he playing?

Was it really conceivable that Holt Fasner might lose a GCES battle over a Bill of Severance?

Softly, almost whispering, Captain Vertigus announced, "It occurs to me, Director Donner, that it doesn't matter whether you're telling me the truth. It doesn't even matter whether you chose me because you think I might win or because you're sure I'll lose." As he spoke his thin voice took on excitement until it sounded almost resonant, almost young. "What you're asking me to do needs doing. It should have been done a long time ago. And the timing may never be more favorable than it is right now.

"I like the idea of having something important to do—for a change. If you're counting on me to lose, you'll have an anxious time during the next few days."

Relief brought up a grin from Min's heart. "Don't lose. If you don't trust me, you can always get me fired later."

Riding a wash of elation, she rose to her feet. After all, the worst that could happen to Captain Vertigus was that he would end his life on a painful political defeat. The Dragon had no history of punishing people who opposed him ineffectively: his malice was reserved for his successful enemies. And if the Bill of Severance passed, Holt Fasner might lose his ability to punish anyone.

In the meantime a little excitement might be good for the captain.

Glancing at the chronometer again, she asked, "When do you expect your people back?"

Captain Vertigus stood as if he barely had the strength to keep his legs under him. "Your timing is good in more ways than one. You should still have about five minutes." As she began to pick up her security devices, he added, "I'll check for you."

Awkwardly he moved around his desk toward the door. Bracing his hands to steady them, he eased the door open a crack.

Min groaned inwardly when she heard him breathe, "Damn. Why is Marthe back so early?" Nevertheless she didn't stop detaching her equipment and stowing it in her pockets.

In the same low voice, he asked, "Now who do you suppose *that* is?"

She felt a sting of tension in her palms. One of the newsdogs? Someone in Maintenance? Just what she needed. Automatically she checked the location of her hidden handgun. Then she joined Captain Vertigus at the door.

Through the slitted opening past his shoulder, she scanned the area where his aides had their desks.

Seven—no, eight—desks; all of them with intercoms, data terminals, hardcopy devices, comfortable chairs; all of them unoccupied. Except one. Slightly to the left of the captain's door and roughly ten meters away across the hall sat a plump, middle-aged woman with graying hair and old-fashioned glasses: Marthe, presumably. She had the air of a personal aide. Maybe she kept track of Captain Vertigus' appointments: maybe she thought she took care of the captain himself. Her desk was positioned so that she could watch the approach to the hall on her right and the Senior Member's office door on her left; so that she could see who came to visit him and when they went away.

At the moment, however, she wasn't looking at the door. Her attention was fixed on a man shambling toward her from the other direction.

As Min Donner scrutinized him, adrenaline slammed through her, and her palms started to burn as if they were on fire.

He was no newsdog. And he wasn't from Maintenance, even though he wore an old worksuit and carried a small tool case; even though the security badge clipped at his shoulder was Maintenance green. The way he moved—stiffly, carefully, as if he cradled something fragile in his chest—told Min at once that he wasn't here for any kind of repair or inspection.

He moved like a man who hadn't healed yet because he'd been operated on too quickly; too shoddily.

She was the director of Enforcement Division, as well as Warden Dios' sometime bodyguard and occasional executioner. She knew a kaze when she saw one.

She didn't hesitate. This was the work she did best. Her impact pistol leaped into her hand as she pulled Captain Vertigus back from the door. "Get *down*," she breathed in an urgent whisper. "Behind your desk."

He stumbled against the edge of the desk, but didn't move to obey. He'd been away from ships too long; no longer recognized an order when he heard one. Instead he gaped at her, his old face full of astonishment. "What . . . ?"

She had no time for his confusion. Her attention focused like a laser through the crack of the door. The man had reached Marthe's desk. He was talking to her, showing her what may have been a work order, gesturing toward the captain's office.

"I said *get down*," Min hissed. "There's going to be an explosion. That man's a *kaze*."

She didn't glance at Captain Vertigus: he understood what a kaze was. She could tell by the sounds he made that he was fumbling around the desk, crouching behind its inadequate shelter.

Abruptly the intercom chimed. A woman's voice said, "Captain Vertigus? There's a man here from Maintenance. He says he needs to test the wiring of your data terminal."

"What about Marthe?" the captain croaked at Min's back. "You've got to get her out of there."

She was Min Donner; familiar with extreme decisions and bloodshed. "If I do that," she articulated so softly that he may not have heard her, "she'll know I was here."

Nevertheless she had to make the attempt.

To serve and protect.

Through the crack, she heard Marthe say to the kaze, "I don't think he's in."

"I'll just check," the man replied. "This'll only take a minute."

As soon as he stepped past Marthe's desk, Min kicked the door open. With her gun aimed as steady as steel for his sternum, she roared at Marthe, *"Take cover!"*

The kaze's eyes widened in surprise; he faltered momentarily.

Frozen, Marthe stared at Min as if she'd just arrived from forbidden space.

Captain Vertigus' voice cracked into a wail: *"Marthe!"*

Then the kaze launched himself toward Min and the door.

Shielding herself behind the door frame, Min shot him in the chest.

She'd waited too long: she should have shot him as soon as she saw him. When the explosives surgically implanted in him detonated, the blast caught her past her shield and flung her against the wall like a handful of rags.

Chunks of concrete sprang off the walls; soundproofing and ducts ripped out of the ceiling; debris whined like shrapnel. Blood burst from Min's nose; impact numbed her whole body. Yet the explosion didn't seem to make any noise. As she rebounded from the wall and sprawled into the wreckage, she already knew that she was deaf.

But she didn't stop. Rolling to get her legs under her, she staggered to her feet.

Swaddled in silence, she checked on Captain Vertigus.

He blinked up at her, his eyes full of powder and shock. His mouth made noises she couldn't hear. If he hadn't been protected by his desk—and if his desktop hadn't been made of crystallized Formica—he might have been seriously injured; might have been killed. As it was, he was only stunned.

Her sheaf of hardcopy was scattered around the office like confetti. Most of the pages appeared intact, however.

Her own voice was nothing more than a vibration in the bones of her skull as she told him, "I wasn't here. No matter what happens, I wasn't here.

"Get that bill ready as fast as you can."

Stumbling as if her neurons were no longer sure of their synapses, she left him alone.

As she passed Marthe's spattered remains and headed for the stairwell, she wondered which of the futures she and Captain Vertigus had tried to make possible no longer existed.

MIN

$\succ$ **B**y the time the shuttle neared UMCPHQ's Earthside dock, she began to recover her hearing.

The process was slow. At first only a high, thin wail registered, barely audible: a sound like someone keening in the distance, grieving for the dead—or like the screech of a shuttle's warning sirens muffled by an EVA suit. For a moment she thought it *was* the sirens; and her palms caught fire again. But neither the crew nor the other passengers reacted. Gradually the sensation of violence faded from her hands. The wail settled into the background until it became almost subliminal; mere neural feedback from her overstressed eardrums.

Then she seemed to hear the muted hull-roar of the drive as the shuttle fired braking thrust. It, too, was imprecisely audible. Unlike the wail, however, it was real. She could feel the same resonance when she touched one of the bulkheads.

Despite the soundless protests of the crew, she unbelted herself from her g-seat and drifted weightlessly toward the airlock. She wanted to disembark the minute the shuttle finished docking.

One of the crew touched her arm; she turned toward him and watched him speak. From somewhere beyond the wail, behind the hull-roar, she heard him—a voice like the whisper of fabric when her arm brushed her side. "Director Donner, this isn't safe."

"If I wanted to be safe"—her voice buzzed in the bones of her

---

skull—"I would choose another line of work." A moment later she ordered, "Flare Director Dios." "Flare" was UMCP slang for "contact urgently." "Tell him I want to see him. Tell him I want to see him *now*."

She would have sent that message earlier if she could have trusted her voice through her deafness.

The crewman saluted and went back to his duties.

Her handgun was back in its familiar place on her hip. She'd restored it as soon as she'd gained the relative privacy of the shuttle. Pains filled her body and her head: the residual throbbing in her sinuses, which persisted although her nose no longer bled; the deeper ache of contusions and bruises. But she ignored them. Other hurts were more important.

She wondered if she would be able to hear Warden Dios answer when she asked him questions.

Hints of noises which might have been dock-alerts reached her. That was a good sign. On the other hand, the crews' routine explanations and announcements were wrapped in silence; baffled by old grief.

When station g pulled her feet to the floor, she keyed open the airlock, equalized the pressure, and cycled the outer doors. By the time the crew had given the other passengers permission to leave their g-seats, she was face-to-face with the nearest guard, telling him to take her to the director.

For all she knew, the familiar authority of her voice came out as hysteria.

Warden Dios must have been expecting her message. Whatever he was doing, he dropped it. No more than five minutes after she left the shuttle, she was with him in one of his secure offices; out of circulation; off the record. Again she temporarily ceased to exist.

Seated behind the desk with a blank data terminal in front of him, he studied her gravely. His human eye and his prosthesis seemed to search her inside and out. Broadly speaking, he must have known what had happened: reports from GCES Security, as well as from his own personnel on Suka Bator, would have reached him faster than any shuttle. But no one except Captain Vertigus could have told him that Min Donner had set off the kaze herself; and she doubted that the captain and the UMCP director had been in contact with each other.

So Warden also had no idea what the outcome of her meeting with the Senior Member was.

Nevertheless he didn't rush her. No matter what he'd dropped to answer her flare, he seemed to offer her all the time and attention she needed. After he'd studied her for a moment, he pointed her toward a chair. As she eased her sore limbs into it he asked, "How badly are you hurt?"

His voice murmured against a keening background. If she hadn't noticed the tension in the cords of his neck, she wouldn't have realized that he was nearly shouting.

She shrugged. "Nothing serious. Bruises. I had a bloody nose. And I can't hear very well—concussion deafness."

"That's obvious." Unexpected strain underlined his whisper. "I've been talking steadily, but you didn't react until you looked at my face. This can wait, you know. I can live with my impatience while you see the medtechs."

"I can't." Heard through her skull, her voice was coarse, almost guttural. "A crazy man killed an innocent woman." She had Marthe's blood on her hands, if not her conscience. "If he'd arrived a couple of minutes earlier—or if I hadn't set him off—he would have killed Captain Vertigus as well as me. I can't wait. I want to know what's going on."

Warden spread his hands. They looked strong in the light over his desk; as steady as stones. "All right. Let's start with this kaze. That's your department—tell me about him."

"A human bomb," she reported automatically. As she spoke she stopped monitoring the modulation of her voice. The director would tell her if she didn't speak clearly. "A terrorist on a suicide mission. We haven't had much trouble with them recently. Most of the fringe groups are in disarray—they can't decide who they hate enough to kill themselves for. Forbidden space scares them too much. About the only group that regularly tries to blow up GCES policy is the native Earthers. But this kaze didn't come from them."

"How do you know?" Warden asked.

"Because he got through Security. He had legitimate maintenance id. That's not easy to come by—especially for a group like the native Earthers, with an established history of"—her mouth twisted— "'opposition' to the GCES. Security is using all kinds of embedded verifications in the id tags of everyone who belongs on Suka Bator.

And we"—she meant Data Acquisition—"supply CMOS-SOD chips for GCES function id. Those chips can't be counterfeited, the same way datacores can't be altered."

Dios knew all this, but he gave no hint of impatience. "What does that prove?"

Min did her best to explain details and perceptions which came to her intuitively. "Assuming it's possible to steal or fabricate the chip to fake that maintenance id—which I don't assume—you can't get the job done overnight. You have to prepare for it. And even if you have the chip, you can't just stamp out that kind of id. You need too much specific information about how GCES Security works— for instance, how they rotate their pass codes. For the native Earthers to pull off something like this, they must have started getting it ready months ago.

"But nobody got that kaze ready. He was in pain when he moved. The surgery was too recent—a day or two ago at most. Why do the kind of long-range work you need to produce fake GCES function id without preparing your kaze at the same time? That part of the job is a hell of a lot easier."

Warden shrugged. "They didn't think they were going to need him so soon." The muffling of his voice made him sound abstract. "The original plan was to use him later, in some other situation. The decision to act now was made suddenly. In response to the events of the past twenty-four hours."

A tingle ran through Min's palms. The muscles at the base of her spine tightened. Without warning the atmosphere in the office seemed to take on threats; obscure implications gathered at the edges of the light. The UMCP director gave her an opening to ask questions—questions which had swarmed like pain through her head ever since she'd taken her seat on the shuttle. Because she needed so much to believe in him, the prospect of challenging him scared her.

But her questions scared her more.

"Then why attack Captain Vertigus?" she countered. "The native Earthers consider him a hero."

"To make him a martyr?" Warden offered impassively. Maybe he couldn't feel her challenge in the air; maybe he couldn't guess where she was headed. The only strain in his demeanor came from the effort of speaking loudly enough to be heard. "To prove that the enemies of the native Earthers are evil?"

Her voice felt like a snarl in the bones behind her ears. "And what has that got to do with 'the events of the past twenty-four hours'? If the native Earthers are involved, why is today different than any other day? Where does the need to attack so suddenly come from?"

His single eye held her gaze. His IR vision must have told him that her nerves were burning.

"This is a crucial time for the Council," he answered. "Issues have come up concerning everything we do in space—and they've certainly come up suddenly. Precisely because Captain Vertigus is a hero to the native Earthers, the attack on him validates his convictions. I mean it validates his opposition to Holt Fasner and the UMC. Remember the captain has always backed us up—and fought Fasner. He doesn't reject our function, he rejects UMC policy. Terrorists have always attacked their enemies—but sometimes they attack their friends in an effort to make their enemies look bad."

Min fought an impulse to lower her head. She wanted to drop her eyes; but the pressure to look away, to fix her attention on anything except the man she served, didn't come from him. It came from inside her: from what she was thinking; from what she feared. The weakness was hers. For that reason she refused to give in to it.

Facing Warden Dios straight, she took a step closer to what she believed was the heart of the matter.

"I've got another idea," she rasped, "one that doesn't require us to assume the native Earthers are capable of faking that kaze's id. We have a high-level traitor—someone so high up he has access to genuine chips, so high up he knows or can get all the pass codes and verifications. Producing valid maintenance id was easy for him. But he didn't have a kaze ready because until today he had no intention of attacking Captain Vertigus."

"Interesting." Warden didn't sound surprised. Aside from his obvious concentration, his face was expressionless. "Then let me ask your question. Why was Captain Vertigus attacked *now*? Why does this traitor suddenly want to get rid of him?"

Shock and keening still occluded Min's hearing. Nevertheless the fact that he hadn't asked who she thought the traitor might be was as loud as a shout.

"Because," she answered past a dryness like ashes in her throat, "we chose him. This traitor wanted to kill him so that he couldn't introduce your Bill of Severance."

Maybe I'm not the only one you talked to about it. And maybe whoever that was leaked the information.

Or maybe *you* leaked the information.

"Alternatively," the UMCP director replied as if she'd engaged him in an exercise of pure speculation, "this traitor may have wanted Captain Vertigus dead for the same kind of reason I ascribed to the native Earthers. Martyr him in order to solidify support for the bill."

Calmly, without apparent premeditation, Dios gave her a reason to think that he might be to blame.

He may have been trying to steer her away from her own ideas.

Without warning, she felt a rush of loathing for him. She hated his calm, his strength, his secrets: she hated this game he was playing, a game which corroded the convictions that made the UMCP valuable—not to mention viable. She was his ED director because she believed in what cops were for. And she'd always been sure he shared her beliefs. But since Morn Hyland's return to Com-Mine Station with Angus Thermopyle—no, before that, since Warden had assented to the quashing of Intertech's mutagen immunity research—he'd given her more and more reason to question the nature of his beliefs; more reason to wonder whether he'd finally sold his soul to the Dragon. Facing him now, with his complex intentions and his subtleties, she burned for the simple service she loved, the clean dedication that kept her whole. And she hated him for taking those things away from her.

Making no effort to mask her anger—she couldn't have concealed it from him anyway—she retorted, "I'm glad you mentioned that possibility. It brings me to your video conference with the Council. While I was talking to Captain Vertigus, I kept asking myself *why*. Why did you do that? Why did you do it now? You've never let the GCES"—or me—"see you in that light before. And I was only able to come up with one answer.

"You did it so the bill would have some prayer of passing.

"But now you've given me another idea." She balanced herself, kept her poise, as if she were a gun aimed at his head. "Maybe you did it so I would be sure to go see Captain Vertigus as soon as possible—so you would have a chance to get rid of the only people who really believe in that bill."

When she stopped, her heart was hammering as if she feared she would be struck down for saying those words aloud. Her hands felt full of killing fire. Yet her eyes never wavered; the muzzle of her accusation held steady.

Just for an instant the muscles of his face tightened; he may have been wincing. Almost immediately, however, he smoothed out his expression. Only a hint of grief around his eye undermined his impassivity.

"I like to think," he articulated slowly, "that if I wanted you dead—if I were the kind of man who solved his problems by butchering subordinates and politicians—I would choose something more honest than a kaze to kill you."

She had trouble hearing him: he was no longer making the effort to speak loudly. Only the slow recovery of her eardrums enabled her to distinguish the blurred vibrations of his voice.

More honest than a kaze.

As soon as he said that, she believed him. That was the Warden Dios she admired; the Warden Dios to whom she'd given her devotion. She couldn't have been so wrong about him for so many years. The whole idea that he might have had something to do with the kaze was smoke.

It was all meant to distract her.

For a moment she was so angry that she couldn't speak.

But he hadn't stopped talking. As if he were still on the same subject, he asked rhetorically, "Has it ever occurred to you that maybe we—I mean all of us, the cops—are responsible for the existence of places like Billingate? That maybe humankind would be better off if we hadn't made ourselves so powerful, or so necessary?"

Min swallowed convulsively. She knew him well enough to know that he didn't expect an answer. Because she was furious, however, she rasped, "That's absurd. We didn't create Angus Thermopyle. We didn't create the Amnion. But if we weren't here, the rest of humanity would have no defense."

A grimace pulled at the corners of his mouth. "I'm not so sure. Human history is full of—I guess you could call them enforcement mistakes. Using muscle to control people seems to make them more determined. Angus and the Amnion are probably a good example.

"Before we got our hands on him, he was caught between two dangers, two enemies. The Amnion and us. They want to change him, take away his humanity. We want to kill him, or at least lock him up. What would you do in his position? We try to get what we want by gunfire. The Amnion trade for it. And they always keep their bargains because they know that otherwise they won't be trusted, which means they won't be able to trade effectively. What *would* you do?"

She stared at him as if she could see mutagens chewing at his genes, changing the structure of his bones.

"It's obvious, isn't it?" he went on. "If you had to choose between being shot by us and risking your humanity with the Amnion, you would be crazy *not* to choose them. They're the lesser danger because they leave you a chance to survive. Once you have us for enemies, piracy is your only sane alternative.

"And *we* make the rules. *We* create the restrictions which define illegality. We *put* Angus in the position where he had to choose between us and the Amnion.

"You can't expect a man like that to have a sense of perspective. You can't ask him to understand that the Amnion are a threat to all humanity, while we're only a threat to people who increase the risks for humankind. He takes everything personally. He *has* to—he's on the run, and his life depends on it.

"The Amnion look good to a man like Angus because from his point of view we're worse. In other words, we *created* him. We created every individual human being on Billingate, on every illegal shipyard, on every outpost or installation that does business with the Amnion. If we didn't work so hard to control piracy—or if we weren't so self-righteous about it—pirates wouldn't be such a danger to the people we're supposed to serve."

As she listened, Min's anger curdled to sorrow. Despite her need to believe in him, he *had* changed. This wasn't how he'd explained her function—and his own—the last time she'd heard him talk about it.

She gritted her teeth to control her sadness. "Then why do it? Why do we work so hard for something we don't believe in?"

Now his voice was no more than a whisper. If she hadn't seen his lips moving, she might have thought the words came from the shadows around her.

"Because the people we're supposed to serve and the people we do serve aren't the same. We don't serve humankind. We serve the

United Mining Companies. And the United Mining Companies profits from piracy. Piracy reinforces the UMC's hold on its markets."

Is that it? she thought. Is that the truth at last? Or is it just another distraction?

Was he casting doubt on the UMCP, questioning the integrity of his own life's work, so that she might believe him capable of aiming a kaze at Captain Vertigus in order to consolidate support for a Bill of Severance?

No, that didn't make sense. If the captain had been killed, no one on the Council would have heard of the bill. It would have been blown up along with its intended sponsor.

And she was morally certain that the kaze had been surprised to see her in Captain Vertigus' doorway.

The video conference may have been a ploy on Warden Dios' part to lend his bill authority, credibility. The kaze was something else entirely.

Clenching her jaws so hard that her head throbbed, she demanded, "Why are you telling me this?"

What makes you think I want to go on serving Holt Fasner, instead of my own species?

What are you trying to distract me from?

Abruptly Warden leaned forward, planted his palms on the bare surface of the desk. His voice was soft, but he pitched it to reach her. His single eye glittered with intensity.

"Min, I want you to survive this. If it can be done, I want you to be the next director of the police."

With those words he bound her to him; caught her in a grip she would never be able to break. Implications came into focus in the light as if his strong fingers held them down on the desktop for her to see. Without transition he restored her convictions; remade himself into the man to whom she'd fixed her heart.

Too astonished for anger or sorrow, she breathed, "You think you're finished." The idea seemed to throw illumination into the most obscure corners of the office. "We need a Bill of Severance— we need some way to change ourselves into what we were supposed to be in the first place, the servants of humankind. But it can't pass because the Dragon has too many votes. So you've decided to sacrifice yourself in order to create the conditions that will enable it to pass. But of course if it passes you'll be removed as director. Nobody will trust you. And if it doesn't pass, the Dragon will get rid of you himself, if only because you've become a liability."

You want to push me away from you, make me keep my distance. That's what all these distractions are for—that's why you're encouraging me to doubt you. You want Enforcement Division to retain its credibility when your position collapses. You want to make me look like the only one the GCES can rely on to pick up the pieces.

Dios seemed to shrink in his seat. Substance appeared to drain out of him, as if her understanding bled his hope away. Or maybe it was her new ferocity which defeated him. Slowly he turned his palms upward.

"I'll tell you why I'm finished," he murmured softly. "As long as I'm telling you things you shouldn't hear, I'll give you one more.

"You've been angry ever since I signed the order quashing Intertech's immunity research. You wanted me to fight Fasner on that one. You probably thought I should have gone public—exposed what he was doing, forced his hand." Hints of ire reached her through her veiled hearing. "But what would that accomplish? If I pushed him far enough, he could always publish the research himself. Tell the GCES I'd misunderstood him. He might be damaged, but he would survive. He would still be here—and I would be gone.

"Of course, I could have just quit. But that would have accomplished even less.

"So I didn't do any of those things.

"I didn't quash Intertech's research. I took it away. The order I signed was just a sham. I took the research and gave it to Hashi. He completed it himself."

Warden's eye was full of darkness. Hints of pain tugged at the muscles of his cheeks. "We have a mutagen immunity drug. It works. Hashi is the only one who knows about it. He's the only one allowed to use it.

"That was *my* idea." The director closed his fists, knotted them on the desktop in front of him. "Fasner wanted to stop the whole project. I persuaded him to let Hashi finish it—to let me have it and keep it secret.

"If *that* comes out, I won't just lose my job. I'll be executed for treason.

"But it's the only lever I have with the Dragon. It's the kind of collusion he understands. It *implicates* me. More than anything I've ever done, that convinced him to trust me—convinced him to let me make my own decisions.

"He would kill me if he knew I'm responsible for that bill. He might kill me anyway, if he thinks the bill could pass—or if he even starts to suspect I might tell anybody else what I know."

The familiar fire in Min's palms seemed to spread up through her body to her face; her eyes burned. Another woman would have been on the verge of tears: Min was on the verge of an explosion. Simply to control the brisance fighting for release inside her, she asked, "But what does he get out of it? How does it help UMC profits if DA has a secret immunity drug?

"What do *you* get?"

Warden took a deep breath. When he expelled it, the intensity seemed to flow out of him. The tension faded from his hands and shoulders; his face resumed its impassivity. He looked like a man who'd taken a desperate risk and lost, and now had nothing left to do but accept the consequences.

"I'm sorry." He sighed. "Sometimes I'm appalled by my own weakness. I should have let you go on believing I simply quashed the research. That would have been easier for you."

Easier? She didn't understand. Easier how?

Did he mean, easier for her to keep her distance? to separate herself from him, preserve ED's integrity?

Was her loyalty such a threat that he wanted—no, *needed*—to drive her away?

"How does it help UMC profits?" he continued. "It preserves the conflict with the Amnion. It scares them—that's what Hashi is using it for—which makes them both more hostile and more cautious. Which in turn makes them more dependent on trade. With the UMC, of course—but also with illegals. And *that* makes the cops more necessary. More violent. More self-righteous. More dangerous. Which produces more hostility and caution.

"Anything that escalates the conflict short of actual war increases UMC profits.

"What do I get? I get to keep my job. Right now that's more important to me than my life."

Min couldn't stomach what he was saying. The ideas sickened her: the thought that her loyalty was hazardous to him sickened her.

Again she asked, "Warden, why are you telling me this?" Where was her clean, simple anger when she needed it? Why couldn't she hate him now? "If you want *easy*, you could have avoided the whole subject. Hell, you could have avoided *me*. There's nothing I can do about it when you decide to sequester yourself."

He didn't look away, but his quiet answer ached with defeat. "That kaze nearly killed you. He nearly killed Captain Vertigus. Knowing you, I assume you feel responsible for the woman who died in the explosion. I owed you an explanation."

She ground her fingers into the tops of her thighs in a fierce effort to contain her distress. She wanted to shout, What kind of explanation have you given me? Do you call supplying me with reasons to distrust you an explanation? Do you call saying you want me to survive an *explanation*? Nevertheless she crushed down her protest. If she gave him another reason to look beaten, she didn't think she could bear it.

"Then I guess," she rasped, "you'll be glad to hear Captain Vertigus has decided to sponsor your bill. He should have it ready by the time the Council convenes tomorrow morning."

The director shrugged. "Too bad. You haven't heard the latest news. Abrim Len has already announced that the Council won't reconvene until Security has a chance to investigate that kaze. Until the Members can be sure they're safe. Another day or two at least."

The keening in Min's ears seemed to grow louder. She began to think it would never go away.

ANCILLARY DOCUMENTATION

TRANSCRIPT OF A COMMISSIONING ADDRESS
DELIVERED BY WARDEN DIOS TO CADETS OF THE
UNITED MINING COMPANIES POLICE ACADEMY ON
THE OCCASION OF THEIR FIRST ASSIGNMENT

Men and women, cadets of the United Mining Companies Police Academy, it's time.

Your training is over, to the extent that the Academy can provide it—to the extent that any of us can ever say our training is over. You've spent many hundreds of hours in classrooms, absorbing advice, memorizing data, squinting at screens and hardcopy, being hectored by pedants, purists, and philosophers—in short, studying until you thought your skulls were going to crack. *[laughter]* You've spent months of real time in simulators and simulations, learning to use our equipment, the best as well as the worst of it, learning the basic skills to survive and function when your life depends on your machinery and your companions—learning everything it's humanly possible to learn from a mock-up. You've been marched, stressed, exercised, taught, and beaten up until even the smallest of you could face entire guttergangs and take less damage than you give. You've been under hard g—you've been through the gap. And some of you— I say, *some* of you—have even contrived to squeeze in a little sleep. *[laughter]*

Now it's over. *[applause, cheers]* Over at last. You've learned what the Academy can teach you. Every one of you is stronger and smarter than you were when you arrived, better equipped to take care of yourselves and the people who trust you, better prepared to meet any future you choose.

It's time you went to work. *[groans, laughter]*

I want to talk to you about that work. *[applause]*

We're the UMCP. In crude terms, we stand against the Amnion: we control their impulse to encroach on our space, our interests, and our survival. And we chase pirates. *[laughter]* In other words, we do what the police have done since humankind started keeping historical records. The only difference between us and the uncountable legions of our predecessors is that our jurisdiction, our "turf," begins where theirs left off—at the limits of this planet's gravity well.

Men and women, cadets, we are responsible for all human space.

That makes us unique in history. It makes us unique in our own time. In every other way, we're just cops. Like every cop before us who ever put his heart into his job or her life on the line, we're here to serve and protect the people who gave us birth, the people who nurtured and educated us, the people who taught us inspiration and imagination, the people who invented our technologies and our arts, the people who made us who we are. In *that* way, we're no different than our predecessors. We're simply another link in the long chain of men and women who took the same oath we do—the men and women who swore to defend what they called civilization against whatever they understood as external and internal threats.

But in *this* way, in the matter of "turf," we are without precedent, in our time or any other. Never before have the police been responsible for the continued existence of their entire species in the whole created universe.

External and internal threats we've had aplenty since the beginning of time. That's inevitable. We're human beings. Most of us can't get out of bed in the morning without causing trouble for somebody. *[laughter]* But the internal and external threats have always been human ones. What one clan or tribe or nation calls civilization, another calls barbarism—or a violation of natural sovereignty. Racial distrust fosters violence. Economic imbalance breeds greed and jealousy. And the planet is a closed ecosystem. Therefore conflicts occur within and between civilizations over the allocation of resources—an understandable struggle which has typically been disguised by masks of religion and politics.

Make no mistake about it. The cops have always had their hands full.

But only on our turf is the continuance of humankind itself at issue. All the struggles of our long, bloody, and unscrupulous past have produced survivors and corpses—but the survivors, like the corpses, have always been human.

That isn't true on our turf.

Of course, the word "turf" is something of an oversimplification in this context. I'm not referring only to questions of jurisdiction. The Amnion exist. They have no discernible desire for war. On the other hand, they're profoundly imperialistic—I say profoundly because their imperialism reaches to the core of our genetic existence, the core of what makes us human beings. All human space is our "turf" because that is our jurisdiction—and because the Amnion will take it away from us if they can. They will take who we are away from us if they can.

For that reason—and no other—we are utterly and essentially unique.

And because we are unique, we have—we must have—a unique relationship with the people we serve and protect. Precisely because we are uniquely responsible for the future existence of our kind, we must also be uniquely responsible to our kind. The sheer scale of the challenge we've undertaken requires of us a special integrity, a commensurate valor, a whole new kind of dedication. You know that. But it requires something more as well. It requires a special responsiveness to the will and spirit of humankind. In the purest terms, we must act *for* the people we serve. If we do not—if the barrier we erect between humanity and extinction *in any way* violates the trust or the desire or the freedom of the people we serve—then we falsify ourselves as cops. We make ourselves, not the defenders of the future, but its arbiters. Rather than simply and cleanly enabling the future, we choose it for men, women, and children who didn't ask us to do that job.

Cadets of the United Mining Companies Police Academy, it is the nature of power to resist restrictions, to seek an unfettered expansion and expression of itself. And it is the function of ethics to impose restrictions on power, to weld and wield the potentialities of power so that they serve but do not control the people in whose name they exist. And we have power, never doubt it. That may seem slightly implausible to men and women who've suffered for years through what we blandly call "training," but of course I'm not talking about *you*, I'm talking about *us*. We, the cops, hold the future of humankind in our care. We must not misuse it. We must be as vigilant in *how* we exercise our power as we are diligent *when* we use it.

I want to be absolutely clear about this. Your oath puts on you a responsibility which extends far beyond the limits of any ordinary employment, any planet-bound or stationer occupation, any less stringent concept of duty. Let me suggest an analogy. Consider the problem of piracy. We don't "chase pirates" just because they're illegal. We don't shoot at them just because they shot at us first—or because they damaged any of the people we protect. We fight piracy for the same organic reason that an antibody fights a virus, because if we don't—and if we don't succeed—the whole vast human organism sickens and dies.

But when an antibody begins to change the shape of the larger organism, when the antibody introduces mutations which the larger organism didn't choose and can't control, we call it "cancer." Like the virus, it kills the larger organism. Unlike the virus, however, the cancer is wrong.

The virus resembles the Amnion. It exists. It seeks to perform the functions of which it is capable for its own honest, genetically coded reasons—because it must. But the cancer is a violation of its own code. It is deadly because its protein chains have become twisted and false.

Those of you who are good with analogies will hardly have failed to notice that piracy also is a form of cancer.

Well, if you're going to die anyway, what difference does it make whether a virus or a cancer killed you? No difference at all—that's obvious. But while you're still alive, while you still have a future, the difference is profound. When you contract a virus, you can always hope that your antibodies will be equal to the task of preserving you. But when your antibodies turn to cancer, you can only survive if you accept some kind of fundamental violence against your own organism—surgery which cuts you open, chemotherapy which wreaks havoc with your polymerase, radiation which threatens the very nucleotides of your existence, genetically engineered predator microbes which attack the cancer, but which can never be trusted to attack only the cancer. Whether or not you survive, the cancer has done you more harm than the virus.

If we are not antibodies, an expression of the humanity of the organism to which we belong, then we are cancer, and humankind would be better off without us.

That is the thrust of your oath, the unique and necessary task you swear to undertake. I must tell you frankly that in the end I don't care whether you succeed at it or not. For the simple and valid reason that we don't try to choose or control the future, we can't guarantee it. Space is immense, and the Amnion mysterious. None of us can know what the outcome of our efforts will be. Our responsibility for and to humankind doesn't require us to know. Ultimately none of us are measured by the degree of our success. We are measured by the quality of our service.

Men and women, cadets of the United Mining Companies Police Academy, it's time.

It's time we all went to work. [*prolonged applause*]

LIETE

Liete Corregio, command third, *Captain's Fancy*, sat at her station on the bridge with the ship's best people around her and a long black wind blowing in her ears.

By ordinary standards, she and the watch she'd selected had nothing to do on the bridge. *Captain's Fancy* was docked, immobilized, both drives and all her energies dead. Even the power to process water and circulate air came from Billingate; from the fusion generator buried beyond reach in the core of the rock. Clamps and grapples held the ship in place, as rigid as the dock itself. Only communications might conceivably demand some attention; but the board could be set to route incoming messages to her in her cabin—or anywhere else she happened to be.

Nevertheless she had her orders. No one aboard could countermand them. And she had no intention of challenging them herself, despite the long black wind and its burden of dread.

She did her best to ignore the wind. It was metaphoric in any case, a habit of mind or a perceptual trick. Ever since she could remember, she'd experienced her life in images of wind: the arctic pressure of necessity which had blown her from place to place and skill to skill until she gusted aboard *Captain's Fancy;* the soaring gale ride of the gap between the stars, the hollow howl of the vacuum; the sweet zephyr of sleep; the solar flare of Nick's virility; the hungry mistral of flight and battle and command. Even the sensations of food and comradeship were like breezes ruffling her short hair, warming her dark cheeks. And when Nick Succorso had finally taken her to bed, after years of longing as poignant and unanswerable as a sigh in a dark cavern, his touch had felt like wind: a scorched blast from an old, baked, and needy desert, raw with sand and so dry it denatured her heart. By the time he left her again, some part of her had shriveled away, desiccated to powder—the only part still capable of questioning him.

Once she realized that now at last she had no remaining needs or desires that didn't belong to him, she began to hear the black wind blowing.

It was the wind of her doom.

It may have been the doom of the whole ship.

Yet it was only a metaphor, an image; a way of thinking: it didn't confuse her. Instead it helped her understand her circumstances. When Nick had burned his way onto the auxiliary bridge and aimed his cutting laser at Morn, the familiar, respected urgency Liete called the mistral had lifted her and flung her at him, carrying him to the floor; saving both him and his ship. She'd ridden breezes and blasts to gain the trust which had made her his command third.

For that reason, she had no difficulty carrying out her orders, despite the sound of the black wind—a prolonged empty echo as twisted as a groan.

She stayed on the bridge, at her station. From around the ship she culled the people she wanted, people she herself trusted: Carmel for scan; Lind on communications; Malda Verone at targ. Helm she gave to Pastille because she valued his abilities more than she disliked his lack of discipline. Engineering sat vacant, of course. And no one was assigned to data and damage control: Morn was lost; Sib Mackern, gone; and Alba Parmute, hopeless. Liete routed those functions to the command console and handled them herself.

Once her people took their g-seats, she told them, "I'm not here to answer questions, so don't ask." Her voice always sounded quiet. Nevertheless it carried: the mistral carried it—or the black wind. She knew that she would be obeyed. "I'm here for the same reason you are—to do what Nick tells us. He gave me orders. I'm giving them to you.

"You probably wish you knew what's going on. So do I. But we don't need that. All we need is orders. As long as he's alive, he isn't going to abandon his ship. That means he isn't going to abandon us. The best thing we can do to keep ourselves alive is follow his orders.

"If you believe you know somebody better *qualified*"—she stressed the word sardonically—"to give us orders and keep us alive, you have my permission to leave the ship. You can go join Mikka. Or hide out on the cruise until this is over.

"But if you can't, then do what I tell you and don't ask questions. Once we start, I won't tolerate anything else."

Steadily she scanned the bridge.

Carmel shrugged; Lind nodded. Both of them had been with Nick too long to start doubting him now. Malda assented for reasons of her own—reasons, Liete suspected, which she and the targ first had in common.

But Pastille grinned like a weasel. "Is it all right," he asked in a rank sneer, "if we *think* while we're working? I mean, it might be useful if we're allowed to at least *think.*"

That didn't deserve a retort, so Liete didn't give it one. Instead she met his gaze until he ducked his head and nodded.

"All right." She took a deep breath, held it for a moment, then let it out softly. "From now on, you're on battle alert until I say otherwise. When I give the word, we'll get started."

The chronometer on her board measured out seconds; minutes. No one spoke. Pastille squirmed in his g-seat. Everyone else sat still.

Ignoring the uncertainty and silence around her, Liete waited until the deadline Nick had set for his return came and passed. Then she began.

While the black wind hinted ruin in her ears, she ordered her watch to run their checklists as if *Captain's Fancy* were bound for deep space.

At the same time, she told Lind to monitor every conceivable channel for messages from Nick, the Bill, the Amnion, or *Trumpet.* And she instructed Carmel to lock scan on *Soar:* if *Soar* gave any sign of leaving the installation, Liete wanted to know about it instantly.

After the checklists were complete, she began to power up *Captain's Fancy* with as much subtlety as she could devise. In order to postpone as long as possible the moment when Operations would notice the ship's status and challenge it, she had Malda use installation current to charge the weapons systems. And Pastille drew on the same source to prime the thrusters for cold ignition, so that drive emission wouldn't betray the ship.

Riding the long black air for reasons she couldn't guess in a direction she couldn't identify, Liete Corregio deliberately deactivated the docking failsafes. When she was done, *Captain's Fancy* could rip free of Billingate without risking shutdown by either the installation's alarms or the ship's own inbuilt survival mechanisms.

She intended to follow Nick's orders no matter where they took her.

MIKKA

Mikka Vasaczk sat at the small table with an untasted drink
clenched in her capable hands, glowering at everything.

She glowered at the false glitter of the lighting, molded to resemble archaic chandeliers; at the walls, which were decorated with
mirrors and holographic nudes; at the painted cruisewalkers who moved
occasionally among the tables, trolling for business. She glowered at
the bar itself, as well as at the young woman who tended it—a girl
so expressionless that she might as well have had no face. She glowered impersonally at the spacers drinking and gibing at the other
tables.

From time to time she glowered at her companion, even though
he hadn't done anything to deserve it.

"Why are we doing this?" Sib Mackern had asked her as soon
as they left *Captain's Fancy*.

Past clenched jaws she'd replied, "He kept my brother."

Confused, he'd begun to say, "That's not what I—" Then he'd
stopped himself. "Your brother? Who is that?"

"Pup," she'd told him shortly.

He'd stared at her as if she'd frightened him. "I didn't know Pup
was your brother."

Now she and *Captain's Fancy*'s data first were in a place called
Paunchys, a nearly clean, almost civilized bar-and-sleep at the fringes
of the cruise. For some reason, *Soar*'s crew liked to come here off
watch.

A sour barkeep deeper in the cruise had told her this. He would have told any paying customer anything which might conceivably encourage them to buy from him. And *Soar* came to Billingate so often, spent so much time in the vicinity of Thanatos Minor, that her people were known.

Ignoring Sib's knotted anxiety, Mikka had led him to Paunchys, seated him at a table not too far from the ones where a small group of spacers already sat, and used some of *Captain's Fancy's* little credit to buy drinks neither he nor she wanted.

Why are we doing this?

Good question. She understood Nick's orders. *I want you to start a rumor about the immunity drug. Say you've heard* Soar's *captain has a drug that protects her from the Amnion. Talk about it until you're sure her crew hears you.* But why he'd given those orders—and given them to *her*—was another matter.

He'd said he wanted to *prime the Bill. To do business.*

She didn't believe that. She had other ideas.

He wanted to get rid of her.

Because she didn't trust him anymore.

Trust him, hell! When he'd turned Morn over to the Amnion, Mikka had realized that she didn't even *like* him. It was possible that she'd never liked him, even though she'd been ready to kill for him ever since they'd first met. But his hold on her had started to fray when she'd seen that he was perfectly willing to sell Morn's son to the Amnion. And it had snapped completely when he'd given away Morn herself.

The knowledge that he could force her to do anything he wanted by threatening Pup filled Mikka with dry, grim rage, as if she'd swallowed a mouthful of alum.

Glowering and bitter, she carried out Nick's instructions just long enough to see tension accumulating in the shoulders at the other tables; long enough to hear strain in the way the spacers tried to pretend they weren't listening. Then she quit. Sitting there in the bar, with Sib's moist, worried eyes on her and nowhere to go, she came to the end of what she was willing to do for Nick Succorso. If one of *Soar's* people had stopped by her table to probe for more information, she might have answered by telling the truth.

She ignored the bugeyes which surveyed the bar. As far as she was concerned, she had nothing left to hide. And they might not be sensitive enough to pick up her voice.

Driven by tension, she told Sib again, "He kept my brother."

Sib hunted for a reply. After a moment he repeated, "I didn't know Pup was your brother."

Gripping herself so that she wouldn't groan, she murmured, "Nick knows."

Mackern's eyes were as eloquent as a kid's: they showed every shade of his fear, his self-distrust. Sweat darkened his pale mustache until it looked like a smudge across his upper lip. Trying to cool his anxiety, he rolled his drink between his wrists. But his fever was too acute for simple remedies—and in any case most of the ice in his drink had already melted.

After a time one or two of the spacers who probably belonged to *Soar* left Paunchys. The rest regrouped themselves at other tables farther away.

Sib rephrased his question. "Why does Nick want us to do this?"

Mikka didn't want to say, To get rid of us. Not here: not now, while Pup was still at risk. Instead she muttered, "To make trouble for *Soar*—for Sorus Chatelaine. It doesn't have anything to do with the Bill. Or the Amnion. Hurting them is just a fringe benefit. He's after her. She's the one who cut him.

"And it's going to work." Her disgust came out in a snarl. "Rumors about an immunity drug in a place like this, for God's sake! The Bill is going to go wild. The Amnion will, too, if they hear about it. We would be safer tossing around vials of concentrated hydrofluoric acid. If we did what he told us—if we kept moving, kept spreading his rumor—the Bill would have us hanging by our entrails before we crossed half the cruise."

Sib stared at her with all his uncertainty and dread showing. "Is that why we're still sitting here?"

"Yes!" she grated. Then she said, "No. I don't know. I just can't do it anymore. I hate it too much."

For the third time, she told him, "He kept my brother."

The data first seemed to consider this part of a ritual to which there was no appropriate response except, "I didn't know he was your brother."

Glaring at him despite the fact that most of her anger was directed at herself, she completed the pattern. "Nick knows." Then, because her heart hurt, and she'd spent most of her life forcing herself to look coldly at whatever hurt her, she added, "His real name is Ciro."

Stiffly, as if he'd decided on suicide, Sib raised his glass like a gun to his mouth and drank.

Mikka didn't touch her own drink until Vector Shaheed walked into the bar-and-sleep. Then she swallowed it all in one long draft because he had Pup with him.

The alcohol wasn't enough to muffle her relief—or her awareness of treachery. She couldn't keep the tears from her eyes as Vector and Pup headed for her table.

"Goddamn him," she breathed to Sib, her voice shaking. "He wants to get rid of them, too."

Apparently Pup didn't understand. His young face showed a relief of his own, showed confusion and uncertainty; but no betrayal. The incompleteness of his gangling limbs—he still didn't have his full growth—made him look vulnerable and precious to Mikka; the only treasure she had left.

Vector understood, however: his clear blue gaze made that plain. Complex perceptions twisted his smile as he stopped at the table. He noticed her tears, but didn't comment on them. "Mikka," he said mildly, "Sib. Imagine my surprise."

"No," Mikka retorted through her teeth, fighting for self-command. "We don't have time.

"Sit down, both of you," she ordered. "Start by telling me how you found us."

Vector turned and waved at the woman tending the bar. Across the intervening tables, he requested coffee for himself, some kind of beer substitute for Pup.

By the time the engineer was seated, Pup had already taken a chair beside Mikka and blurted out, "Nick told us to go talk to the shipyard foreman, but we didn't do it."

She stifled an impulse to put her arms around him. That wasn't what he wanted—and in any case she didn't trust herself. Caught up in her own fear and anger, she'd forgotten that her brother still considered Nick a hero.

"We were supposed to make sure the shipyard was ready to work on *Captain's Fancy*," Pup went on urgently. "That's what Nick told us." Despite his intensity, however, he remembered to keep his voice down. "He found a way to rescue us, get us fixed. He's going to get us out of this mess. We were supposed to be sure the shipyard has the right parts.

"But we didn't do it." He flung an accusing glare at the engineer. "Vector says that isn't what's going on." In a shocked whisper, he said, "We're disobeying a direct order, Mikka."

She made a hushing gesture. "Give him a minute." She wanted to comfort her brother: she needed that more than he did. "He'll explain. But first I want to know how you found us."

Vector tasted his coffee, then grimaced in mock disgust. "Where I come from," he pronounced, "making coffee this bad is a capital offense.

"It wasn't hard," he went on without transition. "I told a data terminal in Reception I wanted a room. The program ran a routine check on *Captain's Fancy*'s credit. I expressed my indignation that the total was so low"—he gave Mikka a round smile—"and demanded a record of recent expenditures. The terminal told me you were using ship's credit to buy drinks here." He widened his eyes humorously. "Expensive ones, apparently."

"But why?" Pup's impatience made him sound younger than usual. "Why are you doing this? Nick gave us orders. If you wanted to talk to Mikka, you could have found her after we made sure the shipyard is ready."

Vector looked at Mikka. The humor slowly faded from his eyes, leaving them cold and hard.

"You might as well say it," she growled. "Somebody has to."

Sib took another drink. When he put his glass down, liquid slopped onto the table.

Vector shrugged; he turned to face Pup squarely. "*Captain's Fancy* isn't going to be repaired. Not now—probably not ever. Nick is finished. He'll never be allowed off this rock. He just doesn't want to admit it." The engineer's tone was quiet and sad. "Anything he says about repairs is crap."

"Then why—" Pup began hotly.

"Ciro." Vector's voice sharpened. "Listen to me. He's weeding out the malcontents. Getting rid of people he doesn't trust. He's fighting to survive. Not for the ship—not for us. He's fighting for himself. And we're a threat to him. The four of us here. Personally.

He might have simply killed us, but that would have made a bad impression on the rest of the crew. So he sent us away. Now he'll make sure we never get back."

This was hard for Pup. He'd inherited too much of Mikka's devotion—and learned too much of his own. For reasons he may not have been able to identify, his face flushed scarlet.

"But *why?*" he demanded. "You still haven't told me *why.*"

Vector shrugged again. "Why is he finished? Or why are we a threat to him?"

Studying her brother, Mikka felt a small leap of pride and relief when she saw that he didn't need to ask why Nick was finished. Pup was young and inexperienced; still growing; barely trained. Nevertheless he was smart enough to recognize that Vector's analysis—or Mikka's—of Nick's fate was secondary.

His cheeks were hot with blood as he said, "Why are we a threat to him?"

Vector looked at Mikka. Mikka glared back at him, avoiding Pup's gaze. Suddenly she found the words difficult to say. She'd given Nick too much of herself for too many years. Even now she was ashamed to admit her disloyalty.

Vector also avoided Pup's eyes and said nothing.

She'd decided long ago that Sib Mackern considered himself a coward. Regardless of his opinion of himself, however, he found the courage to speak before she or Vector did.

Almost wincing, but clearly, he said, "I let Morn out of her cabin. So she could rescue Davies from the ejection pod."

There. The truth at last. Mikka hadn't known about Sib's action. She might not have believed him capable of it. But as soon as he spoke she knew he was telling the truth.

His revelation released the pressure which dammed her voice in her chest. Softly she told her part of the story.

"I nearly ran into her. After Sib let her out. While she was on her way to the engineering console room. I could have stopped her. I mean, I could have tried. At the very least, I could have warned Nick. But I didn't."

Now Vector was ready. "She reached the console room while I was still there. I let her at the pod control board. I'm sure I couldn't have stopped her. I know because I hit her as hard as I could, and it didn't make any difference. On the other hand, I could easily have warned Nick."

As if to steady himself, he took another sip of coffee. "In retrospect, I don't feel good about hitting her. But what shames me most is that it took her so long to convince me.

"Ciro"—he looked straight into Pup's earnest gaze—"I let her at the board as soon as I understood that she would have done exactly the same thing—taken the same chances, risked herself just as much—if *I* were being given to the Amnion."

The flush had faded from Pup's face. Mikka couldn't tell what he was thinking. When Vector finished, Pup studied Sib for a moment, then turned toward her. Without noticing what he was doing, he pushed his drink aside with the back of his hand as if he wanted to clear space for honesty and decisions.

"What about me?" he asked. "Why am I a threat to him?"

Mikka didn't hesitate now. "Because you're my brother, and you work with Vector. Nick is afraid you might start listening to one of us."

For a moment Pup didn't respond. His gaze seemed to shift inward, and he frowned, unconsciously mimicking her customary scowl. As she watched, a new sorrow for him tugged through her. If he frowned like that long enough, it would become permanent; he would begin to look as bitter and grieved as she did.

Then he lifted his head. With a dignity he'd never possessed before, he said firmly, "He's right about *that,* anyway."

Tears ran down Mikka's cheeks again. She couldn't hide them. After a while she stopped trying.

Vector patted Pup on the back, ruffled his hair affectionately. In an avuncular tone, he said to Sib, "Better drink up. We need to figure out what we're going to do and then go do it before somebody comes looking for us to ask about that rumor you were supposed to start."

"What *can* we do?" Sib asked at once. "We don't belong here." He made a gesture that indicated the whole cruise. "We haven't got any allies—or any resources. As soon as Nick cuts off our credit, we won't even be able to eat. And we can't ask another ship to take us. He made sure of that. Nobody will touch the people who started those rumors. They'll leave us to the Bill—or Captain Chatelaine.

And *they* won't care about us. They'll just want to know who's being betrayed."

Inspired by his fears, he'd considered implications which hadn't occurred to Mikka before. With a sting of apprehension, she realized that he was right.

"That means interrogation," Sib finished softly. Visceral dread twisted his face. "I don't want to be interrogated here."

Her lip curled into a snarl. Drugs. Zone implants. BR surgery. She also didn't want to be interrogated here.

"Damn," she muttered. "We shouldn't have done it. We should have kept our mouths shut." To Vector and Sib as well, but especially to her brother, she said, "I'm sorry. I haven't been thinking very clearly."

"So we can't afford to sit here"—Vector sounded strangely jocular, as if he were trying to cheer her up—"and wait for events to unfold. We need a plan. We need to move."

She glared at him. "Don't tell me—let me guess. You've got an idea."

Despite his tone, the engineer's smile was humorless and determined. "Well, for a start," he offered, "it might be interesting to figure out what Nick is up to."

Mikka's old anger was directed primarily at herself. "And how do you propose to do that?"

Vector shrugged. "I don't know. I don't fit in here." Like Sib, he referred to the cruise. "On my own, I probably wouldn't last more than a day or two. I don't know what's possible here and what isn't."

"It has something to do with *Soar*," Sib put in tentatively. "Captain Chatelaine. Mikka says she's the woman who cut Nick. He wants revenge somehow."

Mikka nodded. Nick must have lost his mind. He was in too much trouble himself: he couldn't waste his time on revenge when his bare survival—not to mention *Captain's Fancy's*—was at stake.

Unless he had some reason to believe that causing trouble for Sorus Chatelaine would somehow loosen the stranglehold of his circumstances.

If that were true, Mikka and her companions might be able to benefit from it.

Pup, Vector, and Sib were all looking at her. With her hands locked into fists on the tabletop, she ground the knuckles together, trying to force herself to think.

They couldn't approach *Soar:* that was obvious. The rumor they'd started tainted them; they would end up dead—after the Bill or Chatelaine ripped their brains apart.

But *Soar* and her captain weren't the only players in Nick's game.

Abruptly she put her palms down flat on the table. "Not the cruise," she announced quietly. "Not *Soar. Trumpet.*"

Her companions studied her, waiting for an explanation.

She leaned forward. "Everybody on this damn rock," she whispered intently, "heard her talking to Operations. We know Angus Thermopyle is aboard. Along with a bugger named Milos Taverner, who used to be deputy chief of Com-Mine Station Security. All by itself, that stinks. I'm surprised Operations let them in. Maybe the Bill figures they're less dangerous docked than anywhere else. But that's not the point.

"The point is, Nick has been talking to *Trumpet* ever since Operations cleared her. And Milos Taverner has been bugging for Nick for years. In fact, we wouldn't have been able to frame Thermopyle if Taverner hadn't helped us. Now suddenly the man we framed and the man who helped us frame him arrive here—together, for God's sake!—and Nick is talking to them.

"That's what we need to understand. If there's any window out of this mess, that's it."

"Fine," Vector remarked succinctly. "How?"

"Well"—Mikka fought down an impulse to clench her fists again, pound them on the table—"we might start by watching *Trumpet.* See who goes aboard, who leaves. If nothing else, that'll get us off the cruise, which should make it harder for the Bill to find us."

The Bill's surveillance was everywhere, of course. But the bug-eyes and wires were strictly impersonal: they watched everything in general—and nothing in particular. Without specific instructions to the contrary, the recordings of Mikka and her companions would simply be filed in the Bill's gargantuan surveillance database. And those instructions might not be issued until Nick's rumor had time to spread; generate repercussions. Then more time would be required to run search-and-compare programs on the database. An hour or more might pass before *Captain's Fancy*'s castoffs could be located.

"Maybe we'll get a chance to sneak aboard ourselves," she went on. "Maybe we'll even see Nick. In which case"—she gritted her teeth—"we'll have new options."

"Like what?" Sib asked.

Mikka bit down on her anger until her jaws ached. "Like tying him up and delivering him to the Amnion, just to prove our good faith. Or like making him believe we're going to do it, so he'll think he has to deal with us."

"We can't!" Pup protested as if he were shocked.

She scowled at him harshly. "Why not?"

"You saw him fight Orn." Pup's voice cracked; but he was too shaken to stop. The step from distrusting Nick to attacking him was a large one. "He could beat us all with one hand."

Sib nodded vehemently. He was no fighter.

"Maybe." Mikka shrugged. "Maybe not. And maybe we'll have help. Somehow I doubt lockup has taught Angus Thermopyle enough forgiveness to make him a friend of Nick's."

Vector pushed himself to his feet. "I'm satisfied. Let's do it." He moved as if his joints hurt less in Thanatos Minor's g—as if some of the weight he usually carried had been set aside. "Sitting here makes me nervous."

"But—" Sib scrubbed at the sweat on his face.

"Sib," the engineer asked mildly, "if you were Sorus Chatelaine, how long would you wait before you sent your whole crew to get their hands on the people who started that rumor?"

Mackern blanched. Then he jumped out of his chair as if he'd been poked with a stun-prod.

"Mikka—" Pup's eyes were full of supplication; but he didn't know how to ask for what he needed.

She stood; taking his arm, she pulled him up. Then she hugged him quickly.

"Ciro, I can't promise we're going to get out of this alive—or in one piece," she told him. "I don't know what's going to happen. But whatever it is, you won't be alone. You've got friends."

Despite his trepidation, Sib managed a wan smile. Vector nodded gravely.

"And," she finished, "I'll kill anybody who tries to separate us."

Pup returned her hug long enough to murmur, "All right. I'll be all right." Then he stepped back.

Mikka Vasaczk didn't hesitate. She had no time to spare for doubt—and in her heart she believed she wasn't brave enough for it. She'd depended on Nick Succorso longer than Vector, or Sib, or Ciro; needed him more. With her companions behind her, she left the bar-and-sleep, heading for Reception and *Trumpet*.

ANGUS

Finally his instincts or his data-core told him that the time had come.

He could hardly speak. Blisters covered his tongue; his throat was full of ash. Spasms of nausea pulled at his diaphragm, forcing hot bile into his esophagus, but his zone implants stifled that reflex. The pressure they exerted to control him seemed to cramp his chest. Minute by minute, the pain threatened to become more than his caged mind could bear.

That hurt echoed the condition of his whole body. For an hour now, he'd fought with every gram of his strength and will to break his datacore's hold; find some instance of incompleteness or vulnerability which might allow him to slip free of his zone implants long enough to kill Milos. That was all he wanted: a chance to crush Milos to pulp and splinters; a chance against the abyss. But he couldn't crack the prison which had been constructed inside his skull.

With his mouth full of ash and fatality, he recognized that before long he was going to go mad. Then he would be irremediably lost—a lunatic screaming and gibbering inside his own cranium, helpless to make himself heard, helpless to have any effect at all on anything his body did or his mouth said.

He would be back in the abyss—
back *in his crib*
with his scrawny wrists and ankles tied to the slat

---

while his mother

while howls he couldn't utter clamored against the unyielding bone of his head

while his mother filled him with pain—

Yet he went on fighting. He had no alternative. As soon as he stopped, as soon as he surrendered, he would be swallowed back into the absolute dark from which he'd spent his life trying to escape at the cost of so much fear and blood and loneliness.

Then, a short time ago, he'd received an unexpected touch of mercy. Automatically solicitous for his physical well-being, his computer had taken notice of the damage burning like a slow torch in his mouth. When his distress exceeded acceptable parameters, a gentle electronic emission began to inhibit the pain receptors in his brain. The harm was still real, of course. Nevertheless he was able to continue functioning.

Thickly, as fumble-mouthed as a half-wit, he told Milos, "Try it now."

Machine mercy didn't relieve his despair.

Milos shrugged. Exhaling another stream of smoke into the clotted haze left behind by Ease-n-Sleaze's inadequate scrubbers, he rose to his feet. Completely absorbed in himself, as if he were alone with his supply of nic and his ashtray, he moved to the data terminal. With a tap on the keys, he opened a channel to *Trumpet* and instructed her communications board to relay any messages she'd received.

After a moment he murmured, "Looks like it's here."

"You're the one who knows the code," Angus croaked as if he weren't perilously close to failure. "Is it time to go?"

Milos muttered to himself as he deciphered the message. At last he announced, "I guess." He sounded sad and obscurely bitter, as if something he needed had come to an end.

Angus pushed himself out of his chair. His legs would have trembled under him if his zone implants hadn't steadied them; another kind of tremble, which his datacore ignored, rose from his groin to his lungs and the muscles around his heart. Movement, any movement, was better than remaining still while insanity hunted him down.

He didn't wait for Milos. Striding slowly to conceal his desperation, he moved toward the door, out into the hall. As long as he kept his mouth closed, nothing betrayed his pain except the ashen pallor of his face.

Milos followed him unwillingly. With his second behind his shoulder, Angus took the lift down to the level of the bar and walked out of Ease-n-Sleaze.

The blare and swirl of the cruise hit him like a blast of relief. No wires nearby; bugeyes too far away to pick out individual voices. Most of the people who loitered or shoved along the street were enmeshed in their own needs, their own corruption; they took no notice of him. And the air smelled sweet to him, suggestive and familiar: it reeked of synthetic and natural ruin, but nic was only a small component of its complex assault. Here despair appeared in guises he understood.

For a minute or two he moved along with no particular aim, simply breathing the air, absorbing the glare of color and the muted unstable thunder of boots on the cement floor; tasting the atmosphere for threats. Then he took hold of Milos' arm and pulled his second close enough to hear a whisper.

"We can talk now," he mumbled past his sore tongue. "No wires or guards"—he made a short, harsh gesture—"near enough to hear us. What did Captain Sheepfucker say?"

A twist of disgust lingered on Milos' face. "According to Succorso," he answered softly, "the Bill doesn't have a lockup. He doesn't punish people that—simply. But he has a series of cells for interrogations. Down in his command complex somewhere. That's where he usually keeps people until he decides what to do with them." He looked like he wanted to spit. "The woman didn't know anything else." After a pause he added, "It's not much to go on. He didn't tell us how to find the cells. And we can't be sure the kid is there."

"It's enough." Angus knew where those cells were: he'd spent some time there years ago, during one of his more problematic visits to Thanatos Minor. Apparently the Bill hadn't changed his procedures for dealing with human loot since then. That was all the reassurance Angus needed.

Milos waited for more information. When he didn't get it, he hissed, "All right. Assume you can find the cells. Assume the kid is there. You still haven't told me how you propose to get him out. We can't just walk in there and ask for him." His head twitched a reference to the Bill's ubiquitous surveillance. "And you haven't told me why," he finished almost plaintively.

Good questions, both of them. No more than a minute ago, Angus couldn't have answered either one. And he still had no idea why he'd made this deal with Nick; why Warden Dios wanted him to do whatever he could for Morn. But as soon as Milos said the words *ask for him,* the datalink in Angus' head opened like crossing the gap, and information he'd never seen before came on-line.

Involuntary excitement thudded through him as he received a flood of new knowledge.

Triggered by Milos' words—or the proximity of a crisis—this database informed him that his EM prostheses had capabilities he'd never suspected. They weren't simply able to identify wires and bugeyes; read alarms and locks; analyze technological enhancements. Properly coded, they could also emit jamming fields for a wide variety of sensing devices. He could glitch a monitor until it recorded nothing but distortion, if he got close enough to it.

Or—

Suddenly his excitement became so intense that he forgot Milos and the cruise, Warden Dios and Morn Hyland. The world around him seemed to vanish in discovery.

Or he could bend light.

Not over a large area, of course. His power supply wasn't adequate for that. But he could surround himself with a radiant curve, an electromagnetically induced refraction wave in the visible spectrum, which would make him effectively indistinguishable to most optical monitors. Human eyes would always be able to see him. But neurologic and electronic encoding were fundamentally different, vulnerable to different kinds of distortion. And because the Bill's bugeyes were designed to function over distance under uncertain lighting conditions, they received wider bandwidths—with less accuracy. They would record Angus as nothing more than a slight opalescent ripple in the image, like a blur on the bugeye's lens.

The ripple could still be tracked. An intensive computer analysis of the recordings could follow it as it moved. But first it had to be *noticed:* someone in Operations—or in the Bill's command complex—had to see it and worry about it. And that might never happen. No one on Thanatos Minor had any reason to suspect that Angus carried this kind of jamming equipment—that he or anyone else *could* carry it.

Light-bending fields were known, of course, but they weren't common: their emitters were too bulky, and required too much power, to be effectively portable. And even where the size and power consumption of the equipment weren't a problem, the fields themselves remained too small and immobile to have much practical application. By welding these emitters into Angus, Hashi Lebwohl had accomplished a miracle of miniaturization.

The codes were right there in Angus' head.

Lebwohl and Dios had left him defenseless in the path of madness; he hated and feared them. But that didn't prevent him from experiencing a strange, amazed exultation which bordered on gratitude at their technical abilities. When they'd taken his freedom away, they'd made him into something wonderful.

He hadn't felt an emotion like this since the day an Amnioni had taught him how to edit *Bright Beauty*'s datacore.

He'd earned that knowledge by committing what the UMCP would probably have considered the worst crime of his life—a crime they still didn't know about because none of his human or computer interrogators had possessed enough information to frame an accurate question. Single-handedly he had hijacked a large in-system hauler; but he hadn't wasted his time with the actual cargo. Instead he'd loaded the survivors, twenty-eight men and women, into *Bright Beauty*'s holds and sold them directly to the Amnion on Billingate.

In return for booty on that scale, the Amnion had supplied him with the skill which had kept him alive ever since. Plainly they'd believed he would in turn sell the information to other illegals, thereby doing humankind's defenses incalculable harm.

The memory still brought him a burn of satisfied rage as consuming and addictive as matter cannon fire.

"Listen," Milos protested insistently. "You're probably going to get us killed. At the very least we'll be caught. I won't know what to do—I won't be able to react properly, I won't be able to back you up—if you don't tell me what you're planning."

In the grip of an excitement like glee, Angus stopped, turned. Ignoring the crowds and hawkers, the bright, wild signs, the inviting doorways, the occasional shove, he held Milos' arm with one hand;

with the other, he reached up and clenched Milos' pudgy cheeks so that his mouth gaped like a grotesque kiss.

"Then pay attention." Angus' datacore didn't require him to reassure his second. "I'm only going to say this once.

"I don't need you. You're irrelevant here. I'm keeping you with me because I can't send you away. The fuckers who did this to us don't trust you out of my sight. But all you have to do is stay with me and stay *close*. *This* close." He grinned again, squeezing Milos' cheeks harder. "If somebody shoots at us, try to hide behind me."

An instant later he added, "And keep your mouth shut. Any sound might give us away."

Baring his teeth, he let go of Milos and moved into the crowd.

As he walked, he felt his second behind him, so close that Milos' chest brushed his back. He could hear fear in Milos' tense respiration.

Good.

Almost giddy with exultation and movement, he headed for the nearest lift.

It happened to be one which only served the cruise from Billingate's equivalent of a slum, the habitation levels where the installation's more reduced people lived. That suited him fine, however. He and Milos were still being tracked—or could still be tracked. SAC programs in the Bill's computers could sift the vast body of data from all his bugeyes and wires. Under the circumstances, Angus was perfectly content to let the Bill know where he was. The Bill would think that he was looking for someone here; or that his meeting with Nick had resulted in some task which could only be performed here.

Savoring Milos' tension, he led his second along the grime-crusted halls until he found a small knot of men and women waiting for a lift to the docks.

With Milos pressing against him, he pushed his way into the middle of the crowd.

As the lift opened and people squeezed aboard—while he and Milos passed out of range of one bugeye, into range of another—he activated his refractive jamming field.

He didn't doubt for an instant that it worked. He could trust whatever his databases told him about his equipment. False information could kill him—and then everything Dios and Lebwohl had invested in him would be wasted.

Confident that he and Milos were effectively invisible to the Bill, he left the car when it reached the docks. But he didn't linger there. The pressure of his need for movement swelled inside him: he wanted to run. As if he were eager, he went toward one of the general service lifts used by ships' personnel to reach Operations or the cruise.

Now he had to be more careful: his jamming field wouldn't protect him from guards. And the closer he came to lifts that ran down to the depths of the rock, the more guards he encountered. They paid him no particular attention—which meant they hadn't yet received orders to watch for him—but they were still dangerous, if only because they had eyes and guns.

His heart beat faster and his nerves sharpened as if unknown or unused systems were coming on-line: computer-assisted reflexes; decision-making programs; survival instincts. Beads of oily sweat slid down his temples.

There: a lift that went where he wanted to go.

One guard stood outside, staring dully at nothing with eyes as empty as muzzles. Three people waited for the car to arrive, the doors to open.

The indicators said it was going up.

So much the better.

When the lift opened, half a dozen men and women surged out. With Milos clenched behind him, Angus entered along with the other passengers.

One level up, a man and a woman got off.

Two levels later, the third passenger got off.

No one got on.

Now.

As the doors swept shut, sending the lift upward again, Angus fired a precise laser needle into the control panel, burning a gap in its alarm circuitry.

No warnings sounded, either in the car or in Operations, as he engaged the same locks that Maintenance would have used to take the lift out of service.

For a few minutes, at least, he had a private elevator.

As a precaution, he clamped one hand briefly over Milos' mouth, reminding him to be quiet. Then he sent the car downward like a taste of freefall, toward the core of the rock. Where nothing lived except the Bill in his strongroom and Billingate's fusion generator.

Milos' face looked like Angus' mouth felt: thick with pain; sickened by ground-in ash. Still good. Angus showed his teeth and watched the indicators count the levels.

He knew the one he wanted. His memory of the time he'd been locked up here was as vivid as his databases. *You remember Morn Hyland.* All his memories were vivid. *She had a kid.* Of course, there was no guarantee the Bill still used the same rooms. *That's what we were doing on Enablement—force-growing her kid.* Come to that, there was no guarantee the kid was still alive. *She calls him Davies Hyland, after her pure, dead father.* The whole deal might be a lie. *Now the Amnion want him back.* Succorso's treachery might extend to risking Milos, his only ally, for the sake of some unimaginable leverage with the Bill, with the Amnion. *They want to study the consequences of having a mother who didn't lose her mind.* And the cells would be guarded in any case; watched by human eyes.

Nevertheless Angus' concentration held steady, like one of his lasers. He was *moving.* Personally he didn't believe Succorso had lied—not about needing to get Davies away from the Bill. Succorso's efforts to conceal his desperation only made it more convincing. And Angus' datacore was incapable of doubt: the prospect of trading Davies Hyland to redeem Morn had engaged programming as compulsory as the pull of a black hole.

Five levels to go.

Fourthreetwoone.

Stop.

Milos staggered slightly, shifted away from Angus. A stupid mistake; dangerous. And slow. All Milos' movements appeared tortuous to Angus, clogged with mortality. Reacting at microprocessor speeds, he caught his second by the shipsuit and hauled him close again.

One hand behind him to keep Milos tight against his back, Angus stepped between the opening doors into the corridor.

It was only twenty meters long—a blind passage formed in concrete, with no entrances except to the cells and no exits except by the lifts. Six cells, two lifts. Lighting and bugeyes lined the ceiling; more bugeyes than Angus remembered. With that many monitors, the Bill could study every atmospheric eddy and current—the molecular aftermath of moving bodies.

He'd lived in forbidden space for so long that paranoia had become his ruling passion.

Between one tick of his computer's chronometer and the next, Angus grinned at the idea that he was about to justify the Bill's paranoia.

He was already in motion, already dropping to a crouch as he drew Milos out of the lift. The bugeyes weren't enough for the Bill; of course not: he also had two guards in the corridor. They stood on either side of a door off to the left. One of them cupped an impact rifle with flexsteel probes instead of fingers. The other wore his gun built into his chest—a weapon like a small projectile cannon.

Both of them were wired. Operations would receive everything their equipment saw or heard; would know it the instant they stopped transmitting.

The indicators must have told them the lift was coming. They weren't surprised when the door opened.

Because they weren't surprised—and because they had no reason to expect trouble—they weren't braced for Angus' attack.

Speed. Accuracy. Silence. He'd been designed for such things. His lasers made no noise except the small frying sounds of flesh and hardened plastics as he shot one guard between the eyes, the other through his thoracic gun.

Both men folded to the floor as if the sinews holding their joints together had been cut.

Untouched, their transmitters went on functioning. Operations' visual recordings of the event would show a blur, an odd ruby wink, an unlikely change of perspective. Anyone who saw those recordings would know that something had happened. But most of the time no one watched the recordings: only the computers watched.

The computers might not know the difference between men who sat down or even stretched out on the floor to rest and men who fell dead. The Bill's programmers might not have anticipated this situation. A little time might pass before preselected analytical parameters signaled a warning.

After that, playback would take a few seconds. Whoever looked at the recordings would need a few seconds more to react.

By the time the bodies settled and began to drip blood, Angus stood between them at the door they'd guarded. Milos pressed fright against his back, ground knots of fear into his shoulders, while his lasers probed the lock.

It's got to stop.

As if Warden Dios had foreseen everything, planned for everything, Angus swept the cell open and found Davies waiting.

When he saw his son, he caught his first glimpse of Nick's real treachery.

A shock as visceral as an electric charge fired along his nerves. Nick hadn't said anything about this. And the idea had never crossed Angus' mind. If he'd thought about the matter at all, he would have assumed the brat was Nick's—would have assumed that Morn's transcendent lust for Nick had inspired her to want his kid. Didn't she love him? Hadn't her whole body yearned toward him as soon as they first saw each other in Mallorys?

But for that very reason Angus had not thought about whose son Davies was. The way Morn had given herself to Nick—instantly and without question—had hurt him more than he could admit. So he'd focused his attention exclusively on Morn herself; on snatching Davies as a means to rescue her. He'd closed his mind to everything else.

Yet one look at Davies made the boy's parentage unmistakable.

He had Morn's eyes: they were her color; they held her open fear and revulsion and need. He stared at Angus as if he'd been hit by the same charge; as if they were instantaneously linked and fused by the same burning jolt. And his posture might have been hers as well. Even in dismay, his stance hinted at her suppleness, her grace.

The rest of him, however—

The rest was pure Angus. Slimmer and younger, perhaps, but Angus beyond question.

His son—

And Nick had prepared this surprise deliberately, in unmitigated malice. Which implied that there was more to come, that this was only the first.

—a more vulnerable version of himself—

Caught by shock and recognition like an instant of ineffable brisance, Angus gaped back at Davies and couldn't move.

—another baby for the crib.

"Shit," Milos croaked, strangling on distress. "Shit. *Shit.*"

Then the shock passed. Intuitions as fast and blinding as light blazed through Angus. An involuntary howl built up in his chest, an animal roar of helplessness and outrage.

Davies beat him to it. As if he'd been ripped open with a flensing knife, he started screaming.

At the same time he launched a fist like a missile at Angus' head.

Only Angus' equipment saved him. Microseconds after his son began to scream, he keyed codes to activate a different kind of jamming field.

The bugeyes in the cell went deaf and blind with distortion as Davies' fist slammed into his father's cheek.

DAVIES

E vents were *moving in too many different directions at once.* The woman accompanying the Bill had been ordered to get answers out of Davies, torture him if she had to. He didn't know how much time he had left. After she closed the door and went away, he pretended to relax as long as he could: five minutes at most. Then he surged up off his cot and began to pace the small cell again, six steps on one side, five on the other.

Nick Succorso had given Morn to the Amnion. In all likelihood, he'd handed her over to compensate for his failure to deliver her son. And to punish her. But in the end his reasons didn't matter. Only the fact mattered. By now she was probably an Amnioni herself. Her son was all that remained of her.

He needed some way to control the hurricane of grief and blind white rage storming around his heart.

Six steps. Five.

Morn Hyland. Nick Succorso.

And Angus Thermopyle.

The Bill had told him that Angus Thermopyle had come to Thanatos Minor.

Down in the center of the storm, in the small, clear space created and sustained by the coriolus energies of his distress, he knew the three were connected; intimately bound together. They necessitated each other. He simply couldn't remember how or why.

He'd never seen his father. His only impression of the man came from the things Morn and Nick had told him, as well as from what he could see of his own body; from studying his face in the san mirrors of his room aboard *Captain's Fancy*. He'd spent hours in front of those mirrors, trying to understand where Morn Hyland left off and he began. But those hints had given him no sense of his father as a solid, actual presence separate from himself.

He had no defenses—

Angus Thermopyle's sudden appearance in his cell hit him like a translation across a dimensional gap. Ash-faced and urgent, Angus swung open the door and stalked into the cell as if he'd leaped into being from the core of Davies' blocked memories.

In that instant Davies lost the distinction between himself and Morn. Ambushed by her fundamental desperation, he became her as if he'd never been anyone else.

He hardly noticed the pudgy man clinging like a cripple to his father's back. Without transition, as instantaneous as intuition, he began to remember.

He sat up on the edge of the berth.

Angus reached into one of the compartments along the bulkhead, selected a scalpel, and handed it toward him. "Take it."

Davies' fingers closed involuntarily.

In a voice like acid, Angus said, "Put the edge on your tit."

Helplessness compelled Davies. He didn't need to watch what he was doing. Blindly he moved the scalpel until the blade rested against his nipple, his woman's breast, intense silver against brown. The nipple was erect and hard, as if it were ready to be cut.

"You can understand me," Angus said thickly. "I know you can, so pay attention. I can make you cut yourself. If I want to, I can make you cut off your whole tit. Remember that when you think about breaking my neck.

"I'm going to break you. I'm going to break you so hard you'll start to love it, need it. Then I'm going to break you some more. I'm going to break you until you don't have anything but me to live for."

Davies' depths were full of anguish, a wail he was unable to utter.

Angus tapped buttons on the zone implant control.

Fighting to survive, another part of Davies' mind grappled with information he'd known before and hadn't understood, hadn't appreciated. Angus had given Morn a zone implant. He'd used it to take away her freedom, her will, her self: he'd used it to degrade her utterly.

But comprehension changed nothing. Davies was lost in her.

Obedient to the commands of the radio electrode in his brain, helpless beyond bearing, he replaced the scalpel in its compartment. The zone implant control demanded a smile: he smiled. It told him to kneel in front of Angus: he knelt.

Angus' penis protruded from the open seal of his shipsuit. For some reason, he seemed furious as he forced open Davies' mouth and drove himself into him, gagging his son fiercely until he came.

Roaring with inarticulate revulsion and protest, Davies flung a fist at Angus' head. All his young strength and every gram of Morn's absolute agony went into the blow.

The jolt of his fist on Angus' cheekbone saved him. It was physical, present: he felt it like a kick in his knuckles, elbow, and shoulder. The impact anchored him for a second against the insane violation of Morn's memories; momentarily separated him from her. Without that reprieve, he would have had to kill his father; would have had no choice. Nothing less could protect him from what Angus had done to Morn.

During that instant Angus moved.

He shrugged off Davies' blow as if he barely felt it. So quickly that Davies couldn't see how it was done, Angus blocked his fury aside, spun him around, caught him in an armlock. His own momentum and Angus' charge slammed him at the wall, hammered his forehead against the concrete.

Giddy with pain, he thrashed in Angus' grasp, fought like Morn to break free. If he didn't fight, he would remember more: remember weeks of abuse and contempt; remember abjection; remember selling his soul—

—remember something worse.

But he couldn't get loose. Angus' grip was only more honest than the power of Morn's zone implant, not weaker. Sure as flex-steel, he tightened his hold until Davies could hardly breathe; hammered Davies' head at the wall again. While phosphenes and pain whirled like lost nebulae across his vision, draining the force from his muscles, denaturing the barriers which had preserved him from Morn's cruel past, Angus hauled his head up and hissed like murder into his ear, "Shut up! Shut *up*! You'll get us killed if you don't keep your fucking mouth *shut*!"

The man behind Angus went on moaning, "Shit. Shit," as if he didn't have the strength to cry out.

A trickle of blood ran into Davies' eyes, but he couldn't see it through the phosphene dance. *Angus had beaten him up,* he remembered that, *pounded and kicked and cudgeled his flesh to make him vulnerable, mar his beauty so that it would be less frightening.* "You—" he panted. "You vile—"

"Listen to me." Angus pulled his grip tighter. "*Listen,* you little shit. I can hide us visually, but I can't block sound. Not without distorting every bugeye in range, and then he'll know exactly where we are. He'll track the distortion. I've already set off alarms in Operations, in his strongroom. Goddamn it, *I'm trying to rescue you!* All you have to do is *shut up!*"

Past a chaos of blood and hurt, Davies choked out, "You *raped* me, you sonofabitch!"

"What's he talking about?" Angus' companion begged. "He's crazy. Doesn't he want to be rescued?"

Snarling in frustration, Angus pulled his son off the wall, spun him, hit him in the stomach hard enough to stun his diaphragm. While Davies gaped for air he couldn't get, Angus lashed a hand at the other man, jerked him closer.

"Help me hold him!" Angus whispered hotly. "We've got to stay together. If he opens his mouth, jam your fingers down his throat."

As if he were strong enough to carry them both, Angus heaved Davies and the other man toward the door.

Davies stumbled, but Angus and the other man kept him upright. Blinking blood from his eyes, he forced his legs under him.

In a knot of arms, a tangle of feet, the two men half carried him out of his cell toward the open door of a lift.

Morn must have been someone else, a separate individual, but he couldn't tell the difference.

"Angus," he said, *"Angus, listen to me.*

"I can save you.

"I'll testify for you. When you go back to Com-Mine, they'll charge you with illegal departure. I'll support you. I'm not much of a cop anymore, but I've still got my id tag. I'll tell them you left on my orders. And I'll tell them there was no supply ship. It was a hoax—that other ship set

it up. I'll tell them to arrest Nick Succorso. I can't save your ship, but I can save you.

"Just give me the control." His voice was husky, full of need. "The zone implant control."

And Angus replied, "You aren't thinking straight. You're a cop. It's worse when a cop breaks the law. They'll find out. They have to find out. And then you'll be finished." He may have been crying. "I'll lose my ship."

If there were alarms wailing in Operations, or in the Bill's strongroom, Davies couldn't hear them.

Frantic with haste, Angus and his companion manhandled Davies into the lift. Sweat splashed from Angus' face as he whirled to the control panel, sent the car upward. A red splotch outlined the impact of Davies' knuckles high on his cheek.

"You can't save it," Davies shot back, suddenly angry, more than a little desperate. "I can handle station Security. And the UMCP. I'll think of a way. But nothing can save your ship. It's too badly broken. We'll need a miracle just to get back to Com-Mine alive.

"Please. Give me the control." Now he was pleading nakedly. "I'm not going to use it against you. I need it to heal."

Clamping one hand on the armrest of Davies' seat, bracing his feet on the deck, Angus struck him a blow like the one which had felled Nick, a blow with the whole weight of his existence behind it. If Davies' seat hadn't absorbed some of the impact, he might have been knocked unconscious. Angus might have broken his neck.

"Bitch. I'll never give up my ship."

Who asked you to, you vile bastard? Davies raged. Who wants you to go on living? Succorso should have slagged you while he had the chance!

Morn would have been better off if she'd died then.

But he kept his mouth shut, locked the words and the memories like screams inside his skull. A convulsion was taking place within him, a seismic upheaval, and memory was only one of the tectonic forces Angus had unleashed. *Rescue* was another: escape from the Bill; from the Amnion; from Nick Succorso. And *sound* was the only danger he understood. *I can hide us visually, but I can't block sound.*

Despite the collapse of his protective barriers, he clung to what he understood; to the hard clear need for escape.

Liberated at last, memories yowled and harried through his brain like furies.

While the lift rose he remembered how Nick had tricked and trapped Angus. He remembered the part he'd played in making that possible.

He remembered the impossible yearning which had sprung to fire in him when he'd first seen Nick—the mute, ineluctable, sexless, and almost entirely abstract passion, not for Nick Succorso the man, but rather for the capacity to act which Nick embodied.

He remembered hours of rape, days of humiliation, weeks of the zone implant. He remembered pleading, prostrating himself, offering Angus anything he could think of.

Does that make you feel like a man? he'd asked before he'd learned what was about to happen to him; how savage Angus' intentions were. *Do you have to destroy me to feel good yourself? Are you that sick?*

It's because of men like you I became a cop.

Forbidden space is bad enough. We don't need any worse threats than that. But men like you are worse. You betray your own kind. You prey on human beings—on human survival—and get rich. I'll do anything I can to stop you. No price is too high for stopping a man like you.

And later he'd said, *Even if I can't do it, somebody else will. It doesn't matter what you think of me. Maybe you're right. Maybe I'm as bad as a traitor. But there are better cops than me—stronger— They'll stop you. They'll make you pay for this.*

But Angus had answered, *They'll never get the chance. I told you. I'm a bastard. The worst bastard you'll ever meet. And I'm good at what I do. I've been dancing circles around the fucking cops all my life. If they ever catch me, it'll be long after you're dead.*

In the meantime, I'm going to have some fun with you. You're my crew now. You're going to learn to take orders. And I've got old scores to settle. A lot of them. I'm going to settle them on you. By the time I'm done, you're going to want to run away so bad it'll damn near kill you, but I won't even let you scream.

It was too much in too little time. The car was as claustrophobic as a coffin, too small to contain furies. Davies remembered what Angus had done without being able to believe that he'd done them to Morn Hyland, not to her son.

And he couldn't remember why.

How had his plight become possible? Why had he let Angus have that kind of power over him? He'd always been able to remember the moment when *Starmaster* saw *Bright Beauty* destroy that mining camp, slaughter the miners. Why hadn't *Starmaster* killed or arrested Angus? Why hadn't Davies killed Angus himself?

Nick had told him the answer, but he couldn't remember it. The orogenic forces cracking and shifting through him confused it, confused all recent knowledge: only the past was real.

Blood dripped into his mouth. He bit his lower lip until it hurt like his head.

As the car eased up to the level Angus had chosen, the other man opened his mouth fearfully: he wanted to say something, ask something. Questions and dread haunted his eyes.

As fierce as the pain in Davies' forehead, Angus formed the words, Shut up! As if he were threatening his companion in some way, he shoved his hand into a pocket of the other man's shipsuit, pulled out a packet of nic. Brandishing it in his companion's face, he dared the other man to take it back.

The man winced; his eyes rolled. Nevertheless he didn't reach for the packet—or pull away.

When the doors slid aside, Davies and the other man automatically tried to lurch into motion. Incomprehensibly strong, Angus held them still—

—until he saw that no one was waiting to use the lift; that the corridor in front of him was empty.

Then, with a flick of his hand, he tossed the packet in a spinning arc out the upper left corner of the open door.

Davies didn't realize that the lift was being watched until he saw a guard turn to focus on the object sailing unexpectedly over his head.

Instantly Angus drove Davies and his companion forward. Before the guard could turn back, Angus touched his fist to the man's spine.

The guard fell on his face. After a twitch or two, he stopped moving. A little curl of smoke rose from his clothing and was gone.

Sweat gleamed on Angus' cheeks. Grinning savagely, he impelled Davies and the other man into the corridor.

Twenty meters later, they passed a corner. The lifts which accessed the Bill's private domain were out of sight.

Why? Davies shouted in silence and anguish. Why did I let you do that to me?

What had Nick told him? *He gave her a zone implant to keep her under control.* Talking about Morn as if she and Davies weren't the same person. *That's how he got her pregnant.*

It's a pathetic story. He turned her on until she would have been willing to suck her insides out with a vacuum hose, and then he fucked her senseless. For weeks, he made her do everything he'd ever dreamed a woman could do.

That's your father, Davies. That's the kind of man you are.

And Nick had said, *She'd learned to like it. He'd degraded her so much that she fell in love with it. Eventually she wanted it so much that he could trust her with her zone implant control. It wasn't found on him because he'd already given it to her. She loved using it on herself.*

But that wasn't it, wasn't what Davies needed to remember. The torrent of memories crashing through him had no central *why.*

He needed that absolutely.

At the same time it terrified him so much that he couldn't dislodge it from the blind core of his mind; couldn't break it free to dominate and define the furies.

Struggling for sanity, he took hold of the present long enough to realize that this whole situation should have been impossible. Billingate was thick with monitors. Why didn't the Bill react? *Hide us visually–* How?

And if they were hidden, why did Angus kill the guard?

Impossible or not, Angus' concealment appeared to work. Locked together and nearly stumbling like drunks supporting each other after a binge, the three of them entered an area called Reception. A few men and women were there; but their attention was fixed on the data terminals. And there were guards—Davies couldn't tell how many. But they all had the poleaxed look of men kept awake by inadequate doses of stim. Because of the way Angus and his companion held Davies, with their heads down and their faces toward each other, the guards might not be able to see them well enough to identify them.

Once they passed Reception and entered the corridor leading to the visitors' docks, they were alone again.

Access passages branched off at intervals, serving individual berths. Outside the passages, ship id displays indicated that some of the berths were occupied; others weren't. Davies saw *Captain's Fancy*'s name and had to grind his teeth to keep from howling. Morn wasn't there, she was already lost, already Amnion—but Succorso might be, the man who'd destroyed her.

There was only one evil worse than what Angus had done to her. The ultimate crime had been left for Nick to commit.

But Davies couldn't think about that. *He* was Morn Hyland: the woman who'd been given to the Amnion no longer existed. Rape and ruin ripped through him; furies clawed at his mind. They were going to tear him apart.

Abruptly Angus and the other man swung him into an access passage. He caught a glimpse of the id display: *Trumpet*.

No more guards. He didn't understand that. Angus Thermopyle was a notorious illegal; he'd just escaped from lockup. He should have had guns trained on him every time he took a step. The Bill should have ordered that for his own protection.

But of course the Bill was an illegal as well. Davies was thinking like a cop; like Morn before—

At its end the passage led through a scan field toward an airlock, a ship. Now the Bill would know where they were: that was inescapable. The scan field would register three bodies moving through it. It would show that Angus and his companion had taken someone aboard *Trumpet* with them.

But Angus didn't hesitate. As he compelled Davies and the other man ahead, his face wore a peculiar expression, a look of concentration elsewhere, as if he could hear the voices of the dead.

Together they reached the ship. The other man panted urgently, eager for safety, while Angus keyed codes into the airlock's exterior control panel.

In seconds the lock cycled open.

They blundered aboard.

As soon as the lock sealed behind them, Angus shoved Davies and the other man away from him. Malign triumph and rage burned in his eyes; his features twisted savagely. Slashing his fists at the ceiling, he yelled, "I did it! I *got* you, you bastard!"

He may have been shouting at the Bill.

Davies thudded against the interior doors, stood still with his arms wrapped around his chest to contain the furies.

Gulping for air, the other man gasped, "I don't understand. How did you do that? What did you do? Shit, Angus! The Bill will be here in five minutes. He's going to want blood for those guards you killed."

"No, he won't!" Angus needed to shout; needed an outlet for

his tension and exultation. Pointing his index finger like a gun at his temple, he barked, "I can emit jamming fields! I blinded his bug-eyes—he never saw us! His scan"—he flung his arm in the direction of the access passage—"never saw us! As far as he knows, we aren't here. We've lost ourselves somewhere on the cruise! He'll spend hours looking for us."

Gradually he lowered his voice. "We'll leave communications on automatic. If he calls, the ship'll tell him we aren't here."

"Shit, Angus," the other man sighed again weakly. He inhaled *Trumpet*'s atmosphere as if he'd never tasted anything so sweet. "You scared me. What would it have cost you to tell me what you were doing?"

Angus flashed a predatory grin. "What would it have cost you to force me to tell you?"

Davies couldn't contain so much pressure. The more he confined it, the stronger it became. He wanted to hit Angus, pulverize him, reduce his triumph to powder. His mother's legacy urged him to destroy himself by attacking Angus.

So that he could avoid the central *why*.

Angus and this other man were his allies only to the extent that they opposed the Bill. For all he knew, they were working with Nick Succorso, even though Succorso had betrayed Angus to Com-Mine Security. Or they might be working for the Amnion. Nothing he remembered gave him any reason to think Angus' malice had limits.

But he'd reached his own limits, his breaking point. If he snapped now, he would snap permanently.

Like his father, he needed an outlet.

Tight with suppressed violence, he left the airlock as soon as it opened, strode into the waiting lift to put some distance between himself and Angus. But that was as far as he could go.

Whirling, he cried from the depths of his inherited anguish, *"Damn you, you RAPED me!"*

Angus and his companion froze, staring at Davies as if he'd threatened to immolate himself.

"He said that before," the pudgy man muttered anxiously. "What's he talking about?"

"How the fuck should I know?" Angus retorted. Facing Davies, he demanded, "What the hell are you talking about, I raped you? You must be my kid. I don't know how else she could have dropped a brat who looks like me. I'm going to make Captain Sheepfucker pay for not telling me that. But I've never seen you before in my life."

Unconsciously aping Angus' exultation, Davies brandished his fists, he flailed the air because he had nothing else to hit.

"It's because of men like you I became a cop. I'll do anything I can to stop you."

Angus' yellow eyes widened. "Wait a minute. Wait a minute. I've heard that before. It's a quote. A direct quote."

"Angus—" the other man put in.

"Shut up, Milos," Angus snapped. "Let me think."

Without warning, all the anger ran out of Davies. Anger was essential: it was his last defense. But now the central *why* was too close to the surface; he couldn't fight it down any longer. Involuntary shudders ran through him as his rage turned to panic and helplessness.

"What did Succorso tell us?" Angus asked rhetorically. "The Amnion used some kind of force-growing technique." Mimicking Nick's voice, he drawled, " 'They say force-growing is supposed to make vegetables out of the mother, but that didn't happen to her. They think they know why. So they aren't particularly interested in her. But they want her brat. They want to study the consequences of having a mother who didn't lose her mind.' "

Angus' eyes glittered with intuitions. "I don't know anything about force-growing. They didn't supply me with a database on it. But maybe she was supposed to lose her mind because they gave it to *him*. They *imprinted* it on him. Because he isn't old enough to have a mind of his own."

He let out a guttural laugh. "He thinks he's *her*. He thinks *he's* the one I raped.

"He thinks *he's* the one who killed her whole family."

There.

Why.

Nick had given him a hint, but he hadn't understood it. *After she demolished* Starmaster, *he rescued her from the wreckage.*

Killed her whole family.

Hugging himself like a child, Davies Hyland sank to the floor of the lift and curled into a ball.

ANGUS

Strangely dismayed by the extremity of Davies' reaction, Angus stared down at his son and chewed his lower lip.

He needed a database on force-growing; needed to know what he was up against. Apparently he'd guessed right. The Amnion had copied Morn's mind onto Davies', presumably because knowledge, training, and experience couldn't be force-grown the way bodies could. And apparently some facet of the process—maybe her zone implant, maybe something else—had protected her from going crazy when her mind was ripped away; probably by blocking the memories which had afflicted her with so much revulsion and horror. Now those memories were returning to her son.

His son. The kid was unquestionably his.

Right or not, however, guesses didn't help. They explained Davies' collapse, but they didn't answer the larger questions.

The Amnion want him back. They want to study the consequences of having a mother who didn't lose her mind.

Curled tightly around himself, he lay on the floor of the midship lift. His forehead was crusted with blood. Except for the stertorous rasp of his breathing, he made no sound. But in another minute he was probably going to start whimpering. After that it might be only a matter of time before he began to suck his thumb.

How good were the chances that the Amnion wanted him back now, in this condition? Wasn't it more likely that he'd just become worthless to them?

STEPHEN R. DONALDSON

If that was true, Angus had suddenly lost his leverage. Nick had no reason to exchange Morn for damaged merchandise.

And the memories which caused Davies so much harm were his, Angus', doing.

As he considered the implications, he growled to no one in particular, "Motherfucking sonofabitch."

"Who, him?" Milos asked. His safe return to *Trumpet* left him in a state of brittle relief. Trying to recover his self-confidence, he protested, "Come on, Angus. Give him a break. He's just a kid. It's not his fault he looks like you."

Full of chagrin and bitterness, Angus rounded on Milos. Past his blistered tongue, he rasped, "Not him. Succorso. Captain Sheep-fucker. You aren't thinking, Milos. That's dangerous. It's how shits like you get killed.

"Help me pick him up." He moved to Davies' side. "We'll take him to the bridge until I decide what to do with him."

Riding his relief, Milos stayed where he was. Absentmindedly he reached for his packet of nic. When he realized it was gone, he gave a fleshy grimace.

"Tell me," he said softly. "What aren't I thinking about?"

"We're being cheated." The pain in Angus' mouth made him want to rage. "What kind of game do you think Succorso is playing?" He took a step closer to his second. "Or do you already know? Is that what you were talking to him about before we docked? Setting this up?"

Milos raised his hands to ward Angus away. His eyes hinted at Jerico priority commands. Still softly, he asked, "How do you know Succorso is cheating?"

"Because he's keeping secrets. Somehow he neglected to mention Davies is my son. And he sure as hell didn't tell us Davies has Morn's mind. What do *you* think? Doesn't that sound like he was trying to help us fail?"

Unless the real cheat was on another level entirely; more insidious as well as more profound. In which case, the things Succorso hadn't revealed about Davies were just a distraction.

Milos' eyes dropped; unconscious of what he did, he searched his pockets for nic. After a moment he murmured, "That isn't what we talked about. As far as I know, his problem is exactly what he says it is. He promised this kid to the Amnion. Now he can't deliver." Slowly he looked up to meet Angus' glare. "Everything he said was a demand for help."

Angus wanted to spit his disgust in Milos' face. Grimly he muttered, "Well, we'll know soon, won't we. If Captain Sheepfucker comes here looking for Davies, he wasn't trying to make us fail. He was just playing with us." Distracting us. "If he doesn't, we'll know we're in trouble."

Crowded with vehemence, he pointed at Davies and rasped, "Are you going to give me a hand, or are you going to stand there holding your cock until it falls off?"

A flush of anger highlighted the mottling on Milos' scalp. Nevertheless he swallowed a retort. With a tight shrug, he came to help pick Davies off the floor.

The boy was completely rigid, secured like cargo by the flexsteel straps of his distress. His chest sucked air through his teeth; an urgent, fatal wheeze: nothing else moved. His eyes were clenched shut.

An unfamiliar pang like pity twisted Angus' heart as he felt the pressure of his son's crisis. He seemed to know what was happening inside the boy as if he'd learned it from Morn. Davies was remembering the absolute authority of gap-sickness, the command to commit destruction; remembering the wholesale slaughter of his family.

But it was something which hadn't happened to him—a crime as well as a sickness in which he had no part. And he hadn't lived through the consequences. Yet Morn Hyland, who owned those memories, had taken it better than this. She'd faced this same utter and irreparable horror, and had come back fighting—

In a sense, she'd forced Angus to give her a zone implant. Without it she would have found some way to kill him. Especially if that meant killing herself at the same time.

Her son was being broken by things which she'd already survived.

Angus' son.

Another baby for the crib.

His part in Davies had made the boy weaker than his mother.

And now Morn might be lost because Davies wasn't strong enough to be worth trading for her.

Fulminating uselessly, Angus pulled Milos and Davies into motion. His urge to murder something, anything, was so strong that only powerful zone implants and inexorable machine logic could control it.

Approximately gentle, he and Milos rode the lift with Davies to the midship passage, then lugged him toward the bridge. At the head of the companionway, Milos supported Davies while Angus moved partway down the treads; then Angus accepted the hard fetal knot and carried it the rest of the way. After only a moment's hesitation he propped Davies in Milos' g-seat at the second's station. By the time Milos gained the bridge, Angus was at his own station, keying commands which ran *Trumpet's* communications log across one of the display screens.

The log showed routine operational signals; the message from Nick which Milos had retrieved earlier; and a peremptory demand from the Bill.

This last transmission said, "Captain Angus Thermopyle of *Trumpet,* reply as soon as you get this. My security has been breached. You're in as much trouble here as I am, and I intend to make sure you can't avoid any of it—unless you help me find out what happened and do something about it.

"This is *my* rock, Captain Angus. I'm the Bill you owe. If you don't pay me, you won't live to be paid by anybody else."

"Shit," Milos breathed, staring at the screen. "How does he know it was us?"

"He doesn't," Angus snorted. "He would be cutting our airlocks open right now if he did. But he knows we talked to Captain Sheepfucker—the obvious candidate for a security breach. And he's got a recording of your *activities* while we were waiting for that message. Even if he was brain dead, he would wonder what that was all about.

"The important thing now is to not let him know we're back aboard."

Milos looked at Davies as if he were considering rolling the boy out of his g-seat. "Won't he figure it out?"

"Eventually," Angus admitted. "But maybe by that time we'll be rid of the kid."

If Succorso wasn't cheating.

If the Amnion still wanted Davies.

And if—the unexpected idea shocked him like a static discharge—he could bear to trade his son away.

A more vulnerable version of himself.

He'd spent his life fleeing from his personal abyss. Could he abandon Davies to it now? Could he surrender his son to *the crib—*

with his scrawny wrists and ankles tied to the slats

while his mother filled him with pain

jamming hard things up his anus, down his throat, prying open his penis with needles

and laughing—?

How could he leave any part of himself there?

His datacore might not give him any choice.

Suddenly he felt as weak as Milos. Like Milos, he breathed to himself, *Shitshitshit,* because he didn't have the strength or the words for his dilemma.

"I hope so," Milos said distantly. Then he asked, "What do we do now?"

Angus' datacore didn't care how weak he felt; his zone implants didn't care. "Wait," he muttered. "Until we hear from Captain Sheepfucker."

"In that case"—Milos moved to the companionway—"I need nic."

Go ahead, Angus thought impersonally. Smoke your lungs out. Maybe you'll die of cancer.

But he didn't think anything that good was going to happen.

Davies' clenched respiration was starting to sound like a death rattle.

Welded unbreakably to his equipment, Angus waited like a capped volcano.

Milos returned from replenishing his supply of nic. Smoking like an oil fire, he paced a slow circle around the bridge, passing across the display screens and behind the companionway as if his life revolved on Angus or Davies.

After ten minutes the intercom chimed.

Milos froze in midstride. Angus jerked up his head.

"This is Nick." Succorso's voice, casual and maddening. "Let me in."

On the keypad of the airlock intercom he tapped the id code Angus had given him.

A spasm shook Davies. His breathing sharpened. But his eyes remained knotted shut; he didn't unlock his fetal grip on himself.

Angus silenced the intercom. "I'll do it," he told Milos. He could have opened the airlock from his board, but he didn't. Instead he turned his seat and leaped for the companionway. "I don't want that bastard on this ship unless I'm watching him every second."

The time, his computer informed him, was 04:11:19.07.

Up the companionway. Along the passage past *Trumpet*'s galley, sickbay; the weaponry and computer spaces. Into the lift. Angus' heart hammered; his brain ran lightning calculations. The bugeyes would hear Succorso's voice; would see him enter the airlock. The fact that *Trumpet* wasn't empty might not remain secret much longer. Angus, Milos, and Davies would be safe only as long as it was impossible for anyone to imagine that Angus could emit a refractive jamming field; as long as it was easier for the Bill to believe that Succorso had been given the codes to let himself aboard *Trumpet*.

When the lift opened, Angus moved to the airlock panel and unsealed the doors; then he retreated into the car—out of bugeye range—while the lock cycled.

Succorso stood outside, at the end of the scan field. His eyes were dark and hollow, as deep as gouges; his scars looked like streaks of ash across his cheeks. Nevertheless his mouth wore a buccaneering smile and his arms swung from his relaxed shoulders as if he were afraid of nothing.

He was alone.

Angus raised a warning finger to his lips, then motioned Nick into the airlock.

As soon as the exterior doors closed, Nick asked in a careless tone, "Did you get him?"

Angus waited until Nick joined him in the lift before he pronounced, "You're the one with the death wish, not me. You like treachery so much you would rather sabotage your allies than help them, no matter how desperately you need them."

Hard as a blow, he keyed the car upward.

Nick's smile twisted. "What's that supposed to mean?"

Angus would have hit Nick if he could. His zone implants prevented him, so he did his best to punch with words. "You didn't tell me Davies is my kid. You didn't tell me he has Morn's mind. That was a mistake, asshole—a *big* mistake."

Nick shrugged. A smolder gleamed in the damaged depths of his eyes. "So you did get him?"

The lift stopped, opened. Angus pointed Nick toward the bridge. "For all the good it's going to do you."

A question crossed Nick's features: he let it go. Ambling in Thanatos Minor's light g, he headed along the passage to the companionway.

Close at his back, Angus followed him down the steps.

In Angus' absence, Milos had finally made up his mind to push Davies out of his g-seat. The boy lay curled around himself on the deck between the command stations. His breathing had accelerated: he heaved for air as if he were suffocating. But his eyes stayed shut. If anything his muscles were clamped more tightly than before.

Smoking hard, Milos sat in his g-seat. He'd pivoted his station to face the companionway; but he didn't meet either Nick's gaze or Angus' glare.

"Christ on a crutch, Captain Thermo-pile," Nick drawled. "You were supposed to rescue him, not scare him into autism."

At the sound of Nick's voice, Davies' eyes sprang wide. Wild and white, they stared blind madness at Nick's boots.

Another pang touched Angus' heart.

"It wasn't me." He pushed past Nick to take his own g-seat. Swiveling his station, he confronted Nick with his hands on his board, ready for maneuvers or matter cannon fire. "*You* did this—you set it up. Seeing me triggered a memory crisis of some kind. If you'd warned me, I might have been able to stop it. Instead I made it worse because I didn't know what was going on.

"The Amnion may not want him like this. I don't know about that, and I don't care. It's on your head—*you* can pick up the pieces. We made a deal. Morn for Davies. I kept my end." Grimly he promised, "Now you are going to keep yours."

Nick made a sound like a dying laugh. "Oh, they'll want him, all right. He's still human—he's valuable no matter what condition he's in. And they wanted to study him, see what effect her zone implant had on him. That hasn't changed. They won't be able to blame me if they don't like the results.

"Here." He reached into his pocket, took out an id tag on a fine chain. "This is hers. I'll leave it with you"—his mouth twisted with humor or scorn—"to show my good faith. I'll take him to the Amnion sector." He nodded at Davies. "Then I'll go get her and bring her here."

The id tag was Morn's: Angus recognized the embossed UMCP insignia at a glance.

Too fast for Nick to stop him, he snatched the chain.

"Wrong."

Nick tensed as if he were about to jump at Angus. Almost immediately, however, he forced himself to relax. He may have been taken aback by the speed of Angus' reflexes.

Angus gripped the id tag so hard that his fist shook, daring Nick to spring; nearly pleading for Nick to attack him. Into Nick's face he rasped, "*First* you bring her here. *Then* I'll let you have the kid."

Slowly one of Davies' arms uncurled. His palm pressed flat against the deck.

A tic began to pull at the muscles of Nick's cheek, stretching his scars until they looked like small grimaces. Without shifting his attention from Angus, he asked, "What the hell is going on here, Milos?"

"How should I know?" Milos sighed—a veiled groan. "He's been out of control ever since we docked."

"Then *talk* to him," Nick demanded between his teeth. "Give me some help here. I've done everything I can to make you rich. Right now you're spending money I made for you. You *owe* me, Milos. You got him out of lockup, didn't you? You must have some kind of leverage with him.

"It's time to pay your debts."

Milos dropped his nic on the deck. His hands trembled as he took out another one, lit it. Nevertheless he sounded almost sure of himself, almost calm, as he replied, "You're a dead man, Nick. Only a fool pays his debts to a dead man."

The tic tightened in Nick's cheek. His air of nonchalance changed character: a poised stillness came over him. Not for the first time, he reminded Angus of a viper, supple and deadly. Yet his eyes held a haunted look, a hint of desperation. He might have been drowning.

His gaze flicked around the bridge as if he were looking for a weapon. "Nice ship," he commented appraisingly. "You did yourself a favor when you stole her. She's a lot better than that other hunk of junk."

Then he met Angus' scowl again.

"I don't trust you, Captain Thermo-pile. I know too much about you. How do you expect me to believe you won't renege as soon as you get your hands on her?"

"I don't." Still praying that Nick would attack him, Angus lowered his fist until it rested on the command board. "In fact, I may decide to do exactly that. This is the price you pay for not telling me he's my kid—for not warning me. He doesn't leave this ship until you bring Morn Hyland here."

Now Davies was staring at his hand on the deck rather than at Nick's boots. Painfully, stiff with cramps, he unbent his other arm, straightened his knees a bit.

Nick raised his fingers to rub at his cheek, but he didn't seem aware of it. Darkness filled his eyes. "In that case"—a lopsided smile bent his mouth—"you can kiss her good-bye." He laughed like breaking glass. "I mean, you already have kissed her good-bye. There in Mallorys was the last you're ever going to see of her.

"Don't bother coming with me." He laughed again. Now it sounded like breaking bones. "I can find my own way out."

He turned for the companionway.

Davies pushed himself up onto his knees and lunged forward, grabbing Nick around the legs.

Nick staggered a step; recovered his balance. Angus assumed his son was strong; he'd been strong himself at that age. But the stress of clamping his body into a ball so tightly had left the boy weak. He couldn't pull Nick off his feet.

Nick wrenched himself around despite Davies' grasp. "Let go of me, you little shit."

Davies' mouth gaped open. A croak like a crippled howl came from his straining throat. Driving one leg under him, he managed to knock Nick back against the companionway.

As Nick hit the treads, he snap-punched Davies in the temple so hard that the boy slumped aside.

But Davies didn't let go. He'd lost his hold on Nick's legs, so he clung to one of Nick's ankles. A constricted frenzy flamed on his face.

Quick as a piston, Nick kicked him in the solar plexus.

Davies must have seen the blow coming, however. He had Morn's training—and Angus' instincts. In spite of his weakness and pain, he released Nick's ankle; as Nick's boot slammed into him he flung his arms around that leg and heaved sideways, pulling Nick over him and down.

Milos was on his feet—not to intervene, just trying to put as much distance as possible between himself and the fight.

Angus sat where he was, gripping Morn's id tag so hard the metal cut into his palm; studying his enemy.

Once more he had the dislocated sense of being more than one person; of existing simultaneously in separate realities. One part of him left his g-seat and jumped eagerly into the fray, savage for a chance to use his new resources—to make Succorso pay some of the cost for his long ordeal. Hell, with his welded force he could easily *kill* Succorso. And the strange pangs were growing stronger. Davies was his son—

A more vulnerable version of himself.

Weak with cramps and his mother's absolute chagrin.

Yet Angus didn't move. Prewritten instructions held him still, instructions which denied him the right to hurt anyone with any kind of UMCP connection—and which placed no value on Davies. He sat and watched the struggle as if it were purely of abstract interest, while inside his skull he howled like his son.

Nick was good: Angus had to admit that. The instant he hit the deck, he rebounded to his knees. One two three times he pounded Davies in the face, and again, onetwothree, too fast for Davies to block the blows. Blood splashed from Davies' cheeks, his mouth, his brows. Gulps of air panted in and out of his mouth like aborted screams.

Nevertheless Davies didn't quit. Ducking his head against Nick's fists, he tightened his grip as if he were fighting for Morn's life and strained to haul himself up Nick's body, reach high enough to do some damage.

"Shit!" Milos gasped suddenly. "Angus, Nick's going to kill him!"

With the same abstract abhorrence which kept him still, Angus wondered whether Milos was about to issue a Joshua order.

He couldn't take that chance.

"All right, Captain Sheepfucker," he growled. "You can stop now. If you hurt him any more, even the Amnion won't want him."

Nick flashed a glance at Angus, showed his teeth.

In a spray of blood he hit Davies again *onetwothree.*

Davies' hold on Nick slipped an inch; started to fail—

—and a restriction lifted in Angus' head. Between one instant and the next, his programming shifted along a new logic tree. New implications were considered: new standards applied.

Davies was Morn's son.

Joshua was here to rescue her.

Therefore whatever she valued, whatever she needed or owned, might be important; might be crucial.

He exploded out of his g-seat.

Before Nick reached *four*, Angus caught him by the back of his shipsuit, snatched him into the air, and pitched him against the rear bulkhead.

Nick hit; twisted to land on his feet. Wild and desperate, at the end of his endurance, he charged at Angus as if he meant to prove that he never lost.

Snarling avidly, Angus punched him straight in the forehead with a fist reinforced by implanted struts and plates—a fist as effectively massive as a block of stone.

Nick dropped to his knees like a bull in an abattoir.

He didn't fall; but his eyes glazed, and his head lolled. His hands thrashed like dying fish at the ends of his arms.

Angus felt a rush of raw pleasure as acute as lasers, as clean as matter cannon fire. "That's *twice*, Succorso." Twice he'd beaten Nick physically. "The third time, I won't just tap you. I'll split your fucking skull."

Panting for violence, he bent over Davies to see what shape the boy was in.

Despite his bloody breathing and stunned gaze, Davies was conscious. His hands groped for Angus, plucked at Angus' sleeves. His mangled lips moved dumbly, as if they were trying to form words.

After a moment he managed to moan, "My father— All of them—" Then he choked. "Oh, God."

Roughly Angus picked Davies off the deck. He considered sickbay; dismissed the idea. He needed answers, and he needed them now. Half carrying the boy, he moved back to Milos' station, seated his son there.

With his hands braced on the arms of the g-seat, he peered into Davies' face.

"Pay attention. Try to keep it straight. That was then. This is now. And that was Morn. This is you. Just because you remember her past doesn't mean the same things happened to you.

"All right?"

Davies twitched his head. He may have been trying to nod.

Angus pulled away. The pleasure rush was gone. Seeing his son beaten and bloody was too much like seeing himself in the same state. A sudden pressure filled his throat. Swallowing it harshly, he rasped, "Then let's start making sense. You don't want me to let Captain Sheepfucker leave. I figured that much out. So I won't. He's going to stay until we're done with him.

"Now tell me what the fuck you think you're doing."

Davies groaned softly. A bubble of blood formed on his lips and burst. With a heart-wrenching effort, he brought his eyes into focus.

"I *know* him. We didn't spend all our time fucking. He talked. I wanted to kill him just to make him stop talking."

A new pain pulled like a laceration through Angus' chest. "I said, keep it straight!" As if he were telepathic, he understood Davies perfectly. "That was *Morn*. The kind of fucking he gave you was completely different."

Davies tried to nod again. Abused and urgent, his eyes clung to Angus. "But I *know* him. He doesn't have her."

Angus froze. Milos seemed to be strangling on smoke.

Nick took a breath like a shudder and lowered his head as if he were waiting for the axe.

As clearly as he could, Davies articulated, "He can't trade her for me. He already gave her to the Amnion." A spasm of pain stopped him. When it passed, he finished, "The Bill told me."

Milos covered his face with his hands.

Morn!

Angus' fury was nearly as fast as his microprocessor; nearly fast enough to lash out before his datacore could stop him.

Gave her to the Amnion.

That was the point of Nick's distractions; the real cheat. He'd turned her over to mutagens and ruin. And then he went on using her as a bargaining chip as if he still had her.

Angus would have been willing to die for a chance to hit Nick again.

But his passion slammed into the neural wall of his zone implants: he couldn't move. Outraged and heartsick, he couldn't do anything except stand still and let his programming make Warden Dios' decisions.

Madness crowded his head. Like Nick, he'd come to the end of his endurance. He was on the verge of breaking—right on the edge of his personal abyss—when he heard himself say, "In that case, we'll have to get her back."

"Oh, shit," Milos breathed. He didn't seem to have any other words for his dismay.

"That's crazy." Nick brought the words up from the pit of his stomach as if he were coughing. "She's in the Amnion sector. You'll have to fight them and the Bill and two warships just to find her. And they've already given her their mutagens. She's already one of them."

And you *did that to her!* Angus howled at him. *She gave herself to you, she gave you everything I wanted, and you turned her over to them!*

At the same time he said calmly, "We still have to get her back." He sounded as lucid as a machine. "If she's one of them now, we'll kill her. Otherwise we'll rescue her."

She was a cop: Dios couldn't afford to let the Amnion have her.

"Yes," Davies gritted through his teeth. Behind his mask of blood, his eyes glittered. "Yes."

"I'm going to sickbay," Milos announced stiffly. He sounded like he was grieving. "I'll get some swabs and antiseptic."

Keeping his face turned away, he went to the companionway and moved upward out of sight.

"You're both crazy." Unsteadily Nick gained his feet. "You're going to *get* her away from the Amnion, sure." His eyes were re-covering focus, but his balance remained unreliable. Stress tugged at his cheek like an erratic heartbeat. "You and what army? There's a warship with her guns lined up on us right now. Super-light proton cannon. Even if you can *get* into the Amnion sector and *get* her out"—weakly he tried to hammer the words—"you're never going to get *away.*

"You're as dead as I am." He attempted a grin, but the effort failed, pulled apart by the tic in his cheek. "Unless you let me give them your brat.

"Then some of us might survive."

Even though he was beaten, even though Davies had exposed his treachery, he went on groping for an exit to the cul-de-sac.

"No." Angus dismissed the idea as if he'd considered it seriously for a moment; as if he understood or cared about the need in Nick's voice. "That won't work." He didn't understand or care, however. He paid no attention to Nick's appeal. He was simply talking to fill the silence while he waited for Dios' instructions to come through the gap in his mind. "If I let you take Davies there while I went after Morn, it might be useful as a diversion. But as soon as they lost her, they would keep both of you."

"That isn't what I—" Nick began. But then he stopped. He must have been able to see that Angus wasn't listening.

Squinting through blood and fear, Davies watched Angus. Carefully, trying not to put pressure on his hurts, he straightened himself in the g-seat. In a voice like a metal rasp, he asked, "Why do you want her back? Didn't you get enough out of her the last time?"

"That isn't it." Nick made a thin effort to sound sarcastic. He, too, watched Angus closely. "He likes hurting women—don't you, Captain Thermo-pile?—but not enough to risk himself for it. He's too much of a coward for that.

"He has a different reason." He glanced briefly at Davies. "You've got the mind of a cop. You'll love this. The real reason is, your dear father works for the UMCP. He doesn't want to, of course, but they've got his neck in a noose. He's doing this little job for them to keep them from snapping his spine."

He seemed to think this revelation might upset Angus.

It didn't: Angus hardly heard it. As if Nick's words were a code or a catalyst, the window in his head opened, and data streamed into his mind—a torrent of preconceived plots and needs, exigencies and questions.

"Milos is probably just here to keep track of him," Nick concluded, "report on him if he doesn't do what he's told."

Frowning around his cuts and contusions, Davies asked Angus, "Is that true?"

Abruptly Angus' attention snapped back into focus. He was alive on disparate planes again, existing in separate realities; multi-tasking urgently. But now the data which poured and processed through him required him to concentrate on Nick.

"Well, there's one thing sure," he muttered while his datacore filtered possibilities through the back of his brain, testing options against his experience with Billingate and the Amnion. " 'Report' is what Milos does best." He glanced up the companionway to be sure his second was out of earshot. "You may be interested to hear, Succorso"—his programming kept him too busy for obscenities—"that you aren't the only one he talked to while we were coming in. He also sent messages to *Tranquil Hegemony*.

"They answered before you did."

Nick flinched and turned pale as if he'd been hit in the stomach. His mouth shaped curses which were inaudible because they had no breath behind them.

Angus liked that. He wished he'd done it of his own free will.

"What did they say?" Davies asked.

Angus shrugged. "The codes are too good. I couldn't break them."

The boy didn't take Milos' betrayal as hard as Nick did: maybe he didn't understand it. He pursued the matter impersonally. "Then what's going on? What's he doing?"

"Playing some kind of bugger game." That was obvious. "Me and Succorso and the UMCP and the Amnion, all against each other." Fears and alarms roared in Angus' ears as he thought about the damage Milos could do. Thanks to his zone implants, however, he spoke with untroubled confidence. "Don't worry about it. I can handle him.

"Succorso"—he turned sharply on Nick—"it's time to make up your mind. Shit or get out of the head." For an instant the discrete operations taking place inside him came together. "We're going after Morn. Are you in or out? The truth is, I need you. I need all the help I can get. But I'm not going to force you. It'll be too easy for you to give us away.

"Say yes or get off my ship."

Davies tensed. He may not have understood Milos' betrayals, but he knew too much about Nick's. Leaning forward despite the pain in his ribs, he protested quickly, "Angus, don't let him go. He'll tell them we're coming. That's the way his mind works. He'll think if he shows them his 'good faith' they'll let him off the hook."

Angus didn't hesitate. "I'll take that chance."

"But—" Davies began.

"Shut up," Angus told the boy calmly. His datacore imposed calm. He kept his gaze on Nick. "I said I'll take the chance."

Cocking his fists on his hips, he showed Nick his teeth. "Yes or no, Captain Sheepfucker. Pick one. Pick it now."

Again Nick tried to laugh, but the attempt sounded hollow and beaten—as damaged as his eyes. "You're crazy. I guess I have to keep saying that. You're crazy. No, you stupid, suicidal sonofabitch. *No.* Is that clear enough? I'm not going to help you. I just hope I get to see you again someday—after the Amnion have had time to play with you for a while."

"In that case"—Angus raised the fist gripping Morn's id tag—"get the hell off my ship."

"You're crazy," Nick repeated. "Completely."

Nevertheless he obeyed. His boots stamped loudly up the companionway treads and along the passage until he reached the midship lift. A moment later Angus heard the lift doors close; heard servos hum as the lift descended toward the airlock.

He turned back to Davies. Now he had to fight his way through half a dozen programs, all running simultaneously, in order to talk to his son. Obviously his datacore didn't care how frightened Davies felt.

"He won't warn the Amnion. He thinks that's what he's going to do, but he'll change his mind—as soon as he has time to think about what Milos might be doing."

Davies studied him bleakly. "What's that supposed to mean?"

Demands and instructions thronged in Angus' brain. He was full of scenarios played out against the backdrop of his experience; of possibilities raised and discarded; of outcomes analyzed: simultaneous hope and despair. Tight with stress, he retorted, "I haven't got time for long explanations. We need to get ready. Whatever we decide to do, we need to *do* it and be done before the Bill figures out where you are. As soon as that happens, we're out of choices."

But Davies couldn't let go of his fear. It came from too many different sources inside him: he'd remembered too many horrors. His hands made small, incomplete movements; his gaze pleaded for Angus' attention.

Surprised at his own tolerance—and at his ability to act on it—Angus watched his son and waited. Although he'd spent his life hiding it, he knew exactly how the boy felt.

"It's too much—" Davies murmured. "Too many plots. Too much to remember. I don't know who I can trust."

He shook his head; swallowed roughly, as if he were fighting tears. "Did I—" he asked like a scrape of pain, "did she really blow up *Starmaster?*"

Angus had to resist inexorable machine pressure to continue facing his son. His datacore had other things for him to do. Nevertheless the men who'd designed his commands and compulsions valued his knowledge of illegals, his familiarity with Billingate, his training in extreme situations. On some occasions, to some extent, he was allowed to exercise a little discretion.

He gave Davies a sharp nod. "That's the only reason I'm still alive. And it's the only reason I got her. She was too horrified to defend herself.

"You Hylands need to stop letting yourselves react like that. It makes you too vulnerable."

Drying blood slowly crusted around Davies' eyes. After a moment he said, "Yes," as if he were accepting a legacy.

That was all the time Angus' zone implants let him have. Stiffly he pulled away.

"Where the hell is Milos?" he growled. "We've got to get you to sickbay."

Too late he realized the truth. Like Nick, Milos had left the ship.

SORUS

$\mathbf{S}$orus Chatelaine walked into the Bill's strongroom and found him fulminating like a vial of phosphorus.

"Have you heard already?" he snapped as soon as he saw her. "Does everybody on this bloody rock already know what those bastards did to me?"

Surrounded by computer stations, data terminals, and display screens, he prowled the tight circle of his command center. The rest of the room was as dark and empty as a cavern: every light focused on him and his equipment. In the intense illumination he looked like he was burning. Lean as an ascetic, he might have been a martyr splashed with tallow and set aflame.

She moved closer, stopped just outside his circle. "How can I answer that?" she asked steadily. She had her own reasons for anger—even for fear—but as a matter of policy she never let the Bill see her vulnerabilities. "You haven't said which bastards you're talking about."

"This is your fault!" he barked, sounding more than ever like an outraged child. "You were supposed to be interrogating him." For an instant he paused to glare at her. "Hell, Sorus, I gave you permission to torture him. What more did you need?"

"All right." She faced the Bill squarely. "We're talking about Davies." Her rich contralto betrayed nothing. "But I still don't understand. You said 'bastards,' plural."

"And Davies Hyland himself is a bastard, I know, I know."

Fluttering his hands, the Bill resumed his prowl. His eyes hunted his screens and readouts for answers they didn't provide. "Spare me your sense of humor at a time like this. Why weren't you *with* him, doing what I told you?"

Sorus permitted herself a small sigh. "I needed time to think. I wasn't sure how to tackle him. And"—she skipped a beat or two in order to focus the Bill's attention on her—"I still wasn't sure what Succorso was up to. I've tried to tell you he might be plotting something more complex than we realize. I wanted to learn more about that, if I could. It would be worth knowing in any case—it might be crucial—but it would also help me decide how to approach Davies."

Unnecessarily she concluded, "I wasn't particularly interested in torturing him just for the fun of it."

The Bill snarled through his teeth. "Then why are you here, at this particular moment, if you haven't already heard?"

"Heard *what?*" she countered. Her private anger and alarm took the form of exasperation. "You aren't making much sense."

"Sorus!" he retorted loudly, "I need answers!" His long fingers pointed at screens and terminals all around him. "I already have enough questions."

"All right. All right." It was obvious that she would have to go along with him. She acceded because she wanted to know what had happened. "I'll tell you what I've heard. The only thing I've heard. That's why I'm here.

"There's a rumor in circulation that I'm"—she needed more emphasis—"that *I* am dealing in mutagen immunity drugs. Me!"

The Bill stared at her while she explained.

"Some of my crew overheard two spacers talking about it. In a bar-and-sleep on the cruise. I tried to get my hands on them, but they were gone.

"I want to know who they are. That's why I'm here. I want you to identify them for me, so I can find out what's going on. Is that enough, or do I need to act as upset as you?"

"Oh, spare me your histrionics." The Bill studied her with a seriousness which belied his sour tone. "You're too emotional as it is." He was talking to give himself time to think. "A mutagen immunity drug? Are you sure?"

She shrugged. "That's what my people heard."

"What a coincidence." The Bill raised his hands to his head

like a man who meant to pull out his hair. "What a fucking coincidence."

"That's what *I* thought," she returned shortly.

"I mean, look at it," he went on as if she hadn't spoken. "First Davies Hyland plants the idea of an immunity drug. Well, he's a desperate kid. He might say *anything* he could think of, just to make me reluctant to sell him. But still the idea is a provocative one. Naturally I want to learn the truth, so I ask you to get it for me.

"Then look what happens. A couple of spacers start talking about immunity drugs—and you. Entirely by accident, of course," he snorted, "they do it where your people can hear them. Then they disappear.

"And *then*"—his teeth snapped at the air as if he wanted to tear it into hunks—"Davies himself disappears!"

"What?" For an instant Sorus couldn't control her chagrin.

"Disappears!" the Bill repeated. "I mean literally. Right out of his cell. Leaving behind two dead guards, both of them apparently killed by lasers, and a burned door lock."

Sorus couldn't help herself: she was too badly surprised. "That's absurd," she protested stupidly. "You're making it up."

Full of vehemence, the Bill gestured for her to step inside his circle. "Come see for yourself."

He typed in commands, as fast as scattershot, while she moved to join him. The instant she reached his side, he pointed urgently at two screens.

"The guards were wired, of course. This is what they saw."

Both screens showed an empty corridor from slightly different angles. Sorus recognized the short hall outside the rooms the Bill used as cells. The indicators on the opposite wall told her a lift was on its way down.

The lift arrived: the doors opened.

Like the corridor, the car was empty.

There seemed to be an area of slight distortion, maybe a smudge, in the center of the images: she couldn't be sure.

Abruptly a hand appeared in the air beside the smudge. It disappeared again.

At the same time lines of coherent light ran from the vacant lift to the guards. Both recorded images fell until they pressed against the floor. From their divergent angles, what little they could see of the corridor remained empty.

"And that's not all," the Bill said tensely. "I've got another dead guard. Outside that same lift on one of the upper levels. Apparently he was shot from behind. Another laser."

Sorus felt pressure building in her chest. "What about the bug-eye in the cell?" she asked tightly.

The Bill gave a disgusted snarl; keyed more commands.

The inside of the room appeared on one screen.

Davies stood there, poised and staring in shock. A voice said, "Shit. Shit. *Shit*," but it obviously wasn't the boy's. His mouth was open, but he wasn't swearing: he was screaming. Wild as a tormented animal, he flung his fist at the blank air.

Then the bugeye itself went blank. The screen picked up nothing but distortion: electronic white noise.

After a moment the distortion crackled away, leaving the monitor clear to scrutinize a room with no one in it.

"That," Sorus breathed, "is not possible."

"Did you see the smudge?" the Bill demanded.

She nodded dumbly.

"Operations is working on it. Preliminary analysis suggests it might be caused by a refractive jamming field. If that's true, whoever did this had to carry their own power supply and emitter. And it must have been"—he gestured around him harshly—"about the size of all this. Even if it fit in the lift, it would have been hell to move. And moving it would have attracted a hell of a lot of attention. So that's not possible either."

Sorus shook her head, trying to clear it. Automatically, simply saying the first words that occurred to her, she suggested, "Unless the Amnion can do it. Their equipment has always been better than ours."

"Do you suppose I haven't considered that?" the Bill bellowed. "Do you think I'm so goddamn secure here I can afford to dismiss an idea like that?" Almost immediately, however, his voice frayed to softness. As if he were defeated, he muttered, "I asked them. They say they haven't got him.

"They could lie, of course. But what would be the point? If they want him that badly, they didn't have to steal him. They didn't have to do me this kind of damage. All they had to do was pay for him.

"Sorus"—now he sounded like he was pleading with her—"all

they had to do was give me the money they took away from Captain Nick. They were willing to spend it in any case. What does it matter if I get it instead of him? Stealing his merchandise doesn't improve their position with him. Assuming they have a position they want to improve. It just lets him off the hook.

"Why would they do a thing like that? They've got him where they want him right now—they're squeezing his balls dry, and there's nothing he can do about it."

"I don't know," Sorus murmured, chewing her lip; thinking hard. As far as she could see, the Amnion had nothing to gain by snatching Davies. "Maybe there's more going on here than we know about." She didn't have a theory: she was merely groping. "Maybe this story about an immunity drug is true."

An intuitive frisson ran down her spine.

"I think," she continued tightly, "we need to know who started that rumor about me."

The Bill frowned at her, uncharacteristically puzzled. But he didn't hesitate. "Where? What time?"

"A place called Paunchys." She gave him her best estimate of the time.

At once he swung to another terminal and began running commands.

This kind of data retrieval was rapid. A heartbeat or two after he entered his instructions, the screens above the terminal flickered to life.

She recognized Paunchys easily: the bugeyes gave her several different angles on the room. Everyone sitting at the tables or leaning against the bar showed clearly.

Fortuitously the playback started just as her people left their table to head for *Soar.*

Most of the nearby tables were vacant. From where her people had been sitting, they could only have overheard one particular pair of spacers: a man and woman talking alone with their heads together as if they were telling secrets.

On one screen, the man looked nervous. A streak of dirt on his upper lip may have been a mustache. From another angle, the woman appeared grim and competent, as if she could have had her companion for breakfast.

Sorus didn't know either of them.

She pointed them out to the Bill. Swiftly he stabbed open an intercom to Operations.

As soon as the duty officer answered, the Bill demanded, "I want id on a man and woman. They're sitting together lower right." Distinctly he recited the location, time, and monitor codes displayed on the bottom of his screen.

"Give me a minute," the duty officer replied.

"Do it faster than that," the Bill retorted. "I haven't got a minute." Snapping off the intercom, he glared at Sorus. "What is this going to prove?"

"How should *I* know?" she countered. "You know more about what's going on here than I do."

His scowl made him look murderous as he turned to peer at the screen again. "God knows I'm *supposed* to," he muttered. "Right now I'm not so sure."

The Operations intercom chimed almost immediately. The Bill toggled it hard. "Yes?"

"I have id," the duty officer reported. "The man is Sib Mackern, data first, *Captain's Fancy*. The woman is Mikka Vasaczk, command second, also *Captain's Fancy*."

Brandishing his teeth as if he were inarticulate with rage, the Bill silenced the intercom.

Sorus' guts knotted. "So it was Succorso." She spoke softly, controlling her desire to curse. "I told you he was dangerous."

But she couldn't do it; couldn't contain her visceral panic and anger. She should have killed him when she had the chance. The satisfaction of cutting him, humiliating him, hadn't been worth what it was going to cost her.

"Goddamn it!" she raged, clenching her voice between her teeth, "I *told* you he's up to something!"

"Sorus—" The Bill seemed to flinch away as if her ferocity frightened him. "It wasn't him. Whatever else is going on here, he didn't snatch that brat."

Still shouting, still clenched, she demanded, "How do you figure that? Didn't you tell me he seduced one of your wires so he could find out where Davies was being held? Didn't Davies tell us Succorso has an immunity drug? Didn't he say Succorso and Hyland are in this together? It all fits!

"Succorso and Hyland are working some UMCP plot. They let you have Davies to plant the idea of an immunity drug. Then they took him back. Now they're starting rumors about me. For confirmation. And to make me into a lightning rod, so when the blast hits, it'll be aimed at *me*."

The Bill overrode her. "No. That's not it. He was *here*. Captain Nick was right *here*, trying to talk me into restoring his credit, at exactly the same time Davies Hyland was taken."

Sorus opened her mouth; closed it again. For a moment her brain went numb.

Succorso was here? He couldn't have done it?

What in *hell* was going on?

"Then"—she took a deep breath so that she wouldn't shudder—"it must have been Angus Thermopyle. Him and that Com-Mine Security asshole, Milos Taverner. Where did they go from Ease-n-Sleaze?"

"I'm glad you asked that." Manic and conspiratorial, hiding his fright, the Bill beckoned her to another terminal, another bank of screens. "I've been trying to make sense out of it myself.

"They had rooms." His long fingers were unerring on the keys; he could have run his command center blindfolded. "After they talked with Captain Nick in the bar, they went up to Captain Angus' room. It's all recorded."

Fighting to shove the confusion out of her head so that she could concentrate, Sorus stared at Angus Thermopyle and Milos Taverner in a hopeless little room which could have been in any bar-and-sleep that fed on the less affluent prey of the cruise.

Angus sat in a chair tilted back so that it leaned against the wall. "Make yourself comfortable," he mumbled like his mouth hurt. "We haven't got all night, but you can probably count on at least an hour. You've got that long."

Smoking furiously, Milos checked the room's data terminal. Then he took the other chair and sat down beside Angus.

"You know something about this, Angus," he said. "Something you haven't told me. Maybe something you heard from Dios."

He didn't appear concerned about being overheard.

"I know a lot of things I haven't told you," Angus retorted. "I know a lot of things I haven't told myself. I wouldn't share them with you if I could."

"Well, let me try to guess," Milos replied. "Saying we're here to destroy the Bill is just a trick." The Bill's hand shook as he pointed an accusing finger at the screen. "The real reason is because of me. And Morn Hyland. That doesn't sound very plausible—until you think about what she and I have in common.

"She's been to Enablement. To the Amnion."

Angus' voice was strangely thick. "Don't guess. It just shows you don't know what you're doing."

"Oh, I know what I'm doing, all right," Milos promised. "Open your mouth."

While Sorus stared, Milos dropped his burning nic into Angus' mouth.

Angus chewed and swallowed it. His face was black with rage and nausea, but he didn't refuse or resist.

"Shit," Sorus breathed involuntarily.

"Listen," the Bill hissed.

"It's my neck in the noose," Milos continued, "and I'm not going to let you or anybody else hang me.

"I suppose you really can't tell me what you know. And what you know probably isn't much anyway. You're just an incidental victim. From that point of view, you're worse off than I am.

"We all need somebody who's worse off than we are. Or who can be made worse off."

After that both men fell silent.

Milos went on smoking continuously.

Angus ate each of his nics as he finished it.

Sorus watched him in a state that resembled horror. Dios, she thought numbly. Warden Dios. *Saying we're here to destroy the Bill—*

Suddenly she believed everything Davies had suggested about Succorso and Hyland.

"That goes on for about an hour," the Bill commented. He hit a key to speed up the playback. "Just like Captain Angus predicted. Then the chronology gets interesting.

"In another room Captain Nick finishes browbeating my wire. He gets what he wants out of her. After that he sends a message to his ship—coded so I can't crack it. Then he leaves, goes back to *Captain's Fancy.* Eventually he comes to see me.

"But at the same time—well, almost—we have this." He returned the playback to normal.

Thickly, his mouth full of pain, Angus abruptly said, "Try it now."

As if he rather than Angus were in command, Milos got up and went to the data terminal.

"What's he doing?" Sorus asked. "Talking to Succorso?"

"No such luck," the Bill returned. "He's retrieving messages from *Trumpet*. Coded, of course." Answering her next question before she could ask it, he went on, "We don't have any way of knowing if *Captain's Fancy* and *Trumpet* talked to each other."

Almost sadly Milos murmured, "Looks like it's here."

Despite his characteristically bloated expression, taut with malice, Angus looked sallow and defeated as he said, "You're the one who knows the code. Is it time to go?"

Milos studied his message for a moment before he replied, "I guess."

"And that's it," the Bill announced. He blanked the screen. "They pick up their messages—by some wild coincidence just a few minutes after Captain Nick sends a message to *Captain's Fancy*—and then they leave."

"Where do they go?" Sorus inquired as if her head were full of chaos.

"They don't. They vanish."

She blinked at him idiotically.

"I mean they manage to lose themselves." The Bill made a hawking sound of disgust. "I mean we lose track of them. Once they get out into the cruise and the lifts, the recordings are so full of people that the computers haven't been able to focus on those two. I don't have any idea where they are."

"Then," she said slowly because she didn't know what else to suggest, "they could have snatched Davies."

"I thought of that myself," the Bill sneered. "I'm not completely comatose yet. But if they did, they didn't take him back to *Trumpet*. *That* I would know."

"Unless they have a refractive jamming field and got past your bugeyes."

"Which isn't possible."

New ideas: she needed new ideas. Nothing made any sense; but if she didn't stop floundering soon and begin to understand she was going to be sucked down.

Clutching at straws, she offered, "Or unless they have the kind of help that lets them get into the infrastructure"—which also didn't make sense because it failed to account for the way the guards were killed—"and from there go EVA to their ship."

"What kind is that?" the Bill countered trenchantly. "Captain Nick and Captain Angus have just arrived. What kind of help do you think they could organize in the amount of time they've been here?"

He didn't add, Unless they're getting help from the Amnion. He didn't need to.

"How should I know?" Sorus objected. "I'm just guessing. A portable refractive jamming field isn't possible. Neither is sneaking into the infrastructure, killing your guards without being seen, and going EVA back to *Trumpet*."

Grimly she glared at the Bill. "I don't know where the Amnion stand in all this—but I also don't know where else to look for answers."

He blinked back at her. For a moment his long face was stretched with loss.

"In that case," he said softly, "we're all finished."

Not me, she gritted in return. If you think I'm going down with *this* ship, you're out of your goddamn mind.

To cover her silent promise, she asked, "Are you watching for Taverner and Thermopyle?"

"Sure." The Bill sounded as frightened as a boy. "Of course. The guards have orders to report but not accost." He swallowed so hard that his larynx jumped. "Just in case the Amnion *are* involved. I don't want to give *Calm Horizons* an excuse for a surgical strike."

"And where," she pursued, "is Succorso now?"

He snorted. "You'll love this. He's on *Trumpet*. God knows why—he's there alone. But he went there from here. Apparently Captain Angus gave him the codes to let himself aboard."

Sorus felt pressure writhing like nausea in her abdomen. To herself she growled, Aboard *Trumpet*. That makes perfect sense. Why didn't I think of it myself? But she'd come to the end of what she could endure without taking action. If the Bill wanted to stand here and dither while his world crumbled, he would have to do it without her.

STEPHEN R. DONALDSON

Pulling away abruptly, she left the circle of equipment and strode into the dimness toward the door.

As she moved she said over her shoulder, "Tell Operations I'm leaving dock."

"No, you aren't." The Bill's tone was as soft as the slither of a snake. His fright was gone, sloughed away. "Not until you tell me where you're going. And why."

She swung back to face him. "I'm going to get us some answers. First I'm going to put *Soar* in firing range of *Calm Horizons*. Just to remind them they've got something to lose. Then I'm going to make them talk until I start believing them."

Bright as an auto-da-fé in the concentrated light, the Bill studied her for a long moment. When he finally spoke, he sounded as fatal as a fanatic.

"Good."

The word was a threat as well as a commandment.

Before she could turn away, one of his intercoms chimed.

He hit the toggle. At once the Operations duty officer said, "Sir, we've got Milos Taverner."

With her hand on the strongroom door, Sorus froze.

"Where?" the Bill snapped.

The duty officer was hesitant. "He's just left *Trumpet.*" In a rush he added, "I know it's impossible. I can't explain it. But he must have been there all along."

The Bill's gaze clung to Sorus as if he were begging for help.

Harsh as a cutting laser, she articulated, "That's where Succorso is."

The Bill hammered his forehead with the heels of his palms; he might have been trying to kick his brain into motion. Then he asked Operations, "Where's he going?"

The intercom gave the duty officer's voice a flat, metallic timbre. "Sir, he looks like he's headed for the Amnion sector." After a pause the man asked, "Should we stop him?"

"No!" the Bill jerked out convulsively. "Let him go. If the Amnion are involved, we don't know what's at stake. This may not have anything to do with us."

Without transition he broke into a roar of anger and alarm. "Just don't lose him! If he doesn't go straight there, grab him!"

Then he regained his self-control. Quiet and deadly, he continued, "Put a team together. Get aboard *Trumpet*—cut your way in if you have to. Bring me everybody you find." His teeth chewed out the words like hunks of raw meat. "Except Nick Succorso. I want to see what he does with his freedom. He can go wherever he wants—but not back to *Captain's Fancy*. Do you hear me? Bar him from his ship. I don't care how many guards it takes. I'm going to put pressure on him until he cracks. Then I'm going to toast his testicles and make him eat them.

"Don't fuck up!" he warned the duty officer. "Don't dare. If you do, you won't have to worry about what I'll do to you. The Amnion are going to devour us all."

Stabbing off the intercom, he faced Sorus again.

Through the gloom surrounding her, he said, "Go. Fast. You may be my only hope. I want you out where your guns can do some good before this mess gets any worse. What I need is answers. But if you have to start shooting I'll back you up with everything I've got."

Sorus Chatelaine nodded sharply. She was finished here anyway: Billingate had become as dangerous as a pit of vipers for her. Once Succorso's rumor had a chance to spread, she wouldn't be able to set a foot on this rock without risking her life. Eventually the Amnion themselves would come after her.

Unless she went to them with the truth first.

Unless she convinced them they had nothing to fear from her.

Grimly she left the strongroom to save herself and her ship.

MILOS

If anyone had asked, Milos Taverner might have admitted that
he was scared shitless.

His heart beat so hard that it hurt his chest, and the pressure
seemed to cramp his lungs, so that he had trouble breathing. At
times he swallowed convulsively: at times an odd giddiness came and
went in his head, making him feel that he was about to lose his
footing. Sweat ran incessantly into his palms; so much sweat that he
couldn't rub his hands dry no matter how hard he tried.

Even though his entire life, from the guttergangs of Earth to his
ambiguous position on Com-Mine Station, had been ruled by fear,
he had never been as afraid as he was now.

He was on his way to the Amnion sector; toward an encounter
with creatures that appalled him.

The mere idea made him want to cower and moan.

He had no choice, however. Of course not. He would never
have done something like this, never, if he'd had any imaginable
alternative.

Oh, talking to the Amnion was all right. He could handle that.
How else did buggers survive, when every guttergang was a natural
enemy? By talking to them, that was how. By helping and betraying
them all. And space wasn't substantively different from a city ruled
by guttergangs. On one side stood Com-Mine Security; over there,
the UMCP; over there, pirates like Nick Succorso; and over *there*,
the Amnion. Why shouldn't a man like Milos profit by playing them

off against each other?—especially since otherwise they all would have been quite willing to crush him?

Now, however, he'd run out of choices. His simple, reasonable, and above all secure buggery had been turned against him. Min Donner had taken him off Com-Mine. Hashi Lebwohl had selected him to control and protect Angus. Warden Dios had sent him *here*, to the living hell of Billingate and the cruise.

And then they'd changed all the rules—

You've just been given a rather nasty shock. I regret that, but it was necessary.

They'd lied about the reasons he and Angus were here. Worse than that, they'd built loopholes into Angus' welded priority commands—loopholes which effectively emasculated Milos.

On this one subject, you were misled.

Ignorant of those loopholes, he'd lied to the Amnion.

Everything else you were told concerning Joshua, your mission, and yourself remains true. Joshua has not diverged from his programming. Your command codes still function. You have not been betrayed.

Milos would have found Dios' reassurances easier to believe if the UMCP director had been here to deliver them in person. But he didn't believe them; not for a second. The fact that his command codes still worked didn't convince him. Where there was one lie, there was more than one. Always. Without exception.

He'd been set up.

Now he had nowhere else to turn except the Amnion.

And he had nothing left to offer them—nothing to purchase his survival with—except the truth.

Every step he took was tight with dread. Why didn't Angus come after him? Why didn't the Bill's guards stop him? Why didn't Nick appear out of nowhere, blazing with outraged virility and self-destruction, and attempt to work one of his legendary wonders? Didn't they know what they were *doing* when they risked Milos Taverner in their plots and counterplots?

Apparently not. No one interfered with him as he walked the corridors and rode the lifts toward the place which the Amnion had constructed for themselves at the edge of the installation.

He was scared shitless in more ways than one. Even his limited repertoire of obscenities had been frightened out of him.

· · ·

At last he reached the Amnion sector.

The entrance was only a door in an unmarked wall. Nevertheless this was the location he'd obtained from the data terminal in Reception. And the door had the heavy look of an airlock: when it closed behind him, it would seal him off from the human atmosphere of Billingate.

There was an intercom with a keypad under it beside the door. After rubbing his damp hands uselessly one more time on the thighs of his shipsuit, he punched in the id code he'd been given for his transmissions to forbidden space.

The silence which greeted him was so complete that he could taste it.

A minute passed; maybe two. Waves of giddiness rolled and faded through him until he had to brace himself on the wall. Why was the Bill letting this happen? If Angus or Nick had come after him, they would have caught him before this: therefore they weren't coming. But the Bill could send guards at any time. Surely he knew Angus and Milos had taken Davies, even if he didn't know how? And surely he had recordings of the time Angus and Milos had spent in Ease-n-Sleaze? So where were the guards?

Was the Bill *this* afraid of the Amnion? As afraid as Milos?

Scarcely able to breathe, he entered his id code on the keypad again.

The intercom crackled. "Human, your name is required for confirmation of identity." The alien voice sounded pitiless and unreachable through the tiny speaker.

Milos' throat refused to work. He swallowed spasmodically several times. After a moment he managed to croak out his name.

Another silence. Then the voice said, "Enter the airlock, Milos Taverner," like a distant promise of death. "You are welcome among the Amnion."

With a hum of servos, the door cycled open.

A man stood waiting inside the lock as if he'd arrived from the pit of one of Milos' nightmares.

He was only partially Amnion. One eye and half his face were human, as were his chest, one arm, and most of his legs. But his other eye was lidless, formed for the sulfurous illumination the Amnion preferred. Pointed teeth with no lips over them filled half his mouth. Rust seemed to cover his inhuman arm; rust clogged his knees so thickly that his strange black shipsuit had been cut away to enable him to walk.

In his human hand he held a breathing mask.

"Milos Taverner, welcome." His voice sounded like friction along oxidized iron. "For convenience my name is Marc Vestabule. To spare yourself discomfort, you must wear this."

He offered the breathing mask.

Involuntarily Milos flinched backward.

"Milos Taverner"—the nearly human voice scraped like torn fingernails against Milos' nerves—"we do not know why you have come to us. You may speak here if you wish. Surely, however, it is preferable to ensure against the espionage of this installation's surveillance monitors."

Surely. Of course. That made sense. With a fierce effort, Milos fought down his urge to turn and run. If what he had to say was overheard, Angus, Nick, and Davies were as good as dead; the Bill would kill them. And that might make the Amnion unhappy: very unhappy. Milos' last chance would be wasted.

Somehow he forced himself to step forward far enough to accept the breathing mask.

Marc Vestabule withdrew toward the back of the airlock. Giddiness surged through Milos again as he pulled on the mask; he stumbled as far as the door. But there he caught himself. Clutching his panic to the edge of the entrance, he stopped; couldn't force himself to go on.

Vestabule's human eye blinked as if he wanted to wink but had forgotten how. "Milos Taverner," he said carefully, "you are afraid. What frightens you? Have you not dealt honorably with the Amnion?"

Dealt honorably? Milos wanted to scream. *When did any of you ever* let *me deal honorably?*

He couldn't say things like that, however; not if he wanted to survive. Defensively he muttered, "I've always told you the truth." The mask muffled his voice. "It's not my fault some things I thought were true have turned out to be lies."

The Amnioni appeared to consider the implications of this assertion for a moment. Still blinking, he replied, "But now that you have learned the truth, you have come to offer it to the Amnion. Therefore you are welcome among us, as I have said. Please enter the airlock."

Nearly gagging on the pressure in his chest, Milos Taverner pushed himself past the door.

The lock closed behind him, cutting him off from his humanity. Now he had nothing left to hope for, except that the Amnion would value the things he'd come to tell them.

At once a complex light washed over him: sulfur, scanners, and decontaminants. As far as anyone knew, the Amnion were proof against human diseases and parasites. Nevertheless they didn't believe in taking chances.

He didn't either. On that basis he might still be able to negotiate with them.

Marc Vestabule stared at him stolidly while the light did its work. After a minute or two the inner door of the airlock opened. Milos winced, expecting to see a phalanx of Amnion waiting to horrify him. But the corridor beyond the door was empty. The Amnion trusted Vestabule to do their work for them.

Moving stiffly, as if his joints were rusted inside as well as out, Vestabule motioned for Milos to follow him. "Accompany me, please. I will take you to a chamber where you will feel secure. There you may make your requirements known so that we can discuss how they may be satisfied."

Feel secure. Sure.

Struggling to swallow the labor of his heart, Milos stumbled after the Amnioni.

The chamber Vestabule mentioned wasn't far away. That was fortuitous: Milos couldn't have walked far. Anoxia or stress seemed to gnaw at his balance, chewing it to shreds. If he hadn't caught himself on the strange pheromonic metal of the walls, he might have fallen several times.

When Vestabule ushered him into a room as impersonal and featureless as the corridor, he was dimly grateful to see that it contained chairs. At least he would be able to sit. If he could set aside the breathing mask occasionally, he might even be able to smoke.

Without waiting for an invitation, he lowered his failing limbs into the nearest seat and dug out a packet of nic.

Vestabule studied him as he found a packet, took out a nic and his lighter. The expression on the human half of the Amnioni's face suggested that he didn't understand what Milos was doing. But as Milos repositioned the breathing mask to make room for the nic in his mouth, Vestabule said abruptly, "That is hazardous, Milos Taverner. Doubtless the spark of your lighter—it is magnesium, is it not?—is small. Nevertheless the air of your breathing mask is rich in oxygen—perhaps rich enough to make the spark greater than you anticipate. It is possible that you will harm yourself."

For a moment Milos' brain went blank. He wanted nic, *needed* it: it was the only form of courage he had left. Yet at Vestabule's warning he seemed to see his lighter blaze like a flare, flash-burning his face and eyes— Magnesium was wildly incandescent, usable for lighters only in tiny quantities—and in appropriate atmospheres.

Trembling, he stuffed the nic back in its packet, shoved both packet and lighter down into his pocket. Again he felt a wan gratitude. Vestabule had saved him from hurting himself; perhaps blinding himself. Maybe the Amnion valued him after all.

Light-headed with fear and relief, he insisted through the obstruction of the mask, "I've never lied to you knowingly. You've got to believe that. Everything I've ever told you was the truth—as far as I knew. But there's nothing I can do to prevent other people from lying to me."

Slowly Marc Vestabule picked up another chair, placed it facing Milos, and sat down. When he was settled, his alien knees were only inches from Milos'. Fortunately he didn't lean forward: Milos felt sure he wouldn't be able to stand having the Amnioni that close to him.

Folding his human arm and his rust-covered limb across his chest, Vestabule proposed, "Then perhaps it would be well to begin with the lies and truths which have brought you to speak to us directly."

Milos thought it would be better to start by naming what the Amnioni called his "requirements." At the moment, however, he could hardly imagine what they were. Protect me. Keep me alive. Get even for me. Such things were too nebulous; yet his fear prevented him from thinking of anything else. He understood nothing about the Amnion. How could he ask them to protect him when he didn't know how they would react to his "lies and truths"?

If they were a guttergang—in essence if not in name—why didn't they act like one?

Sweating inside the constriction of his mask, he said, "Maybe you already know. That's a possibility I have to consider. There's too much treachery here. Too many people are lying. For all I know, you're all in it together. Plotting together, using people—"

"Milos Taverner," Vestabule ventured in his rough, oxidized voice, "I cannot respond to these suggestions until you inform me of their content. Clearly you are concerned. However, you have made no mention of the specific issues which concern you."

As if the words had been triggered out of him, Milos retorted, "Why aren't you doing anything about Thermopyle?"

The Amnioni gazed back at him expressionlessly. Only the lid of Vestabule's human eye moved.

"I *warned* you about him," Milos went on in a rush. "The UMCP reqqed him from Com-Mine Security, just like they reqqed me, and they *welded* him, I *told* you that. They gave him computers and zone implants and lasers and God knows what else. And they sent him here to destroy this place. I positively told you *that.*

"Why aren't you doing anything about him?"

Why aren't you afraid of him?

What's going on here?

Now Marc Vestabule nodded. "I see. Our response—or our lack of response—to the threat posed by this Angus Thermopyle causes you anxiety. That is a subject we may discuss.

"Is it your belief that the Bill's defenses are inadequate to deal with this threat?"

"I *know* they are," Milos snorted. "Aren't you aware that Davies Hyland—that kid you want so badly—was taken right out from under his nose? Hasn't he told you?"

Vestabule nodded impersonally. "He has."

"Well, Thermopyle did it," Milos went on quickly. "I was with him the whole time. We simply walked into the cell and grabbed Davies. We took him back to *Trumpet.* And the Bill didn't do anything to stop us. He couldn't—he didn't know what was happening. He hasn't got a clue where that kid is now."

An expression which may once have been a frown plucked at the human half of Vestabule's face. "That statement is not strictly accurate." Turning his head slightly, he touched his left ear. For the first time Milos noticed that the Amnioni wore a small receiver jacked into his ear. "The Bill has been speaking to us from the moment of your arrival," Vestabule explained. "He has reason to believe that Davies Hyland was abducted by Angus Thermopyle and yourself. Presumably he also believes that Davies Hyland is aboard *Trumpet*, for the same reasons. He demands that we deliver you to him, so that he may learn the truth of what has transpired.

"He makes no reference to enhanced capabilities. However, he is aware of your power over Angus Thermopyle. Therefore he believes that you—and perhaps by extension the Amnion, because you have come here—stand at the heart of this treachery."

Milos winced convulsively. Nevertheless, in spite of his alarm, he stuck to the point on which his survival depended. "That doesn't explain why you haven't done anything."

He needed to understand the Amnion—and show them how vulnerable they were—before he could offer them anything that might save his life.

Vestabule didn't hesitate. "Like the Bill," he scraped out as if the Amnion had no secrets from Milos, "we are aware of your dealings with Nick Succorso. Unlike the Bill, however, we know that you do not stand at the heart of this treachery. We believe that the 'plotting,' as you call it, exists between Nick Succorso and Angus Thermopyle.

"We have taken no action concerning this threat for several reasons.

"First, we lose nothing by allowing the Bill to confront Angus Thermopyle on our behalf. Ultimately he is"—Vestabule appeared momentarily uncertain of the word he wanted—"expendable. We are not harmed if he is challenged and made insecure. On the contrary, we gain a greater understanding of the threat itself.

"In particular we hope to gain a greater understanding of Nick Succorso's treachery."

In bitterness and fear, Milos admitted privately that he wanted to understand Nick's treachery himself.

"Second," Vestabule went on without pausing, "Angus Thermopyle and Nick Succorso are natural antagonists. This is a concept which is not comprehensible to the Amnion, but which I have been able to retain.

"I am"—he lifted his shoulders like a shrug—"as you see me. Portions of my former body remain. Similarly portions of my former mind remain. I am able to grasp that Angus Thermopyle and Nick Succorso cannot form an alliance without simultaneously seeking to betray each other. Granted enough scope, they will expose each other's truths and undermine each other's strengths, thereby rendering each other ineffective."

Milos might have sneered at this proposition, but the Amnioni didn't wait for his reaction.

"Naturally the question of 'scope' is critical. It is possible—indeed, it is probable—that the threats they pose, separately and together, will become so acute that we cannot afford to allow them enough scope. Nevertheless while we can we wait, searching for the truth.

"Third, it is our experience that Angus Thermopyle is inherently less dangerous to us than Nick Succorso."

Milos couldn't help himself: he gaped in surprise. "You're kidding. Nick's just a pirate. Thermopyle is the slime of the universe."

Vestabule's alien eye held the yellow light humorlessly. "Both as a cyborg and as a human," he asserted, "we distrust Thermopyle less. As a cyborg, he is limited as well as enhanced by his programming. And as a human his malice is too pure to permit the profounder forms of treachery.

"This is not speculation, Milos Taverner," he said as if he were articulating a fact which had no personal impact. "I have direct experience with Angus Thermopyle, during my life among your kind. At one time I crewed aboard a vessel named *Viable Dreams,* an in-system hauler which fulfilled the support function of transshipping ores discovered by prospectors. It was an unglamorous labor, but profitable. However, we were hijacked by Angus Thermopyle. Twenty-eight men and women, the survivors of our crew, he brought here and sold to the Amnion."

The calm with which Vestabule revealed this detail chilled Milos as much as his rusted flesh and sharp teeth.

"I understand his limits," the Amnioni continued. "His behavior, both on that occasion and subsequently, has made his essential nature plain. For that reason we are disinclined to dispose of him when he may yet serve us against Nick Succorso.

"Finally, you control him, do you not?" Vestabule's human eye blinked rapidly, signaling an intensity which his posture and expression concealed. "Why should we take action against him, when you are able to command him at will?

"Is that not what you wished the Bill to understand when you compelled Angus Thermopyle to ingest your discarded—I have forgotten the word—your nicotine sticks in clear view of the surveillance monitors? Have you not deliberately created circumstances which would lead the Bill to believe that you—and perhaps therefore we— stand at the heart of this treachery?"

"No!" Milos could hardly breathe: his mask was full of fear, suffocating him. "That's not it!" If the Amnion believed that, he was finished, *finished.* "I was just testing him—trying to prove he still obeys my codes. I haven't told you why I'm here. It was all a lie. I believed it, but it was a lie. I came to talk to you as soon as I learned the truth."

"What is the lie? What is the truth?" Vestabule touched the side of his head. "The Bill is passionate in his demand for your delivery. He hints that your presence here violates our agreements with him. How can we answer, except by granting what he wishes, if we do not comprehend what has brought you here?"

Don't do it! Milos fluttered his hands, almost begging for a chance to explain. Don't let him have me.

"I don't know how big it is," he panted urgently, "the lie. I don't know how far it goes. It may or may not have anything to do with destroying this installation. All I know is, it has something to do with Morn Hyland, that woman Nick gave you. Davies Hyland's mother. I told you about her—a long time ago. She's UMCP—an Enforcement Division ensign."

"Nick Succorso made no mention of this," Vestabule observed in a tone as dead as ruined metal. "When he delivered her to us, he retained her id tag."

Milos might have heard hints in Vestabule's words, possibilities of survival; but he was too frightened to concentrate on them. Driven by the pressure of his heart, he went on talking, explaining.

"Thermopyle got his hands on her, gave her a zone implant so he could use her. But Nick wanted her. He took her when we framed Thermopyle. That was a UMCP deal, too. I told you Nick works for them sometimes. They wanted Thermopyle framed. So they could req him. Nick did it in exchange for her."

"What is the significance of this?" the Amnioni asked flatly.

"It's Thermopyle's programming." The sweat on Milos' hands made them feel foul; corrupted. "I'm *supposed* to be able to control him. I'm supposed to guarantee that he does what he was sent here to do. That means I have to know what it is. To destroy the installation. But Hashi Lebwohl was in charge of the whole project. He told me specifically, explicitly, that we were *not* here to rescue Morn Hyland. Even though she's UMCP. Even though Thermopyle wants her back. As far as UMCPHQ is concerned, she's lost, dead. Thermopyle was supposed to ignore her. And I was *supposed* to make sure he did."

The breathing mask seemed to stifle Milos' outrage. He wanted to shout, but couldn't get enough air.

"Do you understand what I've told you about him? His head is full of zone implants, all run by a computer. And his codes and instructions are written in a datacore, where they can't be altered. I have power over him because I know some of those codes, but it's the computer that enforces them. He *can't* make his own choices. It's physically impossible.

"But he *is* making his own choices. He's making choices that violate his programming—that violate what I was told his programming is.

"They aren't what you think." Unconscious of his own actions, Milos scrubbed his hands harder and harder against his thighs. "Nick may be plotting against you—or against the Bill—but Thermopyle isn't. He's plotting to get Morn Hyland back. He snatched Davies because Nick offered him a trade, Morn for the kid. He didn't know you already had her. So now he's planning to come after her. He kept Davies, and the two of them are going to try to get her back.

"Do you see what that means? I'm *supposed* to control him—but Hashi Lebwohl lied to me. Warden Dios lied to me." *On this one subject, you were misled.* "They're using me as some kind of shill. Thermopyle *can't* make his own choices, so he must be acting on the instructions in his datacore, instructions I don't know about— instructions that sometimes let him override my command codes."

Can't you understand that we're all being set up here?

Faintness was beginning to spin through his head like vertigo. With the pressure of his palms against his thighs, he tried to push it down.

"Interesting," Marc Vestabule observed after a long pause. "There are indeed many facets here, many concerns. You speak of some— yet you make no mention of others. Are you unaware of them, Milos Taverner, or does your silence conceal other truths?"

The vertigo seemed to suck Milos' mind away, leaving nothing behind except a fine white panic. Grinding his fingers into his legs so that he wouldn't scream, he asked thickly, "What 'other truths'? I don't know what you're talking about."

For a moment Vestabule's human eye became as unblinking as the Amnion one. "Are you unaware," he inquired, "that both Nick Succorso and Morn Hyland possess a quality which must make them uniquely precious to the UMCP?"

Milos stared back at the Amnioni stupidly. "What quality?"

Vestabule made a small warding gesture with his crusted arm. "Both possess an immunity to mutagens. Twice the same compound which transformed me has been administered to her. She remains human—as Nick Succorso himself once did.

"Unfortunately this installation lacks the facilities for adequate study. We can only determine that her immunity exists. We cannot define how it exists.

"Will you tell me, Milos Taverner, that you know nothing of this?" The rust had been rubbed away: now Vestabule's tone was pure iron. "Will you tell me that the true purpose of Nick Succorso's visits to Enablement Station was not to test his immunity?

"Will you tell me that the true purpose for which he delivered Morn Hyland to us was not to make us aware of the existence of this immunity, thereby informing us that humankind is defended against us—and thereby warning us that humankind is now prepared to en- gage us in war if we do not retreat from our imperatives?

"Will you tell me that the true purpose for which Angus Ther- mopyle was sent here was not to retake Morn Hyland before we could study her—before we could discover the source or nature of her immunity?"

"No!" Milos protested at once. "I'm not going to tell you any of those things! Maybe they're true. For all I know, they could be. What *I'm* here to tell you—"

Abruptly his brain froze. Through his white, blind panic came a black flash like a streak of intuition.

They could all be true.

Then why did Hashi Lebwohl lie? What did he gain by trying to convince me Thermopyle had a completely different mission?

Another flash.

Unless he already knew the truth about me.

He lied to me because he knew I would pass his lies on.

And another.

He sent me here to get rid of me. He wanted the Amnion to do his dirty work for him when they discovered that what I told them wasn't true.

Panting feverishly, Milos said in supplication, "I'm here to give you everything I have. I came as soon as I knew the cops were lying.

"Thermopyle has a secret mission." He wanted to rip off his mask and throw it away; let the Amnion air sear his lungs until all the dread was burned out of him. "It has something to do with Morn Hyland. He's coming to try to get her away from you. And he's bringing her son with him.

"That's it. That's all I have."

With one exception—

"But if you keep me alive—if you back me up—I might be able to stop him. And if I do that, you can almost certainly catch Davies again." He was desperate: he'd reached his own absolute limit. One by one his choices and hopes had been stripped away. Only this remained. "You'll get them both. You probably can't mutate Thermopyle. His datacore will kill him before it lets that happen. But you can study him, learn everything about him. And you'll have Davies to do what you want with."

Vestabule regarded Milos steadily: the Amnioni sat as still as a tombstone, untouched by Milos' appeal.

"Isn't that *enough*?" Milos cried. *"What more do you want from me?"*

Vestabule stirred; shifted his legs. "Milos Taverner," he said like cold, cleaned metal, "I urge you to refrain from fear. It gains nothing. We will keep you alive. We will give you our support. I do not mean to frighten you when I say that your usefulness is at an end."

His human hand slid into the pocket of his shipsuit.

"These are concepts which no Amnioni can process without great difficulty. For many of my people they are impossible. Even for me they stretch the limits of comprehension. Nevertheless it is necessary to comprehend them.

A DARK AND HUNGRY GOD ARISES

"While serving both Com-Mine Security and the United Mining Companies Police, you have dealt with us, trading your knowledge of them for credit. Though it is difficult for us to understand, we must assume that you have dealt similarly with them, trading your knowledge of us for credit."

No, Milos wanted to protest, no, of course not! But Vestabule's alien gaze held him; Vestabule's iron tone struck him dumb.

"After the events which have taken place here," the Amnioni continued, "this network of dealings will no longer be fruitful for us. Therefore our relationship must be altered. Between you and us, Milos Taverner, conformity of purpose will be achieved through the mutual satisfaction of requirements.

"You require life and support.

"We require you."

From out of his pocket, Marc Vestabule pulled a hypo.

The vial of the hypo held a viscid liquid, as dark as poison.

Screaming, Milos flung himself out of his chair. Vestabule caught him easily, however. One Amnioni hand gripped him, as tight as a flexsteel band; one human fist drove like a piston into his solar plexus.

Fear as fathomless as the gap between the stars shocked Milos' nerves. Locked in spasms while his neurons misfired, he couldn't defend himself as Vestabule pierced his forearm with the hypo and released mutagens into his veins.

ANCILLARY
DOCUMENTATION

WARDEN DIOS: EXTRACTS FROM THE PRIVATE
JOURNALS OF HASHI LEBWOHL, DIRECTOR,
DATA ACQUISITION, UNITED MINING COMPANIES
POLICE

*[This extract is dated several months prior
to Angus Thermopyle's arrest by Com-Mine Security.]*

N owhere is the particular and pe-
. . . culiar genius of the man more
evident than in his handling of the matter of the Intertech immunity
drug.

I have had occasion to note in previous entries that he is my
superior because he possesses a quality of charisma—the ability to
lead by inspiration—which I lack. In other ways, however, I consider him my only peer—certainly my only peer in the hallowed bas-
tion of UMCPHQ. Yet I must acknowledge that I would have been
hard-pressed to manage the crisis which Intertech's immunity research represented as well as he did. Perhaps because I lack charisma,
I might not have been able to obtain—as he did—the most desirable
of all possible outcomes. . . .

. . . the issue is difficult to explain because an understanding
of its parameters requires an understanding of Holt Fasner, and an
explication of Holt Fasner's motivations is not a challenge to be undertaken lightly. Speculation is both easier and less useful than true
insight.

I might, for example, consider the possibility that the common view of the Dragon is inadequate. Of course, I do not refer to the public perception that he is simply the most wealthy, dominant, commanding, glamorous, and therefore necessary man living. Rather I mean to cite the view which commonly underlies the public perception—the view that he is a man driven by avarice, impelled by greed to risk all human space against the Amnion for the sake of the UMC's profitability. This view is inadequate because the difference between unimaginable riches and even more unimaginable riches is ultimately trivial.

Instead I might speculate that his avarice is not for wealth, but for power—that he is driven by a desire for godhood, a yearning to attain the stature of unquestionable as well as unavoidable fate for the whole of humankind. And I might further observe that all human aspirations to godhood must fail while the Amnion and death exist. Finally I might conclude that it is this ineluctable failure which both confirms Holt Fasner's lust for power and erodes his ability to control it.

But having said all that, what have I accomplished? Have I shed any light into the dark heart of the Dragon in his lair? Have I altered any of the decisions which must be made, the actions which must be taken, concerning him? I have not. I have only constructed a guesswork edifice for my own edification and amusement. . . .

. . . accept, then, the underlying common view that Holt Fasner is cemented to his own fate by ordinary acquisitiveness—that all his great attainments and cunning are dedicated to the uninteresting goal of acquiring meaningless increments of wealth. Does this imply a concomitant acceptance of the commonly held underlying view of Warden Dios, that he is nothing more than the perfect instrument of Holt Fasner's will? that he is at once so brilliant and so mindless that he can serve Holt Fasner purely, untainted by needs and desires of his own? that he lacks both of those glorious human foibles, scruple and ambition?

Certainly not. It is patent that brilliance and mindlessness cannot coexist, that ambition metastasizes exponentially in the absence of scruple. Holt Fasner QED. Therefore it follows as naturally as humans fear pain that Warden Dios is not the Dragon's instrument, but rather his natural enemy.

This explains the Dragon's selection of him as director of the

UMCP. How better to both defang and profit from a natural enemy than by binding him to yourself, sealing him away within your own structures and exigencies, so he cannot serve himself without also serving you? If Warden Dios were not the director of the UMCP, Holt Fasner would have to kill him.

Yet this is a paradox—at once fertile and dangerous—because Warden Dios' needs and ambitions can never be identical to the Dragon's.

Intertech's immunity research provides a case in point.

Grant for a moment that Warden Dios is another Holt Fasner—less confirmed in his lust for power, less eroded in his ability to control it—but another Dragon nonetheless. Precisely because he has been less confirmed, less eroded, he cannot aspire to supplant his nominal master. Yet what other outlets remain for his ambitions? What other needs or priorities might his brilliance serve? And—do not neglect this point—how else can his natural enmity to the Dragon express itself?

Perhaps by identifying himself with the UMCP rather than with the UMC. By assigning to the UMCP an importance which he denies to the vaster and less specific domain of the Dragon. By affirming the stated purposes and restrictions of the UMCP at the expense of Holt Fasner and the UMC.

Now consider the matter of the immunity drug.

The moment Intertech's research threatens to succeed, the Dragon perceives a threat. If humankind may be immunized against mutagens, the peril of the Amnion recedes. Therefore the necessity of the UMCP—and of its corporate host—recedes. Therefore the logic which sustains that host as the sole conduit for alien trade and wealth loses its syllogistic inevitability.

At once the Dragon moves to quash the research. It must be removed before it can become the means by which his hold on human space frays away.

So much is predictable, hardly worthy of comment.

But how does Warden Dios respond? Does he permit himself spasms of self-righteousness, as a lesser man might? Does he fall prey to scruples or fainthearted alarms? Does he oppose his putative master, either openly or privately?

He does not.

Instead he persuades the Dragon that Intertech's research must be permitted to continue in secret—in my care, in fact. Employing his considerable resources of eloquence and charisma, he convinces the Dragon that an attained immunity drug—if it were kept secret—would be a tool of unmatched power. He does not stake his argument on the proposition that such a drug could be used to secure the safety of his own people. Instead he suggests using, not the drug itself, but knowledge of the drug against the Amnion. By "leaking"—odious term—that knowledge, he can induce them to be more fearful in their dealings with us. They will be at once confirmed in their distrust of humankind and eroded in their ability to act on that distrust. And this development will conduce to the security of the UMC as the sole conduit for alien etc.

How can the Dragon resist such blandishment? Its virtues are too plain to be refuted. The current state of poised but inactive hostility between humankind and the Amnion is reinforced. UMC profits are maximized. And Warden Dios' purity as the instrument of Holt Fasner's will is demonstrated. His natural enmity to the Dragon is apparently defanged by his implication in the Dragon's disdain for humankind. Once again Warden Dios is subsumed by Holt Fasner's avarice.

Inevitably the Dragon cedes his approval. And so the Intertech research comes to me, to complete and use as I advise—and as Warden Dios sees fit.

Therefore the commonly held view that Warden Dios is the perfect instrument of Holt Fasner's will is affirmed, is it not?

I think not.

Consider the beauty of this outcome from the perspective of the UMCP. Certainly the Dragon is given what he most desires—the immeasurable and ultimately meaningless satisfaction of his greed. But the more significant, the more effective, benefits belong all to the UMCP. We have the drug itself, to use both for our own security and for the consternation of our opponents. The risks of actions we have already taken are reduced. The risks of actions which we have heretofore declined are made acceptable. We can manipulate the defensive postures of the Amnion almost at will. The consequences of humankind's quite natural and comprehensible impulse toward piracy are diminished. We are given a bulwark against the depredations of politicians, protected by the mere existence of our secrets from ham-fisted tampering. Only Protocol suffers under the burden of secrecy—

and such men as Godsen Frik are born to suffer. Both Enforcement Division and Data Acquisition are made stronger.

Warden Dios has gained all this—and at what cost? At no discernible cost at all, apart from the delicious expense of allowing the Dragon to retain his illusions. And failures of godhood will—they must—derive from any illusion. Thus Holt Fasner has been at once confirmed in his lust for power and eroded in his ability to control it by his most necessary subordinate—his most natural enemy. . . .

. . . having no scruples myself, I do not hesitate to call myself a genius. However, I am more cautious when I apply that name to others. . . .

. . . because of victories such as his handling of Intertech's immunity research, as well as countless others, I state categorically that Warden Dios is a genius.

GODSEN

Godsen Frik sat in his office and stared at the orders he'd just received. As he read the official hardcopy for the third time, he tried to believe that he wasn't afraid.

Things like *this* weren't supposed to happen to him. What was the advantage of being Holt Fasner's protégé—what did he gain by his efforts to serve the United Mining Companies as much as the United Mining Companies Police—if things like *this* could still happen to him?

Where did Warden Dios get the nerve? Didn't he understand that Holt Fasner was his *boss*—that the Dragon could simply *fire* him?

But if Warden fired Godsen himself first—and the Dragon didn't consider the Director of Protocol worth losing the Director of the whole UMCP for—

That was the possibility Godsen concentrated on, so that he wouldn't think about his real fear. A man who'd been fired by the UMCP for insubordination—or worse—wasn't a likely candidate to succeed Abrim Len as president of the Governing Council for Earth and Space. All of his ambitions—not to mention his long years of patience and ass-licking—would come to nothing.

The other possibilities were too disturbing to consider.

What if this quicksand of plots and counterplots proved too thick for him; too subtle and deadly? What if he drowned in it? He could survive being fired. And if he was fired in Holt Fasner's name, the

Dragon would eventually reward him. But what if the plotting actually killed him?

There was blood in these orders. He knew without asking that they were a response to the attack on Sixten Vertigus. People were going to die before this tangle of betrayals sorted itself out. Somewhere, somehow, the decision had already been made that the stakes were worth killing for.

Godsen Frik didn't want to be one of the casualties.

He reread the hardcopy obsessively in an effort to prevent himself from wondering whether his loyalty to Holt Fasner at Warden Dios' occasional expense was reason enough for nameless madmen to want him dead.

Or whether he distrusted Dios enough to call the UMCP director a madman.

His orders were as clear as they were unexplained. Until further notice, Godsen Frik, Director of Protocol, United Mining Companies Police, was restricted to UMCPHQ.

What was Dios trying to do? Prevent Frik from taking one of his sporadic junkets to the fleshpots—Godsen loved words like that— of Earth, where he would presumably be an easy target? Well, in all honesty that wasn't much of a hardship. Protocol was full of attractive women—he'd seen to that as a good PR director should—and some of them found him attractive in turn, for their own reasons. If they lacked the seductive perversion of the fleshpots, they were still women. Some of them were bound to be worth teaching.

In fact, being restricted to UMCPHQ wasn't a hardship at all, in any obvious sense. His quarters were luxurious in ways which satisfied his sense of his own worth, ways which suggested that he was accustomed to wealth and status, but not ruled by them: his rooms were spacious; full of subdued art, quiet holograms, data terminals, and video screens; furnished with costly but understated rugs, sofas, chairs, tables, beds. And his office was spartan only by comparison with the official room which Warden never used except on occasions of public display. From where he sat he could perform all the necessary functions of his job: issue bulletins, hold meetings, fend off or gratify newsdogs; brief the votes either in session or in private, by public transmission or secure downlink; support or oppose the policies of his fellow directors.

So why did he feel trapped? Why was he *scared*?

Because there was so much at stake, sure, of course, that was the reason. Angus Thermopyle had been set loose against Billingate. Controlled by none other than Milos Taverner, in the name of heaven! And explicitly programmed not to rescue Morn Hyland. That was bad enough. But Dios' explosive video conference with the GCES made everything worse. A nightmare for Protocol, impossible to clean up or sweep under the rug. He had "curled the moral hair" of the votes with a vengeance. Godsen had already received four calls from Maxim Igensard, *five* from UWB Junior Member Carsin, and two more from Abrim Len—none of which he'd answered, for the simple reason that he didn't know how.

And the attack no *on Sixten Vertigus* no *made everything MUCH worse* no, don't think about that. Absolutely not.

It would be better to answer his calls than think.

Restricted to UMCPHQ.

Suddenly he felt sure that the only conceivable way to minimize or at least contain the damage to the UMCP—and by extension, Holt Fasner—was to go to Earth, visit Igensard and Carsin and Len and even dear old outdated Sixten Vertigus in person. In person he might be able to talk them down from their hysteria, swaddle them in blather; mop the sweat of paranoia off their brows, so to speak. He was at his best in person. Any technological interference, even by video downlink, neutralized the charm which made him good at his job, the ability to spin gossamer illusions and make them seem substantial.

It was intolerable that Warden Dios seemed determined to commit seppuku in this bizarre fashion; taking his director of Protocol with him.

Immersed in fears he didn't want to recognize, Godsen flinched involuntarily when his intercom chimed. He dropped the hardcopy of his orders as if it were hot enough to burn him. His hands shook as he toggled the intercom.

"Yes?"

"Director Frik, I have a call from Holt Fasner."

His secretary had been chosen because she had the kind of dulcet and accessible voice—this was Godsen's phrase—which gave newsdogs wet dreams. He hated it and her down to the ground.

He kept his loathing to himself, however. In an avuncular rumble, he answered, "Put him through, my dear. It doesn't pay to keep the High and Mighty waiting."

"Yes, sir."

At once one of the speakers on his desk—the channel he used for his most private conversations—came alive.

"Godsen." The name wasn't a question. And the voice didn't identify itself. It didn't need to: Godsen would have recognized it in his sleep. "What the hell's going on down there? The votes are pissing pure alum."

"Mr. Fasner—sir," Godsen blurted out while his brain fumbled for the first consecutive sentence it could find, "I'm glad you called. I was just about to contact you. I've been working on a report—"

"Spare me the bullshit," the Dragon retorted. He sounded incongruously cheerful. "Put it where it might do all of us some good. If you wanted to talk to me, you would have called by now.

"Try telling the truth instead. What—I mean this literally, Godsen—what in hell is going on?"

Old reflexes kicked in. As if he were behind a podium facing a hostile news conference, Godsen countered, "Can you be more specific?" Real dignity was beyond him at the moment, but at least he could sound starched and irritable at need. "There are any number of 'hells' going on. Which one do you want to talk about first?"

"Oh, stop it." Holt may have been enjoying himself. "You know perfectly well what I want to talk about."

Quailing inside, Godsen clung to his reflexes. "The first that comes to mind, sir, is the attack on Captain Vertigus. Do you want to hear my usual speech about the diligence and integrity of UMCP investigations? Or perhaps a sidebar on the merits of GCES Security? I'm afraid that's all I have to offer. Only the Enforcement Division director or Warden Dios might know more, but if they do they haven't revealed it to me."

"My, my, you *are* in a state today." Holt sneered. "One might almost think that kaze was aimed at you." Without transition his tone became a snarl. "No, that is *not* what I'm asking about."

Godsen winced. What else was left? As stiff as cardboard, he suggested, "Then I suppose you're interested in the director's video conference with the GCES?"

"Good guess," Holt returned trenchantly.

Godsen resisted the impulse to come up with other possibilities. They wouldn't distract the Dragon. Instead he said, "In that case I'll suppose as well that you already know what actually happened—who said what to whom, that sort of thing."

Holt Fasner waited. His silence sounded even more ominous than his voice.

"I'm going to suppose that what you want to know"—Godsen hung fire momentarily—"is why the director did it. What he hopes to gain."

The Dragon still didn't speak.

"Mr. Fasner—" Without meaning to, Godsen stopped. What could he say? More to the point, what could he say over a communications link which was inevitably being recorded somewhere in the bowels of UMCPHQ?

I think Warden Dios has lost his mind.

Good choice.

I think he's trying to sabotage Data Acquisition. He's too pure to like operations like the ones we've launched against Thanatos Minor, so he wants to get them prohibited in the future. Hashi only went along with it because he's too full of his own cleverness to realize the truth.

Even better.

I think he's trying to *hurt* you, Mr. Fasner, you and me and maybe everything the UMC stands for, God alone knows why.

No, that was definitely too frightening to say. Even recognizing the existence of such issues was dangerous.

It was typical of the Dragon to be careless of other people's security considerations.

Swallowing heavily, Godsen began again.

"Mr. Fasner, you don't really want to talk about that now. In any event, I probably don't know the answer. The director"—even now he couldn't stifle his rhetorical impulse—"hasn't taken me into his confidence on this subject."

While Godsen sweated, the Dragon remained silent. Then he replied with unexpected good humor, "So don't talk to me. You're probably right—I don't want to hear it like this.

"Grab a shuttle," he commanded, "and come over here." *Here* meant his "home office," his corporate station orbiting Earth only erate—Warden had forced him to choose between the UMC and the UMCP.

The UMC *owned* the UMCP, for God's sake! That was the only clear thought in Godsen's spinning head. Of *course* he should do what the Dragon wanted, and damn the consequences. Otherwise everything he'd ever done or suffered was wasted.

But in his weighted stomach he believed, *knew*, that Warden Dios didn't kill the people he was sworn to protect.

If a kaze could get into the Members' wing of the GCES complex on Suka Bator to attack Sixten Vertigus, no one was safe. Godsen Frik had to ask himself which he distrusted more, Warden's self-destructiveness or Holt's consuming disdain.

His ten minutes were almost up when he finally summoned the courage to chime his secretary.

"Communications must have recorded the conversation I just had with Holt Fasner," he said to her. "Tell them I want a copy of it on Director Dios' desk immediately. Tell them to *flare* it. I want him to look at it right now."

His voice didn't shake. In fact, he sounded more dignified than he would have thought possible.

That small victory gave him the fortitude to begin looking at his messages from Len, Igensard, and Carsin so that he could figure out how to answer them.

MIN

Min Donner had also received orders.

Like Godsen's, hers made her feel strangely misused, as if she'd been cheated or thwarted in some way; neutralized or disenfranchised.

Like him, she sat in her office and chewed them like gristle, trying to imagine what they meant.

Unlike him, she knew what to do about them. And she wasn't scared. She was angry. She was battered and tired, stretched too thin to react with anything except anger.

She'd recovered her hearing: that was the good news. Except for a small high-pitched whine far back in the audible spectrum, sounds and voices reached her without distortion. But everything else—

Her whole body ached from the force of the kaze's bomb. For a while that pain had settled into a dull, steady throb: noradrenaline and serotonin had made it easy to ignore. But now it was growing stronger, more acute, as her body demanded attention for its needs. Her shoulders and hips felt arthritic, nearly immobilized. The corners of her jaw hurt as if she'd been grinding her teeth hard enough to dislocate the joints. Her mind felt muzzy and numb, packed with polypropylene insulation. At unpredictable, infuriating intervals, fresh blood dripped from her nose, demonstrating her weakness for anyone to see.

If she'd stopped to think about it, she would have realized that she hadn't slept since before Warden had briefed Angus Thermopyle and Milos Taverner; hadn't eaten since the crew of the shuttle to Suka Bator had given her a sandwich. She didn't have time to think about such things, however.

By itself the attack on Captain Vertigus would have been enough to consume all her attention. But in addition she needed time as well as emotional space to consider the implications of her conversation with Warden.

Unfortunately those weren't her only responsibilities—

She also had a disaster of staggering proportions on her hands.

Godsen Frik was dead. Less than twenty minutes ago, he'd been blown to pulp and splinters by a kaze.

Men and women still ran and shouted in the corridors; clearing away wreckage and a few bodies; making way for damage control workers and investigators; hunting for more kazes.

Too late, all of UMCPHQ was on defense alert.

She felt that she could still hear the explosion, even though she'd been too far away to distinguish anything except an impalpable shock through the muffling walls and infrastructure. The whine in her ears seemed more like an echo of Godsen's death than a residue of the attempt on Captain Vertigus.

She was Min Donner, director, UMCP Enforcement Division. Her domain included UMCPHQ Security. She couldn't blame herself if a kaze got into the Members' wing of the GCES complex; but there was no one else to hold accountable for Godsen's murder.

And how many more of them were on station? Who or what would they destroy next?

Her people had already reconstructed the attack as well as they could. Godsen's secretary had been injured by flying debris, but she remained alive—still conscious. She'd been able to tell Min's Chief of Security that a communications tech had come to her and asked to see the PR director. The request was an odd one, so she'd checked both his id tag and his communications credentials. Both had looked good. More to the point, both had passed routine verification by the Security computer. So she'd chimed Godsen. The PR director had told her to admit the tech.

Five seconds after the door closed, the kaze had set himself off.

She did her job, the Chief of Security reported. Can't blame her.

I don't, Min snapped. I don't even blame you. I just want to know how it happened.

I want to know if it's going to happen again.

It happened, the Chief explained, because she did a routine verification, not a full background. Everybody in the chain did the same thing. Dock security did a routine verification when he got off the shuttle. Before that, port security did a routine verification when he boarded. Before that, GCES Security did a routine verification before they let him into the port.

Wait a minute. GCES Security? You mean this kaze came from Suka Bator? From the GCES complex?

That's right.

The Chief of Security waited while she swore to herself. Then he continued.

His id was legit—all the correct verifications, all the right pass codes—everything written in the CMOS chip was right. He had orders from GCES Communications to report to UMCPHQ Center. They're legit, too, even though GCES Communications denies issuing them. As long as no one got suspicious—as long as no one ran a full background—he could have gone anywhere once dock security let him in.

What did the full background show?

Nothing. He doesn't exist. I mean there's no record of him. His id tag and his function id were never issued to anyone. The tag was real—I mean it fit him, its data matches what the lab has gleaned so far from blood and tissue in Frik's office—but it was never issued.

Min wanted to demand, Then who was he really? You've got gene id—who *was* he? She didn't bother, however. The Chief of Security would pursue that inquiry as a matter of course—and would probably learn nothing. On Earth thousands of people every year avoided id processing. Most of them lived in guttergangs and had no reason to desire any of the so-called benefits of being an identified member of human society.

Instead she asked a different question.

So have we suddenly become stupid around here? She made no effort to tone down her fury. Don't we learn from experience anymore? It's only been a few hours since a kaze tried to kill Captain Vertigus. His id was legit. He passed routine verification. But a full background would have caught him. Didn't it ever occur to any of us that there's no such thing as *one* kaze? If there's one, there can always be more. Why weren't we doing full backgrounds on everybody who sets foot on this station?

The Chief of Security was ashamed of himself. Nevertheless he didn't flinch.

Because I didn't think of it. Ten minutes after the attack on Captain Vertigus, I advised GCES Security to do full background on everyone they let past any checkpoint on the island. But then I assumed anyone who came here from there had already been screened. And I guess I assumed one attack on a GCES Member meant more attacks in the same place. The Chief shrugged grimly. Dock security would have run full background if he'd come from anywhere except Suka Bator.

Simply because she blamed herself more than him, Min offered the Chief a way to soften his shame.

So GCES Security let us down.

By which she meant that someone in GCES Security had been suborned; had deliberately let the kaze through to the UMCPHQ shuttle.

Treachery was spreading.

How many kazes were already loose on station?

Director, the Chief said hesitantly, I don't understand. If whoever did this has the resources to make kazes and equip them with legitimate id and send them here, why waste all that on Protocol? Why bother? What's so important about Godsen Frik? Why not you, or Director Dios? Why not Center, or Communications, or Data Storage—why not something vital, something that would really damage us?

Min had no idea. Unlike Captain Vertigus, Godsen would have done everything in his power to oppose a Bill of Severance.

What was Godsen doing? she asked.

He had a call from Holt Fasner about ten minutes before the kaze hit. That's all I know.

The Dragon, she thought bleakly. Godsen's mentor and nemesis. How had the PR director failed to understand that dragons always devoured their servants?

Everyone in UMCPHQ would be devoured if they didn't start defending their own better than this.

Chief, I want you to—

Trying to recover some of his self-esteem, the Chief of Security interrupted her.

I know. Full background on everyone who's arrived by shuttle, starting with the past twenty-four hours and working backward for at least a month. My people are already running it. And from now on no shuttle gets within twenty thousand k until we have full background on everyone aboard. Nobody gets into any sensitive part of the station without being absolutely checked.

It wasn't enough, but it would have to do. Min was too angry to say anything else, so she sent him back to work.

She was angry at herself for a number of reasons. Pain was one— the mortality which inhibited her when she needed to be at her best. A sense of failure in her duty was another. She should have seen the necessity for the precautions which her Chief of Security had missed. And she recognized one more: she was glad Godsen Frik was dead. That unctuous weasel had done the UMCP incalculable harm by serving the Dragon more than Warden.

Because she was angry at herself, she would have pursued the investigation of these kazes with every gram of tenacity, intelligence, and bloody-mindedness she had in her.

But she wasn't given that choice. She had orders—

They lay in front of her as she sat at her desk, wrestling with fatigue, pain, and confusion as if they were her personal furies. Warden's instructions had been cut with a precision which hadn't been necessary between her and the director for a long time. Clearly and effectively, they prevented her from doing her job as she saw it— from uncovering and rooting out the treachery which had sent kazes against the GCES and the UMCP.

Instead she was forced to leave the investigation as well as the aftermath to her Chief of Security; and to the strange young woman Hashi had sent over from DA. All of Hashi's people were good: Min admitted that. And this one was an expert—so he claimed—in tracing CMOS chips, presumably by identifying where, how, and when they were manufactured. That might prove invaluable—assuming, of course, that any recognizable particle of the kaze's id had survived the explosion. Nevertheless Min hated being barred from the investigation; hated trusting it to subordinates for whom she felt responsible and to experts she couldn't trust because they shared Lebwohl's involuted priorities.

Now, of all possible times, she hated being sent away from UMCPHQ.

Was Warden trying to protect her by getting her out of the way? Trying to keep her alive so that she could succeed him as UMCP director?

Or was he getting her out of the way for a completely different reason? Perhaps because he feared that she might actually be able to track these kazes to their source?

The orders themselves gave her no answer.

They were superficially simple. The stark hardcopy required her to take command of the first available UMCP warship and proceed immediately to the asteroid belt served by Com-Mine Station. Using the belt to cover her, she was instructed to watch for and respond to developments from the direction of Thanatos Minor.

In this case, the "first available UMCP warship" happened to be *Punisher,* a Scalpel-class cruiser which had just arrived in UMCPHQ's restricted gap range after nearly six months harrying pirates out beyond Valdor Industrial. Min's command would be a battle-scarred and ill-provisioned vessel with an exhausted crew.

She and *Punisher* were supposed to get as close as they could to Thanatos Minor without violating forbidden space and then just sit there, hoping that they could react appropriately when something happened.

No doubt subsequent communication would make clear what constituted an appropriate reaction. Nevertheless it galled her that *these* orders didn't spell out the answer. Was she being sent to rescue whoever survived Joshua's attack on Billingate? Or was she supposed to make sure there were no survivors?

Was Warden trying to protect her by wasting her in this way, or did he have some better use in mind?

The idea that his only purpose might be to spare her from sharing his doom made her want to howl with fury.

Is that all he thinks I'm good for? Picking up the pieces after he's gone?

Rubbing her sore, red eyes and her throbbing temples, she called him to demand an answer.

Despite her anger, she was taken aback when she reached him immediately. His readiness to face her questions and challenges nonplussed her.

"I got your orders," she said unnecessarily; then she faltered. As soon as she heard his firm, sure voice, her ability to focus her ire at him began to dissolve.

"Good." He sounded brisk and unreachable through the speaker on her desk. "How soon can you and *Punisher* be on your way?"

Her eyes blurred for a moment; she couldn't rub them clear. "They're decelerating now. As soon as they brake enough, they'll head back toward the gap range. I'll be on a shuttle in fifteen minutes—I should be able to catch them in two hours. Once I'm aboard, all we need is enough velocity, and we can go into tach."

All we need is a reason that makes sense—a reason I can believe in.

"Good," he said again.

For a moment he was silent. Then he said gently, "That isn't why you called, Min. You might as well say it now. You may not get another chance for a while."

A new trickle of blood tickled her upper lip. She scrubbed it away with the back of her hand. Her anger had suddenly become grief. She didn't know how to cross the gulf between her and the man she served.

Swallowing harshly, she answered, "The whole time we were planning this operation, you didn't say anything about sending me or any ship out there." *The next kaze may be aimed at you. It's my job to protect you.* "What's changed?"

"Nothing yet," he replied promptly. "But it will."

Almost immediately, however, he amended, "I don't mean that literally. What I mean is that nothing has changed where Thanatos Minor is concerned. Things are changing here, obviously. I didn't expect kazes"—hints of his own anger showed in his voice—"and I definitely didn't expect to lose Godsen."

"Also," he continued without pausing, "there's one other change I ought to tell you about.

"We're expanding our communications web out where you're going. Every gap courier drone and listening post we have or can get is being sent to intercept transmissions from Thanatos Minor. In fact, I'm trying to expand the web enough to cover several cubic light-years in that quadrant—I'm covering as much sheer space as I can, and still be sure messages and data get back here in a matter of hours. You should be able to stay in contact."

This information seemed to leave her numb. She had no idea what it meant. "Warden"—why was she so weak in this situation, when she desperately wanted to be strong?—"we spent months getting this operation ready. If you wanted a bigger communications web, why wait until now to do something about it?"

"Because," he replied succinctly, "I'm not the one who wants it. This is the Dragon's idea. In fact, he was talking to me about it when that kaze hit Godsen.

"Now there's a coincidence for you," he remarked almost casually.

"Anyway, he thinks we're too exposed in this operation—he's worried about containing the damage if something goes wrong. So he wants to maximize our ability to find out what happened in time to do something about it. He ordered me to put everything we have into the web. On top of that, he's giving us access to UMC communications resources."

Still casually, Warden concluded, "I think he's trying to dissociate himself from the things I told the GCES."

Min nodded to herself. Of course. Expanding the web was Fasner's idea. Suppressing the mutagen immunity drug had been his idea. He'd talked to Godsen shortly before Godsen was killed. He was talking to Warden when Godsen was killed.

She was beginning to think that neither she nor the UMCP director existed. They were both figments of the Dragon's fevered and acquisitive imagination.

"Warden, listen to me." It couldn't be put off any longer: it had to be said. "I'm your bodyguard. That's part of my job. What can possibly change on Thanatos Minor that's so important you have to send me to deal with it, instead of letting me stay here to fight those kazes?"

He was silent for a long time; so long that she thought he might have walked away from the intercom, leaving her alone with her speaker's empty circuits. But then past the thin constant whine of neural feedback she heard him sigh.

"You're going to think this is strange." He sounded so distant that she imagined she was overhearing a conversation with someone else; perhaps with himself. "I'm not going to explain it. But I have reason to think"—he stumbled momentarily, as if he already regretted his decision to speak—"Morn Hyland may survive what's happened to her. She may even get away alive.

"If she does, I want someone to make sure she stays alive, someone I can trust. That means you.

"Good luck."

Her speaker clicked clearly as he silenced his intercom.

She'd been concentrating so hard that she hadn't felt her nose bleeding. When she glanced down, she saw damp red spatters on the hardcopy of her orders.

ANCILLARY DOCUMENTATION

G U T T E R G A N G S

Until humankind came into contact with the Amnion, it was easy to believe that guttergangs would eventually rule the Earth.

In one sense, their roots were as old as crime. "The poor you have with you always," said Christ, not inaptly. However, he might have gone on to observe that poverty had no meaning in the absence of wealth: where all have nothing, all are equal—and none poor. From the moment when human evolution first stumbled on the concept of *having*, some individuals or tribes or people *had* more while others *had* less. Predictably the disparity bred tension. In due course that tension led to violence—the *taking away* from those who had by those who had not.

As in all human endeavor, concerted action proved more effective than individual effort: groups could take *more*.

Gangs of one kind or another became inevitable as soon as *having* was invented.

In another sense, however, guttergangs were more recent. They were a product of modern mechanization and urbanization. More specifically, they were a symptom of as well as a reaction against the slow collapse of Earth's social infrastructures.

Because the services of well-meaning but overtaxed communities could no longer feed or care for their young adequately; because educational systems tried harder to control than to excite their students; because transitional life-styles and intense technological changes eroded the ability of families to provide stability for their children;

because humankind's rush to exploit the planet and consume its resources led to a rising tide of poverty which no one could stem; because the fiscal policies of governments were designed primarily to defend the comfort of the few against the hunger of the many; and because, finally, no one could pay for enough police to combat crime: for all these reasons and more, guttergangs flourished throughout Earth's sprawling urban structures with a vigor unprecedented in human history.

The gangs were starving, loveless, abused, despised, cornered: therefore they fought back. And they were able to fight back successfully because they wrested their survival from the same crumbling infrastructure which had created the conditions for their existence— thereby, of course, hastening the decline of that infrastructure; worsening the state of people who lived within rather than against Earth's social compacts; encouraging the growth of more guttergangs.

Much like corporations or governments, they bred chaos around them for the sake of creating order for themselves. Creating nothing, producing nothing, they took away what other people produced or created. More than that, they took away the very constructs and compacts which enabled creation and production to occur. They were parasites on the body of human civilization, just as civilization itself was a parasite on the body of the planet. Some cynics argued that they represented the inevitable outcome of humankind's imprecise moral sense: rapacity and selfishness carried to logical extremes.

Sooner or later, parasites usually lose. They feed on their host until the host dies; and with the death of the host, the parasites themselves starve away. But the guttergangs were too entrenched to be rooted out by anything short of complete cataclysm or absolute tyranny. And the development of the gap drive made their existence more secure rather than less.

Interstellar travel supplied humanity with the opportunity to exploit distant asteroid belts and planetary systems; in other words, with a vast increase of available wealth. Naturally the influx of new resources shored up Earth's tottering infrastructures—which in turn gave the guttergangs more to live on. By prolonging the life of the host, the gap drive gave the parasites more time in which to spread and multiply; increased the rate at which the parasites devoured the host.

It was easy to believe that guttergangs would eventually rule the Earth.

This entire societal equation was altered, however, by contact with the Amnion. The discovery of a fundamental, insidious, and above all external threat to humankind's existence turned the tide of history against the guttergangs.

The effects of this discovery were not simple. Obviously the struggle for the survival of the race would take place hundreds or thousands of light-years away, and would be carried on by the forces of the infrastructure. The fate of humankind would be decided elsewhere: the guttergangs would live or die with their host. By the ordinary laws of parasitism, therefore, neither society nor the guttergangs had any reason to change. Yet the knowledge of an enemy they could not see and would never have to fight changed the guttergangs profoundly.

They did not suddenly discover patriotism, of course. They did not put aside their clenched internecine attack on all social structures outside their own for the sake of humankind's greater good. Nevertheless they were human beings—genophobic to the core. Like patriots and religionists, environmentalists and native Earthers, nations and corporations, politicians and cops, they could not stifle the visceral frisson of their revulsion against imperialism by mutation.

By degrees too small to be measured, too small even to be noticed in the short term, the guttergangs began to erode.

This process took any number of forms. As one crude example: thanks to the Amnion, the appetite of the UMCP for young bodies was as intense as, and inherently more comfortable than, the guttergangs'. Active recruitment by the police gave the hungry youth of Earth a choice distinct from the more passive, as well as more brutal, accretion of the guttergangs.

Or a more subtle instance: hating and fearing the Amnion, the ordinary people of Earth—the natural prey of the guttergangs—had less hatred and fear to spare for those gangs. Therefore in complex, almost indefinable ways the guttergangs began to lose their mystique, their attraction for the lost and disenfranchised of the planet. In comparison to the Amnion, the gangs were perceived as more bearable, more manageable, more normal; therefore less threatening to humankind—and less appealing to humankind's downtrodden. Over time, no human enterprise could oppose—or remain unchanged by—this kind of perceptual shift.

Slowly across the decades, genophobia united humankind against its common foe.

Cynics saw this turning of the tide as a demonstration that prejudice was the only true survival instinct humanity had left. Less cynical observers had difficulty deciding whether to be grateful or terrified.

NICK

By the time *Trumpet*'s airlock cycled shut behind him, and he
crossed the scan field to the complex of passages which accessed the
visitors' berths from Reception, Nick Succorso knew that Milos had
told him the truth.

You're a dead man—

When he'd left *Trumpet*'s bridge, he'd been sure of what he
meant to do. Thermo-pile and that bugger, Taverner, had cut him
off from every recourse, every line of escape: all but one.

Only a fool pays his debts to a dead man.

Like Sorus Chatelaine, he was going to enlist in the service of
the Amnion. He would tell them what Angus and Milos were doing;
warn them that an attempt would be made to rescue Morn Hyland.
He would let them have his ship and his skills and his knowledge of
the cops in exchange for his life.

That option stank. He hated it. Not because it was any different
than the dealings he'd had with the UMCP for years: he saw no
reason to think he wouldn't be able to serve the Amnion with the
same misleading loyalty he'd given the cops. Not because some of
his crew would hate it, or would hate him for doing it: he could
always get a new crew. And not even because it was the same choice
Sorus herself had made: nothing he was forced to do now would
change his revenge on her.

No, he hated enlisting with the Amnion because that would

affect his reputation. It would cost him glamour: it would make him appear as mortal and outmaneuvered as he felt.

He intended to ensure that Thermo-pile and Taverner suffered the tortures of the damned for doing this to him.

That determination lasted until he crossed the scan field and started along the passages toward Reception.

Then some things Angus had said to him hit home; they went off inside him like timed grenades.

"Report" is what Milos does best.

You aren't the only one he talked to while we were coming in. He also sent messages to Tranquil Hegemony.

They answered before you did.

Milos was *playing some kind of bugger game. Me and Succorso and the UMCP and the Amnion, all against each other.*

Nick felt himself breaking up inside. Sweat stood like blood on his forehead; the whites of his eyes glared at the walls; pale as bone, his scars pulled at his face like fresh cuts. *Some kind of bugger game.* Apparently his brain had shut down when Angus hit him. He must have been stunned. *"Report" is what Milos does best.* He hadn't really understood those words at first. *They answered before you did.* After his initial rush of panic, he'd forgotten them. Maybe his skull was cracked: it hurt badly enough for that. And since then he'd been reacting on pure instinct.

But now he began to think again.

Where did Angus get that kind of strength?

What if everything he'd assumed about Angus and Milos had been wrong from the beginning?

Oh, shit.

What if Milos and Angus weren't working for the cops? What if they were just faking it? What if the whole point of this shuck-and-jive was to get Morn back to UMCPHQ and make it look like they rescued her?

What if the Amnion had turned her into some kind of genetic kaze, and now they wanted the cops to have her so she could go off where she would do the most damage?

Of course the Amnion knew the cops wouldn't trust her, wouldn't let down their defenses, unless they were sure she was innocent. What if Angus and Milos were working for the Amnion to make Morn look innocent?

Oh, Christ!

Nick was momentarily frozen with panic, not because he cared about the threat to humankind, but because he'd just lost his last option.

If Angus and Milos were working for the Amnion, Nick didn't have anything to offer that might save him.

Frightened motionless, he stood where he was and tried to believe Angus had lied to him.

You aren't the only one he talked to— He also sent messages to Tranquil Hegemony.

They answered before you did.

It was too tidy, too convenient. Angus must have invented it, trying to pressure Nick into helping him.

Nevertheless it was inherently credible. Milos Taverner was exactly that kind of buggering sonofabitch.

How was it possible for Thermopyle to be so fucking *strong*?

Goaded by chagrin, Nick broke into a run.

He had to get back aboard *Captain's Fancy* before the full weight of the Bill's anger and Angus' treachery and his own miscalculations came down on his neck.

Displays at the ends of the access passages indicated ship id for the berths they served. Half the signs were blank: some of the others showed names he recognized. When he noticed *Soar*, he took charge of himself, slowed his pace to a walk. He would see himself in hell before he risked letting any of Sorus Chatelaine's people witness his panic.

Soar's display flashed at him. Under the ship's name ran the words SECURE FOR UNDOCK.

Good. Despite his fear, his mouth aped a predator's grin. His plan was working. Whatever else happened, he was going to *get* that bitch.

In command of himself now, even though he couldn't control the muscles spasming in his cheek, he continued on his way.

There: around a corner; twenty meters past the only other display in this section of the corridor: *Captain's Fancy*.

His alarm turned instantly to fury when he saw that the access to his ship was guarded.

Two men stood there, both gripping impact rifles. One had a video prosthesis in place of his left eye; the other looked like a gorilla that had been rebuilt so that it could dismantle concrete with its bare hands.

They were both breathing hard, and their faces were flushed, as if they'd just arrived running.

They'd already seen Nick; they watched him as he approached. Their rifles pointed ominously at his chest.

He should have turned and run himself. Those men had come to arrest him. Either the Bill wanted to confront him with the rumors Mikka and Sib had started about Sorus, or he'd been connected to Davies' rescue somehow. He was finished if he didn't get out of here; didn't get out of here fast—

He was finished without his ship.

And he had nowhere to run.

His head hurt as if he had splinters of bone sticking into his brain. Driven by momentum and outrage, he walked straight toward the guards as if they had nothing to do with him; as if he could simply brush between them and go on to his ship.

His thin bluff was wasted on them. They shifted to block the passage completely. The one with the bugeye in his head raised his rifle to his shoulder and tightened his finger on the firing stud.

Nick stopped. He had no choice.

Somehow he was going to kill at least one of these men before he was taken.

"What the fuck are you assholes doing?" he snarled. "That's *my* ship. I'm going aboard."

"No, you ain't." The gorilla smiled to show his bad teeth. "You been barred."

Barred?

"Pending a resolution of your disagreements with the Bill," the other guard explained as if he were quoting, "you are denied access to your ship."

Barred?

"Asshole," the gorilla finished happily.

He might as well have said, The Bill has decided to kill you. He just hasn't decided how yet.

For an instant, Nick believed that he was finished. He had nowhere to go, no defenses left. All his options had failed. The pressure of defeat rose up in him like a cry.

But then he realized that the guards weren't here to arrest him. He still had his freedom of movement.

Without transition a fighting calm came over him. *You're a dead man.* Milos had told him the truth. Here in Billingate, he was nothing without *Captain's Fancy.*

Nothing except himself. Nick Succorso. The man who never lost.

The man whom Sorus Chatelaine had cut and then abandoned aboard the original *Captain's Fancy;* the man who had resurrected himself from that death to become the stuff of legends.

He measured distances; estimated his chances of knocking both rifles aside in time to land a few blows.

The gorilla looked like he could absorb a punch which would pulverize Nick's fist, and go on smiling.

Nick returned a grin of his own. His scars curved blackly under his eyes; the tic was gone from his cheek. As if he hadn't just received a death sentence—as if in the face of Amnion threats and the Bill's muscle, UMCP treachery and Angus' malice, he'd at last recovered his true immortality—he asked almost casually, "I don't suppose the Bill happened to mention what he wants me to do before I can have my ship back?"

The guards shook their heads. "You got to ask him," the gorilla sneered.

"I will," Nick said for the sake of his self-image, "as soon as I can spare the time."

Turning his back sharply, he strode away.

Thermo-pile and Taverner and the Bill and Hashi fucking Lebwohl were out of their minds if they thought they could do this to him.

Grinning hard enough to stretch his scars, he rounded the corner, passed out of sight of the guards—and nearly collided with Mikka Vasaczk.

She put a hand on his chest to ward him off. He didn't need to look into her eyes to see how angry she was; how desperate. The force of her thrust and the set of her hips told him that she'd come close to hitting him.

Sib Mackern and Vector Shaheed stood behind her like bodyguards. They had Pup with them. But as soon as Nick registered their presence he ignored them. He didn't have time to consider the implications of the fact that they were together. The orders he'd given them should have kept them apart: therefore they hadn't obeyed him. That was dangerous, but secondary. They would pay for it later. Mikka and the guards outside *Captain's Fancy* were his immediate concern.

"Just the people I was looking for," he announced softly. His sardonic assurance was so complete that he almost believed it himself. "Come on. We've got work to do."

He moved past her as if she had no choice except to follow him.

"Nick." She caught his arm, pulled him to a halt. "Listen to me." Her grip was as hard as she could make it. For some reason it reminded him of the strength of her legs when he'd had sex with her. "This is the last chance you're going to get."

Deliberately he glanced at the nearest bugeyes. "Save it. The Bill won't hesitate to use anything you say against you."

Against me.

Apparently Mikka didn't care. "*Listen* to me." The lines of her face were clenched and bitter. She looked like a woman who'd decided to step in front of matter cannon fire. "We're not taking any more orders. We don't work for you. We're not your crew any longer. You've made it too obvious we're expendable. And we don't much like what you're expending us for.

"Now we're going to stop you."

She didn't let go of his arm.

Nick couldn't help himself: he gaped at her. "Say what?"

Sib Mackern edged closer to her shoulder, as if he wanted her to protect him—or as if he'd decided to die with her.

Nick's incredulity didn't touch her. "The bugeyes are part of it," she grated. "A little trick we learned from you. The strategic use of recordings. No matter how fast you are, you can't kill all four of us before one of us manages to tell the Bill at least some of the things you don't want him to know."

"That's right," Vector put in. He sounded calm and a little sad. "In fact, I don't think you'll be able to kill any of us before Operations sends those guards"—he nodded in the direction of *Captain's Fancy*—"to find out what all the noise is about."

The engineer was right. Unless Operations or the Bill had too many other things to concentrate on, the guards were probably already headed this way.

"But if you don't kill us," Mikka continued as Nick stared at her, "you won't be able to prevent us from talking to anybody we want. Captain Chatelaine for one." Like his scars, her eyes were full of blood. "Captain Thermopyle for another."

Despite the danger of the guards, Nick stood still, let his heart beat two or three times while he met her fierce glare. She'd always been the best of his crew—the most capable and intelligent; the most loyal. If only she'd been better looking, she might have held his interest longer. He still didn't understand how he'd lost her.

Abruptly, as if he could do such things without effort, he twisted his arm free. In the same motion he shifted a few steps to the side. Involuntarily Mikka, Vector, and Sib turned to face him; they moved as if he were steering them, positioning them between him and the corner.

Lazily he swung up his hand and pointed his index finger into Mikka's face. "I'm not going to try to kill you," he said distinctly. "I told you—I need you. We've got work to do.

"You don't really want to talk to the Bill. He hasn't got anything to offer you except a grubby life in this stinkhole. Personally I don't think he's going to be able to offer even that much longer."

Are you listening, you bastard? Are you *sure* you want to bar me from my ship?

"And you don't want to talk"—Nick sneered the name—"to Captain Chatelaine. She works for the Amnion. Directly for the Amnion. Before she changed the name, her ship used to be called *Gutbuster*. She did covert operations for forbidden space back in the days when Billingate didn't exist."

Another small step to the side. Now Pup was in range. He would make a good hostage. A quick grab; quick pressure on the carotid arteries in his neck. Then Mikka would do anything Nick wanted. For a minute or two, anyway.

Her brother pressed against the wall as if he were cowering. His eyes flinched back and forth between Nick and Mikka.

"As for Captain Thermo-pile—"

Sib took Nick by surprise. Nick had decided long ago that Mackern was no threat: the same fear which enabled him to go beyond the limits of his training and talents at the data station would also paralyze him. So Nick focused his attention exclusively on Mikka. He couldn't react in time as Sib whipped forward, caught Pup's wrist, and jerked the kid out of reach.

Mikka swung Pup behind her and faced Nick as if she meant to hurl herself at his throat.

Nick adjusted his balance slightly, let her see that he was ready. Like an avatar of the man he used to be, he remarked, "I think I've finally figured this out. You're the ones who let Morn out of her cabin so she could rig that ejection pod. You've all been working against me at least that long.

"But you know something? I don't care. I really don't give a shit. You still haven't got a *clue* what's going on here. You're floundering around in the dark, instead of using your brains to keep yourselves and maybe *Captain's Fancy* and all the rest of us alive."

"Why don't you tell us, Nick?" Vector countered steadily. "Why don't you give us one of your so-called *clues*"—he compressed more venom into that one word than Nick had ever heard from him—"instead of keeping them all to yourself?"

"Because," Nick drawled back, "I don't want the Bill to hear me.

"But you mentioned Captain Thermo-pile. As it happens, I'm on my way to see him right now. Why don't you come along? Once we're aboard his ship, you'll get more *clues* than you know what to do with."

"Mikka, no," Pup panted urgently. "It's a trick. You said yourself this stinks. Why are Thermopyle and Taverner together? What's going on? He's trying—"

"Answer the kid," ordered the gorilla as he stepped past the corner, waving his impact rifle, "asshole. Tell everybody what's going on."

Gasping, Sib jumped to the illusory protection of the wall. As if he were sliding, Vector eased out of the way.

As solid as a boulder, the guard planted himself beside Mikka and Pup, and aimed his gun at Nick's belly.

Nick was ready for that, too. Even the pain in his head had receded: he felt ready for everything. All he cared about was that the guard was alone. The gorilla had left his companion behind to keep watch on *Captain's Fancy.*

"Mikka," he said in a conversational tone, "I'm only going to give you one more order. This is the last—then we're quits.

"Take this shithead's gun and stick it up his ass."

At once Mikka moved.

Not to obey: she pulled back to show her empty hands, avoid the line of fire, cover Pup.

Nevertheless it was enough. Ponderous and brutal, the gorilla wheeled to track her with the muzzle of his rifle.

By then Nick was already in motion.

He took two lightning strides and leaped.

Swinging up his left knee to lift him higher, he snap-kicked the toe of his right boot into the guard's larynx.

Convulsively the guard flung his gun away as if the metal had shocked him. Gagging on crushed cartilage and torn muscle, he slammed to the floor.

With negligent ease, Nick caught the rifle out of the air. His hands settled on the barrel and the firing stud.

"Goddamn it, woman," he growled at Mikka, "I *told* you what I wanted."

Instinctively she braced herself. Pup seemed to thrash at her shoulder, trying to get in front of her. Vector held Sib so that he couldn't move.

Nick would have loved to shoot her. She deserved it: they all did. But he needed her.

"I figure," he breathed maliciously, "you've got about ten seconds to reach a decision. After that the Bill won't let you make any choices ever again."

Despite the fact that his head suddenly hurt as if someone had hit him with an ax, he turned and ran for *Trumpet* as smoothly as a hunting cat.

With his peripheral vision, he saw *Soar*'s id display flash red: SHIP UNDOCKING.

Crimson and pain seemed to fill his ears. He couldn't hear anything except the hammer of his boots and the labor of his lungs. Until he reached *Trumpet*'s access passage and turned, he didn't know that Mikka and Pup, Vector and Sib, were all following him, running hard.

"Nick," Mikka panted before he started down the passage, "there are more guards coming. A lot of them." She stopped so abruptly that Pup blundered into her. Sib's boots skidded out from under him; he nearly fell. Vector was ten or fifteen meters back: his arthritis made him slow. "They would be here already, but they're lugging some kind of heavy equipment. Looks like mining lasers."

Nick reeled for a second; caught his balance. "They're not going to *Captain's Fancy*? They're coming here?"

"*I* don't know." Mikka shrugged stiffly. "They're headed in this direction."

Which meant the Bill knew where Angus and Milos were. He knew where Davies was.

Racing ruin, Nick dashed along the access passage and across the scan field to *Trumpet*'s airlock.

With the heel of his hand, he toggled the external intercom.

"This is Nick." In spite of his urgency, he managed to sound almost relaxed. "Let me in. I've changed my mind. And I've brought some help."

No one answered. The speaker emitted an impalpable whisper of static. The lock didn't open.

Bootheels thudding, Mikka came to his side. Sib and Pup joined her; Vector doggedly brought up the rear.

"If I were you," Nick drawled into the intercom, "I would listen to me. You could use help.

"Oh, by the way, I think I should mention that there's a platoon of guards heading this way. They've got mining lasers. The Bill is going to peel you open like a vein of cesium."

You flagrant sonofabitch, you'd better know what you're doing!

With a whine of servos, the lock began to cycle.

Mikka shoved Pup headlong through the opening; nearly dived after him. Nick nodded Vector and Sib ahead of him as if he meant to cover them with his rifle; as if he cared what happened to them. Pirates with swashbuckling reputations did things like that. As Mikka keyed the lock to close the outer door and open the inner, he stepped briskly inside.

Before the lock sealed, he caught a glimpse of guards at the end of the access passage.

They were definitely coming this way.

"Now what?" Mikka demanded, breathing hard.

Nick didn't bother to answer. As soon as the inner door opened your gonads. But now we've got help." He nodded at Mikka and her companions. "Seven of us might actually be able to do it.

"I'm willing to give it a try. Unless you want to pretend you can pull it off on your own."

"Pull *what* off?" Mikka demanded harshly. "What operation? What the fuck are you bastards talking about?"

Angus gave a brutal grin. His eyes didn't shift from Nick's. "These your people?"

Nick nodded.

Angus snorted through his teeth. "I don't think they like you very much anymore."

"I said, *what* operation?" Mikka yelled. Her anger and desperation seemed to burn in the air of the bridge.

Nick didn't look at her. He met Angus' grin with a smile of his own.

"You'll like it," he answered as if he were happy at last. "We're going to rescue Morn."

Mikka's stunned silence at his back was as loud as a shout. Sib Mackern took a shuddering breath like a man on the verge of tears. Softly Vector whispered, "Oh, my aching joints."

Nick stood still, waiting for Angus to reject his help; daring Angus to say no.

But Angus didn't. Over his shoulder, he said to Davies, "He's right. We need the help."

Nick went on smiling like his scars.

on *Trumpet's* lift, he entered the car. What was left of his crew, the surviving remnant of his ship, crowded after him. He sent the lift upward.

Mikka and her group weren't literally all that was left of his crew. But the rest had become even more expendable than she was: *Captain's Fancy* herself was expendable. The Bill had made that necessary.

Nick imagined that he would exact more recompense than anything the Bill could afford to pay.

The lift let him out into *Trumpet's* core passage amidships. Moving with long, confident strides, he led his people to the bridge companionway and ran smoothly down the treads.

Angus and Davies stood between the command stations, facing him. Except for their shipsuits and the swelling bruises on Davies' face, they looked like a video trick—time-elapse replicas of each other.

Mikka clattered down the companionway, with Pup, Sib, and Vector behind her. Because they didn't know what they were getting into—or perhaps because they'd always known Angus Thermopyle as a dangerous enemy—they arrayed themselves at Nick's back as if they were on his side.

Nick met Angus' glare, Davies'. Angus' was yellow with old, irreducible malice. But Morn's limpid eyes in Davies' face made the boy look more intimately murderous. His father hated everybody: Davies hated only Nick.

With all the insouciance he could produce, Nick asked, "Where the hell is Milos?"

"Captain Sheepfucker." Angus didn't move a muscle. "If you think you can walk in here and take over with only one gun and four people to back you up, you've been eating your own shit too long."

Nick glanced down at the impact rifle; he nearly giggled. With a shrug, he tossed the gun to Angus.

Angus caught it; held it as if he didn't need it.

"You were right," Davies muttered to Angus as if that were the worst insult he could level at Nick.

Nick ignored the boy.

"You've got it wrong," he said steadily. "I told you I changed my mind. I didn't want any part of this operation because I didn't think it had a chance. I didn't feel like getting killed for the sake of

ANGUS

A ngus watched Nick smile and tried to find some way to squeeze murder through the interstices of his programming.

It was insufferable that Captain Nick bloody Sheepfucker stood there smiling as if he'd just won again, beaten Angus again. It was intolerable that Nick brought his own people aboard Angus' ship; that Angus had to accept them because he needed them. It was utter and absolute craziness to let them in here, to trust them—

Nevertheless his datacore issued its instructions, and he obeyed, ruled by the pitiless compulsion of his zone implants.

Nick's UMCP connection made him effectively immune to any real harm from Angus. And his offer of help satisfied the prewritten logic of Dios' exigencies. Rescuing Morn took precedence over everything—Angus had no idea why.

It's got to stop.

He didn't understand that either.

He was so full of hate that his blood seemed to steam and boil in his veins; so eager to break Nick's neck that his hands burned and his temples throbbed. Hate was all that sustained him in the cage which his mind had become—hate and a strange, ineffable terror at the thought of Morn Hyland. He paced inside himself like an imprisoned predator, driven and helpless; haunted by killing.

Unfortunately his passions meant nothing.

"So who the hell are they?" he demanded of Nick. "What're they good for?"

The intercom interrupted him. From outside *Trumpet*'s airlock, a voice blared, "Captain Thermopyle, open up. We're coming aboard. You get to choose how we do it—that's as much courtesy as the Bill has left—but we're going to do it. If you don't let us in, we'll cut our way. We'll do a little BR surgery on your ship, free gratis no charge. You can get it repaired when you have enough money—if you're still alive.

"You hear me? I said *open up*! You've got one minute. Then we start cutting."

Davies flinched involuntarily. He'd been through too much in too short a time. Eyes like Morn's pulled away from Nick, came to Angus' face as if they were wincing: eyes exactly like Morn's, full of fear and need and revulsion. Swelling and contusions distorted his features.

Angus stepped to his command board, tapped a key which silenced the external intercom. Then he turned back to Succorso.

A woman, two men, and a kid about Davies' age stood behind Nick: his people. At a glance, the woman looked too hostile to admit she was out of her depth, and one of the men had the round, calm appearance of a cat addict. But the other two were scared out of their skins. The kid twitched nervously from one foot to the other; he was practically holding the woman's hand. The man with the abject mustache sweated and gaped as if he was being rendered down for grease.

"Come on, Nick." Angus' programming left him no more space for insults. "I'm waiting. They look like you picked them at random on the cruise. What makes you think they can help me?"

Nick's gaze sharpened. Behind his grin, the lines of his face tautened across their bones. Color ebbed from his scars.

"Angus," he said softly, "don't you think you should do something about those guards? They aren't bluffing. We saw mining lasers."

"Nick," Angus returned, you shit-faced fucker, "we haven't got time for this. We can't get started until I know who your people are and what they can do."

For an instant Nick seemed to lose control. "Then do something about those guards!"

Angus rolled his eyes, shrugged. With a flick of his wrist, he tossed the rifle to Davies. Then he leaned over his board and typed in a quick command.

A moment later a recording of his voice played over the bridge speakers.

"This is Captain Angus Thermopyle. I'm not aboard right now. To protect the security of my ship and my associates, I've rigged *Trumpet* for self-destruct as soon as her sensors detect any forced entry. The simultaneous explosion of her thrust and gap drives and other power systems will produce destructive force on the order of"— the recording recited a number which sounded too high, but which Angus knew to be conservative. "I estimate that will reduce approximately one third of Billingate installation to powder. If you want confirmation, analyze my incoming particle trace." This is no ordinary Needle-class gap scout, you sonofabitch. "Codes to enter and leave *Trumpet* safely are known to my associates. Codes to disable *Trumpet*'s self-destruct are known only to me. Until I return to my ship, I can do nothing to save you if you try to break in. My associates—if they're unlucky enough to be aboard—can do nothing to save you in my absence.

"Message repeats.

"This is—"

Angus silenced the playback. "That's on automatic. I set it when you came aboard. Those guards have been hearing it ever since they arrived." To Nick he growled, "Thanks to you and Milos, the Bill thinks I'm here. But he can't be sure. And he probably thinks I'm bluffing—but he can't be sure of that, either. Which buys us a little time. Maybe it'll be enough."

Everyone around him could see that *Trumpet*'s systems were up and active. Operations had the same information.

Nick couldn't hold Angus' gaze. To conceal his relief, he glanced at his people, scanned the bridge. Without bringing his eyes back to Angus, he asked, "So where is Milos?"

He may have been trying to regain the upper hand.

Angus' programming didn't require him to answer that question. Its logic moved in another direction—toward possibilities of coercion which made Angus' veins throb with hunger.

"Nick, you've got a bruise the size of my fist on your forehead. When it's done swelling, it's going to turn purple." The mildness imposed by his zone implants amazed and appalled him. "You'll look like you lost an argument with a steel piston. Stop asking questions. Start answering them."

Abruptly the woman muttered a curse and pushed past Nick. Despite his reputation as a man for whom women were willing to drop dead, she shouldered him aside contemptuously so that she could confront Angus and Davies herself.

Fury flickered like a static discharge in Nick's eyes, but he didn't try to stop her.

"Captain Thermopyle," she announced in a voice made for shouting, "I'm Mikka Vasaczk, command second, *Captain's Fancy*—or I was until recently. He"—she indicated the frightened man with the mustache and the staring eyes—"is Sib Mackern, data first." Next she nodded at the cat addict. "Vector Shaheed, engineer." That left the kid. "Ciro Vasaczk is Vector's second. Also my brother. Nick wants to get rid of us. He was planning to abandon us here.

"I'll tell you why. We don't like what he did to Morn." She shifted her scowl to Davies. "We all tried to help you. Sib let her out of her cabin. Between the two of us, Vector and I let her at the ejection pod controls. That's why the pod brought you here, instead of to *Tranquil Hegemony*—why you're still human.

"But we weren't able to help her." She swallowed once, roughly. "Or we didn't try hard enough. Maybe we all thought we were alone. Or maybe we just couldn't believe he would really go that far."

"*I* knew it," Davies rasped back. "I knew it from the moment I was born—and that was before I remembered anything about him."

"Yes." Mikka nodded slowly. "But you're a cop. You think differently than we do."

Her glower swung back to Angus. "The four of us are interested in rescuing Morn. If the Amnion haven't already finished her. But Nick isn't. You've got to understand that. He hates her—he *wants* them to have her. If he told you anything else, he was lying.

"He's only here because the Bill barred him from *Captain's Fancy*. He doesn't have anywhere else to go."

Neither of the men behind her moved. Only the kid nodded.

Angus believed her. Her face looked as honest as a fist. If she'd helped keep his son away from the Amnion, he could count on her to help him reach Morn as well.

Somehow the virile and invulnerable Captain Succorso had succeeded at driving his own people to mutiny.

"Too bad, Mikka," Nick snarled. "Nice try." His air of casual superiority had deserted him: he looked frayed and vicious. "But Angus already knows my reasons don't matter. If this is the only choice I have left, so much the better for him. He wants my help. Now he's got it.

"The truth is," he finished, "*you* haven't got anywhere else to go either."

The engineer, Vector Shaheed, spoke for the first time. "You're wrong, Nick." His tone was like his face and his eyes, too calm to be normal. Nevertheless Angus didn't hear cat in it: he heard old pain; pain which had been suppressed so long that it dulled everything around it. "We've already told you—we could have gone to the Bill. We could have gone to Captain Chatelaine. Either of them would have been"—he smiled wanly—"fascinated to hear about your adventures on Enablement."

Angus would have been fascinated himself. Old instincts shrilled at him, warning him that what Nick had done on Enablement was important. Unfortunately his programming had no instincts. The countdown running in his mechanical mind ticked inexorably shorter.

"Discuss it later," he demanded. "Right now I need answers.

"Have any of you done high-tension work?"

Vector, Mikka, and the kid all nodded.

"Angus," Nick put in, "I'm going to help you, but only on one condition." Without transition his manner changed again. He was like a kaleidoscope, different at every turn. Now he sounded companionable and relaxed, as if he were among friends. "I need to talk to *Captain's Fancy.* I can do it while you get organized. My command third doesn't know what to do. She probably doesn't know I've been barred. As long as she thinks she has to wait for me, she's paralyzed."

Angus wanted to snap, Shut up, asshole. If you ever talk to your ship again, it'll be over my dead body. His datacore had other priorities, however. Apparently its unintuitive logic had assigned Nick the status of a UMCP officer in need of assistance.

Helpless to do anything else, Angus pointed at Milos' station. "You can access communications there. Just don't screw up—don't let Operations hear you."

Grinning ferally, Nick slid into the command second's g-seat and put his hands on the board.

The abyss lurking at the back of Angus' mind taunted him. He wondered if his programming had just forced him to make a terrible mistake.

But he couldn't think about that. As if it were recircuiting neurons, his zone implants tuned one ear to listen to Nick. The rest of him focused on Nick's people.

"Have you got EVA training? You know how to use guns?"

Davies shook his head, then nodded in confusion as he remembered Morn's experience in the Academy.

"We aren't exactly trained for it," Vector answered, "but we've all done EVA. Pu—Ciro and I've never had to use guns."

"All right." Pieces clicked into place in Angus' plans. "You're my high-tension crew. Davies, you're with them. It's your job to keep them safe. When you're done, you can cover our retreat."

"I don't understand," Davies put in. "You haven't told me what you're planning."

Angus ignored him. "The rest of us—Nick, Mikka, Sib, and me—are going to get Morn out." Brutal as impact fire, he added, "Or kill her if the Amnion have already mutated her."

At the same time he listened hard to what Nick was doing. But Nick addressed his ship entirely in written code: he didn't say a word. His fingers raced on the board, typing like volleys in a barrage. Under his concentrated gaze, his scars hinted at darkness.

"We're going EVA," Angus explained, "so we don't have to deal with the Bill's muscle. We'll cross the docks and the rock to the Amnion installation—roughly three k. We'll cut our way in. That's the easy part. The hard part will be finding her."

And surviving. Angus had already realized that he was effectively powerless against the Amnion. If his datacore hadn't ordered otherwise, for its own reasons, he would have been tempted to protect Vector and Ciro himself, and send Davies after Morn.

"Once we find her, we either deal with her or grab her. We'll take an EVA suit for her—that's your job," he told Sib. It wouldn't hurt to encumber Mackern with an extra suit. He didn't look like he was good with a gun in any case. "As soon as she's in it, we'll come back the way we went."

And if we can do all that, if you're still alive, and I come back in one piece, and the Bill hasn't burned *Trumpet* open, we'll try to figure out how to get away from here.

"You make it sound a little too simple," Mikka remarked through her teeth.

Davies nodded urgently. Sib's eyes showed white.

Angus grimaced at her. "There are only three dangers—aside from the chance the Amnion will shoot us before we can shoot them." Or the chance that Angus himself would be paralyzed; perhaps turned against these people. "The Bill might decide to send his guards EVA. Or some ship might pick us up on scan and warn Operations. *Calm Horizons* could do it."

"*Soar* could do it," Nick put in while he worked. "She left dock just a few minutes ago."

"Or," Angus continued, "the Amnion might call out the Bill's dogs after we attack. In fact, they'll do that for sure.

"Vector and Ciro are going to solve all those problems for us."

Mikka, Davies, and the others waited. Angus didn't elaborate, however. He didn't want Nick to know what he had in mind; didn't want Nick to tell his ship. Everything Succorso touched had too many possibilities for treachery.

"*Finish* it, Nick," he demanded. "We've got to *go.*"

"Done." Nick keyed off the board and stood up. "I'm ready. I like simple plans—they leave room for inspiration." As if he'd recovered his superiority, he faced Angus with his fists on his hips and a grin on his teeth. "There's just one more thing you have to explain.

"Where the fucking hell is Milos?"

Nausea twisted in Angus' guts, but he shrugged as if he didn't care. "I'm not sure. I think he's gone to the Amnion."

Nick's people were stunned: Nick himself looked poleaxed. "He *what?*"

Since leaving UMCPHQ, Angus had gained only one thing he actually wanted: he'd gotten rid of Milos Taverner. The cost of that victory was probably going to be more than he could bear. Warden Dios, may he rot in hell, hadn't planned this operation well enough.

Scowling acidly, Angus pointed at the companionway. "You heard me. Let's get going."

"But that means he's told them we're coming!" Nick protested raggedly.

No, it means he's told them my priority codes. He's told them how to turn me off.

"Sure," Angus agreed. "But he hasn't told them how. He doesn't know."

And the Amnion don't know I've got help. They won't try to stop us because they're planning to shut me down. That way they think they can catch me *and* Davies.

Angus could protect his son. Unfortunately his datacore didn't let him do what was necessary to defend himself.

"Wait a minute," Nick insisted, "wait a minute," as if he were on the verge of panic. "You told me he talked to them—even before he talked to me. How long has he been working for them?"

"How the fuck should I know?" Angus could feel the mouth of the abyss closing around his heart. "But he must have started before you bastards framed me." Before you got me into this. "He's been too busy since then to start anything that complicated."

"But *that* means—" Nick's mouth hung open in shock.

"It means," Mikka grated, "the Amnion knew the truth about you when we went to Enablement. Your bugger must have told them. They already knew you were cheating them. That's why they tried to kill us in the gap—why they used us for an acceleration experiment. And *that's* why they tried so hard to get Davies before we left. They assumed he was going to die when we did."

Cold with concentration, as intent as his father, Davies watched her as if he were testing what she said against what he could remember. "But that doesn't explain why I'm so important. What do they want me *for?*"

Angus wanted to howl in frustration. Maybe his zone implants would have let him. Before he could make the attempt, however, an automatic relay tripped on his command board, opening a channel to Billingate Operations.

At once the Bill's voice burst from the bridge speakers.

"Captain Angus, you motherfucking sonofabitch, you're finished!" He sounded frantic, almost hysterical. "I'll get you for this—I'm going to *fry* you as soon as you try to leave.

"In the meantime, I'm cutting you off. No more power, no more air, no more operational data. Live with *that* if you can, you shitbag! You can supply your own life support, but you *need* operational data."

Then the transmission ended as if he'd silenced his pickup with a hammer.

Full of artificial calm and native horror, Angus announced, "I'm only going to say this one more time. If we don't go now, we'll lose our chance."

Leaving Nick's dismay and Davies' concentration and Sib's chagrin behind, he headed up the companionway.

Light and quick in Thanatos Minor's g, Mikka followed on his heels.

By the time he reached the passage running through *Trumpet's* core, boots rattled on the rungs as more people came after him.

His son must have been immediately behind Mikka. As Angus strode toward the weapons locker, he heard her answer Davies' question.

"The Amnion want to solve the problem of mutating human beings without destroying their minds." She was trying to help the boy again. "They want to make Amnion who look and talk and remember exactly like human beings. When Morn survived giving you her mind, they started to think zone implants are the answer. You're their chance to study the consequences of what she did. So they can refine their mutagens."

"Which is why," Angus said over his shoulder for no reason he could name, "I want you to protect Vector and Ciro, instead of coming with me. I don't want to risk letting those fuckers get their hands on you."

He had no idea if that was the truth.

On the other hand, he knew exactly how Morn would react if he rescued her—and lost her son in the process.

He'd never looked in *Trumpet's* weapons locker: he hadn't had time. But a database gave him the codes. He tapped them into the keypad of the lock and swung open the door.

"Jesus!" Mikka breathed. "That's not a weapons locker, that's an arsenal."

Angus saw armaments of all kinds: handguns, rifles, lasers, blasters; a variety of knives; mortars, grenades, and other explosives; enough destructive capability to equip an expeditionary force. An inventory scrolled through his head, but he ignored it. The countdown ran remorselessly. He picked out a couple of limpet mines, a small, precise laser, and a miniaturized matter cannon. In this case "miniaturized" meant the gun was longer than his leg and twice as heavy; if he was lucky, it carried enough charge to fire three times. Hefting it, he stepped aside to let other people at the locker.

Mikka took an impact rifle and a laser. Following her example, Davies added a laser to the rifle he already carried. Sib chose two handguns, but wasn't comfortable with them; he put one back. Vector grabbed a couple of stubby projectile launchers—weapons which were useless at any distance, but which could hardly miss at close range. He gave one to Ciro and pulled the kid past the locker.

Nick didn't linger over his selection. He helped himself to two handguns, an impact rifle, a clip of grenades—

Angus slapped the locker shut, nearly catching Nick's fingers, and headed aft to the compartment where the EVA suits were stowed.

Except for the ones which fit him and Milos, they were of standard sizes—more of them than *Trumpet's* official passenger capacity would ever need. One glance told Angus he'd never seen suits like them before. They were normal in most respects: flexible Mylar and plexulose constructs with polarizing faceplates, air tanks, power-packs, helmet radios, belt clips for tools or guns. But he couldn't see how the maneuvering jets worked.

Impersonally efficient, a database supplied the answer.

"Take a suit," he told Mikka and the others. "Set communications for"—he named a frequency at random. "That way we can talk without being heard—unless somebody stumbles on our setting.

"This won't be zero g, but you should know how to use the jets. They're more responsive than you're used to—more maneuverable. They work like waldos. Inside the suit there's a harness. It clips around your waist and through your crotch. Toggles are on the chest plate. When it's active, it reads how you move your hips and fires the jets, left, right, up, down, whatever you want.

"They take practice, so you'd better hope you don't need them."

Angus didn't doubt that his computer already knew how to control the jets perfectly.

Cramped in the narrow passage, Mikka and the men began stumbling into suits. Davies kept himself as far from Nick as possible. Ciro and Sib both needed help with the unfamiliar equipment: Vector and Mikka assisted them. Nick talked aimlessly about *Trumpet's* resources; but no one paid any attention to him. Angus' programming supplied a checklist. He put down his weapons to run through it.

From the pocket of his shipsuit he took out a small transmitter like a zone implant control, transferred it to one of the pouches of his EVA suit. Then he pulled on his suit and sealed it; clamped the limpets and laser to his belt. The cannon was too heavy for that, so he cradled it in his arms. At once he moved toward the lift.

He was trying, *trying*, not to listen to the claustrophobic hiss of air in his ears. It told him that he'd just sealed himself into a crypt, a crib; tied down so that the woman looming over him—a woman as vast as space, who should have been his mother—could fill him with pain like the void between the stars.

EVA always terrified him.

The countdown continued. His bluff wouldn't hold much longer. As soon as the Bill panicked he would order his guards to start cutting. Then *Trumpet* would defend herself—but not with self-destruct. Instead she would trigger a power shutdown across as much of the installation as she could reach. Angus had arranged that during Nick's absence.

At the same time he'd done some extensive mapping of Billingate's power supply, using equipment which no known Needle-class gap scout possessed. What he'd learned was of no use to him at the moment, however. For now only the shutdown mattered.

It would keep *Trumpet* intact for two or three more minutes, no more. And it would be fatally premature if it happened before Vector and Ciro had carried out his plans.

He was already sweating like a whole herd of swine, and he hadn't even left the ship yet.

Mikka joined him in the lift almost immediately, with Nick close behind her. "Are you sure all this stuff works?" Succorso's voice sounded too loud in the confines of Angus' helmet. Through two faceplates Nick looked like a ghoul: his scars resembled open wounds. "It's so damn new, I don't think it's ever been tested."

"It works, Nick," Mikka muttered. "Give us a break."

Nick regarded her steadily, as if he'd already decided how to kill her.

Davies was ready, but he waited for the other men; entered the lift last.

Fighting his impulse to gasp, Angus sent the lift upward to *Trumpet*'s other airlock.

Now Davies was the first one out. He positioned himself inside the lock beside the control panel, with his back to the wall and his rifle ready. He kept its muzzle pointed at Nick's belly.

Angus expected treachery from Succorso as much as his son did. But not here; not like this. It might happen once they reached the Amnion installation—or maybe when the group returned to *Trumpet*. Where Nick was concerned, Angus' greatest fear wasn't that Nick would betray him, but that his prewritten restrictions would prevent him from making Nick pay for it.

With seven people packed together in the airlock, Angus gave Davies a nod. Davies turned to the control panel, tapped keys.

The inner door slid shut.

Compressors whined, pumping air out of the lock to avoid a burst of release into the vacuum. Angus' EVA suit tightened around him, inflated by its internal atmosphere; his companions seemed to puff up as if they would float away as soon as the airlock let them go.

He turned down the gain on his pickup so that Nick and the others wouldn't hear him panting. EVA terrified him, small places and vast ones terrified him, but his zone implants didn't give him any choice. Biting his lower lip hard, he faced the ladder to the outer door and waited for the airlock to open.

When *Trumpet*'s servos pulled the door aside, he climbed up to it, stuck his head out, and got a glimpse of what Nick's treachery entailed.

The whole region of the visitors' docks was awash in stark white light. This was normal: as fierce as fire, arc lamps on tall poles blazed in all directions, giving incoming ships visual confirmation of their approach attitudes and trajectories.

Etched in illumination so intense that it seemed nearly phosphorescent, the landscape was at once ordinary and strange. For kilometers across the surface of the planetoid, Thanatos Minor's native rock had been replaced by concrete—the reinforced outer face and abutments of Billingate.

Unlike the cargo docks and shipyard, this section was unmarked by gantries or cranes, loading- or service- or power-bays, airlocks for freight haulers or stevedores. Instead the only features were the berths themselves, cones inset in the concrete and surrounded like maws with banks of grapples and cables; a couple of huge radio dishes positioned to cover this quadrant of Billingate's control space; scan antennae and receptors, as tall and brittle as burned trees; occasional access hatches for the emergency airlocks; and a number of gun emplacements, offering matter cannon fire to the void.

By themselves the emplacements looked massive and murderous, immeasurably destructive. However, seen next to the fathomless dark which covered Thanatos Minor instead of sky, they appeared no more distinct or effective than the old stone they'd replaced.

The light—or the contrast between the unnatural, human light and the natural, inhuman void—gave the landscape its strangeness. Against this black and absolute background, any arc lamp, no matter how intense, was nothing more than a small flare. Human senses insisted that so many millions of tons of concrete, so much fusion-generated power, so much evidence of conscious intention, should have been large enough to mean something. The surrounding emptiness disagreed.

Angus wore EVA suits for the same reason that he wore ships and stations: to protect his body and his life from the vacuum, of course; but more to protect his sanity from the abyss. Space itself appalled him.

It may have been the only thing he truly understood.

Because of the light, he could see *Captain's Fancy* clearly, even though she was a hundred meters away.

He caught sight of her just in time to see her rip herself out of her berth. Riding a spray of lost air and torn grapples, a corona of sparking power lines, she drifted away from the docks as if she were lost.

LIETE

elted in her g-seat at the command station, Liete Corregio rode jolting thrust and complex winds as *Captain's Fancy* blasted loose of her berth and sailed free.

At once new forces pulled at her: acceleration; maneuvering thrust; internal spin. They tugged her body from side to side, hauled against each other inside her like nausea. She didn't need internal spin: the ship's movements would be easier to stomach without it. But she engaged it because the magnetic field generated by centrifugal g would be legible to Billingate Operations; to *Tranquil Hegemony* and *Calm Horizons*; to *Soar*. It would make *Captain's Fancy* look less threatening. A ship that intended to do battle wouldn't hamper herself with internal spin.

Liete was concentrating too hard on other things to name the wind in her ears. It felt like the mistral of urgency, but it might have been the long black pressure which called her to doom.

The emptiness of the engineering and data stations nagged at her. The bridge was incomplete; *Captain's Fancy* was incomplete. Liete had to make up the lack caused by Nick's absence and his secrets out of herself.

"Operations is screaming," Lind reported from communications. His own urgency made his voice crack and his larynx bob. "They aren't threatening us yet. They're too incoherent."

"Ignore them," Liete ordered. "Cut them off if you have to— you've got too much else to do.

"Have you sent Nick's message to that listening post?"

"Don't bullshit us," Pastille put in, nearly cackling with tension. "You mean, has he sent Nick's message to the UMCP? That won't do any good. We'll be dead before it reaches them."

Liete ignored the helm third; waited for Lind's answer.

Lind checked a readout. "It's done. Tight-beamed to the same coordinates he used last time."

"Then concentrate on the ships," she told him. "*Trumpet, Soar, Calm Horizons, Tranquil Hegemony.* We're going to hear from at least one of them."

The air around her felt leaden, humid with stress. The scrubbers seemed unable to keep up with it.

"What am I listening for?" Lind asked.

"Nick's priority codes—the old ones." Liete accessed them on her board, relayed them to him. "Tell me the second you hear them. I want to know immediately, exactly, what the orders are."

"But Nick won't—"

"No, he won't," she snapped. "He's already told us what to do. He won't change his mind. And if he does, he'll use the new codes. But when you hear the old ones, I want to know what the computers are being instructed to do. Give that precedence over everything else.

"Don't waste time talking about it. Route it straight to me."

"Right." Hunching to his console, Lind tapped keys as fast as he could.

With every tick of the command chronometer, the wind in Liete's ears felt more like the mistral. Nevertheless it didn't unclog the atmosphere of the bridge.

"Malda, weapons status," she demanded.

"Up and ready," the targ first replied. "Give me a target, and I'll hit it."

Hardly pausing for breath, Liete turned toward scan. "Carmel, it's your job to keep us alive. Watch those ships, *watch* Billingate. If anybody decides to fire, we need warning. If anything comes after us, we need warning."

"I'm on it," Carmel muttered stolidly. She didn't glance at Liete: her attention was focused on her readouts. "Speaking of warning, there are people coming out of *Trumpet.* I count five—six—now seven."

People, Liete thought with her heart in her throat.

Coming out of *Trumpet*.

How could that be?

How could there be so many?

Which one of them was Nick?

But such questions had no bearing on what she had to do; they changed nothing. She let the wind carry them away; tug them to tatters and disperse them like smoke.

Slowly, controlling herself so that she wouldn't panic, she turned her g-seat to face the helm station.

"Pastille, you're insufferable. You're undisciplined and insulting, and you smell bad. This is your chance to prove you're really worth what you cost.

"I want one-g acceleration, no more. We're not trying to go anywhere fast. Follow *Soar*—she's our target." Her nerves still burned cold whenever she thought about Sorus Chatelaine. "Whatever else happens, we're going to make sure she ends up dead.

"But stay between her and the installation," Liete warned. "*Right* between. Make sure she and Billingate can't try to hit us without hitting each other. That should protect us from *Calm Horizons* as well. *Soar* will block their targ.

"I want to make it as dangerous as possible for any of them to fire on us."

Pastille obeyed without looking at his hands. G changed vectors; *Captain's Fancy*'s attitude and trajectory shifted; but he didn't drop Liete's gaze.

"You know that can't work, don't you?" His tone was at once sarcastic and insinuating. "As soon as we hit *Soar*, Billingate won't have any reason to hold fire. We can't stand up to those guns—not this close."

Liete glared at him while darkness and necessity gathered around her. "Go on," she told him softly, as if she were calm. "Say it all— get it out of your system."

Tell me whether I can trust you.

Abruptly the helm third lowered his eyes to his board as if his hands had lost their place. In a thin voice he articulated, "This is a suicide mission. Nick doesn't want us to come back."

Lind's fingers paused; his larynx lurched as he swallowed convulsively. Malda looked at Liete with a frozen expression on her face. Even Carmel raised her head to listen.

Liete surprised and pleased herself with a short laugh. "Does that sound like him to you? Has he ever done anything that made you think he wouldn't mind seeing his ship destroyed?" Prompted by the scorched and hungry memory of Nick's touch, she added, "Have you considered the possibility that he's one of the people who just left *Trumpet*? That he's got Mikka and Sib and Vector and Pup with him, and they've gone EVA to sabotage the guns?"

Pastille continued running helm commands. Liete's stomach twisted as g altered in several directions simultaneously. One of the display screens showed tracking blips for *Captain's Fancy*, *Soar*, and *Calm Horizons*. *Soar* continued moving steadily, unhurriedly, toward the Amnion warship. By degrees *Captain's Fancy* swung into line behind her. In moments *Captain's Fancy*'s course and speed would match *Soar*'s.

Defensively Pastille muttered, "Well, *somebody* had to say it. So we can all stop worrying about it."

"I think," Carmel put in like the cut of a shovel, "it's unexpectedly considerate of you to take such good care of us."

"Oh, go fuck yourself," Pastille retorted.

The scan first acted like she hadn't heard him.

The desert blast of Nick's lovemaking held Liete; it went moaning past her ears, ruffling her hair, drying her eyes.

"Just to be on the safe side, Malda," she said in the same tone, "fix targ on *Tranquil Hegemony*. If worst comes to worst, we can always use a stationary target."

As Malda complied the clicking of her keys sounded dull, muted by the weight of the atmosphere.

"I don't know what they're doing down there," Carmel remarked impersonally. "They've split up. Three of them are going in one direction, four in another."

At once Pastille asked, "Are they heading for the guns?"

At this range Billingate had only two emplacements which could be brought to bear on *Captain's Fancy*.

"Maybe," Carmel grunted, "maybe not. It's too soon to tell."

"Liete"—Lind sounded like he'd just swallowed his Adam's apple—"here it comes."

"Analysis!" she barked. "Fast!"

Lind was fast. Almost instantly one of her readouts sprang clear.

The message came from *Calm Horizons.*

It invoked Nick's priority codes, the ones Morn had given Enablement Station.

Using the authority of those codes, *Calm Horizons* instructed *Captain's Fancy* to lock open this communications channel and link it directly with her command computer.

Then the Amnion warship ordered *Captain's Fancy* to shut down her drive and kill all power to the weapons systems.

As if her synapses were on fire, Liete hit overrides which disabled both helm and targ.

New g crawled through her guts as the ship lost thrust. She could almost hear the impalpable groan of the matter cannon and lasers powering down.

"Shit!" Malda cried involuntarily. "What—?"

Pastille's protest smothered the targ first's. "What the fuck are you *doing,* Liete?"

Liete couldn't breathe. Her nerves still burned; spasms locked the air in her chest. Does that do it? she asked the silence. Was I fast enough? Do they believe me?

Nick, tell me I was fast enough!

"Orders from *Calm Horizons,*" Lind explained in a high, tight voice. He was too frightened to keep his mouth shut. "They told us to shut down drive and weapons. They used Nick's priority codes—the old ones."

Malda slumped in chagrin or relief.

"And you *did it?*" Pastille protested wildly. "They used the old codes, and you *obeyed?* Are you out of your *mind?*"

A shudder ran through Liete. She took one tentative sip of air, then another. Abruptly her muscles unclenched, and she could breathe again.

"They think we're helpless," she said hoarsely, as if she were losing her voice. "Now we can really go to work."

The wind in her ears had become as black and fatal as the gap.

ANGUS

Swinging his matter cannon up with him, Angus climbed out of the airlock to stand on *Trumpet*'s hull.

The surface was complex: deformed with receptors, antennae, and dishes; warted with gun ports designed to look like supply hatches. Thruster tubes splayed at the ship's tail, arising from the heavy bulge of the drive housing. Only to a spacer's eye did she look swift or beautiful. Her lack of sleekness as well as any obvious symmetry would have crippled her as an atmosphere craft; nevertheless it meant nothing while she sailed the vacuum—or the gap.

Angus wished he could see the starfield. Even little lights billions of k away would have given the encompassing dark features, softened its utterness; ameliorated the abyss. But the arc lamps, like small suns, blinded him to any other stars.

Adjusting his faceplate's polarization to improve his depth of field, he scanned the docks quickly, searching for guards or witnesses. Of course, he had no guarantee the other berthed ships wouldn't see him. If they thought to use their sensors, they could pick him out easily. That was unlikely, however. Thanatos Minor's visitors trusted the Bill for security. The more obvious danger came from Operations; but that, too, was unlikely—at least for a few more minutes. The installation was trained and equipped to protect itself from threats which emerged from the gap and the dark, not from men crawling like mites across the surface of the rock.

White under the burning lamps, Billingate's blunt concrete looked as empty and inhuman as a wilderland.

Angus kept one eye on *Captain's Fancy* as he moved away from the airlock to make room for his companions.

Belying the violence of her undocking, Nick's frigate moved as if she followed routine departure protocols.

Mikka Vasaczk swarmed up the ladder, burst out of the lock to stand beside Angus. Like him, she scanned the area. When she caught sight of *Captain's Fancy,* she bit down so hard on a curse that her voice sounded like she'd drawn blood.

So she hadn't known this was going to happen. Nick hadn't taken her into his confidence: he trusted his own crew to roughly the same extent that he trusted Angus.

Nick himself came next: from the airlock he executed a neat flip and landed on his feet. Then Vector and Ciro emerged. Hampered by the burden of an extra EVA suit, Sib climbed more slowly. And his awkwardness delayed Davies.

Angus didn't wait for them. Their suit communications would pick up everything he said.

Grabbing Succorso's arm, he pointed out *Captain's Fancy.*

"What the fuck are you doing, Nick? Answer a civil question while it's still civil."

"I'm not doing anything." In the constriction of Angus' helmet, Nick's tone cut like mockery. "Liete's in command—she's doing it."

Angus ground his fingers into Nick's arm as if he meant to rupture the suit. His welding made him strong enough to pull a wince from Succorso's face.

Obeying the pain, Nick explained tightly, "It's a diversion. I'm giving the Bill something else to worry about. He knows I have a grudge against Sorus. I told Liete to make it look like she's going after *Soar.* He'll believe that. And it'll scare him—he depends on Sorus. Meanwhile Liete can cover us."

This had to be a lie. It was too pat, too convenient. Nevertheless Angus' programming accepted it.

In any case it might work.

He let go of Nick and turned toward Vector and Ciro.

"We're in a hurry now. Every minute counts, so don't fuck up." He gestured toward the nearest radio dish. "That's your target.

"Here." Quickly he moved to an access hatch he'd unlocked earlier, while he and Davies were getting ready. Set inside the hatch was a high-tension cable a hundred fifty meters long—a line thick enough to carry the power for a dozen ships. It was already connected at one end and rolled on a drum so that it would feed out when it was pulled.

He picked up a tool kit and the free end of the cable, and shoved them at Vector.

"Take this to the dish, wire it in. Let me know as soon as you're done. We're going to short out the Bill's communications so badly it'll take him hours to unscramble it. Once you're clear, I'm going to hit that dish with every gigawatt a fusion generator can pump down this cable."

When power on that scale slammed into Billingate's communications, every failsafe in Operations would shut down to protect the computers from being slagged.

As a diversion, that would make *Captain's Fancy's* gambit look trivial.

Vector accepted the cable, the tools, and stood staring at Angus. Angus could see his mouth moving, but no sound came from his pickup.

"Great idea," Nick sneered. "Too bad it can't work. Didn't you hear the Bill say he's cutting you off from installation power? All by herself this little ship of yours can't generate enough jolt to do him any real damage."

"That's what he thinks"—Angus sounded mechanically calm—"but he can't do it. He doesn't know how much I know about his computers. I've been embedding codes in my operational transmissions—ordering his computers to give *Trumpet* emergency priority. They won't accept a command to cut her off until he figures out what I've done and cancels her priority."

His datacore didn't require him to mention that he'd done all this in the past half hour; or that it was a gamble which might easily fail. If the codes were inaccurate—or if Operations had already noticed them—

Vector made a whistling noise through his teeth.

In a frightened voice, Ciro asked the engineer, "Can he do that? I mean, can he really trick the Bill's computers?"

"We don't have time to *discuss* it," Angus snapped. Every passing second seemed to increase his visceral alarm, as well as the compulsions of his programming. "You'll never find out what I can and can't do if you don't *hurry*."

Then he wheeled back to face the others.

"Davies, go with them. Keep them safe. Call me the instant you're clear.

"The rest of us are going to *burn*."

He saw the white glare of uncertainty from Davies' eyes, the skepticism on Nick's face. Mikka glowered at him like a threat; Sib's fright was as open as his mouth. But Angus ignored them: he had no more time. He hefted his matter cannon, toggled the jet control on his chest plate. Trusting Thanatos Minor's g, his reinforced joints, and his prewritten knowledge to protect him, he flung himself in a long leap off *Trumpet*'s hull.

As if they were trained for it, his hips cocked upward. At once the suit's jets cut in, braking his drop to the concrete. He landed easily, bounded a few steps ahead, then turned to make sure that Nick and the others were following.

"Angus!" Davies shouted. Too much volume hurt Angus' ears. "She's my mother! She's all I have!"

Angus didn't answer. Dread and prewritten exigencies consumed him.

Like Angus, Nick sprang from the ship. His control of his jets was awkward, but he managed them well enough to land safely.

Mikka shook her head. Snatching the extra suit from Sib, she lobbed it toward Angus; then she located a series of zero-g handgrips circling *Trumpet*'s girth and lowered herself rapidly down the side.

Angus caught the suit: he couldn't risk letting it be damaged. Morn would need it.

Or she wouldn't.

Or he might not get to her at all.

Grinding his teeth, he forced himself to wait until Mikka and Sib caught up with him. Then he pushed the extra suit into Sib's arms and started running.

Low g made running easy, if not effortless. Three k was too far, but he couldn't help that: the Amnion sector was where it was. In truth he didn't know why he wanted to get there so fast. Milos Taverner was almost certainly waiting for him—and Milos had his priority codes. Yet he ran without the urging of his datacore or the pressure of his zone implants.

He ran because he was a coward. More than anything else, he needed to arrive at the end of his fear.

Over his shoulder he saw Vector, Ciro, and Davies nearing their destination. The long cable snaked behind them, black against the blaring white of the concrete. Surely Vector would know how to wire the dish; surely Nick's engineer would be at least that competent. Angus could have done the job himself in his sleep—

His helmet seemed to echo with the sound of Sib's labored breathing. Mikka's flat, grim stride gave the impression that she could sustain it for hours. But Sib was too scared; he moved with bands of trepidation tightening around his chest.

Too bad. Angus didn't slow his pace.

"Use your jets, Mackern," Nick suggested. "Turn them on and poke with your hips like you're fucking. That should give you a lift forward."

Good Captain Sheepfucker, still trying to create the impression that he cared what happened to his people.

If Sib had stopped to think, he might not have tried it. But he was frantic. His free hand flopped at his chest plate; locking his legs, he tried to thrust his hips up and forward.

At exactly the wrong instant he stumbled. The sudden pressure of his jets carried him straight at Angus like a cargo sled gone out of control.

Riding enhanced reflexes, Angus spun out of the way; grabbed Sib by one arm and leg, and hauled him to a stop before he could strike the concrete and tear his suit.

"Shit," Sib panted in deep gulps. "Shit."

He sounded too much like Milos. Angus slapped at his jets toggle for him, then left him and ran on.

Now Davies' group had reached the dish. Vector handled the cable while Ciro dug tools out of the kit. Davies braced himself with his impact rifle in his hands as if he were willing to burn down the heavens in order to defend the engineers.

Two k to go.

Mikka dropped back to pace Sib. Angus and Nick rushed ahead together.

"Angus." This time Davies didn't shout. His voice was hushed, as if he were afraid of being overheard. "Vector has the junction cover off. The wiring looks simple—I could probably do this myself. We'll be ready in a minute or two."

"Get clear when you're done," Angus ordered between breaths. "There's going to be one hell of a static discharge."

"They used to call it a corposant," Vector remarked in a concentrated tone. "Or St. Elmo's fire."

"Who is 'they'?" Ciro asked. Angus' helmet speakers were tiny, but they picked up the undercurrent of dissociation in the boy's words. He was too young to know what to do with his fear.

"Ciro," Mikka gasped as if she were coughing, "stay with Vector. I'll be back. That's a promise."

"Sailors on oceangoing ships," Vector answered calmly. "Back on Earth a long time ago. The ships were wood, and they used wind for drive. Sometimes during storms the atmosphere generated so much static it seemed to gather in balls and roll along the masts and spars."

After a moment Angus realized that Vector was talking in order to steady his second; distract the boy from his fear.

For some reason this recognition filled him with such rage that he seemed to go blind. His computer could still see: his zone implants kept him running flawlessly. Nevertheless his eyes registered only red fury. The crib turned the inside of his faceplate opaque, and the only defense he had left against the molten, helpless agony which the looming woman had inflicted on him was a mad and murderous hate.

That must have been why he wanted so intensely to rescue Morn. She, too, had a zone implant: he'd used it to abase her in every way his desperation could devise. Therefore he needed her; depended on her to the same extent and for the same reason that he'd been dependent on the looming woman—for his survival. That woman could have killed him: Morn could save him. Her zone implant had enabled him to reverse their positions in and above the crib; to fend off the abyss.

And like that other woman, she knew his most necessary and fatal secret—

His suit's climate controls couldn't cool him fast enough. Sweat ran down his collar, congealed in his armpits and crotch.

One k to go.

Abruptly he and Nick passed the last arc lamp and came to the

end of the concrete which had been poured for the docks. From here
he could see the entrance to the Amnion sector crouching like a
bunker in Thanatos Minor's surface; but he would have to cross bare,
raw rock to get there.

Now any fall would be much more dangerous. Mylar and plexulose could resist a variety of punctures, or reseal around the holes;
but the suits might not stand up to being torn on this old, sharp
stone.

Angus turned to look for Mikka and Sib.

They were at least two hundred meters back, still lagging. She
held one of his arms, supporting him as well as she could: they ran
together awkwardly, bouncing against each other and stumbling away
as if they were exhausted.

"Angus." Davies' voice seemed to come from the black void
overhead. "We're done. It's ready."

Angus saw three small shapes hurrying to distance themselves
from the radio dish. "Are you clear?" he demanded.

"Clear enough," Vector reported. "Do it now—if you still can."

Angus Thermopyle might have hesitated: ordinary mortality might
have slowed his reactions in a situation like this.

If the Bill had detected the trick—

If Operations had disabled the embedded codes—

If someone somewhere had witnessed what was happening and
warned Billingate—

But Joshua had no mortality. From a pouch in his EVA suit he
took out the small transmitter he'd prepared for the occasion.

In one smooth motion, he aimed the transmitter's antenna and
thumbed the switch.

Picoseconds later an incandescent conflagration as feral as lightning and as noiseless as nightmare caught the dish and etched it
against the black heavens.

Then every illumination across the whole of the visitors' docks
went dark.

Midnight seemed to slam down on Thanatos Minor like an av-
alanche. No stars, no light, no movement, Angus saw nothing, heard
nothing, he was alone, the abyss had swallowed him utterly. Nick,
Mikka, and Sib; Vector, Ciro, and Davies: they were all stricken
from existence; even their broadcast breathing couldn't reach him
across the vacuum.

Locked in the silence of his zone implants, he began gibbering to himself because he couldn't wail aloud.

Then Nick drawled suddenly, "Well, *that* worked, anyway."

At the sound, Angus felt an instant of inconceivable gratitude.

Nevertheless his datacore didn't know and couldn't care what he felt. It paid no attention to his fear—or his relief. Impelled by artificial emissions, he stowed his small transmitter. Next he unclipped a hand lamp from his belt and flashed it for Mikka and Sib.

"Ciro," Mikka gasped hoarsely, "are you all right?"

"Sure. Of course." For a moment the boy wasn't afraid at all. "That was *incredible.*"

"We're fine, Angus," Davies reported. His voice was rough with relief. "We're moving toward you now. We'll come about halfway and wait for you."

"No!" Angus called back. "Stay close to *Trumpet* and cover us from there! I don't want you cut off."

Davies' reply came like a farewell out of the dark.

"Right."

"I see them!" Sib gulped unexpectedly.

"We see your light, Angus," Mikka announced. "We're coming."

Before Angus' programming could send him off across the rock, the arc lamps came back on.

LIETE

Liete sat perfectly still, sweating while she waited for more orders; waited for the Amnion to believe that their first instructions had been obeyed.

"All right," Pastille panted. "I understand. I think I understand. You want us to look helpless so we can keep our options open. You don't want them to know Nick has already replaced those codes—"

Sounding tense, nearly feverish, Malda Verone put in, "Because if they know those codes don't work they'll be afraid of us. They'll try to kill us before we can do anything."

But Pastille wasn't done. "Was that all they told us? Shut down thrust?"

"And targ," Malda informed him.

"But what do they get out of it?" he protested. "We're still moving—still on the heading we want. All we've lost is acceleration. We're still getting away."

"Don't you ever use your head?" Malda's voice shivered. "We're coming into range for Billingate's guns. They'll be able to hit us soon—and we can't maneuver. Or shoot back."

"This is just the beginning," Liete pronounced as if she were sure. "They'll send more orders when they're sure the last ones were effective. They don't know our systems—even with those codes, they can't control us precisely. So they started crude. As soon as they're ready, they'll try some refinements."

If they get the chance. If they don't already have too many other things to worry about.

"Their first order," Lind offered nervously, "was to keep open a link between communications and the command computer. What they'll probably do next is use the link to demand information so they can plan their 'refinements.' "

Could they tell the difference? Liete wondered. Did they know *Captain's Fancy* had lost thrust and weapons power, not on their orders, but on hers?

Probably not. They weren't trying to pull data back out of her board; not yet. They'd simply issued instructions and then watched to see what would happen.

She had no time to waste. The wind was blowing: like Nick, it burned away her choices. She needed to prepare *now*, before *Calm Horizons* took the next step.

"In case you're interested," Carmel remarked from scan, "I can tell you where those seven people from *Trumpet* are headed."

Liete couldn't help herself. Nick was almost certainly one of the seven.

And she needed another minute or two to think.

"Go on," she told Carmel.

"None of them are anywhere near the guns," the scan first said flatly. "Three of them stopped at one of the radio dishes. They're dragging something. It's too small to scan accurately—Billingate emits too much garbage—but it might be a cable.

"The other four are moving fast—I mean running—straight across the docks. They aren't together anymore. Two of them have pulled ahead. But the other two are following.

"There aren't any ships in that direction—if you don't count *Tranquil Hegemony*." Carmel paused, then remarked bluntly, "At a guess, I would say they were headed for the Amnion installation."

Liete's stomach churned. The Amnion installation.

Nick! What're you doing?

"So much for your theory about the guns," Pastille snarled.

Without warning the scorched heat of the desert took her, and she lost control.

She flung off her belt, jumped out of her g-seat. "Will you *shut up?*" she yelled at the helm third, "or do I have to send you off the bridge?" Any of the people around her could have shouted louder than she did, but none of them could make their voices carry and cut like hers. "I'm *sick* of listening to you whine because you can't second-guess Nick! Believe it or not, Ransum can do your job—and she won't bitch all the time!"

Pastille didn't look at her: he faced his board as if he were concentrating hard. "Give me something to do," he muttered past his shoulder. "I'm just sitting here."

"I want *noise!*" Now that she'd started shouting, she couldn't stop. The wind in her ears seemed to carry her out of herself. "I want emission chaos, as much as we can put out! I want to look exactly like a ship that's fighting to figure out what went wrong—fighting to bring up power somehow—fighting like *hell* to break loose!"

Abruptly vehemence and urgency let go of her. A strange stillness like the center of a storm filled her.

"I want camouflage," she explained calmly. "I want to emit so much confusion that Billingate and *Calm Horizons* and *Soar* won't be able to tell the difference when we power up."

Carmel didn't hesitate. "I can run a feedback loop for some of our scan systems. Doppler sensors, radiant power emission receptors, particle sifters, things like that. Use them for broadcast instead of reception. We'll look like we're going critical—like we're suffering some kind of meltdown."

"Good." Liete nodded. "Do it."

Lind was already working. As his hands typed commands, he barked into his pickup, "*Captain's Fancy* to all ships. *Captain's Fancy* to Billingate Operations. *Captain's Fancy* on all bandwidths. Emergency. Emergency. We are out of control. We have lost maneuvering power. Stay clear. I say again, do not approach us. We have a thrust emergency." He hit more keys, then turned to Liete. "That's on automatic across the operational spectrum."

"Good," she said again. Bracing herself on the command board so that she wouldn't tremble, she lowered herself slowly back into her g-seat.

Malda chewed her lower lip. "I might be able to dummy a short into one or two of the lasers." A taut vibration cut through her tone. "Make it look like I'm trying to tap maintenance power, but the lines can't carry the load."

Liete nodded once more. "And while you're doing that, start leaking a little power back into the matter cannon. Keep it slow—

maybe it won't show. I want to be able to hit something in five minutes, if I have to.

"The same goes for you, Pastille. Bring the drive back up, but do it *slow*. Get ready to burn when the time comes.

"Lind, keep watching for orders from *Calm Horizons*. Just like before—I want analysis the same instant we hear from them."

Lind opened his mouth to reply; but before he could find his voice, Carmel cried out, "Holy shit!"

"What?" Liete demanded. "What is it?"

"That dish just went up like a flare!" Carmel shouted.

Almost immediately, however, she recovered her poise. In an oddly formal tone, she announced more quietly, "Billingate has experienced a complete power shutdown."

"Operations is dead!" Lind gasped. "They aren't making a sound."

Liete's heart thudded with admiration. Oh, Nick!

She fixed a look on Pastille. "Got any more complaints?"

But she didn't give him time to respond. As if she were singing to herself, she said happily, "Analysis, Carmel."

Carmel took a deep breath. "Nick must have hit the dish with enough juice to trigger every failsafe in Operations. That won't stop them long. I mean they'll be able to get power back up almost immediately. Life support, weapons, things like that. Those systems are designed to protect themselves and come back on-line. They should be functional again in less than a minute.

"Communications is another matter."

Lind was so excited that he hopped against the belt of his g-seat. "Nobody designs communications gear to take that kind of jolt! If we're lucky, their central systems have been slagged. If *they* are, they'll still need hours to unscramble the damage. They may have to reprogram every computer in Operations—and that's after they find and fix anything that burned."

Carmel peered at her readouts, then said, "Right. Billingate has power back."

Lind tightened the receiver in his ear, listened hard. Nearly crowing, he reported, "Nothing from Operations. They're still dead."

"And"—Liete's heart went on singing, even though her voice was calm—"we have exactly what we need. A diversion. Suddenly we're nobody's biggest worry. We're helpless—we don't matter anymore. What matters is what's happening to Billingate.

"This is our chance." She faced Pastille squarely. Nick has given us our chance. "Let's not miss it."

Pastille nodded as if he were in awe.

"Malda?" Liete asked.

The targ first hunched over her console, keying commands as fast as she could. "I'll be ready," she murmured distantly.

Simply because Nick and his people were out on Thanatos Minor's surface and therefore vulnerable, Liete ordered, "Fix targ on *Tranquil Hegemony*. That comes first. We'll tackle *Soar* when we know more about what's happening."

Malda nodded.

Liete looked at the display screen which showed *Captain's Fancy's* position behind *Soar* on her way toward *Calm Horizons*. In silence she promised Nick that she wouldn't let him down.

Not after this. Now she understood completely that he could never be beaten.

ANGUS

The arc lamps were dim for a moment; they flickered as if they were sizzling inside. Then they came back up to brightness as if someone in Operations had dialed a rheostat.

Angus remained still on the edge of the concrete, waiting for his datacore to send him into motion again; plunge him back into a headlong rush toward Milos and doom.

"What went wrong?" Sib Mackern panted raggedly, as if he had no background in data and damage control.

"Nothing," Angus muttered. I hope.

"Power doesn't matter." Nick sounded abstract, thinking about something else. "What matters is communications." His head tilted back: he stared upward as if he could see *Captain's Fancy* receding from him. But of course he couldn't: even with all her running lights ablaze, she would be invisible now, washed from sight by the intensity of the lamps. Nevertheless an odd note of yearning in his tone suggested that he spoke not to Sib, but to his ship. "If we've fried enough of their circuits, they'll be paralyzed. They won't be able to talk to anybody."

The Bill would be effectively helpless. Trapped in his strong-room, completely dependent on his communications network, he would have no idea what was happening. He would have to leave his reinforced hidey-hole, ride the lifts up to Operations, simply in order to obtain information. *Calm Horizons* and *Tranquil Hegemony* could talk to each other: they could talk to *Soar*. But none of them could reach Operations or the Bill.

Which meant that the threat to *Trumpet* would be temporarily neutralized.

And the Amnion would be cut off from the Bill; they wouldn't be able to call him for help—

Without transition, as if he didn't know how he'd passed from immobility to motion, Angus found himself running across the gnarled and whetted rock.

He wasn't hampered like Sib: because of his zone implants, he breathed steadily, strongly, despite his instinctive EVA panic and the knowledge that he was lost. Strutted muscles and joints carried him easily across the treacherous surface, as if he could never fall. The matter cannon in his hands might as well have been weightless.

Sib's hoarse gasping seemed to fill his helmet. He could hardly hear Mikka's labored respiration: he couldn't hear Nick at all.

Bounding between igneous outcroppings and glazed planes, Nick ran as if he didn't need welding to match Angus. In reaction Angus' lips pulled a snarl across his teeth. He wanted to run faster, leave Nick behind; outdo him somehow. Then he noticed that Nick was experimenting with his jets: teaching himself how to control them; using them to keep pace.

Their destination loomed ahead. Distance reduced the glow from the arc lamps; in their faded brilliance the concrete of the Amnion sector silhouetted itself against the absolute void. Above Thanatos Minor's surface the installation was like a bunker in size as well as configuration. The part which protruded from the ancient splash and swirl of the rock was nothing more than a small section of roof—an emergency exit. It gave the Amnion a way out. The dedicated berth where *Tranquil Hegemony* rested was half a kilometer away on the left. Docking lights picked the high bulk of the warship out from the dark; guns and antennae articulated her bulbous shape.

If her crew was running scan—if the Amnion were that cautious—they would see Angus and Nick, with Mikka and Sib lagging behind. *Tranquil Hegemony* might not be able to contact Operations—perhaps not even her own people in the installation—but she could send out forces of her own.

Between her and this bunker, the raw stone was marked only

by a flat metallic sheet nearly thirty meters on each side, the sliding hatch of a shuttle port. It protected a small dock which could launch and receive personnel craft.

"Be more careful, Sib," Mikka ordered tightly. "They'll wait for us when they need us. You won't do anybody any good if you fall and tear your suit."

Sib didn't answer. He was panting too hard.

Nick waved a hand at the bunker. "I presume," he said between breaths, "you've got a plan for this, too."

Angus didn't need a plan. He needed a design diagram. His databases and his own experience suggested that this installation was large enough to quarter a hundred or more Amnion. Where would they keep Morn? How could he find her?

Assuming he survived that long, how could he locate the other thing his programming required, a way into Billingate's infrastructure?

On the strength of welded muscles and lesser g, he leaped in one long stride to the top of the bunker.

His immediate goal was on the far side. When he dropped over the edge, he landed on a concrete apron in front of the outer door of the airlock.

He hardly noticed as Nick sprang down beside him: his concentration had focused in like the beam of a laser as he studied the exterior control panel and intercom. Under different circumstances the locking mechanism would have been no obstacle. If he'd been willing to open the installation to the vacuum—and warn the Amnion that they were under attack, give them time to seal their interior doors and marshal their defenses—he could have simply blasted his way in. But to rescue Morn he needed a better approach.

"Now what?" Nick sounded impossibly close, as if he were inside Angus' helmet. "If you use the intercom and ask nicely, they'll probably just open up. Why not? That way they can get their hands on all of us at once."

"Shut up," Angus muttered. His tension showed in his voice. Apparently his programming no longer cared how much dread he betrayed.

From a distance of half a dozen centimeters he glared at the control panel.

With his EM vision, he should have been able to read its circuitry exactly. For some reason, however, his prostheses had gone blind.

His heart lurched in panic, and his hands ran with sweat inside his gloves. What was going on? He couldn't *see* what he needed; his datacore had switched off his enhanced sight; Dios or Lebwohl had sent him this far only to make him fail—

Then an artificial calm slowed his pulse. From the window in his head came a flood of information about his prostheses.

He couldn't *see*, he was informed, because the polarization of his faceplate distorted his EM vision.

Shit! Just what he needed.

Urgently he adjusted the degree of polarization. At the same time he scaled it up and down the spectrum, hunting for a wavelength which would let him read the control panel. He didn't need polarization at all, not here in the shadow of the bunker, protected from the burning glare of the lamps; but the faceplate induced a distortion of its own, blurring EM emissions. Scrambling through databases while he made his adjustments, he searched for settings to counteract the inherent refraction.

"What're you doing?" Nick inquired sardonically. "Trying to unlock it by willpower?"

There: an imprecise flicker of electromagnetic tracery like a circuit board seen under a disfocused microscope. Too much detail was lost; accuracy would be almost impossible. But Angus might be able to cut into the lock wiring without setting the whole installation afire with alarms.

As he reached for his laser, he told Nick, "Get Sib and Mikka here. We can't wait for them."

Nick didn't move; didn't obey. He stood still and watched while Angus narrowed his laser down to its smallest focus, aimed it into the center of the control panel, and fired.

A pinprick of metal flamed crimson, then denatured like smoke into the vacuum.

With luck, the alarm circuits were disabled.

Now a second shot, millimeters away from the first.

A moment later the outer door of the airlock irised open like a dilating eye.

"You amaze me." Nick's tone was too cold and dangerous for awe. "The Bill doesn't know how much you know about his computers. The Amnion don't know how much you know about their airlocks. What's next, Angus? Are you going to simply wave your hands and undo what they've done to Morn? Do you know that much about mutagens, too?"

Mikka rounded the corner of the bunker and came to a stop on locked knees. Through her faceplate, she looked frantic with exertion. When she saw the staring airlock, she gaped at it.

"Where's Sib?" Angus demanded.

"Here." Sib stumbled onto the apron and caught himself on Mikka's shoulder. His handgun hung from his belt; he carried the extra EVA suit wrapped to his chest with both arms.

"We're going in," Angus announced harshly. "Shoot anybody you see, Amnion or human." Shoot Milos, if you can. "Be ready to shoot yourselves—unless you like mutagens.

"If you've got some idea how to find Morn, I'm listening."

Sib shook his head. His features twisted as if he were about to puke.

"As far as I know," Nick remarked slowly, "there's only one entrance from the rest of Billingate to the Amnion sector. She'll be near there. Unless she's one of them now, in which case she could be anywhere."

"Why?" Angus rasped. "Why there?"

"Because they don't trust me." Nick grinned like his scars. "They don't trust her. There's more than one kind of kaze. They've learned to be careful. They won't risk, say, an explosion that might do them real damage. They won't let her anywhere near their operational center, or the shuttles, or that damn warship"—he nodded toward *Tranquil Hegemony*—"or any of the places where they work or live, until they're sure she's safe."

Damn. Angus had to admit that Nick was right. But the airlock into Billingate was probably farther away from where he stood now than any other part of the Amnion sector.

The longer he stayed inside this installation, the more vulnerable he would be. He knew in the marrow of his bones that his programming would never allow him to kill Milos.

Too bad. Prewritten logic compelled him. It left no room for hesitation.

Bracing his cannon in both hands, he stepped into the airlock.

At once his fear turned the color of sulfur.

Outside Nick tilted his head again to study the featureless dark. As if he were talking to himself, he murmured softly, fervidly, "Do it. Don't wait. Do it now."

Then he followed Angus.

While Mikka and Sib joined him Angus made new adjustments to his faceplate, refining away the wavelengths which the Amnion liked best as if he could tune out panic and ruin.

Nick didn't wait for orders: he thumbed keys on the inner control panel. An almost subliminal groan carried to Angus' external pickup as the airlock cycled shut. A moment later he heard the hiss of pressurization as atmosphere pumped into the lock. Displays inside his helmet told him that he could breathe the air—if his life depended on it.

As soon as the airlock pressure had been equalized, the inner door irised.

It opened on an empty lift.

"Down," Nick said unnecessarily. "I don't know how far. Your guess is as good as mine."

Angus' computer ran complex calculations, comparing what he knew of Billingate and Thanatos Minor with the estimated size and depth of the Amnion sector; he let numbers spin through him while he entered the lift. By the time Nick, Mikka, and Sib had left the lock, his computer had come up with its own guess.

The lift's controls showed twenty-five indicators: he had that many levels to choose from. Holding his breath involuntarily, he keyed the tenth.

Servos closed the iris like a shutter. A heartbeat or two after the door shut, the car dived for the depths of the rock.

Angus positioned himself against the back wall so that he could level his cannon. "I'll lead, but I want you beside me, Nick." His voice distressed the inside of his helmet. "Don't make me use this thing if I don't have to."

Matter cannon had been developed for use in the void, where the secondary and tertiary quantum discontinuities could be discounted. No man in his right mind would fire such a gun within walls.

Nick replied by showing his teeth.

"Mikka," Angus went on, "you and Sib cover my back. You cover *him*—don't let anything happen to that suit."

Through her faceplate, he saw her nod. "We *are* going to get out of this alive, aren't we?" she asked grimly. "I promised Ciro I would come back."

"If I survive, you probably will, too. They may have a whole fucking arsenal handy, but it won't include anything like this." Angus waggled the end of his cannon.

That was as close as he could come to telling her the truth.

The lift seemed to plummet like a stone, but it didn't scare him. Instead he felt a small piece of his visceral dread break away, lost in the fall. At least now he was no longer EVA. He was *inside*, where the vast dark couldn't reach him—

With a palpable wheeze, the car braked to a halt at the tenth level.

Sib snatched his handgun off his belt. Mikka tightened her grip on her rifle. Nick and the muzzle of Angus' cannon faced the door as it slid aside.

Apparently the unauthorized use of the lift had attracted attention. An Amnioni with several arms and at least four eyes stood waiting. A bandolier across its shoulders carried spare charges for the heavy, rust-caked weapon in its hands.

Nick's reflexes were almost as fast as Angus'. Before the Amnioni could twitch, he slammed it in the chest with impact fire.

His gun made a muffled sound like dynamite buried in cement, and the Amnioni staggered backward. Spraying strange, greenish blood from a massive hole in its chest, the creature hit the wall and fell onto its face.

Together Nick and Angus sprang out of the lift.

Sib made a choking noise, as if he'd swallowed his tongue. Mikka grabbed his arm and shoved him into motion ahead of her.

Angus scanned the corridor in both directions, wheeled to orient himself. His computer scrolled design hypotheticals through his head. To the right, the passage stretched empty for a considerable distance. To the left, it turned a corner out of sight after ten meters.

That way, his computer said—to the left; away from *Tranquil Hegemony's* berth.

He pointed Nick in that direction. "Go!"

Nick sprinted toward the corner; then dived skidding onto his belly as two more Amnion armed with heavy rifles came into sight.

They were ready: they'd heard the distinctive concussion of an gone, ripped open on service shafts snarled with wiring and conduits. So much concrete and steel had been torn from the walls and ceiling that Angus could see little else: the bodies of the Amnion had disappeared as if they'd been atomized. He might have been looking at a bomb crater in one of Earth's embattled slums.

Through the neural reverberation in his ears, he heard alarms of all kinds—wails of structural damage; warnings of bloodshed; calls to battle.

A diversion wouldn't do him any good if he stayed there to see what would happen next. "Come on!" he shouted. Too loud, he knew he was shouting too loud, his companions could hear him without that. But if he didn't shout, he couldn't hear himself.

Mikka helped Sib back to his feet. At a run Angus led them and Nick to the lift.

They jumped aboard, and he sent the car down one level.

The corridor it opened on was completely deserted. Apparently every Amnioni in the vicinity had already left to deal with the emergency above.

If one diversion was good, two would be better. Give the Amnion reason to think they were under a completely different kind of assault. Angus thrust Nick, Mikka, and Sib out of the lift. From his belt he detached a limpet mine; he set its timer for thirty seconds, clamped it to the side of the car, hit controls to send the car on downward. Then he jumped out as the doors closed.

Nick muttered, "I guess we won't be coming back this way." He sounded amused.

Angus consulted his computer. Already its design hypotheticals had gained definition, detail. It measured the dimensions of the corridors, the lift's apparent rate of travel between levels: it compared that data to what he knew about Billingate's scale and orientation within Thanatos Minor. For the first time it offered him close order estimates.

Two hundred fifty more meters.

On this level.

Assuming Nick was right.

Angus started into a fast trot. He would have run harder, but now he couldn't afford to leave Sib or Mikka behind.

They passed one corner, then another, before he heard the disimpact gun. As soon as they caught sight of Nick, they began to lay down fire.

Energy beams sizzled in the air like frying flesh. Reacting at machine speed, Angus jumped backward, blocking Mikka and Sib out of the way. But he couldn't shoot: at this range his cannon's blast would reduce Nick to pulp and grease.

Nick's dive carried him under the blare of beams. Before the Amnion could correct their aim, he hit them both.

Echoes rolled like distant thunder down the corridor, calling for the Amnion to notice that they were under attack.

Angus ran. By the time Nick regained his feet, Angus had reached the corner.

Beyond it the passage went straight for twenty or twenty-five meters, past several closed doors and one lift. There it met another door as high and wide as the entrance to a meeting hall. From that point it turned left again.

Nick came up beside Angus; started to pass him. Instincts squalled in Angus' head: he stopped Nick with an arm like a steel bar.

This was why Hashi Lebwohl and Warden Dios had chosen him. Trained by a lifetime of cowardice and violence, he had instincts which no computer could match.

"Now what?" Nick demanded.

At that moment the high doors opened. Reacting to the sounds of detonation, six or eight Amnion crowded outward to see what was happening.

"Time for another diversion," Angus snarled tightly.

Planting his weight, he fired his cannon at the Amnion.

The blast nearly deafened him: the gain on his external pickup was set too high. If he hadn't braced himself—and if he hadn't been welded for this kind of work—the concussion might have ripped him off his feet.

Mikka staggered backward. Sib fell on his back with an inarticulate cry that seemed to echo like the blast through the devastation in the corridor.

For an instant pulverized concrete clouded everything; the lighting flickered as automatic relays rerouted power. Then the dust cleared, sucked into the air-scrubbers, and the effects of matter cannon fire in an enclosed space became visible.

Only rubble remained of the meeting hall. Even its far wall was tant crumpling explosion of the mine; felt the vibration nudge against his boots.

At his back Mikka's gun hammered twice, three times. Amnion must have emerged from one of the doors behind him. Sib's handgun emitted an aimless whine, as if he had no idea what he was shooting at.

More corners. Angus' computer revised its estimates.

Somewhere the creatures were marshaling their defenses—enough Amnion to simply overrun the human intruders. He had to hope that they were confused about the kind of danger which threatened them. Otherwise he could only believe that they knew what he was after—and knew how to stop him.

Abruptly he found a wide passage running straight in the right direction.

Dozens of other corridors T'ed off from it, every one of them as threatening as the mouth of a pit. Nevertheless it offered him a chance to make better progress. He couldn't refuse.

A winking red indicator inside his helmet told him that his suit's climate controls had exceeded their tolerances. He was sweating too hard: they couldn't process so much humidity. Soon he would be in danger of dehydration.

Growling to himself, he sent Nick along the left wall, Mikka and Sib down the right. With his cannon he covered the view ahead. From the center of the passage he drew his companions along as fast as they could go.

Nick, too, had been trained for fighting: he also had good instincts. At the first intersection on his side, he unclipped a grenade, armed it, and threw it hard along the corridor. Then he slung his rifle over his shoulder and picked up his handguns. They made less noise.

Mikka followed his example.

Almost at once she triggered fire into the gullet of a corridor. When she was satisfied that her target was dead, she pulled Sib forward.

The blast of the grenade sounded shrouded and small, too minor to do much damage.

Ninety meters, Angus' computer estimated.

Seventy.

With both guns Nick blazed a barrage down one of the side passages. "Got you, you bastards," he growled softly.

Sixty.

"Time to start looking." Angus' voice seemed to scrape in his throat. He could hardly squeeze up enough spit to swallow. "Slow down. Watch for doors with guards."

He was too exposed, too easy to spot. Grimly he sent Nick and Mikka ahead of him; he waited for them to signal that the corridors were clear before he crossed the intersections.

Where are you, Morn? How am I going to find you?

Are you still human?

Do you still want to kill me?

He should have turned off his external pickup completely. Milos was here somewhere; he *had* to be. All he needed was an intercom or a loudhailer, and Angus would be finished.

But his programming rejected that elementary precaution. He needed to hear what happened outside his suit.

It's got to stop.

Goddamn you, Dios! If you really wanted me dead, you could have done it easier than this!

Warned by nothing but instinct—the pressure of intuitive panic between his shoulder blades—he whirled suddenly, wrenched the mass of his cannon around and brought it to bear just as five Amnion surged into the passage. From fifty-five or sixty meters away, they hurtled in his direction. Their crusted skin and their quasi-organic weapons made them look more like engines of destruction than sentient beings.

Like artillery his cannon howled at them. In an instant they were gone, effaced by rubble and dust.

So much for stealth.

The blast seemed to multiply in his ears as if he were at the bottom of a cavern, buried in reverberation. He barely heard Mikka hiss from the corner of an intersection, "Angus, here!"

Thirst parched his tongue; his throat was clogged with sand. Slowly, disoriented by echoes, he lowered the cannon, took up his laser. As smooth as a cat, Nick came to his side; together they moved to the wall behind Mikka and eased forward.

Past the corner he saw a short hall—thirty meters at most—open at the far end. Several doors marked the wall at regular intervals. Unlike the entrances he'd seen until now, these were heavily reinforced, as massive as the doors of cells.

An Amnioni laden with weapons guarded the middle of the hall.

The creature must have known the installation was besieged. It wore a headset which presumably kept it in contact with the sector's operational center—and presumably the sector's communications functioned separately from Billingate's. But the Amnioni's stance betrayed no anxiety.

Maybe its understanding of its role was so precise that it didn't worry about anything else.

Or maybe it knew something Angus didn't.

He'd come too far to falter now. In any case his prewritten exigencies no longer left room for instinct. Before dread or doubt could interfere, he told Nick to shoot.

Nick raised his gun and burned the Amnioni through the head.

By the time the creature tottered to the floor, Angus was on his way to the door nearest it.

Stupid, crazy, you asshole, you *shit*! As if he had no instincts and no fear, as if decades of mortal terror had taught him nothing, he put himself in his companions' line of fire.

They couldn't shoot when Milos Taverner appeared at the far end of the hall.

Joshua's tormentor and nemesis; stun and interrogation, live nic butts and excrement—

Angus knew instantly that Milos had been pumped full of mutagens. It showed in his eyes.

Nothing else about him had changed. He looked as human, as pitifully ordinary, as ever. His hands were yellow with nic; his shipsuit slid across human skin when he moved. Distinct in the sulfurous light, splotches defined his scalp through his sparse hair. The smile on his pudgy features was calm, as if at last he'd come to terms with treachery.

Joshua. I'm going to give you a standing order. Jerico priority.

But his eyes were lidless and unblinking; they had deformed irises, as narrow as slits; their balls were the biting yellow color of mineral acid.

When I tell you to open your mouth, you will always obey.

And he breathed the air comfortably.

After that you'll chew and swallow normally.

Helpless and appalled, Angus froze.

Every lurch of his heart seemed impossibly slow; the gaps between the seconds were imponderable and vast. Events which must have taken virtually no time at all stretched and dilated as if they became infinite at the speed of light.

Open your mouth.

Use your laser, you shit, use your *cannon*, for God's sake, blast him, fry him, burn him *down!* Before he says anything!

Carefully Milos dropped his burning nic onto Angus' tongue.

Angus remained still, paralyzed, as if Warden Dios and Hashi Lebwohl had left him for dead.

"Joshua," Milos articulated contentedly. "This is a Jerico priority order." His eyes fixed on Angus; despite their alienness, they were full of a malice so intense and pure it could only be human. "Stop. Turn. Kill the people behind you."

As if he'd already been obeyed, he added, "I knew you would come here. It was inevitable. Dios and Lebwohl cheated both of us. All I had to do was wait."

Angus lifted his laser slowly, as if it weighed dozens of kilograms.

Open your mouth.

While the gun came up—during the supernal gap between one second and the next—a link opened in his head.

As if the message were emblazoned on his brain, he heard or saw or felt his programming speak to him.

You are no longer Joshua.

Jerico priority has been superseded.

You are Isaac. That is your name. It is also your access code. Your priority code is Gabriel.

Priority code is Gabriel.

Gabriel.

In that instant he was set free of Milos.

Dios or Lebwohl had seen this crisis coming. They'd planned for it. When his life depended on it, they released him from all control but their own.

The change must have warned Milos: he must have seen the sudden ferocity on Angus' face, or the blaze of hate in his eyes. As

Angus brought up his laser and fired, Milos pitched himself backward around the corner.

Too late, Nick's guns blared past Angus' shoulder. Like Angus, he missed.

Raging with murder, Angus charged after Milos.

He reached the corner in time to see a door across the next passage slam shut. Milos was gone.

Angus would have chased after him, flamed that door to cinders in order to reach Milos. He felt sick with relief and fury: now more than ever he needed someone to kill. If he didn't let the violence inside him out somehow, his heart would crack. But his datacore had other ideas. Turning hard—and trembling as acutely as his zone implants allowed—he strode back toward Nick, Mikka, and Sib; toward the door in the middle of the hall.

" 'Joshua'?" Nick asked tightly. " 'Jerico'? What the hell was that all about?"

Angus ignored the question. Aiming his laser, he burned out the door lock. Then he returned the weapon to his belt.

Morn was here; she *had* to be. Milos had made no effort to lure him anywhere else: the Amnioni had probably assumed that Angus' databases and detectors enabled him to know where she was. Therefore she must be here. That made sense, didn't it?

Didn't it?

Fuming to contain his fear, he pushed the door open.

He saw a small, sterile cell full of light and need. Because of the polarization of his faceplate, he couldn't identify any monitors; but he didn't care about that. He didn't care who saw him now: Milos would tell the Amnion where he was if the bugeyes didn't. He cared only that the room contained nothing except a small san and a couchlike chair which was cushioned and adjustable like a sickbay table.

Morn Hyland sprawled there as if she were dying.

He recognized her instantly, despite the breathing mask that covered the lower half of her face. Her eyes staring at him were deep and damaged; bruises discolored her cheekbones; her torn and dirty hair straggled as if it were falling out, killed by uncontrolled chemical reactions. Since he'd last seen her, her whole body had become as scrawny as an anorexic's: emotional and physical brutality had dismantled her poignant beauty in the same way that *Bright Beauty* had been dismantled.

Nevertheless Angus knew her. He seemed to know her more intimately than he knew himself. Her addiction, her zone implant withdrawal, was plainly written in the stretched lines of her face and the stark anguish of her eyes. She was Morn Hyland: hurt beyond bearing, abused to the verges of madness and death; but still human.

He had no idea why she was still human. At the moment the fact itself transcended everything else. He had no attention to spare for the explanation.

When he saw the horror in her gaze, the presumption of more harm, his own eyes went blind with tears.

Dismantled like *Bright Beauty*—

His datacore ruled him in every other way, but it placed no restrictions on weeping. Apparently Lebwohl or Dios had never considered the possibility that he might be capable of grief.

But like *Bright Beauty* Morn had been his; she'd served him utterly. Her beauty and her humiliation had belonged to him. Under his control she'd given to him and done for him anything he could name.

That made her precious.

And she'd saved his life—

Until Hashi Lebwohl and zone implants ripped it from him, he'd kept his bargain with her.

The sight of what that bargain had cost her sent tears as hot as blood scalding down his cheeks.

On a literal level, Nick had done this to her. But the underlying truth was that Angus himself had caused it all. It was on his head.

Caught and held by the sheer scale of her suffering, he remained still. For several seconds no one moved. Morn stared and stared at him as if she'd fallen into cerebral palsy. Nick had taken one quick look through the doorway and then withdrawn: now he stood like Mikka, guarding the ends of the hall. Sib's arms and legs seemed to yearn toward the room; yet he didn't take a step.

Then Angus' datacore compelled him to break his stasis. His time was running out.

His zone implants eased some of the tension in his lungs. As if he were wincing he raised his hand to the controls on his chest-plate and activated his external speaker. Blinking hard to clear his eyes, he husked softly, "Morn, listen. I've got a ship. And I've got Davies. He's there—at the ship. We're going to get you out of here."

When he said her son's name, her head jerked up. Darkness smoldered in her gouged eyes, as if her head were full of the gap; as if her mind had gone into tach and couldn't get out.

"Can you stand?" he asked; almost pleaded. "Can you walk? We'll carry you if we have to, but we're all more likely to survive if you can walk."

Her eyes went on smoldering at him as if he spoke a language she no longer understood.

"Morn, please. Say something. Answer me."

In another moment he was going to fall on his knees and beg her for a response.

Without warning, Sib pushed past him into the room.

"Morn," he panted, "it's me. Sib Mackern." His tone was fraught with concern and fear. "We're all here—all the ones who didn't want Nick to sell you. Mikka, Vector, even Pup. Vector and Pup are with Davies. Angus is telling the truth. They're guarding the ship.

"Nick is here, too. We needed him. But he's lost *Captain's Fancy*. He doesn't have anywhere else to go.

"Morn, I helped you once. So did Vector and Mikka. We didn't give you what you needed, but we did as much as we thought we could. Let us help you now.

"Davies can't hold the ship for long. If we don't get back soon, we'll lose him. We'll lose everything."

Morn gave no sign that his words meant anything: she reacted only to her son's name. Yet that was enough. Each time Sib said, "Davies," she moved farther. First she sat up; then she shifted her legs off the chair; finally she stood.

Muffled by her mask, her voice sounded as frail as mist.

"Don't let Nick touch him."

"I've got a better idea," Angus grated. Morn's words triggered a change in him: as soon as she spoke, his grief became a cold, settled, and familiar rage. He stepped out into the hall. Too quick to be stopped, he snatched the impact rifle off Nick's shoulder, then reentered the cell and thrust the gun toward Morn. "Here. *You* don't let Nick touch him."

She took the rifle and clutched it as if it were the only real thing in the room. Her fingers settled on the firing stud.

"We have to go EVA, Morn." Sib's voice seemed to sweat concern. "It's our only way back to *Trumpet*. I brought you a suit." He opened his arms to show her his burden. "I'll help you put it on."

Abruptly Angus swung away. He couldn't watch anymore. And his programming had other requirements for him to satisfy. Ignoring his distress, databases opened in his head, feeding him everything the UMCP knew about fusion generations; everything he'd learned by mapping Billingate's power systems.

Charged with other men's purposes and his own violence, he left the cell.

At once Nick confronted him. "You sonofabitch. Now she's going to kill me."

Angus had no attention to spare. "Not as long as she thinks you'll help keep Davies alive."

Turning his back on Nick, he faced Mikka.

She met his gaze with the bitter glare of a woman who was ready for anything. Her hands cradled her weapons as if she'd known how to use them all her life.

"I'm leaving now," he announced bluntly. "I've got other things to do. You're in command until I get back."

Her eyes widened slightly, but she didn't interrupt; didn't protest.

"It's up to you to take her to *Trumpet*." He meant only Morn. He didn't care what happened to anyone else. "Get her aboard—her and Davies. Then seal the ship. I can open the airlock whenever I need to.

"Remember, you're in command, not *him*." Angus jerked a nod at Nick. "Don't let him get in your way. If he gives you any trouble, shoot him for me."

Nick's chuckle sounded wild; a little crazy. "Captain Thermopile, you're out of your fucking mind."

Angus ignored him.

"I need an hour," he told Mikka. "If I'm not back by then, leave without me. Rip *Trumpet* out of her berth and run. You won't be able to defend yourselves worth shit, you don't know enough about her, but you won't have any other choice. If you stay here after that, you're finished."

Mikka's glower seemed to promise that she would obey him as long as she remained alive.

"One hour," he repeated harshly.

Then he strode away as if he'd been turned loose.

He was temporarily at peace with his programming. A keen joy like a paean of murder began to sing in his heart as he moved alone into the clenched, threatening emptiness of the corridors which led toward Billingate and destruction.

MORN

She couldn't think. Words meant nothing: there were no words which could contain the long silence of her cell while the Amnion waited for their mutagens to transform her. And nothing else made sense.

Angus was here—but of course that was impossible. How much suffering did she have to endure before she would be free of him?

He said he came to rescue her. That wasn't just impossible, it was stupid: a man like him would never place himself in this kind of jeopardy to rescue anyone, especially not a cop who knew so much about him.

He told her where Davies was, he seemed to imply that he'd already rescued her son—which wasn't so much impossible as entirely inconceivable.

Yet Sib Mackern was here as well. That was true, wasn't it? She could recognize him through his faceplate, couldn't she? He was trembling to help her: solicitude seemed to pour off him in waves, despite the interference of Mylar and plexulose. Unless the whole thing was an hallucination—unless the reality of what Nick had done to her and what she'd done to humankind had at last become so unbearable that she'd fled from it into dreams—

Some of *Captain's Fancy*'s people wanted to help her? They'd come to rescue her? With Nick? And *Angus*?

She clung to her son's name and the grips of the impact rifle so that she wouldn't break into mad, lost sobs.

STEPHEN R. DONALDSON

Sib tried to help her; he urged her limbs into an EVA suit. She wanted his help, wanted the suit itself. But Angus had said, You *don't let Succorso touch him*. She couldn't release the rifle long enough to put on the suit.

Gently Sib took hold of her left hand and tried to urge her fingers loose.

As sudden as a figment, Nick appeared in the doorway. Keying his external speaker, he snapped, "If you clowns don't hurry, none of us are going to get out of this alive."

As if it were cued by his voice, a concussion shuddered through the cell. For an instant the sulfurous lighting flickered. Dust sifted from the corners of the walls. Somewhere nearby a powerful explosion had taken place.

What had she seen in Angus' hands? What kind of gun was that? It'd looked like a scale model of a matter cannon.

Was he fighting for her escape with a *matter cannon*?

He was capable of that. The same indomitable cowardice which made him a rapist also made him deadly.

A small mewling sound came from her mouth as she forced open her fingers, let Sib pull her arm into the EVA suit.

Next the right: she transferred the rifle to her left hand, then shoved her right urgently into the glove of the suit. Second by second a nameless desperation mounted in her. Each of her forearms bore the marks of a tiny wound where the Amnion had injected her with mutagens—and another where they'd drawn blood. All the norepinephrine and dopamine and immunity had been sucked out of her into those small vials, betraying her whole species. She had nothing left except fear.

She thought that Sib would seal her suit, but he didn't. Instead he began to strap some kind of interior harness around her hips. "It's a new system for controlling your jets," he explained as he worked. "It's like a waldo—you move your hips, and the jets fire. You may need it." Lamely he added, "I can't control it myself."

Now she knew she was dreaming. She'd trained with suits like this in the Academy: *Starmaster* had been equipped with them. But the technology was recent. No one except the UMCP had it.

As quickly as he could, Sib finished with the harness, then sealed her into the suit. Last came the helmet. He held it in front of her, waiting for her permission to put it on.

Because this was all a hallucination, and she knew it would soon end, leaving her as doomed and damned as ever, she pulled a deep breath through her mask, then nodded.

Sib swept the mask off her head and replaced it with her helmet.

As soon as the helmet was sealed, its indicators came to life, giving her oxygen, temperature, and vital sign status; assuring her of its integrity against hard vacuum.

"Let's go, Morn."

Sib's voice through the internal speakers sounded too close, too intimate. Nevertheless she didn't raise her hands to reduce the gain: they were locked onto her rifle, and she didn't intend to remove them again. Like a madwoman she believed that as long as she gripped the gun she could keep the dream of rescue from ending.

Anchored by the pressure of her fingers on the rifle, she allowed Sib to take her arm and draw her out of the cell.

"Finally!" Nick snarled. "Come *on.*"

Without waiting for an answer, he broke into a run toward the end of the passage.

Hadn't Sib said, *Mikka, Vector, even Pup?* But only Mikka Vasaczk stood in the hall. Where were Vector and Pup?

And where was Angus? Morn expected to find him there, keeping the whole Amnion installation at bay with his strange gun. But he'd gone somewhere.

Blurred by the polarization of two faceplates, Mikka peered at her. Mikka's face was distorted and familiar: her glower looked like the anxiety of an old friend.

"Are you all right?" she asked. "Did we get here in time?"

Morn's throat worked convulsively, swallowing sobs. "They took my blood." That was the worst accusation she could level against herself. "They've got the drug."

"When we have some time"—Nick's voice carried clearly from the end of the hall—"you can tell me how *you* got the drug."

Morn hardly heard him. She was talking to Mikka.

"I betrayed—"

She fought to control herself, but she couldn't keep her weeping down. Small sounds leaked like whimpers from her throat. Without her zone implant control, she was nothing.

"Maybe not." Nick's tone was harsh. "I told you, it only stays in your body for about four hours. Whether they got it depends on when you ate the capsules and when they drew blood.

"Now *come on,* goddamn it! Someday even *these* fuckers are going to figure out what happened and do something about it."

When and *when.* Morn clung to the idea the same way she clung to her rifle. Was it possible that her dream included hope? Was it permitted in this hallucination that she'd saved herself without betraying humankind?

Maybe she could remember what she'd done; figure out the sequence of events and time. It was a fact that Nick had once told her the immunity drug stayed in the body for about four hours. If she could recall when she'd taken the capsules in relation to when the Amnion had taken her blood—

All right, think. *When* did she take the first one? *When* did she take the second? the third?

Obsessed by time, she let Mikka and Sib pull her forward.

Everything she'd suffered for days or months felt like a swirl of nightmare: she couldn't distinguish one day from the next, certainly not one hour from the next. Nevertheless her need for this one hope was absolute. She wrestled her sore, brutalized mind for clarity, despite the fact that she was running now, that Sib and Mikka had dragged her into a run along a wide hall full of cruel illumination and intersections like maws; despite the fact that Nick and Mikka seemed to blaze away with their handguns almost constantly, and even Sib brandished fire as if he thought he could hit something that way.

An energy beam scorched past her head. Nick yelled as he fired; Sib gasped, "Christ!" For an instant the air sang with streaks of coherent force and light. Then Nick veered into a side passage. Mikka and Sib kept Morn close behind him.

Because she hadn't known what was going to happen, she'd taken one capsule as soon as she found the vial in Nick's cabin. Of course that immunity had passed out of her body during the long hours when she'd been kept drugged. But she'd taken another dose after Mikka had awakened her, before Mikka had delivered her to Nick. After that Nick had walked her to the Amnion sector and given her away. How much time passed then before she was injected with the mutagen? Half an hour at most? Roughly an hour since she'd eaten the capsule?

She'd been too terrified to measure time; but she had the impression that the Amnion had waited quite a while before drawing her blood.

She shook her head. Not good enough. *Quite a while* could mean anything. She would never be able to figure out the exact interval.

Sobs or gasps seemed to burst delicately inside her helmet, like bubbles.

Then a new idea entered her head like a ship crossing out of the gap.

This place had no research facilities. Maybe the Amnion hadn't drawn her blood promptly because they couldn't test it in any case. And *maybe* her immunity—artificial, like all her other resources—was simply sitting here, sealed in sterile containers to await transportation to Enablement.

That was another kind of hope.

Almost immediately Nick led the way to a lift. The instant the doors opened he herded Mikka, Sib, and Morn into the car. It rose so swiftly that Morn's knees nearly failed.

Where was Angus? Why couldn't she hear his matter cannon?

Taut with exertion, Sib's voice strained in her ears. "This isn't the way we came, Nick."

Nick replied with a growl of disgust.

"That makes it safer," Mikka panted tightly.

"We've got to stop those warships," Morn breathed. "*Calm Horizons. Tranquil Hegemony.* Stop them."

Sib gaped at her.

"Why?" Mikka demanded.

At last Morn noticed the desperation in Mikka's eyes. She saw that Sib was close to exhaustion. Pale and bloodless, Nick's scars gleamed as if they'd been cut to the bone.

"So they can't take my blood back to Enablement."

"How?" Now Mikka sounded as weary as Sib looked. "We've lost *Captain's Fancy.* Our ship is a gap scout. Assuming we get back to her, she doesn't carry the kind of guns that stop warships."

"We aren't going to stop anybody," Nick rasped at Morn. Through his faceplate his eyes burned with the desire to inflict pain. "Just staying alive is going to be the best trick we've ever pulled off.

"Your Captain Thermo-pile told me a little secret. Something I had no idea about. When we went to Enablement, the Amnion already knew you were a cop. They knew I was working for the cops."

In shock, Mikka barked, *"What?"*

Nick ignored her. "That's why they were willing to kill us in the gap. They knew we were going to cheat as soon as we started talking to them. And it's another reason they want your kid so badly. He has your mind. Just getting you wouldn't be good enough. They want your mind intact—a cop mind that isn't protected or distorted by zone implants."

The lift stopped; opened. Balancing his guns in his hands, he sprang out to scan the corridor.

"Oh, Nick," Mikka said like a moan. "You fool. You fool."

"I don't care," Morn murmured while she followed him. As far as she knew, she was talking to herself. "They've got to be stopped. There must be some way to do it."

She didn't care what it cost. She wanted to burn her long pain clean in a blaze of destruction. If Davies died in the process, at least he would die human.

And he would understand. He was more than her son: he was an undistorted replica of her reasoning and knowledge, her passions and needs. He would feel the same way she did.

Off to her left, an Amnioni appeared in a doorway. Sib flung fire in that direction; but he stumbled, and his shot scored the floor. As he fell, he lost his grip on Morn's arm.

She squeezed the firing stud of her rifle; heard a detonation like the sound of shattering stone. The Amnioni sprawled backward in a splash of rust and green.

Sib caught up with her as fast as he could. "Thanks," he gulped. "I'm no good at this."

The blast seemed to ignite her body. Shrugging off Mikka's support, she ran on her own strength after Nick.

Now she was ready to fight. Her hands ached on the rifle, hungry for use.

The passages were empty, however. The Amnion had mustered their defenses elsewhere.

Nick led the way as if he knew exactly where he was going.

For his own reasons, he stopped at another lift. The car was slow to answer: according to its indicators, it had to come from several levels below. He swore steadily under his breath while he waited; as the doors finally slid open, he braced himself to fire.

Like the corridor, the car was empty.

"Is this it?" Sib asked urgently.

Nick entered the car without answering.

Mikka prodded Sib and Morn ahead of her. "I think so," she panted.

Upward again. Now Morn rose as if she were going to sail through the top of her head; as if her spirit could soar straight on out of the lift and the installation, carrying only her rifle into space to do battle with the warships.

Unfortunately the rules of gravity held. When the car stopped at its highest level, her body still contained her. Abruptly the energy of impact fire drained out of her. She felt leaden and mortal, weighed down by the consequences of withdrawal and the implications of weakness. She hardly knew what she was seeing when the lift opened on the iris of an airlock.

An airlock. Her thoughts struggled slowly, clogged by old prostration. EVA.

We have to go EVA. It's our only way back to Trumpet.

If she could have escaped the rock's g, she could have flown her fate altogether; could have used the suit's jets to waft her effortlessly out into the dark. Even against g the jets might be powerful enough to bear her away.

But the pressure might trigger her gap-sickness.

In any case, Davies was waiting for her; he needed her. For his sake she had to remain confined to her flesh a little longer.

As the iris dilated, it seemed to suck Nick into the airlock. Immediately he moved to the control panel and keyed the cycle. Mikka sent Sib and Morn after him, then paused to immobilize the lift by firing a laser into its controls.

The inner iris was already closing. She had to dive through it to reach the airlock.

Morn listened to the sibilant whine of depressurization and tried to believe that she was strong enough to reach *Trumpet;* that she would be able to find the strength somewhere, without the help of her black box.

As soon as the outer door irised, Nick strode onto the concrete apron of the airlock. Without waiting for anyone, he hurried out of sight around the corner of the bunker.

Beyond the lock loomed the planetoid's black rock. A powerful illumination came from behind the head of the lift: the apron lay in shadow, but cold white streaked the fractured surface where Nick had gone.

Again Mikka paused to slag the controls. No one would follow her and her companions out this way.

Gripping the rifle as if it could keep her on her feet, Morn went after Nick.

Almost at once she caught sight of *Tranquil Hegemony*.

The ship's docking lights defined her against the impenetrable heavens; the cold white glare etched her guns and antennae. The bulbous, inhuman shape which the Amnion preferred made her look squat despite her size. Past the metallic hatch of a shuttle port, her bulk lowered like a thunderhead over the raw stone.

Now Morn could see that the white illumination came from the arc lamps of the visitors' docks. Nick ran in that direction, bounding over the rocks as fast as he could. Because she knew him intimately—because she understood that he was as treacherous as the surface—she suddenly grasped why he was in such a hurry.

He wanted to reach *Trumpet* in time to take command before Angus returned; in time to lock Angus out.

A new sting of fear swelled her heart. Nick had her black box. She preferred Angus.

Could Davies hear her? If she called her son's name into her pickup, would he be able to receive her voice? Could she warn him?

She didn't try. Her throat locked, holding her silent, when she saw Nick stop suddenly.

Planting his feet, he raised his arms to the dark. His helmet tilted back.

"Do it!" he cried. Fury and desperation made him frantic. "You little bitch, I gave you an order! I want you to *do it!*"

The dark didn't answer.

Mikka and Sib came up beside Morn; they drew her with them toward the harsh light. For a moment or two, however, she could hardly move her legs. The intensity of Nick's cry closed around her chest like a clutch of panic.

She was wrong about him.

Oh, God, what was he doing? What was he *doing?*

"I wish Liete didn't worship him," Mikka muttered bitterly. "She should have better sense."

"What did he tell her?" Sib gulped.

"*You* ask him," she retorted. "I've got too many other things to worry about."

Without warning the light changed color. Morn saw sulfur lick like yellow flames across the side of Mikka's suit.

At the same time she felt the rock under her boots rumbling.

"Nick!" Mikka yelled. "Get down!"

Morn turned toward the new glow.

The hatch of the shuttle port was in motion; it ground open like a window, spilling yellow illumination and a froth of atmosphere frozen to ice in an instant.

Simultaneously Mikka and Sib called, "Morn!" Mikka caught her arm, dragged her flat on the serrated knuckles of the rock.

A heartbeat later, the blast of thrusters shook the surface like an explosion, and a shuttle shaped like a g-stretched ball rode atmospheric ice out of the port. At full burn the craft hurled herself upward.

Morn and her companions were too close. Thrust dispersion hit them so hard that it might have torn their suits. Fortunately the vacuum leeched most of the force away. She felt the pressure wave slam along the length of her body and pass on.

All the status indicators inside her helmet showed a reassuring green.

Through her teeth Mikka hissed, "Now!" She sprang upright. "Let's go."

Panting raggedly, Sib hauled himself to his feet.

Morn stayed where she was.

For some reason, she couldn't take her eyes off *Tranquil Hegemony.*

Right in front of her the ship's running lights came on.

"Morn?" Sib choked out. "Are you hurt? Do you need help?"

"Oh, *shit,*" Mikka moaned as she saw what Morn was looking at.

Batteries of searchlights stabbed abruptly off the sides of the warship. For a moment they wandered aimlessly; then they pulled into focus and swept toward the airlock bunker and the docks. Almost immediately they began to quarter the surface.

They were looking for the people who'd attacked their installation.

Morn saw the ship's guns swivel as they came to bear.

Tranquil Hegemony intended to blast her enemies off the face of the rock.

LIETE

    Controlling herself fiercely, Liete resisted the impulse to demand premature reports from the bridge crew. She could feel a pressure building in her chest, an inchoate frenzy accumulating like the force of a storm. G had simplified since *Captain's Fancy* lost thrust. Nevertheless she had difficulty breathing. Nick had been inside the Amnion sector too long. If he stayed there much longer, the strain of holding her emotions down would rupture the lining of her lungs.

At last her restraint failed. She couldn't wait out the silence. Like a poised whip, she asked, "Status?"

Lind looked over at her. His board was already putting out all the garbage it could; he had little else to do but listen. "*Tranquil Hegemony* and *Calm Horizons* are talking to each other. *Soar* is in it, too. They've turned up the gain so much they sound like they're yelling, but we don't know the code." Lamely he added, "I'm no cryptographer." Then he finished, "They're going to do something, that's for sure. But I can't guess what."

Liete nodded. She didn't care what answers she received. All she wanted was the distraction of hearing people speak.

"Malda?"

"I've got a twenty-five-percent charge on the matter cannon." The targ first seemed stretched too thin, near her breaking point. Her hair straggled past her eyes, but she didn't have the energy to tie it back. "We can fire one gun hard, or let all of them dribble."

"Pastille?"

Pastille snapped his fingers as if he resented the interruption. "Maneuvering thrust, that's it. I can take us back to dock like this, but we can't burn."

"Good enough," Liete asserted. "The point is, it's more than they think we can do. Keep at it. The longer they wait, the more we'll be able to surprise them."

Abruptly Malda swung her g-seat to face Liete.

"Liete, we can hit *Soar* right now. She's our target, isn't she? If we fire at this range, we can blow her guts out. Why don't we do it now and get it over with?"

Liete started to say, Because I'm hoping we can find a way to do this and stay alive.

She started to think, Because Nick went into the Amnion installation in an EVA suit, and he hasn't come back yet.

But Carmel interrupted her.

"Liete!" Rigid in her g-seat, the scan first stared at her readouts while her fingers ran commands which focused instruments and sifted their data. "We've got people coming out of the Amnion sector. One, two—I see four of them. They look like the same four who went in."

"I can't be sure," she muttered apologetically. "Our scan isn't that precise. But their suits reflect the same way."

"Where are they headed?" Liete fought down her urgency, struggled to keep her voice calm. "What about the three who went to the dish?"

At the same time Pastille demanded, "What in hell did he *go* there for? I thought he wanted Morn back. He's been sick ever since his gonads got a taste of her."

Liete was instantly furious at him for asking the question she most wanted answered herself. But Carmel didn't let the helm third deflect her.

"Back toward *Trumpet*," she reported. "One of them's ahead of the others, moving faster. The other three are staying together, but they're going in the same direction."

"The three from the dish are back at their ship. Just standing there. I assume they're waiting to cover the others."

Four people entered the domain of the Amnion: four came out. Had they failed to get what they went in for? Or had someone been lost?

Had Nick been lost?

Deserts and doom filled Liete. She refused to believe that Nick had been lost.

As if she were prescient, she asked Malda, "Have you got targ on *Tranquil Hegemony?*"

Malda nodded just as Carmel announced sharply, "The Amnion are opening their shuttle port!"

At once Liete sat forward, began pulling data from scan, helm, and targ to her board; getting herself ready.

"*Now* what's going on?" Pastille growled. "Are they abandoning the installation? Did Nick do them that much damage?"

Fortunately he didn't appear to expect an answer.

"You want targ on that?" Malda asked. "If we hit it now, we can cripple the port. Or we can get the shuttle when she blows dock."

"No," Liete ordered. "Leave her alone. She's not our target.

"Power up faster. Pastille, do the same. *Now*, while *Calm Horizons* and *Soar* have something else to think about."

"Port open," Carmel reported. "Here she comes." An instant later the scan first barked, "Jesus, she's in a hurry! That's a full-burn launch." Almost immediately, however, she reverted to stolidity. "She's coming right at us. If she doesn't correct, we're going to collide."

A heartbeat later, Carmel added, "She's correcting now." Liete saw the figures on her own readouts. "She doesn't want us—she's heading for *Soar*. Or *Calm Horizons*. But she won't miss by much. They must really believe we're paralyzed.

"They can't abandon the installation that way," she continued steadily. "She isn't big enough. I estimate she only carries ten of them."

Liete called for status again.

Matter cannon charge had reached forty percent. Thrust was up to thirty-five.

"Message from *Calm Horizons!*" Lind gulped. "New orders. Complete shutdown—everything, even maintenance. They want us to stop putting out all this noise."

Too much, it was too much, Liete couldn't think about so many conflicting priorities. The wind in her head had become a swirling buffet, full of confusion—

"Oh, shit," Carmel breathed. "*Tranquil Hegemony* just put on her running lights. She's powering up."

Liete could hardly breathe; pressure seemed to pull all the air out of her lungs.

Where was Nick? Where was *Nick*?

One thing at a time, she told herself. Just one. You can do it if you take one thing at a time.

"Is she undocking?" she demanded. "Are they using her to abandon the installation?"

"No," Carmel responded quickly. "That's not thrust emission, that's matter cannon." In shock she pulled away from her board, faced Liete across the bridge. "She's charging her guns. And she's using searchlights. She's going to blast those people down there. She's going to blast *Trumpet*."

Just for a second, Liete's courage failed.

Blast.

Those people.

And *Trumpet*.

Nick was a dead man—

Her whole body flinched as if a stun-prod had been fired into her chest.

—unless she found a way to save him.

In that instant the long black wind swept all her fears and conflicts out of her.

Steadily she asked the scan first, "How long before she's ready to fire?"

"How should I know?" Carmel gritted. "I'm no expert on Amnion warships." Then the passion in Liete's eyes stopped her. Abashed, she murmured, "A minute? Two at most?"

Liete nodded. "How long before that shuttle passes us?"

"At that acceleration?" Carmel consulted her board. "A minute and a half. But she won't keep burning—she'll cut thrust any second now. Otherwise she won't be able to brake in time for *Soar*. Maybe not even in time for *Calm Horizons*."

Liete couldn't wait that long. *Calm Horizons* was trying to shut *Captain's Fancy* down: Liete's subterfuge was about to be discovered. And her target was *Soar*. Nick had ordered her to kill that ship. At any cost. No matter what else happened. Somehow he'd maneuvered

Sorus Chatelaine into this position so that she and her ship would be vulnerable. If Liete didn't attack now, *Soar* or *Calm Horizons* would realize they'd been duped; they would understand their danger and open fire.

But *Tranquil Hegemony* was charging her guns to smash seven people and their ship off the face of Thanatos Minor.

And one of them was Nick. He was out there, exposed like a dummy in a practice range. He couldn't survive against those guns— couldn't survive without *Trumpet*—

Liete Corregio considered his life more important than his orders.

"Pastille." Her voice was only a whisper, but it carried like a cry. "I want braking thrust. Stop us—head us back the way we came."

"What the hell for?" he objected. "I thought you said we're after *Soar*."

To silence him, she explained, "I want us closer to that shuttle. We'll use her for cover."

Pastille glared back at Liete, then turned to his console. Swallowing protests, he went to work.

At once braking g slammed Liete against her belt as *Captain's Fancy*'s thrusters roared.

She shrugged off the stress. "Malda, targ on *Tranquil Hegemony*. Aim for her guns—hit her with everything you've got. On my order."

Malda's hands shook. Fighting to control them, she pounded her keys vehemently, as if she were furious.

"Carmel, how far away is that shuttle?"

The scan first understood combat: when it came, she had no hesitation in her. "She's cut thrust—she's coasting. Alongside in thirty seconds or so. Depending on Pastille."

Thirty seconds. Liete snapped a look at her chronometer. *Calm Horizons* didn't have a clear field—*Soar* was in the way—but *Soar* could fire at any time. If Sorus Chatelaine feared hitting the shuttle, she might hold off.

On the other hand, if she thought *Captain's Fancy* was about to ram the shuttle, she would certainly attack.

At this range and speed, evasive maneuvers would be useless.

And Carmel wouldn't be able to give any warning. Liete would know that *Soar* had fired when *Captain's Fancy* took the hit, not before.

Carmel and Lind had been with Nick for a long time: in their separate ways, they had come to terms with death and desperation. And Malda loved Nick with her own private urgency. Liete could rely on them all. Only Pastille would fail her.

When he realized what she meant to do, he would try to stop her.

The black wind blew like a song through her heart. Everything that held her back was gone: she was alive with scorched fidelity and doom. As if she were inspired by music, she began dummying helm function to her board; secretly routing control of *Captain's Fancy* away from Pastille.

So that she could save Nick.

MORN

Morn watched helplessly as *Tranquil Hegemony*'s guns came into line as if they'd already found her; as if she were as distinct as a beacon against Thanatos Minor's dark stone. Matter cannon at this range— She told herself that if she'd had the strength she would have climbed to her feet and fled; she wouldn't have given up; while she could still draw breath and move her legs she would have done her best to survive. Nevertheless she knew it wasn't weakness which held her down.

It was futility.

From her dedicated berth, *Tranquil Hegemony* could destroy everything between her and the planetoid's horizons. One barrage would reduce the docks to rubble: it would be more than enough to wipe out four people in EVA suits and a single gap scout.

"Run!" Mikka shouted as if she were raging.

Sib didn't move. Like Morn, he seemed to have come to the end of his strength; his will. "We can't outrun that," he said softly.

"They're starting cold!" Mikka yelled. "They need a minute to bring up power, maybe two!" She grabbed at his arm, at Morn's, tried to heave them into motion. "Come on!"

"Mikka." Sib sounded calm, almost resigned. He'd worn out his fear. "Two minutes or twenty, it doesn't make any difference. We can't outrun those guns. Even if we reach the ship—even if we get aboard. One hit will crumple her like an empty canister."

He looked back toward the lift bunker, then returned his gaze to the warship. "I wish Angus was here. I would like to hear him tell us why he thought this was ever going to work."

"I don't care!" Mikka cried. "You can't just stand here and watch yourself die! You've got to at least *run!*

"I promised Pup I was coming back!"

Wheeling away, she sprinted over the stones in the direction of the docks and *Trumpet*.

Nick went on peering upward as if he thought he should be able to see his ship somewhere.

"Morn, are you there?"

The voice in her helmet sounded like Angus'. But it couldn't be; he was gone; and anyway it was too young for Angus, too scared.

"I heard Nick. I heard Mikka and Sib. Are you with them? Where are you?

"Morn, where *are* you?"

Davies.

He was nearby—within reach of her suit's receiver. Angus had told her the truth.

She'd believed that she would never see her son again. Now he was about to be killed. Like Sib and Mikka and Nick, like Morn herself, he would be hammered to pulp among the rocks. Then the rocks would melt in the after-heat of the blast, and the pulp would burn down to ash and cinders until it fused with the stone.

"Jets," she panted. "The jets." Her hands and legs came under her as if they were in someone else's control; she tottered upright. "They're faster. It's worth a try."

Slapping at her chest plate, she activated the jet harness.

The first burst of compressed gas lifted her in a long bound past Sib. One careful cock of her hips; another burst: restrained only by g, she vaulted to Mikka's side just as Mikka activated her own jets and sprang ahead.

But Sib wasn't coming.

"Wait," he muttered distantly. "I don't know how to use these things. I can't handle them."

Morn turned to help him—

Davies, I'm sorry!

—turned in time to see a piece of the void catch fire.

It was too sudden to be understood: the synapses of her brain couldn't keep up with it. Nevertheless training and experience identified what was happening as she witnessed it.

Two separate cannon blazed almost simultaneously—guns from different ships. The first burned toward the source of the second: it hit, spewing coruscation like a solar flare, emissions on every conceivable wavelength. If Thanatos Minor had possessed an atmosphere, the concussion might have deafened her.

At nearly the same instant the second cannon drove a lance of light-constant destruction down on *Tranquil Hegemony*.

That blast reached Morn: it rolled through the rock, staggering her. A noiseless visceral shriek poured off *Tranquil Hegemony*'s sides as if the ship were dying; as if she were being scorched alive.

The heavens went immediately black; the void engulfed the embattled ships. But *Tranquil Hegemony* remained visible in the glare of the arc lamps and the glow of her own running lights.

The first shot must have affected the targ of the second by some small fraction of a degree. *Tranquil Hegemony* hadn't suffered a direct hit. One bulging section of her side had been torn open: the shriek was the tangible tremor of escaping atmosphere commingled with warning sirens, battle klaxons, and the automatic yowl of interior seals. She was hurt; badly hurt.

Yet Morn knew at a glance that the warship hadn't been crippled. She may still have been space-worthy: she was certainly capable of firing her guns.

After faltering for a few seconds, her searchlights stopped quartering the surface and swept away to focus like targeting lasers on *Trumpet*.

Without warning, Nick began to howl:

"You bitch!"

"Morn!" Davies' voice rang in her ears. "Are you there?"

"Yes." She could hardly force herself to speak; her voice scraped her throat like a wounded thing. "We're coming."

"That must have been Liete," Mikka gasped. "Goddamn it, how could she *miss*? Even Simper can run targ better than that. Malda could do it in her sleep!"

"*Captain's Fancy* was hit," Sib breathed thinly. "I saw it. That must be what went wrong."

"Take cover." Morn did her best to make Davies hear her. "I

don't know where. Not on *Trumpet*. They're going to pulverize her as soon as damage control seals that hole and reroutes their systems. Try one of the empty berths. Maybe you can find an access hatch and get inside."

"Morn, there's no point." She recognized Vector easily. "It'll be like trying to take cover on a battlefield. Operations was ready to kill us before all this started. Now they've lost communications. They're desperate in there. They'll ash anything that moves first, and wonder what it was later."

In spite of what he'd just said, she could tell that he was smiling as he added, "Still, it's nice to hear your voice."

Nick had stopped howling, but he didn't move. Rigid with fury or despair, he faced the dark heavens and remained motionless, gripping his fists at his sides.

"Come on," Mikka breathed into her pickup. "Even if I'm as good as dead, I want to keep my promises."

In a gust of compressed gas, she headed toward the docks and *Trumpet*.

Morn made no effort to get Nick's attention. Let him stand there until his ship turned cold and came apart. There was nothing she could do for him—and she wouldn't have done it if there had been. He still had her zone implant control.

Instead she went to help Sib manage his jets.

She didn't need to hurry now: she knew that. She would die when *Tranquil Hegemony* was ready to kill her. Nothing could change that. Nevertheless she wanted to get as far as possible from the warship and everything Amnion; she wanted to stand beside her son, and the few people who had taken pity on her, when she died.

Mikka had already reached the concrete by the time Morn got Sib moving. Riding their jets, she and the data first left Nick behind. As if they were alone on the rock—as if they were ghosts with nothing left to trouble them—they let the hiss of compressed gas carry them toward *Trumpet*. Sib had dropped his handgun; after a moment Morn realized that she'd lost her rifle somewhere. But they didn't need weapons anymore. Like Mikka ahead of them, they took no notice of the possibility that the Bill or even the Amnion might send guards out after them. That danger had ceased to have any meaning.

Once she paused to look back at Nick. Small and slumped against the looming bulk of *Tranquil Hegemony*, he'd broken out of his rictus and was moving slowly away from the warship. Maybe he, too, had decided he didn't want to be alone when he died.

After she and Sib gained the concrete, they were able to travel more quickly. As his handling of his jets improved he began to skim forward as if he were skipping. With a shrug and a ghost's smile, she scudded beside him. When she died, she would be free, at last and forever.

No doubt *Tranquil Hegemony* was holding fire until the Amnion could be sure they would hit all their targets with one blast. Skimming and prancing like lunatic children, Morn and Sib crossed the arc-lit docks until they were close enough to see Mikka and three other people illuminated by searchlights in front of a Needle-class gap scout which must have been *Trumpet*.

She deactivated her jets and slowed to a walk. A step or two later, Sib did the same.

"Morn?" Davies asked. He sounded plaintive; scarcely able to believe that she was there. "Morn?"

She didn't know which of the four he was: she was still too far away to recognize individuals through the polarization of their faceplates. She raised a hand to identify herself. When he also raised his hand, she smiled quietly, even though he couldn't see it.

"Why don't they get it over with?" Pup muttered tightly. "What are they waiting for?"

No one answered him.

As if she were at peace, Morn turned to watch *Tranquil Hegemony* kill them all.

From a distance of at least three k, the warship looked smaller; less fatal. Morn could no longer distinguish the gun ports: she could barely see the guns themselves. If her faceplate hadn't protected her from the stabbing intensity of the searchlights, she wouldn't have been able to see the ship at all. Nevertheless the range was trivial for matter cannon. Even badly designed guns wouldn't suffer enough dispersion to weaken their impact for several thousand k—and nothing the Amnion made was badly designed.

At least a thousand meters away across the concrete, Nick also had turned to watch. Some intuition must have warned him to look back at the charged shape of the warship.

Like Morn, he must have seen the flame of thrust like a torch in the void.

At once he began to howl again as if his heart were being torn out.

Suddenly the searchlights cut off. For an instant the changed illumination confused Morn's vision. Through the residual incandescence, she thought she saw *Tranquil Hegemony*'s guns wheel in their ports, fighting to reorient themselves.

The torch overhead grew longer, plunging like a comet.

Misaimed and useless, lasers from the warship's sides emblazoned the heavens. She'd been taken too much by surprise. And she was already hurt. She couldn't defend herself.

At the last second Mikka cried frantically, *"Liete!"*

Thrust flaming, *Captain's Fancy* came down like a scream out of the deep dark. Lasers caught up with her before she hit, but they were too late. Truer than her own targ, she sledgehammered straight into the center of the damaged warship.

Without transition both vessels were transformed from poised, rigid metal to pure fire and brisance.

Morn lost sight of the cataclysm momentarily: she was falling and couldn't look. The uncontained detonation of *Captain's Fancy*'s drive and *Tranquil Hegemony*'s weapons sent a shock wave through the rock and the concrete as if they were water. Stone shattered; concrete cracked and buckled like ice; the surface under Morn bucked so hard that she stumbled to her knees. Arc lamps fizzled and spat; some of them died. Steam plumed from wounds like volcanic vents in Billingate's structural integrity.

By the time she lurched back to her feet, *Captain's Fancy* and *Tranquil Hegemony* had collapsed into each other. Visual echoes of flame streaked the dark, but the fire itself died rapidly as its energy and the vacuum devoured the last of the spilled oxygen.

Nick was closer to the point of impact: the shock wave had knocked him flat on his back. Except for the palpable grinding of concrete as it settled into new shapes, there was no sound anywhere but the prolonged outcry of his anguish.

Then Mikka sighed, "Oh, Liete." Tears filled her voice; but Morn couldn't tell whether they were tears of relief or loss.

"Come on," Sib murmured. He plucked at Morn's arm, touched Mikka's shoulder. "Let's go aboard. We still have to get out of here somehow."

Finally Nick's protest choked away into silence.

Instead of moving toward the ship, Mikka went to her brother and wrapped her arms around him fiercely.

"Sib's right." Vector spoke in tense bursts, as if he had difficulty breathing. "*Calm Horizons* is still out there. So is *Soar*. And the Bill—probably isn't feeling very charitable. They won't want to let us get away with this."

Leftover flame seemed to echo in Morn's head. She feared that if she tried to move, she would lose her balance again. *Captain's Fancy* was gone: nothing remained of the place where she'd abandoned herself to Nick, perfected her zone implant addiction, and fought for her son's life except twisted metal and ruin. Liete Corregio, Pastille, Simper, Alba Parmute, Carmel, Karster, Lind—the dead were too many to be numbered. At last she understood that it was all too expensive. This terrible expenditure of lives and pain had to stop.

"She's Angus' ship," she breathed like a memory of fire.

"But he put Mikka in command," Sib said as if that changed everything.

Mikka, Morn thought, not Nick. Angus hadn't given her away again. He was still himself enough to distrust Nick.

When she turned, she found Davies beside her.

"Where is he?" her son asked. "Is he coming back?"

"I don't know." If she could have forgotten the blaze and concussion of impact, she might have wept. "He broke into my cell." *He gave me a weapon, but I lost it.* "Then he went somewhere."

"He's going to rejoin us if he can." Mikka's tone was harsh; as guttural as a groan. Scourging herself into motion, she let go of Pup and faced Morn. "He set a time limit. If he isn't back by then, we're supposed to leave without him.

"Come on." She gestured stiffly toward *Trumpet*. "Let's see if we can keep his ship in one piece until his time runs out."

Through his faceplate, Morn saw Davies nod grimly. With her vision distorted by polarization, she couldn't tell the difference between him and his father.

Pulling Pup after him, Vector went first. His suit didn't disguise the arthritic stiffness of his movements; his joints must have hurt acutely as he climbed the handgrips up *Trumpet*'s side. When he rounded the curve, Sib and then Mikka followed; Morn and Davies brought up the rear.

From the elevation of the airlock, Morn looked across the docks to see what Nick was doing.

He'd regained his feet; turned his back on the charred wreck of his ship. Alone and awkward across the riven concrete, he picked his way toward *Trumpet*. Every step was slow—even from this distance, he appeared to be in pain—but he came steadily, carrying his loss like a pallbearer.

Distinctly Davies said, "This is our chance to get rid of him. We can seal him out. Let the Bill have him—if he can find his way inside."

Seal him out—

A pain of her own twisted around Morn's heart. Like Angus, Nick had done things to her which she would never forgive. And he had her black box.

Coming to help her had been Angus' idea, not Nick's.

Get rid of him—

Her desire to close the lock against him was so intense that she nearly moaned.

Yes! Let him die outside and be damned!

But it was too expensive. She'd seen that with her own eyes, felt it with her own heart's pain. The Amnion had tried their mutagens on her. Like treachery and lies, revenge cost too much; grudges and hate cost too much. Nick and Angus had taught her that.

She didn't hesitate.

"No," she told her son. "You're a cop. From now on, I'm going to be a cop myself." Not the kind of cop Warden Dios and Hashi Lebwohl were: the kind her father and mother had been. "We don't do things like that."

"Are you sure?" Mikka demanded from the lock. "We're better off without him. We're *safer*—he's made too many enemies. And he hates Angus too much."

"I'm sure," Vector put in softly. "Morn's right. The rest of us aren't cops, but we have enough other problems without doing things that will make us sick of ourselves."

"Besides," Sib observed, "he still has his guns. If he tries to blast his way in, we might not survive the damage."

Morn took Mikka's silence as assent. She gave Davies a quick hug, then lowered herself down the ladder into the ship.

Davies rather than Mikka keyed commands into the control panel, shutting the airlock so that it would reopen for Nick. He gave the impression that he was already acquainted with *Trumpet*. Morn wondered how long he'd been with Angus; how long ago Angus had rescued him. But she didn't ask. For the moment, at least, all her questions had been burned out of her.

And she was overtaken by a strange sense of recognition, an unaccountable impression of safety. From the airlock and the lift down to the central passage and along it to the EVA suit compartment and the weapons locker, she *knew* this ship. Details were different, of course, if for no other reason than because *Trumpet* was new; but she'd done some of her training in Needle-class gap scouts. For the first time since *Starmaster*'s death, she found herself in a place where she felt she belonged.

Davies must have had the same reaction—

After her long hours in an Amnion cell and her hazardous escape, *Trumpet*'s poignant familiarity nearly overwhelmed her. She had to remind herself forcibly that this was Angus' ship, Angus Thermopyle's; that when she entered *Trumpet* she was reentering the domain of the man who had raped and debased her to the core of her being.

If she could have believed that she or any of the people with her—even Nick—were capable of taking *Trumpet* away from Billingate intact, she would have prayed for Angus to fail his deadline; beseeched the uncaring stars to grant her that one last mercy.

Mikka was in command; but Davies stowed his suit and weapons first. Once he unsealed his helmet, Morn saw his face clearly for the first time since the day he was born.

Her heart seemed to stop when she saw that he'd been beaten up.

The damage was recent. Blood still crusted his forehead; bruises which hadn't had time to turn livid swelled his cheeks, puffed around his eyes.

The Bill had done that to him. Or it'd happened in the struggle to escape.

Or he and Angus had fought over her; over the things Angus had done to her.

An inarticulate protest died in her throat as she studied her son.

Apart from his battered face, he didn't appear hurt. He was noticeably thinner than Angus: in fact, he was thinner than he'd been when *Captain's Fancy* had left Enablement. And his skin looked hot, as if he were burning up inside; tension poured off him like heat. Nevertheless he was physically intact.

His eyes hid whatever he was feeling. He glanced at Morn quickly, but didn't meet her gaze. He may have been angry at her for refusing to doom Nick. Or he may have been ashamed of himself for wanting to lock Nick out.

Or he may have begun to recover the pieces of her past—

The thought that he might be able to remember how she'd abandoned herself to Nick made her own skin burn. Yet that chagrin was small compared with other, more profound shames. He might recall how Angus had raped and brutalized her—or the way she'd saved his life—

Or how she'd killed *Starmaster*—

As he wheeled away and hurried toward the bridge, he seemed to take the last of her strength with him. Without warning her legs became so weak that she nearly folded to the deck.

She'd been terrified that how he was born and what he knew about her might drive him insane; that only the strange blockage of his memories kept his mind in one piece. Yet he was whole now, whatever he remembered. Angus had given that to him—or done it to him.

His mind was no longer hers. He'd begun to inherit the legacy of his father.

And he'd had to fight for it.

Suddenly she wanted Angus to come back so that she could force or beg him to tell her what he'd done to her son.

She stood in the passage without moving, too beaten and exhausted to remove more than her helmet.

Fortunately Vector seemed to understand her condition. As soon as he'd put away his suit and projectile launcher, he knelt in front of her despite the pain in his joints to unseal her suit, unstrap the harness from her hips, tug the tough fabric off over her boots.

Mikka had already finished storing her gear. She scrutinized Morn for a moment, then turned to her brother. Her old scowl was etched into her features, but fatigue and concern had worn off every other expression. "Ciro, find the galley," she told him. "A ship like this, the foodvend probably works by magic. Make coffee, cocoa, hype— anything hot. And sandwiches. Bring them to the bridge."

Ciro? Morn thought wearily. She'd never heard Pup's real name. Like Davies', his face had changed since she'd last seen it: danger and fear had aged him by several years. For the first time, his resemblance to his sister was obvious.

He opened his mouth to protest, then closed it when Mikka pushed his shoulder gently. "Right away would be good," she murmured, unconsciously copying Nick. "Right now would be better."

Ciro ducked his head and went to obey.

With Sib behind her, Mikka followed Davies toward the bridge.

Vector smiled wanly at Morn. Pain or exertion left a sheen on his round face. When they were alone, he said, "I owe you an apology."

She blinked at him dumbly. Her brain was full of Davies and weakness: she had no idea what he was talking about.

He levered himself up from his knees. Old hurts hampered his gaze as well as his joints. "If it weren't covered by so much other damage," he explained quietly, "you would have a bruise where I hit you."

As careful as velvet, he stroked the ridge of her cheekbone with his fingertips.

Instinctively she flinched away. He was male, like Nick; like Angus. His touch and his gentleness seemed to impact her like a blow.

He smiled again as he lowered his hand. In a tone like a shrug, he said, "I like to think I would regret that in any case. But as it happens I have more reason than you may realize. You forced me to look at the implications of my life, and I didn't like what I saw. If I were wiser—or perhaps simply braver—I would have hit myself, not you.

"I don't understand any of this. How it comes about that a man like Angus Thermopyle is here to rescue you from Nick and the Amnion—well, it's beyond me. But it's given me a chance to see things differently. That's my other reason for regret. In retrospect, it seems"—his smile broadened slightly—"downright callow of me to have hit the woman who changed my life."

What he was saying must have been important, if he made such a point of it; but its significance eluded her. Once she realized that he didn't mean to hurt her, she could no longer focus on him. In her thoughts she'd already joined Davies. On the bridge of a ship

she knew—a UMCP ship, whether Angus had any dealings with the
police or not. Only her weakness held her back; only the immeasurable cost of her hours in an Amnion cell.

She needed her zone implant control. Without it she had too
little substance, too few resources, to change anyone's life, even her
own.

"I'm sorry," she began. "I need—" Unable to say the words, she
stopped.

Apparently he had his own ideas about what she needed. He
nodded as if he were amused by his personal follies. "So do I."

Then he took her arm and helped her into motion.

As frail as a derelict, she shuffled through the ship.

When she reached the head of the companionway, she heard
voices below her.

"If anyone tried to break in, the computer didn't record it,"
Davies reported, presumably to Mikka. "I checked the communications log. There's a whole series of threats, some from the Bill, some
from Operations. They get more hysterical as they go along, but they
aren't very specific. Then they stop. The channel goes dead. No
more demands, no more threats—and no more operational data.
Nothing but static. *Calm Horizons* could be right on top of us—there
could be half a dozen ships coming in on Billingate—and we wouldn't
know it." He gave a sardonic snort which reminded Morn of Angus.
"On the other hand, we're still getting installation power."

"Ship's status?" Mikka asked brusquely.

"Up and running," Davies said. "All systems green. I went
through the checklists. We're ready."

"Then give me scan," she ordered. "Let's find out who's in range
to hurt us."

Morn pulled away from Vector. Bracing her arms on the rails
and locking her knees, she lowered herself down the treads. She
wanted her son to believe in her. If he saw how weak she was, he
might not trust her.

He sat at the command station. His hands on the console were
accurate, but cautious; not particularly adept. Morn's memories and
his time with Angus familiarized him with the ship, but they couldn't
take the place of experience. He was probably competent to run
Trumpet under normal circumstances: the present danger required
someone with more expertise.

Mikka was the best choice Angus could have made, even though she knew less about *Trumpet* than Davies did.

She and Sib stood on either side of the command station, watching for data as Davies activated scan and fed the results to the display screens. In moments blips appeared on a schematic of Billingate's control space. Davies typed a few guesses based on the ship's last operational input. The blips took on ship id.

"That's all we can see," he muttered. "Thanatos Minor blocks us from the shipyard. We're blind past the horizons."

Holding her breath, Morn moved to the back of his g-seat. If she braced herself there, she could stay on her feet and study the screens.

Five blips. Two of them were off in the direction of human space, one incoming, the other heading out. *Trumpet* had picked up their demands for traffic data and navigational protocols had obtained ship id from those transmissions. The incoming vessel called herself *Gambler's Luck*. Unless she slowed her approach, she would be in range to have an effect on the action around Thanatos Minor in twenty minutes. The outgoing ship, *Free Lunch*, was burning hard, obviously on the run from trouble.

The other three blips Davies had identified by guess: their transmissions, if any, were all tight-beamed. Nevertheless Morn was sure he'd named them correctly.

Soar. Calm Horizons. And the Amnion shuttle.

"It looks," Davies pronounced, "like *Soar* is moving to pick up the shuttle. Its course is erratic, and there's a sputter in its emission signature. I'm assuming it was *Soar* that fired first. The shuttle must have been right beside *Captain's Fancy*. It got caught in the discontinuities. I think it's out of control. But *Soar* won't have any trouble catching it."

His father's voice and Morn's training made him sound certain.

"*Calm Horizons* is coming this way," he went on. "Probably wants to improve her field of fire."

"Will she attack while we're still docked?" Sib asked tensely. The calm or resignation he'd felt earlier was gone. "She can't hit us without damaging Billingate."

"If I were the Amnion," Davies rasped, "I wouldn't worry about that right now. They've lost *Tranquil Hegemony*—in fact, they've lost most of their installation. And they know Nick works for the cops."

Complex vibrations sharpened his tone, like whetted knives. Morn heard anger, revulsion—and a strange note of pride. "They know about his immunity drug."

As he said that, a small sun of fear and shame went nova in her heart. They know— Of course they knew. Nick had told her that. But how did Davies know?

"They're bound to assume," he continued, "that's why their mutagens didn't work on Morn. So they have to believe he set them up. He and Angus must be working together—he gave them Morn to bait some kind of UMCP trap.

"Stopping this ship probably takes precedence over everything else."

Morn's knees failed: she sagged against his seat. "You remember." If she'd ever needed her zone implant control, she needed it now. "Your memory came back." How else could she face the things her son knew about her? "You remember Nick telling me about the drug."

No wonder he wanted to lock Nick out of the ship. He remembered the things she'd done with him; the lies and desperation; the sex—

"Yes." He spoke over his shoulder without facing her. "I remember it all." He sounded far away, too far to be reached; doomed by knowledge. "It started coming back as soon as I saw Angus."

He remembered the people she'd killed.

He remembered what Angus had done to her.

Did he want Angus' death as much as he wanted Nick's? Or was all his remaining rage and revulsion fixed on her? Had he given his loyalty to his father because he couldn't bear the memories he'd inherited from his mother?

Anger and revulsion made perfect sense to her; but what had he found in her experience—or his own—to be proud of?

If she lost him—or he lost her—he would have nothing left except Angus.

Vector had moved to stand behind her. Although he didn't touch her, he seemed to lean toward her as if he wanted to shore her up somehow.

"Speaking of Angus," he put in quietly, "how much time does he have left?"

"He told me an hour." Mikka's tone was abstract: most of her attention was on the screens. "I checked my suit chronometer when he said it. He's got"—she glanced at the command console readouts—"eighteen minutes."

Davies swore under his breath. "That gives *Calm Horizons* time to position herself right over us. We won't have any kind of escape trajectory to get out of range."

"Then we'd better go now," Nick drawled mordantly.

Sib and Mikka whirled; Davies twisted his head toward the companionway. Supporting herself on the command seat and Vector's shoulder, Morn turned as Nick started down the steps with Pup in front of him like a shield.

Pup moved as if he had cramps in his arms. His eyes seemed to roll, showing flashes of white; his young features were stretched taut.

His hands were empty. Apparently Nick had interrupted him before he finished in the galley.

Nick had taken the time to remove his EVA suit. He was grinning sharply, but a spasm in his cheek clenched one side of his grin into a snarl. Blood filled his scars: they looked black and vengeful. Above them his eyes glared wildly, as if he were cornered.

He descended the companionway without haste. Keeping himself behind Pup, he reached the deck.

"We can't afford to wait," he announced like a splash of acid. "Davies, this is your chance to convince me you're worth keeping alive. Disengage from dock. Give me a normal departure lift-off. Get thrust ready to burn. Put the gap drive on standby."

Davies' lips pulled back from his teeth. Deliberately he took his hands off the command board and gripped the sides of the console.

"Do it *now*," Nick warned. "You're fucking dispensable, you know that?"

"Nick." Mikka took a step forward, cocked her hips belligerently. "I'm in command here. We're not taking your orders anymore. None of us are."

There was something wrong about the way Pup stood. His posture was too rigid; the line of his spine was too acute. Morn opened her mouth to caution Mikka, but her throat locked down on the words, keeping her silent.

Nick waggled his eyebrows grotesquely at his former second. "I'll give you one chance. Tell him"—he jerked a nod at Davies—"to do what I just said. Make him obey. Then I'll let you be in command.

"Otherwise—"

He lifted his left hand from behind Pup's back.

He was holding Morn's black box.

"I've got my fingers on enough buttons," he said cheerfully, "to fry her brain.

"You hear me, you little shit?" he flared at Davies.

Then he relaxed. "One squeeze, and she's a null-wave transmitter. Which would just about count as justice, don't you think?

"Let's start over again." He spat each syllable precisely. "Disengage from dock. Give me—"

Mikka flung herself at him with all her strength.

Pup's whole body flinched in panic. Morn tried to cry out, but she couldn't unclose her throat.

Quick as a snake, Nick snatched his right hand into sight and jammed his handgun at Pup's ear.

Mikka stopped as if she'd slammed into a wall.

"That's better." Nick grinned and snarled. "Now we're getting somewhere."

He ground the muzzle of his gun into Pup's ear until Mikka retreated past the command station. Then he released the pressure. Gasping through his teeth, Pup stumbled away. At once Nick caught him by the back of his shipsuit, swung him to the side, and pulled him into the command second's g-seat.

Pup braced himself there with his hands on the padding down inside the arms; but Nick didn't give him a chance to jump free. Pivoting the second's station, he put Pup and the console between himself and the others.

Shielded again, he rested his forearms on the back of the g-seat, his handgun propped against Pup's head, Morn's zone implant control poised.

"Are you listening now?" he inquired comfortably. "Are you paying attention? I can kill you all from here if you so much as twitch. And dear old Captain Thermo-pile can't sneak up behind me." He nodded to show that he had a clear view of the companionway. "In any case, he won't get the chance. We're leaving.

"Davies Hyland, you slimy little asshole"—he faced Davies squarely—"you'd better start following orders. Morn goes first if you don't. For the last time"—without warning he broke into a shout like a scream—*"disengage from dock!"*

"No." Morn was astonished that she could speak. She was too weak to remain locked, however. And Davies needed her. All these people needed her. Nick was her problem.

"I don't care what happens to me. I'm useless anyway, with-out—" She flicked a gesture at his left hand. If she could have moved toward him, she would have done so; but she was too exhausted to let go of Vector and the g-seat.

She'd driven Nick to this. With her lies as well as her convic-tions—with her false sexual abandon and her honest commitment to her son—she'd cost him his invincibility, his belief in himself. That also was expensive. Now she had to deal with the consequences.

"Go ahead and fry me, if that's what you want. Kill us all—try to get away on your own. Or wake up and face the truth. You're finished.

"The stories are over. Nick Succorso the famous swashbuckling hero doesn't exist anymore. You've lost your ship—you've lost every-thing. Isn't that true, Nick?

"Isn't it?"

Pup squirmed as if something in the g-seat had poked him.

Nick responded by slapping the side of Pup's head with the handgun. The boy slumped, so pale that he might have been about to faint.

However, Nick had reacted without really noticing Mikka's brother. The spasm spread across his face as if Morn had burned a nerve; he was all snarl. His eyes were as dark and hidden as caves.

Softly Morn asked, "What happened to your mission against Thanatos Minor?"

He couldn't refuse to answer: his loss was too great. Bitterly aggrieved, he replied, "I failed. Is that what you want to hear?" His scars looked like scabs on his cheeks. "I *failed.*

"I was supposed to sabotage the Bill with that immunity drug. I was supposed to set him up with it and then substitute a fake. De-stroy his credibility. That was the plan, Hashi Lebwohl's plan. You were my failsafe. You were ruined anyway, Angus fucking Thermo-pile saw to that. Lebwohl let me have you so that if everything went wrong I could sell you instead of giving up the real drug."

He spoke like a fuel fire in a constricted space. Flames fed on themselves, mounting toward an explosion. "But that was before I saw Sorus.

"Do you know who she is?" His eyes ached at Morn, as hungry as black holes. "Of course you don't. I never told you her name. Sorus Chatelaine. Captain of *Soar*. She's the woman who cut me.

"As soon as I saw her, I gave up on the Bill. Let Lebwohl do his own dirty work. I went after her. I drove her off Billingate, got her out in space where she was vulnerable. Then I sent *Captain's Fancy* to finish her off."

No one on the bridge appeared to breathe. Sweat ran unnoticed down Sib's face. Davies sat at the command station like a knot of violence. Fear and fury struggled back and forth across Mikka's features, paralyzing her. Vector's blue eyes had gone wide, as if he were bemused by wonders.

Morn watched Nick gravely, waiting for his hand to tighten; waiting for the neural apotheosis which would extinguish all the synapses of her brain; bring her responsibility for what she'd done to him to its natural end.

"Thanks to you," he growled viciously, "the Amnion thought they had my priority codes. They thought they could control my ship. That's why they didn't hit her as soon as she blew dock. And *that* gave Liete her chance. I set *Soar* up. I would have gone after her myself, if the Bill hadn't barred me. So I took the only chance I had left. I told Liete what I wanted. I sent her to kill Sorus for me.

"But she didn't do it. She knew what I wanted, and she didn't do it. I *failed*, all right? You *goddamn* women are all the same. You use me for all you're fucking *worth*, and then you cut me and leave me to die.

"*It's not going to happen again!*" His cry was an echo of the lost howl with which he'd watched Liete betray him. "*This* time—*this time*—I'm going to kill every one of you who doesn't *do what I want!*"

For some reason Pup met Davies' eyes. Through his pallor and panic, he gave Davies a tiny nod.

"Bullshit, Nick!" Slowly, almost unthreateningly, Davies stood up from the command station. Without appearing to move, he placed himself between Nick and Morn. "You aren't going to kill any of us. If you do, you won't have an audience for all this self-pity. You won't have anybody left to blame."

Nick flinched; his face twisted into a mask of anguish. "That does it." His tone was pure bloodshed. "You're first."

Leaning over the top of the g-seat, he aimed his gun at Davies' face.

As frantic as a convulsion, Pup brought up a stun-prod no bigger than a dagger and stabbed it into Nick's armpit.

That close to his heart the stun-prod had enough impact to knock him to the deck in a pile of dissociated limbs and spasms.

Burning forward, Mikka snatched Pup out of the g-seat and hauled him back.

Like the stroke of a piston, Davies drove at Nick: he kicked the handgun out of reach, grabbed up Morn's black box. For a moment he crouched over Nick's twitching, unconscious form as if he intended to break his neck.

"Davies," Morn panted, "don't!"

Then she seemed to run out of transitions.

Between one heartbeat and the next, she found herself on the deck in Vector's arms.

Without leaving Nick, Davies appeared at her side.

Unexpected and unannounced, Angus swung down the companionway rails onto the bridge.

He'd removed his helmet, but he still wore his EVA suit. Streaks of dried sweat grimed his face; his eyes bulged as if he were in the last stages of dehydration.

She blinked once, and several people were in different positions. A voice which might have been Angus' demanded water. Pup was gone. Woozy with stun, Nick climbed to his feet. Sib had retrieved the handgun: he held it in both fists, pointing it at his former captain. Angus sat at the command station. Mikka stood in front of him with her mouth open.

"Tell me later," he said. His tone was raw with thirst. "We're leaving right now."

She pointed at the display screens.

He nodded brusquely.

"Find cabins," he ordered. "We're going to burn in about five minutes. The g-seals on the bunks are your only protection.

"Davies, for God's sake, put her to sleep. She's in withdrawal— it could kill her. And hard g triggers her gap-sickness. Take her to a cabin. Stay with her. I'll tell you when it's safe to wake her up."

At the edges of her vision, Morn saw Davies raise her black box and peer at the function labels.

You know as much about it as I do, she tried to say. All you have to do is remember. But she couldn't speak. Her failures welled up from the bottom of her heart. She'd endured too much—was in too much need. She lasted long enough to see Pup hurry down the companionway carrying a g-flask for Angus; long enough to hear Mikka order Sib and Vector off the bridge.

Then Davies touched buttons, and she fell into darkness as if it were the gap between her abilities and her desires.

ANGUS

A ngus emptied the g-flask while he watched Davies carry Morn up the companionway. He wanted to go himself; wanted to hold her in his own arms for a while. Her condition still brought glints of fury and grief past the control of his zone implants. His desire to kill Nick had settled in as if it were the definitive passion of his life. But of course his programming wouldn't let him harm anyone connected with the UMCP. And he had too many other threats to juggle—

The new countdown running in his head left no room for mistakes.

He could pull data from *Trumpet's* logs faster than Mikka could put it into words. A glance or two told him why Morn, Nick, and the others were still alive—why *Captain's Fancy* and *Tranquil Hegemony* didn't appear on the display screen in front of him. He couldn't understand what had possessed *Captain's Fancy* to sacrifice herself like that. At the moment, however, he didn't need to understand: the fact itself was enough.

Two less threats to worry about. That left *Calm Horizons*, *Soar*, and the Amnion shuttle. It left *Gambler's Luck*, *Free Lunch*, and at least half a dozen other ships trying to get out of trouble by breaking away from dock.

It left the countdown.

He needed help. He could run *Trumpet* indefinitely on his own: he was built for that. But he and his ship would stand a better chance if he had help.

Sib Mackern and Vector Shaheed had already gone to find cabins where they could ride out heavy g. Davies would stay with Morn. That left Mikka Vasaczk, Ciro—and Nick.

His thirst was too fierce to be assuaged by one g-flask. Nevertheless his zone implants enabled him to ignore his craving for more water. His computer had concluded that he was no longer in immediate danger from dehydration.

Mikka was the obvious choice. She was Nick's second; already trained. But Angus didn't trust Nick out of his sight—

Ignoring the possibility that anyone who was taken by surprise might fall and get hurt, he tapped thrust. A hard jolt rang through the ship as he blew the docking clamps and ripped *Trumpet* free from Billingate's cables.

Mikka caught herself on the front of the command console; Ciro grabbed at his sister's shoulders. Nick staggered, nearly lost his balance. His eyes were glazed, and his mouth hung slack; stun still confused his neurons.

Angus grinned at the thought that someone had found Milos' weapon and used it on Nick.

"You two get out of here," he told Mikka and Ciro. "You haven't got much time—I want you safe.

"You," he cracked like a lash at Nick. "You're my second. Sit down and get to work."

Protest flared on Mikka's face. With an effort, she smothered it. "Come on," she growled at her brother's alarm. "Angus can handle Nick. If the two of them can't get us out of here, we were never going to make it anyway."

Ciro brandished Milos' stun-prod in Nick's direction, warning him; then followed Mikka off the bridge.

Nick ignored the boy. He was blinking rapidly at Angus, trying to focus his eyes.

Angus keyed attitudinal thrust, orienting *Trumpet* along a departure trajectory toward *Calm Horizons*. As the ship pulled slowly away, Thanatos Minor's g eased.

"I said—" he rasped.

"I heard you," Nick panted. "I'll do it. Give me a minute."

Breathing hard to clear his head, he leaned into the second's g-seat. His hands fumbled as he attached his belt.

"What am I supposed to do?"

Angus toggled controls. "You've got helm. Scan data is on the screens. I'll do the rest." Simultaneously he brought up targ and communications. "Run us out on a heading for *Calm Horizons*. No more than one g.

"Evade if anyone fires. Use as much thrust as you need. Otherwise stay on a slow intercept course for that warship."

The countdown clicked ahead like a timing fuse. Nick rubbed his hands over his eyes, ground the heels of his palms into his scars. A moment later a surge of acceleration tugged Angus against the back of his seat as Nick heated the thruster tubes.

The pressure stabilized near one g. Nick typed a subtle correction. Almost at once the scan plot on the screen showed *Trumpet* moving in a straight line for *Calm Horizons*.

Good. Maybe Nick was smart enough to realize that if he didn't take orders now he wouldn't live long enough to get a second chance.

Trumpet's guns were charged, but Angus didn't intend to use them if he could avoid it: he didn't want to be caught in a fight here. Instead, despite the drain on thrust, he activated her shields—reflectors to fend off laser fire; particle sinks to protect against matter cannon. Then he keyed his console pickup and began hailing *Calm Horizons*.

Six minutes. Not nearly enough time for *Trumpet* to get away safely. Even through vacuum, the shock wave would hit her like a fist. Gap scouts weren't designed to stand that kind of stress.

On the other hand, it ought to be possible to persuade *Calm Horizons* to hold fire for only six minutes.

"This is Angus Thermopyle," he announced into the pickup, "captain, Needle-class gap scout *Trumpet*, to Amnion defensive *Calm Horizons*. Don't fire. I say again, do not fire. My ship has no offensive weapons. I can't threaten you.

"I have prisoners I wish to trade for safe departure. I'll hold course and acceleration steady to intercept your position at—" His computer ran a lightning calculation: he named the time it gave him. "I'm prepared to offer Nick Succorso, Morn Hyland, and Davies Hyland in exchange for permission to depart Amnion space. Captain Succorso ordered his vessel, *Captain's Fancy*, to destroy *Tranquil Hegemony*. Morn Hyland is a UMCP ensign. Davies Hyland is her son, force-grown on Enablement Station.

"They mean nothing to me. You can have them if you'll let me go."

Firmly he silenced the pickup.

Nick's hands had frozen on his board, poised for obedience or sabotage. "You sonofabitch," he murmured.

In case Nick tried something desperate, Angus braced himself to deactivate the second's station.

But Nick appeared to know that he didn't have any choices left. "What makes you think you can bluff your way out of this?" he asked thinly. "What kind of scam are you and Milos running?"

Five minutes.

As *Trumpet* pulled away, her scan field past the planetoid's horizons improved. Now he counted ten ships out of dock. Some were fleeing. Others converged on his trajectory purposefully, sent by the Bill—or the Amnion. *Soar* had matched course and velocity with the shuttle to take the craft aboard.

"Me and Milos?" Angus wanted to laugh. "You're out of your mind.

"Let me guess what happened to you," he countered. For reasons of its own, his programming didn't require him to explain himself. "I put Mikka in command. You didn't want to wait for me, so you tried to take over. But you let a kid with a stun-prod beat you. Another triumph. Nick, you're a walking success story. No wonder your brains are scrambled."

Nick's face twisted, but he didn't retort.

"I'm going to give you two orders," Angus went on. "Try not to scramble them, too. The first time I say *now*, veer off and burn. I don't care what heading you choose. Just get us away from as many of those ships as you can. They can't all be coming our way by accident.

"The important thing is maximum thrust. She won't want to do it—I'm bleeding power for her shields. Push her red if you have to.

"The second time I say *now*, give me one of your famous blink crossings."

Four minutes.

"Can you handle that, or should I do it myself?"

"I'm not sure I care," Nick growled. "It might be fun to see you get out of this on your own."

Nevertheless Angus' readouts told him that Nick had begun to plot new courses while he readied the gap drive.

Abruptly the bridge speakers blared to life.

"*Trumpet*, come about. This is *Stonemason*. I have orders from the Bill. If you don't reverse thrust, I'm going to open fire. You have sixty seconds to comply."

On the display screen ship id appeared beside *Stonemason*'s blip. She was already in range to attack, and gaining fast.

Almost immediately, however, *Trumpet* picked up the mechanical sound of an Amnioni transmission.

"Amnion defensive *Calm Horizons* to human ship *Stonemason*. You are required to withhold fire. You transgress Amnion space. Therefore Amnion purposes take precedence. The destruction of *Trumpet* is unacceptable. She carries individuals which are necessary to the Amnion.

"If Captain Angus Thermopyle intends treachery, your assistance in preventing *Trumpet*'s flight will be rewarded. However, if he deals with the Amnion honestly, he will be permitted to depart. The Bill will be offered"—the metallic voice appeared to hesitate—"other compensation."

Angus bared his teeth. "It's like I always say. One good lie is worth a thousand truths.

"Hold course and acceleration steady. Even if the Amnion know I'm lying—even if they want you dead—they can't pass up a chance to get Morn and Davies back."

Nick nodded grimly. He'd chosen his new heading. All the gap drive's status indicators showed green.

Three minutes.

If *Stonemason* hesitated that long, she wouldn't live to regret it.

On the other hand, if she fired before then, the Amnion would learn more than Angus wanted them to know about *Trumpet*'s shields.

"Negative on that, *Calm Horizons*," *Stonemason* returned. "I can't tell the Bill you want me to hold off. Operations has lost communication. If I don't follow his orders, he won't let me back in dock."

Before *Calm Horizons* could reply, *Trumpet*'s antennae picked a new voice out of the crackling dark.

"*Calm Horizons*, listen to me! This is the Bill! I'm on a cargo shuttle. This is the only radio I can get my hands on.

"Don't trust Thermopyle! He's lying. He's going to try to skip past you somehow.

"Ask him how he got Davies Hyland! Ask him how he got Morn Hyland. He won't let you have Succorso. He and Succorso are in this together. They snatched the Hyland kid from me. Then the three of them took his mother from you. They're the ones who broke into your installation, killed your people, destroyed *Tranquil Hegemony*.

"Don't listen to him, *Calm Horizons*! It's a trick!"

Two minutes.

Before the Bill stopped shouting, the speakers picked up *Calm Horizons'* transmission again.

"*Calm Horizons* to all human ships in the vicinity of Thanatos Minor." The alien voice held a note of urgency which Angus hadn't heard before. "You are required to converge on the human ship *Trumpet*. *Trumpet* must be captured. Human ships which assist in *Trumpet's* capture will be given the greatest rewards the Amnion can offer. Human ships which do not assist in *Trumpet's* capture will be presumed hostile and destroyed.

"Message repeats. *Calm Horizons* to all—"

Nick cut through the broadcast. "This isn't going to be easy." Strain shone like a sheen of sweat in his tone. His hands held steady on his board, but his eyes flicked and rolled like a cornered beast's. "No matter how we veer off, that fucker will have a clear shot at us. Her targ can handle our acceleration, you can count on that. And those other bastards are all moving faster than we are."

Angus now counted four ships in addition to *Stonemason* driving hard to form a cordon around *Trumpet*.

Harshly Nick went on, "We'll need at least thirty seconds to pick up enough velocity for an effective blink crossing. In thirty seconds every asshole out there will have time to hit us."

One minute.

Angus mimicked the superior drawl Nick had lost. "Then I guess we need a diversion.

"Get ready. I'm going to cut this fine."

Heavy g: pressure that would drive Morn into gap-sickness, if Davies didn't take care of her; enough pressure to squeeze Angus and Nick like sponges in their seats. Nick wasn't familiar with *Trumpet* yet: he didn't realize how hard she could burn. Nevertheless he was right that *Calm Horizons'* targ could handle it. And he was almost right about the amount of time *Trumpet* would need before she could attempt a blink crossing. For the first twenty seconds she might as well be a stationary target.

Unless she rode the shock wave.

If Dios and Lebwohl had miscalculated—

If their understanding of Billingate's fusion generator wasn't accurate enough—

Or if *Trumpet* couldn't take the stress—

"*Calm Horizons* to human ship *Trumpet*," the speakers reported. "You are required to discontinue thrust. Do so immediately. Commence braking. This will be taken as evidence of good faith. If you do not comply instantly, you will be presumed hostile. For the purposes of the Amnion your destruction will take precedence over the value of your prisoners."

A wail that Angus couldn't utter filled his chest—a cry of fear which his zone implants and prewritten instructions refused to permit. He sounded as bleak as a grave as he told Nick, "Now."

Nick slapped keys with his palms.

A structural roar seemed to deafen the speakers as *Trumpet*'s thrust leaped to full power. Despite his reinforced strength, Angus slammed back in his seat, then fell sideways as *Trumpet* cut to her new course.

Away from *Calm Horizons.*

Between *Stonemason* and two other ships.

On an oblique heading for the fringes of human space.

Scan detected targ from several sources tracking the ship, swinging guns into line.

Two seconds later a nuclear blast tore the heart out of Thanatos Minor.

A theoretically impossible fusion accident had become possible when Angus, deep in Billingate's infrastructure, had cut his way through the failsafes and rewired some of the circuits. If the Bill had remained in his strongroom, and Operations had been able to restore internal communications, he might have received warning of what was about to happen; but he wouldn't have been able to stop it. Not without a complete overhaul of the power station's control.

When a fusion generator sufficient to run all of Billingate exploded, it produced more than enough destructive force to break open the planetoid.

Impact screamed through *Trumpet*'s hull as the shock wave struck. Rock like a maelstrom ripped the vacuum in every direction. In seconds, fractions of seconds, the stone storm would catch her, tear her shields apart like vapor, twist her to scrap in the vast dark. Already half the human ships were gone, punched to pieces by Thanatos Minor's ruin.

Through his ship's screaming Angus also screamed:

"Now!"

Against the brutal kick of the blast, Nick pitched at his board, slapped keys with his open hands.

Scant meters ahead of the rock, *Trumpet* went into tach; plunged like Morn into the gap.

WARDEN

In the aftermath of the kaze's attack on UMCPHQ, Warden Dios was summoned before Holt Fasner.

He'd been able to prevent Godsen Frik from answering such a summons. For that reason he was indirectly responsible for Godsen's death. But he couldn't refuse himself. The Dragon was his boss.

If he'd been susceptible to vain regrets, he might have cursed the naïveté or blind idealism—or perhaps the arrogant ambition—which had inspired him to accept Holt Fasner's offer of service in the first place. He wasn't that kind of man, however. Instead he shrugged his shoulders ruefully and went on with his job. Time and experience had worked few changes in the nature of his motivations. Such as it was, his naïveté had dissolved; he was no longer blindly idealistic; his ambitions had shed their arrogance. Nevertheless he did what he did now for much the same reasons which had originally led him to accept positions in SMI Security and then the UMCP.

He believed that problems should be solved by the people who became aware of them. Devotion, labor, and care couldn't be expected from human beings who saw no need for such things. Therefore they had to be supplied by men like himself and women like Min Donner.

At one time he'd privately considered this conviction admirable; hence the suggestion of arrogance in his ambitions. Now, how-

---

STEPHEN R. DONALDSON

ever, he saw it as the means by which Holt Fasner had manipulated him.

Unfortunately he couldn't give it up. The fact that he hadn't been wise enough to prevent his beliefs from being used against him was no reason to surrender them. And to a significant extent the problems of the present had been created by his own actions; his own compromises and misjudgments.

Those compromises and misjudgments had proved exceptionally fertile ground for the Dragon. He'd sown many things there.

Warden Dios had no intention of shirking the harvest.

So he took his personal shuttle from UMCPHQ to the "home office" of the United Mining Companies—the orbital platform from which Holt ran his complex enterprises. He disembarked into an escort of what Holt called "Home Security"—more accurately Fasner's bodyguards. Although Warden knew his way, HS accompanied him to the secure center of the station, where—so the conceit ran—the Dragon lurked in his lair.

When the doors and walls and screens had sealed behind him, rendering the lair and its secrets impregnable to espionage, he came face-to-face with the man who had made him what he was.

Delicate and insidious fears took hold of him whenever he contemplated his boss.

Stay calm, he told himself.

Stay clear.

Remember what you're doing.

Holt Fasner's aura was disturbing. Despite his one hundred fifty years, he looked younger than Warden; superficially in better health. Subtle drugs wiped eighty or ninety years off his skin; lifted at least half that many from the tissue of his heart and lungs, the marrow of his bones. Only the advanced ruddiness of his cheeks, the occasional tremor in his hands, the way he blinked as if he had difficulty keeping his eyes in focus, and the hint of mortality in his IR emissions, conveyed the impression that he wasn't entirely well.

He smiled a cold greeting past the surface of his utilitarian desk. Like the desk, his office was crammed with data terminals, video screens, and communications gear of every description—as ready for information as a living brain—but it wasn't particularly expansive; or even notably comfortable.

"Well, Ward." He waved a hand at a chair across the desk from him. "Sit down. Let's have a chat."

Schooling himself to conceal his anxiety, Warden took a seat and folded his arms over his heavy chest.

"We'd better do more than chat," he said as if he could afford to be impatient with the most powerful man in human space. "This is a bad time for me to be away. There's too much going on.

"You know that, of course," he added, "so I assume you have something particular in mind. Ordinary channels are secure enough for chats."

Holt gave a gesture like a shrug; his aura was tinged with tension. "Come on, Ward—humor me. Let's not rush into this. You can spare a few minutes. How's the weather over there?" He smiled humorlessly. "Have you found any leads on those kazes? What's the news from Thanatos Minor?"

Warden sat like a sphinx. "Rush into what?"

Unruffled by directness, Holt countered, "What in heaven made you think it was a good idea to restrict Godsen? I can't honestly say I liked him, but he did his job well, and he'll be missed." The Dragon blinked in small bursts like shivers. "I'm sure by now you must have realized that he would still be alive if you hadn't given him those orders."

"Yes, actually." If Holt had possessed a prosthesis like Warden's, he would have seen regret and useless anger swarming like insects under the surface of the UMCP director's skin. "I did realize that."

"And . . . ?" Holt prompted.

Warden steadied himself with the pressure of his arms. "I did it to protect him. That's what I thought I was doing, at any rate. I asked myself how the kaze who attacked Captain Vertigus could have obtained legitimate id, and I concluded it must have come from a traitor in one of three places—GCES Security, UMCPHQ, or here. With all due respect, I discounted my people."

"But not mine," Holt said for him.

Warden nodded. "And not the Council's—although yours are more likely. Between the two of us, you and I supply GCES Security with virtually everything. And you have a lot more people than they do—or I do. More people means a greater chance that one of them is a traitor.

"Until I located the source of that kaze's id," he continued, "I thought I could minimize the danger by restricting Godsen. He was more vulnerable than anyone else, since he has so many reasons to visit Suka Bator."

And you.

"Of course, I couldn't have foreseen that you would call him— or that you would suddenly need to see him in person."

Blinking furiously, Holt asked, "Do you think there's a connection?"

Stay calm, Warden recited like a litany. Remember what you're doing.

"I hope you can tell me. In fact, I hope that's why you sent for me. The timing is certainly curious. Godsen would still be alive if he'd answered your summons. Did you know he was the next target? Did you know who's responsible?"

That was as close to honesty as he chose to come.

"Of course not," Holt snapped in irritation. "If I knew 'who's responsible,' you would already have his head on a platter. Weren't you listening when I said I'm going to miss Godsen?"

Almost immediately, however, he recovered his humorless poise. "But since you mention it, that does bring me to one of the subjects I wanted to chat about. Godsen's replacement. It's an important position. In fact, I predict it's going to be crucial. Have you had time to think about it? I have a good candidate in mind."

Warden drew a slow breath past the pressure of his arms. "I've already promoted someone."

Holt dropped his jaw to emphasize his surprise; acid colors swirled in his aura. "My, my, Ward. Whatever possessed you? You know how vital I consider PR. Why else do you imagine I insisted on Godsen in the first place?" His tone sharpened. "What made you think I wouldn't want a say in his replacement?"

Warden seemed to feel the Dragon's breath on his face, hot and fatal; but he kept his face impassive. Dispassionately he lifted his shoulders. "As you say, PR is vital—especially now. I needed someone right away. And I had no way of knowing you were about to suggest a replacement. I suppose I assumed you had too many other things on your mind."

Holt studied him hard. "Who did you promote?"

"One of Godsen's assistants. A woman named Koina Hannish."

"You and women." Holt snorted. "The next thing I know, you're going to replace Hashi with some young flirt who makes you feel all warm and cuddly."

"Wait a minute." Warden knew his boss well enough to understand that Holt used insults as camouflage for his true intentions. Still the UMCP director needed some kind of emotional outlet. "Is that your opinion of Min Donner? She's a 'young flirt' who makes me feel 'all warm and cuddly'?"

Holt ignored this protest. Still sharply, he ordered, "Demote Hannish. Tell her it was temporary—you've found someone better."

Warden tightened his grip on himself. "I can do that," he replied, resolutely mild. "But don't you think you're being a little obvious? Her promotion is already on record. She's already presented her credentials to the Council." Despite his determination to remain calm, however, Holt's implicit threat galled him. Goaded by loss and anger, he began to speak more strongly. "You predict PR is going to be crucial. Are you sure you want to let the Council see you meddle in UMCP internal affairs at a time like this?"

The Dragon braced his hands on his desk as if he wanted to prevent them from shaking. His emissions curdled like sour milk.

"You know, Ward, when I look at you these days I sometimes wonder if I haven't created a monster."

Warden swallowed a retort. Stay calm. He disliked being called Ward.

"What about me seems monstrous to you?"

Holt put equanimity aside. "That video conference," he articulated trenchantly.

Stay clear.

"What about it?"

"What *about* it? My God, Ward, if I didn't have so many reasons to trust you, I would turn you into dog food. Don't think I'm not tempted in spite of your record." He meant, Don't think I can't do it. "Do you have any idea what kind of hornet's nest you've stirred up among the votes? Did you do it on purpose, or did you just not consider how they would react?" His breathing was shallow and flurried. "You should have listened to Godsen. I'm sure he would have warned you. He was damn near frothing at the mouth when he told me about it."

Warden faced Holt stolidly. "You've seen the recordings," he answered. "I'm sure you've talked to people—I mean people besides Godsen. You know as much about it as I do."

"Oh, I've *seen* the recordings," Holt sneered. "I know them by heart. They're full of gems. Here's one."

Glaring at the UMCP director, he quoted, " 'It appears that Captain Thermopyle has left our solar system for forbidden space. If he does not alter his course, he is headed toward a planetoid called Thanatos Minor, which we believe to be the location of a bootleg shipyard catering to the needs and transactions of pirates.'

"Or how about this one? 'Com-Mine Security allowed Ensign Hyland to depart with Captain Succorso on your orders.'

"But those aren't the best. I especially enjoyed it when Hashi said Succorso was sent 'to Thanatos Minor armed with a drug which he would claim supplied an immunity to Amnion mutagens.' And I practically had an orgasm when he admitted you gave Hyland to Succorso 'so that he would have something to sell if he were trapped or caught.'

"I *know* about the video conference. I *know* how the votes are reacting. What I *don't* know is what possessed you to tell them things like that.

"Who are you trying to sabotage here, Ward? Who is this aimed at?"

"Stay calm," Warden said aloud. Slowly a smile softened the clenched expressionlessness of his features. He raised one hand to the patch over his left eye. "You look like you're about to have an infarction."

Blinking spasmodically, Holt leaned back in his chair. A sting of apprehension shaded his aura.

"As you say," Warden went on, "it's sabotage. Smoke. It's aimed at Special Counsel Maxim Igensard."

He'd prepared for this as well as he could. Now he had to put himself to the test.

"The Council has been debating us for years," he explained. "All the issues are old and familiar. Only Igensard is new. But he's already made up his mind about us. Hashi and I just confirmed what he thinks. And we did it without quite telling him the truth.

"Complete lies are too easily uncovered. Almost-truths are much more effective."

Holding down his self-disgust with the strength of his arms, he went on, "The risk, of course, is that I've cut the ground out from under my supporters. But I'm willing to take that chance for the sake of blowing smoke in Igensard's eyes.

"Holt, that man is dangerous. If anyone is capable of pushing and prying hard enough to get at the facts, he is. I know his brand of outraged righteousness. He's so sure he's right and pure that he'll relish bringing both of us down and opening the borders of forbidden space to prove it.

"I can stand tarnishing my reputation a little to stop him.

"I know you don't like that. Your whole empire rests on the UMCP. If we don't at least look like our integrity is unimpeachable, you're in trouble. But before you decide I've gone into meltdown, think about what that conference accomplished."

"Which is?" Holt demanded shortly.

Warden didn't hesitate. He'd gone too far to falter now.

"I gave Igensard lies so accurate he won't be able to distinguish them from the truth. From his point of view, if we really let Succorso have Morn Hyland just for the insurance, the last thing we would do is say so. From his point of view, if we actually released Thermopyle and sent him against Thanatos Minor, the last thing we would do is reveal his destination.

"From his point of view, if we truly had a mutagen immunity drug which we decided to keep secret, the very last thing we would do is call attention to it by saying we've faked a drug to use against Billingate.

"And that's not all. In addition I've set things up so that if anything goes wrong nobody gets the blame but me. If I look culpable enough, you're in the clear. You can always protect your interests by letting Igensard have me."

At last he stopped. For better or worse, he'd said what he came to say. Now he had to face the outcome.

Holt regarded him sourly for a long moment before rasping, "Is that supposed to reassure me?"

Warden shrugged. "I don't know how you feel," he replied despite the fact that his IR sight read Holt's concern, anger, and fear plainly. "I'm just doing my job.

"What else would you like to chat about?"

That was the wrong thing to say. It set Holt off like the spark of a magnesium lighter.

Surging forward in his seat, he snapped, "Don't mess with me, Ward. I'll have your balls for truffles.

"You planned all this before you ordered Godsen to admit publicly that Thermopyle was gone, but you didn't bother to mention it. You decided to climb out on this limb without consulting me. Now I'm going to tell you what it means if you fall. Then you're going to go back to UMCPHQ and leave the rest to me.

"If anything goes wrong on Thanatos Minor—*anything at all*—your precious Joshua is finished. Morn Hyland is finished. Nick Succorso is finished. Milos Taverner is finished. Do you hear me? I want them dead. I want them and their ships and every scrap of information about them *extirpated* from the universe.

"That includes the immunity drug. Especially the immunity drug. If I'd known you were going to give the votes any hint it exists, I would *never* have let you talk me into preserving it.

"Have I made myself clear? You've already sent Min Donner out that way. I assume you want her in position to intercept what comes out of forbidden space. Give her this job. If anything goes wrong out there"—his hands knotted into fists and pounded each word onto the desktop—"you make goddamn sure she kills them all!"

Warden found it unexpectedly easy to remain calm. He'd done what he came for. And the result didn't surprise him. He'd helped create this problem: now he meant to solve it; meant to reap the consequences.

Releasing his arms, he rose to his feet.

"It's clear, all right," he said quietly. "I think it will stay that way from now on.

"I'll report as soon as I know what's happening."

Holt growled a dismissal and keyed the door seals so that Warden could leave.

As he walked out of the Dragon's lair, Warden closed the door distinctly behind him.

It's time, he thought. This has got to stop.

Please, Angus. Don't fail.

This is the end of *A Dark and Hungry God Arises*.
The story continues in
The Gap into Madness: Chaos and Order